# *High Heels*
# *& Bicycle Wheels*

## JANE LINFOOT

Harper
impulse
we're just below

HarperImpulse an imprint of
HarperCollins*Publishers* Ltd
77–85 Fulham Palace Road
Hammersmith, London W6 8JB

www.harpercollins.co.uk

A Paperback Original 2014

First published in Great Britain in ebook format by HarperImpulse 2014

Copyright © Jane Linfoot 2014

Cover images © Shutterstock.com

Jane Linfoot asserts the moral right
to be identified as the author of this work

A catalogue record for this book is
available from the British Library

ISBN: 9780008105501

Automatically produced by Atomik ePublisher from Easypress

*For my own personal hero and tandem partner, Phil*

# Chapter 1

'Eeek!'

Hot naked tush alert!

Careering round the corner of a hedge in the car park, Bryony Marshall, *Sporting Chances'* TV production assistant on-the-run, dug hers heels into the gravel and skidded to a halt. Clutching wildly as the coffees she was carrying flew in all directions, she balked at the startling rear view that confronted her.

Damn. Embarrassing or what? Crashing into today's bike race celebrity guest-of-honour as he tucked in his shirt in the shelter of his car tailgate was not the ideal way to discover what men wore under their cycling shorts, even if she was delivering resuscitating caffeine. There was no way she was going to live this one down, except… Her eyes locked onto the most delicious butt ever.

Talk about all her Christmases coming at once. *With definite emphasis on the 'come' bit.*

So that would be nothing on then… Underneath the kilt as it were. No boxers, no briefs, not even a teensy-weensy mankini. And all those rumours about professional cyclists waxing their backsides weren't holding up, either.

*Bryony, behave. Look away. Now!*

One hard mental kick got her rampant inner-woman back in line. Almost.

But hey, there was every excuse to go wild given the shape of him. This guy was ripped enough to double as a super-human – one hell of a toned back, broad shoulders bursting with muscles under that slippery Lycra top he was finally dragging on.

That was the great thing about being a production assistant – the job was full of surprises. Fighting to rein in her saggy lower lip, Bryony sucked in the drool. Hurriedly arranged her best 'I'm soooo sorry' face as he spun around to face her.

Wham! Too late. Her mouth had gone again. This time her whole jaw.

Beautiful didn't begin to cover it.

All cheekbones and stubble shadows, the laconic twist of his smile instantly acknowledged the eyeful she'd just enjoyed. Permeating the air with delicious early-morning hot-male scent. Body spray mixed with a double dose of testosterone. She watched as he scraped his fingers through his tousled hair. Then, almost as if in retaliation, he surveyed her through narrowed eyes, and sent a shock-shiver zipping down her spine.

Beautiful, hot, with a full torching of arrogance.

Like he was certain he was best.

*At everything.*

The thought was so far out-of-line that it sent her knees weak.

And he was giving her one thorough, blatant, top-to-toe, mental undressing, which she was lapping up, God help her. Only the sub-zero breeze, slicing off the North Sea was saving her from melting into a syrup pool on the tarmac.

She was so far off her game plan, she couldn't believe it.

Scarborough in June, 10 a.m. on a Saturday morning and cold enough to freeze...

OMG. Errant nipples leaping to attention under scrutiny was the last thing she needed. One sensitive area and she'd been dying of embarrassment for her Fembot tendency ever since Year 8 – thanks-a-bunch Austin Powers. A desperate glance to confirm her double-padded bra and down jacket were on top of the job.

*Thank you to the God of Wonderbra for that.* Then, grappling her 'professional' back with one designed-to-be-dazzling smile, she bounced in for an introduction.

'Bryony Marshall, *Sporting Chances TV* – you must be Jackson Gale?'

Not that much of a wild assumption, given the way the decal-covered car was hollering it to the world. And something about the whole Teflon arrogance of the guy told her not to go in making excuses.

He thrust a hand in her direction.

'Bryony! Hi, I'm Jackson.' Riveting her to the spot as his face split into a grin the width of the promenade. 'Going commando, as you just discovered.'

*What?*

'Erghhh…' Clinging onto his lean tanned hand under the tray of coffees as, for once in her life, words failed her.

'No worries. At least now you can quash the rumours. Tell your viewers that I don't shave my backside. Seems to be a subject of endless fascination to them. '

If he was deliberately trying to wind her up, no way was she going to let him get the better of her.

'I'll certainly do my best to pass that on.'

'And if you've finished with it, I'll have my hand back please.'

'Oh, yep.' She unlocked her fingers. Shucks. Had she really been clinging onto him?

'So what's your preference? Shaved?' Where the hell had that deep, gravelly growl come from? His dark eyes twinkled with mischief. 'Or not?'

'What?' she squeaked. Damn it! Was this guy for real?

'Just wondering where you stand…' His narrowed eyes locked onto her chest again. 'In the rough-versus-smooth debate.'

She grappled a moment, to get control. 'In that particular debate I'd say I stand firmly outside of the room.' There – that told him. She tossed her head deliberately, shimmied him an unmissable

3

'keep your distance' smile. 'Fancy a coffee?'

She thrust the tray under his nose.

'Great. Thanks.' Finally he unstuck his gaze from her boobs, allowing it travel to her face. 'Got any black, without?'

Her stomach did an unexpected triple-flip as his dark eyes collided with hers, and she looked away quickly.

Reeling a bit at that molasses voice. Getting her breath back. 'Sorry…?'

'Mind still stuck on the underwear issue then?' He let out a short guffaw. 'Sorry to confuse you. I'm talking coffee here. No milk, no sugar.' He flashed her another grin. 'Keep up.'

*Rude or what?* And definitely pushing it.

'Try the one with the green lid.' Determined not to rise. So that was how he stayed in shape. She nudged a plastic cup towards him. 'Muffin?'

His smirking snort with a triple shot of incredulity suggested she was talking dirty. Very dirty.

'Do I look like I eat muffins?'

Good thing she hadn't gone for pure porn cupcakes then.

'Raspberry and white chocolate chip, freshly baked…'

And still he shook his head.

*Whatever.*

Muffins were today's healthy option. She'd done a mega-order to ensure the crew stayed sweet, though no doubt by the end of the day she'd be hitting the cupcakes as usual, wading through an inch of buttercream for an instant sugar rescue.

'Later perhaps.'

Was that him trying to be conciliatory?

'Good luck with that given the gannets here; otherwise known as cameramen.' Damn. She didn't mean to let that beam get away. People who refused her muffins didn't deserve smiles that effusive, even if they did have a great ass.

'Did someone say white chocolate?'

Bryony turned to see Cressy swooping around the wing of

the car, and coming to her own swooning halt right by Bryony's elbow. 'Lordy! Phwoar! Don't mind if I do! Loving you for the muffins, Bry.'

Bryony, lips twitching, let her gaze skim firmly over the top of the OMG face Cressy was shooting sideways at her.

Cressy was so generous and warm, Bryony had forgiven her years ago for having the pint-sized figure she'd always wanted herself. But she was also a total man-magnet. Men falling at Cressy's pretty, dainty feet was something else Bryony was totally inured to, even though it had landed them in a whole load of trouble more times than she cared to count.

And today could be shaping up for another Cressy train-wreck.

According to last night's background research, fitted in by Bryony at two in the morning in her childhood bed after that shocker of a dinner with her Mum and Stepdad, it seemed that Jackson was exceptionally available. Apparently, cycle race podium-girls weren't the only females he got up-close and personal with. Completely on the market by all accounts. Grabbing whatever he could wherever he could, and the more the better. Quality *and* quantity. Oh, and his nickname was The Howler, for three exceptionally good reasons: a) after howling gales, b) because of the way he howled as he crossed the finish line, and c) because…

The last reason went straight in the too-much-information bin. No way did she want to imagine his girlfriends' ecstatic screams at the crucial moment.

More so, since she'd seen the guy in all his naked glory.

*Especially since…*

Bryony re-spun her brain cogs and landed, randomly, on last night's crazy family dinner. Ouch! That would have to wait for later, when she had a whole lot of time and at least a full psychology department on hand for support. She had to remember: however hurtful the suggestions sounded, her mother was only trying to be kind.

*Take one second to clear your head of all things family…And*

5

*another to forget exactly why you've volunteered to bury yourself in work when you could've been shopping...*

The frantic catch-up background reading was just one of the drawbacks of ending up working on a sports programme when you were the least-sporty person on the planet.

World famous cyclist Jackson Gale...

Getting up to speed for this sporting gig was time-consuming, not to mention stressful. Oh, and yawnsville too.

In theory TV production was the same regardless of the subject, but somehow it was a whole lot easier if you were in tune with what you were filming. It came naturally to her to be enthusiastic about filming pretty things and country houses, whereas with sport... even the word made her cringe. All wrapped-up with memories of humiliation in games lessons at school when she was not only a head taller than everyone else, but also terminally uncoordinated. At least the money for this job was top-whack and it was helping Cressy out of a hole, seeing as how the crew had all gone down with some unmentionable virus, which accidentally coincided with some ferocious stag-night celebrations.

Although, talking of Cressy and holes; despite Jackson's penchant for play and the way Cressy was warming up her full-bodied come-hither wiggles right here on the car park, she didn't give much for Jackson's chances today. Bryony looked up, expecting to see Jackson's tongue lolling out in Cressy's direction, and started sharply as his eyes sidled up her own body then clashed with her gaze.

All grey brown and smokey.

*Shades of irresistible.*

Except she always resisted. Other people had relationships, not her.

So, Jackson was still pursuing the undressing thing, then. Anyone else and she'd have rottweilered them by now. Why the hell had she let him go this far?

He inclined his head and narrowed his gaze a fraction, sending

6

her pulse into overdrive.

Why didn't he realise he was honing in on the wrong person here?

This *so wasn't* how it worked when Cressy was around. And it wasn't only because of Cressy. Bryony didn't do flirting, for goodness sakes. She rarely did men. She had her rules, and that included no flirting. Especially not at work.

Especially not in Scarborough, of all places.

Scarborough was too cold and too northern to be auspicious for any sort of romance – *and* it was laden with back-story.

Oh my. He was still looking. Would he never give up?

She took a large gulp of air. Given the way today was shaping up, she was starting to wish she'd bitten the bullet, stayed home in London and faced her demons. At least then she could have had the soothing benefit of retail therapy.

Beside her, Cressy's wiggle had escalated into overdrive, apparently to zero effect.

Time for action. Not necessarily evasive action. Any action at all would do.

'Here, have that muffin.' Bryony stuffed a cake at Cressy, who jerked to a standstill, staring at her open-mouthed. Then Bryony strode purposefully to find refuge on the far side of the car, pulled herself up to her full five foot nine plus heels, put on her best production-assistant-in-control voice and motioned to the rack on the car roof.

'So is this the bike you and Annie are going to ride today then?'

Annie, being Annie Brooks, one time super-athlete, turn-her-mind-and-body-to-anything-and-win, morphed into mega-successful presenter of *Sporting Chances*, who always wore state-of-the-art running shoes. Bryony squinted down at her own wedge-heeled trainers which she'd panic-bought in an attempt to fit in with the gym bunnies on the Sporting Chances team. Four-inch heels rather than five was the only concession she'd been able to make towards a sensible appearance. It wasn't her fault; she'd had an addiction to towering heels since the age of three. At least she'd made an effort with her Sweaty Betty Zero Gravity Leggings – not that she understood the technical spec, but at least the name was cool. Whatever. Annie was a super-brave, super-talented, super-woman. She was going places. And she was beyond crazy if she was ready to get on the back of a push bike for a ten-mile ride with this guy.

Based on the knowing way he was slow-blinking at her, Bryony guessed that he knew he'd got to her.

'Yep. The tandem. That would be the one.' He leaned a shoulder on the car and shot her one long, laid-back, wicked grin. Zap! One electric bolt arrived on target, oblivious of the cycles zooming round the car park, the gathering crowds and the milling pedestrians hovering around the car bonnet. 'It's the tandem challenge I'm contracted for. Champion cyclist teams up with famous sports presenter; it's a golden ratings combination for the sponsors.'

Whatever. She got the joke, though the last part had a curiously hollow ring to it.

'It's shaping up to be a great day.' She flashed him another PR smile to counteract any wobbles he might be having. It was her job to smooth things here, and celebrity ego-massaging was something she could do in her sleep. 'You're going to be a great pull.'

The fraction of a second pause was long enough for her to kick herself for what she'd just said, not long enough for her to jump in with something to neutralise the statement.

'Sounds like an offer I can't refuse…' His face split into a slow grin, even more wicked than before. 'Thanks, we'll discuss the details later.'

Jeez, this guy was a nightmare. She prayed her cheeks weren't entirely bright-red and opted for flat-out dismissal as the best tactic. 'We all know I'm talking crowd-pullers here, Jackson.' An eye-roll and a deep sigh hopefully emphasised the put-down.

'Fine, no need to get your Nikes in a twist.' He was straight back at her with a low rumble of laughter and enough smoulder in his eyes to bring the back of her neck out in a hot sweat.

Definitely time to get this show on the road.

'Okay. You get the bike down; I'll go and find Annie,' she barked, and he jumped.

Nice work.

Great. The power had shifted. She was back on top. Business as usual.

'That's still the best proposition I've had this morning.' He gave her a smirk.

She raised one eyebrow at him and gave him an icy stare, to finally put him in his place. So, even though he might be King of the cycling world and distantly related to the Prince of Darkness when it came to pulling women, he didn't miss the bit about her being in control.

Here. Today. Now.

Behind the car Cressy erupted like a one-woman volcano.

'Annie? Jeez, sorry. That's what I came to say. How the hell did I forget?' She slashed a raspberry muffin smear across her cheek, inadvertently spraying a shower of cake over Jackson as she spluttered. 'Annie's in the Ladies being sick. There's no way she'll be able to ride.'

# Chapter 2

So Annie was out.

And given that they needed a female on the tandem with Jackson – orders from on high, after a rush of phone-calls – that left Cressy as the only option. Or Bryony. And the message from the top was that they could fight it out between them, but one of them was going on the back.

'There are times when I hate this job.' Bryony grimaced, rolling her eyes around the car park. Bike riding was so not her thing. 'The way we always go the extra mile to make things work.'

'Ten miles looking at that butt may not be so bad.' From the way Cressy was grinning, Bryony could tell that she was well up for it. 'I was in love with choppers when I was a kid. Did stunts and everything. It'll be like old times.'

Cressy in love with choppers? No change there then.

'Phew. I'm pleased that's settled.' Bryony released one sigh of relief. She would have died rather than ride on that tandem.

Cressy stooped, rifling enthusiastically through the bag Annie had thrust into her hands as she left.

'It's all very rosy in here…' Cressy screwed up her face, squinting up at Bryony. 'But there's one teensy problem.'

Bryony's stomach sank.

'Namely?'

Cressy waved a cycling shoe in her direction.

'Look at the size of this. It has to be a seven. These beauties clip on to the pedals, and my mini-feet will slip right out of them.' She shrugged, gave a guilty grimace. 'Sorry babe, but it looks like this one's down to you.'

'Can't you borrow some that fit you?' Desperation was mounting in Bryony's chest.

'Maybe I could have done if we'd known about it earlier, but right now I can't see anyone in cycling shoes with small feet.' Cressy gave a hopeless shrug as she scanned the car park. 'If I could I'd have grabbed them already.'

'Can't you change the pedals or something?' Bryony's voice rose to a squeak.

'I doubt we'd get any others in time,' Cressy glanced at her watch and sighed. 'But even if we did I'm still in heels, and there's no way that fits with Jackson's major champion look.'

*Damn and double damn.*

This couldn't be happening, could it? Bryony chomped her lip, determined not to scowl. Scarborough was so not her lucky place, but it wasn't Cressy's fault.

'Talk about Cinderella in reverse.' One last desperate ploy to wriggle out of the hot seat. 'There's no way I'll fit into that Lycra, though.'

'It's not as if you've got a choice. At least Lycra's stretchy.' Cressy gave Bryony's hand a pat; if it was meant to be comforting, then it failed. 'It'll squeeze you. Make the most of your assets for The Howler.' Cressy shot her a wicked smirk as she shoved the kit towards her. 'You know he's called that because he's so great in bed that he makes women...'

Bryony cut her off swiftly. 'Yep, I did the reading too. *Blowing In, Jackson Gale, The Official Biography.*'

Trust Cressy to zero in on the bedroom side of things; although, something about this particular guy had her own brain hanging in exactly the same place. Great minds...

She made a mental note to stop that. And fast.

'Aww, Bry, tell me you haven't been reading biographies again?' Cressy grimaced at her. 'There's no need to take it so seriously. *Hot Stuff* magazine has all the low-down and it's so much more readable. And that Lycra certainly made the most of *his* assets.'

Cressy and her obsessions again.

Although she had a point.

In spades.

Not that she was about to admit to Cressy she'd noticed. No point getting the girl any more over-excited than she was already.

'Probably just padding.' Bryony added a derisive sniff to reinforce the deception.

'That particular bit of him had nothing to do with padding, Bryony Marshall, and you know it.' Cressy shook her head despairingly. 'And lucky you for having that rear view for elevenses.'

Bryony shrugged, aiming to look completely disinterested. 'Whatever.'

'Don't knock me out with your excitement. Glory, what I wouldn't give to be in your saddle.' Cressy's teasing nudge hit her full in the ribs. 'C'mon on then. Unless you want to strip off here like Mr Smart-ass, we'd better head to the Ladies. I'll pour you into your finery.'

'Fuchsia! And so tight! What the hell was Annie thinking?' Bryony, emerging into the sun from the Ladies tripped on the step and landed in a heap on Cressy. 'At least this dreadful stuffing round my bum will come in handy when I fall on my butt.'

'Careful!' Cressy grabbed Bryony's arm hastily. 'And in her defence, Annie probably chose the shorts to match the Charity top. They wouldn't have been quite such a snug fit on her. And the padding is to stop you getting wedgies and saddle sores.'

Snug? That had to be the polite way of putting it. Indecent was more like it. And saddle sores were *so* not on her agenda. An already-bad day was turning into an indisputable nightmare and it wasn't even eleven o'clock yet. Bryony grimaced down at her boobs, morphed to melon-size, and her cleavage, squished skywards by the bursting zip.

'Who'd have thought a stretchy top three sizes too small would zoom a girl to a double G? I look like I'm promoting Breast Enhancement, not Sport for Teens. And it's not very warm either.'

*Nipple alert!*

Bryony squinted down, to examine her profile.

'Don't worry, it's an erection-free zone – this far at least.' Cressy shot her a grin. 'And you look fab. So lucky we found that matching lippy. I can think of someone not a million miles away who'll appreciate the look.'

'Just the kind of support I need.' Not. Cressy could wiggle her eyebrows all she wanted. That one wasn't happening. Jackson Gale, with his smouldering, stomach-flipping brand of uninvited flirtation, had already made it onto her personal list of guys to be avoided at all costs. Bryony snorted, determined to distract her. 'These shoes are crazy. I'll never be able to walk in them.'

'Sorry to state the obvious.' Another rueful grin from Cressy. 'But you're not exactly going to be walking...'

*Ahhh, shucks.*

'Don't remind me.' Another worry zapped into her brain. 'You have told Jackson that it's me on the back?'

Ominous silence. Cressy shuffled.

That would be a 'No' then.

'It's a great opportunity. You need to lighten up, Bry; we both know that. This could be your chance. Look at it as a gift.'

More animated eyebrows.

'Cressy...' Was there even any point in admonishing her?

'At least it'll be brilliant for that career path you're so obsessed with. They'll really owe you after this.'

Bryony dragged in a breath and clutched at her stomach. Somewhere along the line it had dematerialised. 'This is such a bad idea.'

Why did she say always say 'yes' like some over-enthusiastic, cliff-fixated lemming? Why did her irrational need to prove herself override her sensible head every time? Why did she always need to show that she could pull off the impossible? Scared stiff of two wheels and she'd still let herself be railroaded into this. She'd barely ridden a bike since she was six and, even then, she'd been wobbly.

'Don't worry, it'll be over before you know it.' Cressy, sensing her wavering, whisked into Producer-mode. 'Let's go and find Mr Delicious and get you on this bike.'

# Chapter 3

As Jackson wheeled the tandem out along the edge of the car park half an hour later, the trickle of spectators was increasing, all heading in one direction towards the race start down the road.

Damn to the way today was going.

Damn to how he'd felt obliged to traipse to this wind-lashed desert of a town, simply in an effort to try to reinforce his cleaned-up reputation. His aunt had begged him to come as a favour to a friend of a friend, who was masterminding the event. Accidentally mentioned to Team HQ, who seized on it as part of his personal character-whitening campaign, and here he was. Along with a film crew, also courtesy of the whitewash brigade, who were ostensibly about to begin charting his progress as he returned to fitness with the team.

Guaranteed to annoy the hell out of him, more like. But all the more reason to appear like the new good boy and not the old bad boy. Truth be told, he was beginning to miss bad-boy Jackson more than a little himself. All this 'best behaviour' was wearing very thin – his screaming libido could vouch for that. Why the hell his aunt had convinced herself that he'd be a huge draw at what seemed little more than an out of the way fun-run and tandem race was beyond him. Who in their right minds would want to see some washed-up cyclist with a crapped-up knee?

And in Scarborough?

Whichever marketing exec was pushing it as a new-found trendy resort needed their head examining. The location's charm had certainly by-passed him.

He didn't even have anything he could give as an excuse right now. It was his fault for letting things slide, for not getting his life sorted, for sitting in limbo, waiting endlessly for his dratted knee to heal. Although the TV talk, vague as it was, did have the whisper of a promise of being financially rewarding down the line. Depending what developed. Not holding his breath on that one either. So, apart from the TV possibilities, the only spark on the dismal grey horizon that purported to be the North Sea was the woman who'd caught him with his shorts down earlier. Literally.

She was the one thing all week that had made him smile. Possibly all year. Worth it for the look on her face and the excuse it gave him to give her the once-over in return.

And PHWOAR to what was waiting for him body wise, even if she was doing an Oscar-worthy performance of making out that she was a superior ice maiden.

Not that he'd needed any encouragement. Far from it. With a body like that wafted in front of him, he practically needed a restraining order. Big shame he was on his mission of self-improvement. The Jackson Gale that the press portrayed, Jackson Gale as he was before the whitewash, would have whisked her into his bed, or possibly not even that far. Hell, that Jackson Gale would most likely have had her in the car park, there and then, up against the wall. In broad daylight.

*Ignoring the electric shocks that the image powered to his groin. Ditto his blood, fizzy as shaken cola, since she zoomed into his view-finder.*

Ironic, then, that today's Jackson Gale wasn't about to run loose, with voltage like that scrambling his radar. Having spent the best part of a year cleaning up his act, he wasn't about to squander the efforts, however hot the woman. He found it disconcerting that it was even on his mind. The press wrote rubbish about him on a daily basis and he realised that the press guys who knew the truth were lined up, waiting for him to fall off the virtue wagon, just so they could seize a scoop. No way was he going to hand them that satisfaction. He had too much to lose.

But there was something about the lilt of those lips, the quiver of those eyelids, not to mention the oh-so-full-on nipples he'd glimpsed as her coat fell open that sent more shocks zapping south. Doubly ironic given what his out of control libido was howling at him to do. ASAP. If not sooner. He gritted his teeth. Drove the thought of that tongue, teasing a raspberry muffin crumb from her finger end, right out of his...

A light touch on his shoulder jolted him, and he spun.

'Cressy! You're back!'

And look what she'd brought.

Bryony. Shuffling to hide behind Cressy and failing spectacularly, like trying to hide Everest behind a molehill. And talking of mountains, in one gulp he lost all the air from his chest cavity.

Bryony. Shrink-wrapped in shimmering bubble-gum-coloured Lycra, cleavage as deep as...

'And I've bought you your partner in crime.' Cressy's words floated over his shoulder.

Unzipped was the word which stuck in his head. And beautiful. If Barbie and Wonder Woman had their genes mashed up, this would be it. With a shake of that filthy rock star, who liked to wear cowboy chaps and not much else on a dirty day. Talk about hot... Scorching more like. Fluro pink perfection, down to every last blonde, tossed tress, entirely eclipsing how stuck-up she was.

And entirely unsuitable to ride a bike of any kind, especially a tandem.

Someone had to be taking the mickey here. Okay, he understood the presenter with the sporting credentials had taken a vomit-check, but surely they could have found someone more suitable than this. Eye-candy was for bedrooms, not bike riding, and this woman looked about as fluffy as candy-floss.

Somewhere deep in his psyche, the twanging ache of lust morphed into the molten lava of anger.

'You are joking?' His words slammed off the tarmac louder than he'd imagined, shot through with bitter tarnish that had so much more to do with resentment for what he'd waded through these last eighteen months than the woman standing there now.

Through the apparition-haze he sensed her flinch, and the slight drop of her jaw wrenched his twisted guts another turn. Was he feeling guilty? Sorry for her? Then motor-mouth beside her jumped in.

'Sorry to disappoint you, but due to the kit problems, this is the best we can come up with.' The dizzy one, suddenly not so ditsy any more. Ostensibly apologising, but packing a punch; spinning him a resounding smile, presumably to sweeten the awful truth. 'This is it, Jackson. Take it or leave it.'

So that told him. Whose mouth was gaping now?

'She's just not the girl for the job.' When in trouble, make the same point a different way. This would never have happened in his victory days.

'And you think I don't know this?' Bryony cut in, eyes flashing. 'At least we agree on that. And please stop discussing me as if I'm not here.'

He clawed back control of his jaw. Prepared to negotiate.

'Have you ever even ridden a bike, Britney?'

From her speech hesitation, and shrug, that'd be a 'No'.

'For God's sake, it's not Britney, it's Bryony. And of course I've ridden a bike.' Avoiding eye contact, she studied her feet feverishly. 'When I was younger.'

Younger? She already looked like she belonged on a nappy night. Close up, she couldn't be more than twenty-six.

'At playgroup?' He gave a hollow laugh. 'What do you know about cycling, anyway?'

One flash of her eyes told him Barbie had left the building

and Wonder Woman had sprung into action. It warned him that he might need to take cover and fast.

'What? Do I have to have qualifying times to sit behind you?' She gave a disparaging sniff. 'For crying out loud, it's a bit of fun, not London bloody 2012!'

Ouch. One sideswipe that hit him full in the thorax.

He caught Cressy landing Bryony a swift kick on the ankle and shooting her a 'face', no doubt telling her she'd jumped in with both feet about the London Games that he'd missed.

Damn. The last thing he wanted was to be saved. Saving went hand in hand with pity and he had zero time for that either.

Hell, he should be beyond all that now. Served him right for failing on all counts there. Failing by having that stupid accident in the first place, failing to make the damned Games and then failing to come to terms with it all. He should have put it behind him when it happened. All those years of work, all the anticipation, one careless slip, and he'd missed the whole damn show. The event of a lifetime, ten years working towards it, and he stuffed it up.

Swallowing a mouthful of sour saliva, he braced himself for total climb-down.

'Okay, point taken.' He watched Bryony's pale curls flick as her chin whipped up, no doubt marking some kind of personal victory, which was going to be short-lived. 'So, if you're that experienced, then you'll know you need a helmet…'

'Oh, damn.' Her confident flounce was instantly replaced with the squawk of panic. 'Cressy?'

Point to him. Worth it, if only to see the whites of her eyes as her face crumpled. Not so sure of herself now, was she?

'No worries, the helmet's in the kitbag, Bry.' Cressy posted him a mocking dead-eye as she triumphantly pulled the hat out of the holdall and thrust it at Bryony.

'One last thing—' And it had to be said. 'From your VPL I'd say you're wearing a thong?' From the way she coloured up, he knew he'd scored a bulls-eye there. 'Are you sure that's wise? Cutting in and all that? There's a reason I go commando.'

'Too much information.' She vaulted in, glaring at him like she'd love to throttle him and finish off with a happy dance. 'I know you think you're God's gift, Jackson, but, honestly, my underwear choice is up to me.'

'Okay, it's your call, I'm only trying to help.' Eyes snagging on Bryon, as she fiddled alternately with her chin strap and – God help him – her thong elastic, he wheeled the tandem out to an open patch of car park. 'If you insist you're up for it, then climb aboard.'

He braced himself. Stood back, holding the handlebars at arm's length as she approached. Something about the way her steps hung back screwed up his stomach again. What was it with this woman and the way she tipped his guts upside down?

Definitely committed then. His pulse picked up speed as she arrived beside him, grasped the rear handgrips and shot him a hesitant scowl; yet he was still totally unprepared for the scent of her. One sweet, warm, blast of pure sex hit him as she bumped against his hip and swung her leg up, fumbling her way onto the saddle.

*Guts on full spin now.*

'Seat at the right height?' He had to ask, though getting in close enough to raise it might be beyond him.

'Errr. I guess so.'

'Bemused of Scarborough' speaking there, but giving the right answer from his point of view. No way could he cope with the up close and personal that adjusting her saddle would involve. Even though it was obviously too low, he wasn't about to force the issue.

She sat up shakily, one toe on the ground, and stopped biting her lip long enough to manage a slip of a smile. 'So where do I put my feet?'

A question to make his heart sink if it hadn't been pounding so fast. Experienced bike rider? What a load of...

'You need to clip the cleats on the base of your shoes into the pedals.'

Easy. If you weren't a high-maintenance female who couldn't tell a bottom bracket from a chainset.

'What?'

Nice move. Neatly making it sound like he was the one over-complicating this.

'Twist your feet and attach them to the pedals.' Watching the clouds scudding across the bright blue sky, he counted to ten.

'No, not happening.'

No surprise there then. *Dammit.*

His pulse already in overdrive, anticipating the next bit. Taking the weight of the bike on one arm, he bent to help, sliding his face down, mentally blocking the slippery heat of her Lycra-clad thigh perilously close to his cheek. Grasping her foot and yanking it into place on the pedal.

'Not so hard, is it?' Not for her, at least. 'Twist your foot on and off. Get the idea?' He aimed for nonchalant, rather than ready-to-take-her-against-the-wall.

'Cool. They seem to be clipped in now.' She dragged in a deep breath, pushed him an accusing stare.

The full heat and weight of her body plus the bike rammed up against his as he straightened to stand, and the surge in his groin came as a firm reminder to him to somehow sort the desert of his sex life as he disentangled himself from the scent of clean hair. Moved hand over hand, towards the front of the tandem.

Why the hell was he going ahead with this? More to the point, why was she? She could act as feisty as she liked, but he'd felt the nerves juddering through her, heard the rattle of her chattering teeth, even though her jaw was clamped tight shut. He had an idea that, despite her bravado, Cherry Bomb was silently freaking out here.

He was suddenly aware as he swung his own leg over the crossbar and clipped a foot onto his own pedal that they had an audience. Winding the pedal into position, he raised his eyebrows to the arc of bystanders.

'Right, I'm going to push off. All you need to do is to sit still and pedal along with me, okay? And stop pedaling if I stop.' Throwing a glance over his shoulder, he saw Bryony clinging onto the handlebars, eyes wide with terror.

Anything but okay, then.

'Yep.' She gave a wobbly nod and threw a desperate grimace at Cressy. 'Great.'

Lying through those perfect teeth and hyper-ventilating too. She was about to get a whole lot more than she bargained for. For a nanosecond he considered stopping, taking pity and letting her off, but the caveman in him overrode that. Now that he'd got her jammed in behind him, he was loath to let her go. True, she might turn into a complete liability on the back, but some strange part of him was relishing the thought of spending a half-hour with his buttocks thrust between her hands on the bars, the two of them rushing through the air together. Despite the fact it was barely eleven in the morning, he felt a sudden compulsion to forget all about the race and pedal off into the sunset, dragging her behind him. It was only a fun bike race after all. Fifty tandems racing ten miles along a road, a linear course rather than laps, and judging by the fancy dress he'd already seen charging round the streets, most of the entries were about the fund-raising, not the speed. But an overwhelming desire to go AWOL, taking the Cherry Bomb with him? Weird, or what? He put it down to too much caffeine.

'We'll have a trial run. A couple of turns around the block, see how it goes.' Laughing over his shoulder in a desperate bid to block out the sunset image, he decided to join in the lie-fest. 'You'll be fine.'

As he pushed off, a crescendo of yelps from Bryony rose over the cheers and wolf-whistles of the small crowd. Too bad. He powered on the pedals, clicked up the gears.

'Go Bryony!' Cressy's yell followed them across the car park. 'You're gonna have the ride of your life!'

At least someone thought so.

# Chapter 4

Three swift laps round the block later and she was shaping up better than he thought possible. His barked instructions to sit still and move with him had worked. Now they were coasting down a quiet residential road lined with elegant terraced houses, the screaming had stopped, she'd lost the attitude and her gasps had subsided into small moans. Although this was good news for his aching ears, it was pretty disastrous for his good-behaviour policy, given the way the small mews that she was emitting now sounded sexual enough to drive his libido wild.

He tried to close his ears to the distracting noises behind him. She needed to man up. If she couldn't take the heat, she shouldn't go in the damn kitchen in the first place. That was better. Quiet was good. Although maybe she was too quiet.

'Are you alright back there?'

The reply, when it finally came it was more of a whisper than a groan. 'No…'

Not sounding good. One glance over his shoulder confirmed that she was green.

Damn. He'd known this was a ridiculous idea; it was his fault, he should never have set off. Just another example of the disaster area his life had become.

Bad decisions, bad calls. When did it all go so wrong? And why did bad follow bad like a toppling cascade of dominos, making it seem like all the good years had been down to luck and nothing else? Yanking the bike into the side of the road, the tourniquet tightened around his gut again as he watched her struggle onto the pavement.

'Why didn't you say something?' That sounded way harsher than he intended no doubt as his own self-recrimination spilled over.

He caught the flare of surprise in her eyes as she sank down to squat on the kerb. With a big shrug, she shook her head. Gulping for air, she brushed a hand across her cheek and a slash of tears streaked the dust. Oh, shit, she was crying. The woman who seemed so goddamn sure of herself, and he'd broken her in three blocks. She swallowed again, rubbed her nose and sniffed hard.

'Something wrong?' May be best to act like he hadn't seen the tears.

'I don't want to wimp out.' Her bottom lip juddered. 'But I feel sick.'

Unbelievable. 'Not another one.' He let out a slow breath. What was with everyone today?

'I'm too scared to look forward, so I look sideways, but then everything flashes past and makes me dizzy.'

Pulling herself together might help. 'You need to look forwards over my shoulder.'

She grimaced. 'It's all so fast.'

Now he'd heard it all.

'The speed's the best bit. The exhilaration. It's the closest to flying you'll get without wings.'

'I don't do thrills. Or flying.' She chomped hard on her thumb-nail and gave what looked like an involuntary judder. 'I hate sledging, I refuse to ski, going downhill fast is my worst nightmare, because I hate not being in control.'

A control-freak to boot. Today just got better and better. 'Great. You'll just have to postpone your enjoyment until you get back in your armchair then.'

'I thought that with the flat course it would be okay.' Her eyes staring up at him were gut-wrenchingly blue.

'Flat? Whoever told you that?' Someone clearly forgot to mention the gentle ten mile climb to a big final descent and he wasn't about to enlighten her. Biting back his exasperation, he pulled his water bottle out of its cage on the bike frame and thrust it towards her. 'Have a drink, it might make you feel better.'

The shake of her hand as she grasped it sent an unexpected jolt of sympathy through him, making him want to reach out, rub a comforting palm across her back. Yet he held back, firmly, as he watched her lips close around the bottle top. Chasing sunsets? Reaching out? Not him. Not in this life. Even though the vulnerability of her neck as she tipped her head back to drink sent his stomach crashing to hit the deck. She took a long draft, then pulled her legs up and tucked her chin onto her knees.

'Too many raspberry muffins, maybe.' Flicking a strand of hair away from her mouth, she gave a rueful grimace and tapped the drinking bottle with one, perfectly manicured, russet nail.

Polished nails and tandems? He should have known better. 'You don't have to do this. We can walk back; it's only round the corner.'

She flew back at him in an instant. 'There's no way I'm giving up.'

So, that put him in his place. Again.

'Okay. We'll give it one more go. I'll raise the saddle, so you'll sit higher. This time you face forwards and we'll take it steady. You only have to say the word and we'll stop.'

Hopefully, that would placate her.

'You don't understand.' She fixated on him with narrowed eyes as she unfolded her legs, rubbed her nose again and clambered to her feet. 'Giving up isn't what I do.'

Got that now. And staring down your top isn't what he did, except the way she was standing, tugging at her jacket. He couldn't help but notice. He swallowed hard, trying to dispel all thoughts of rolling his tongue around what had snagged his attention; but he failed, just as he failed to avert his eyes.

'Are you cold?' That was enough to break the spell.

'Oh, drat.' She flung her arms around herself, and, dammit, he lost the view of what had the potential to be the most promising set of nipples in the history of the world. Although, on the plus side, he gained an insight into how fast a blush could splash across a girls cheeks – also sexy as hell. Somehow he didn't have her down as a blusher, but her grimace was telling him she was dying here.

'Here. Take this.' In a flash he'd unzipped and flung his own jacket round her shoulders. 'I'm warm anyway.'

Ever the gentleman, as long as he wasn't mesmerised, obviously. Warm had been an understatement. Overheated more like.

'Thanks.' Absentmindedly, she pushed an arm into a sleeve. 'If you're sure.'

Not looking at him when she was talking to him, then. Following her sightline downwards, he saw that her eyes had locked onto something a lot lower than his face.

'Aw, damn.'

Length and width – and plenty of both – bulged against the glossy black sheath of his shorts on proud display, and still more to give. Thanks to the God of Lycra for the stretch. His attempt to whack the bulge into submission with the heel of his hand failed.

'Gotcha.' Bryony, eyes shining, proving she could serve an ace return.

Cheeks pinker than ever now that he'd caught her, her lips twisting into a grin that lit up the world, as she zipped herself into the safe haven of his jacket. And not backing down.

'So you did.' He gave a snort. 'No place to hide in Lycra.'

Not backing down. And sharing the joke. He liked that in a woman, even a high maintenance one.

'Come on.' He glanced swiftly at his watch. 'We'd better get moving if we're going to catch this race.'

'Made it!'

Bryony caught the grin Jackson flung over his shoulder as they whizzed under the start banner, chasing the other riders who were already a hundred yards down the road. At least now her seat was higher and she could see ahead, she was less queasy. Getting travel sick on a tandem…she'd never live that one down. In a blur out of the corner of her eye, she caught Cressy, arms flailing like windmill sails, yelling.

'The camera bike will catch you up!'

Then she was gone, her words lost in the rush of air. And who even cared about cameras? *Damn it to that, in spades.* A TV production woman who forgot about filming?

In front of Bryony, Jackson was up on the pedals now, bouncing from side to side, giving chase. Navigating, steering, and zig-zagging alarmingly between the other tandems as they caught up with the bunch.

'Oh, my. This so wasn't my best idea.' One groan to comfort herself, perked up by the view.

Wow, that was one toned butt. As for the muscles in those thighs… Nudging her hand too, as he sank back onto his saddle. OMG. I just touched Jackson Gale's…

'Blimey.' A bump in the road threw her out of the saddle, cancelling all wayward thoughts.

'You okay back there?' He slung a grin over his shoulder. 'Don't forget to hang on.'

She locked her fingers more tightly on the handle bars. If she didn't concentrate here she'd be off the flaming back. Her wrists were already burning with the effort of holding on, and they'd hardly even begun. If it had been achingly scary going slowly round the block, now they were weaving in and out of other bikes right across the road – it was terrifying.

'At least I haven't chucked up.' Yet.

'It'll soon be over, it's only ten miles.' Another nugget tossed in her direction. 'We'll get ahead of the rest of the field and keep out of trouble.'

So comforting. Not.

'It all feels like trouble.' It was alright for him. He was used to it.

'There's no serious competition. Most people are in fancy dress.' Another spurt, and he gave a loud guffaw as they accelerated past a custard-yellow cloud. 'We ruffled Donald Duck's feathers there!'

What crazy place had she landed in?

'Only a guy could be that competitive about overtaking cartoon characters.' Craning her neck as she shouted, she peered past his ear and saw capes up ahead. 'Batman and Robin – they'll give us a run for our money.'

She should have shut up. Like a red rag to a bull. Jackson was up again, and her feet were flying around on the pedals in time with his as they soared past them.

'Batmobiles can't keep up with me.' He was shouting back with the enthusiasm of a five year old. 'I top sixty miles an hour downhill on a good day.'

Not what she wanted to hear. If it hadn't already been in free-fall, her heart would have sunk.

'Can't we ride with the rest?'

That groaning appeal fell on deaf ears.

'The faster we go, the quicker we get there.' One flash of a backwards grin told her he had no intention of slowing down. He might even be enjoying tormenting her. 'It'll all be over in another twenty minutes. Keep pedaling.'

As if she had any choice.

When had she ever been this out of control? Another bump sent her rocketing skywards.

'Ouch!' The dull ache in her butt exploded as she crashed back onto the saddle, the padding in her shorts doing nothing to save her bottom. As for her legs, they were on fire.

Twenty minutes more? She'd be dead.

Gritting her teeth, she clamped her eyelids shut and sent a juddering prayer to the God of accelerated-career-progress, to make it end soon.

'Hey, Cherry Bomb, time to wake up.'

One more jaunty comment flung in her direction and she might just throw up after all. This one penetrated her self-induced trance deeply.

'If you're expecting me to open my eyes, think again.' She growled through gritted teeth as no way would her bone-shaken jaw unclench.

'We're almost there. You need to wave to the spectators. The camera bike is lining up ahead of us too.'

Weakly, she opened one eye a crack. She couldn't have ached more if a forty-four wheel pantechnicon had driven all the way over her then reversed back again.

'Smile! It'll make a perfect shot, us flying down this hill to the finish.'

It was so like this joker to be mocking her.

'Hill…' The shock of the word unlocked her jaw. 'What hill?'

She snapped her eyes open in time to register a hairpin-bend sign whooshing by. Blinked to bring the blur into focus and saw the road dropping away in front of them, dipping sharply like a roller coaster, then corkscrewing round. She hurled out her mental anchors.

'Hold on tight!' Another superfluous instruction from Jackson.

If she'd had any breath left, she'd have hyperventilated. 'If I hold on any tighter my arms will drop off.' Angry enough to find the strength to protest. 'Slow down. Pleeeeeeease.'

Downhill. Accelerating. Out of control. All her nightmares. To the power of ten, at least, if not to the power of a thousand.

'JACKSON! SLOW DOWN!'

The only upside to freewheeling was that the pedals were still. The noise of people on the pavement edge bounced off her head as the washing-machine thump of the world switched onto full-spin.

Why the hell wasn't he doing as he was told? People *always* did as she asked. That was the effect she had. The ability to make people do as they were told was her special power and always had been; now was not the moment for it to fail her.

Colours flashing past, faster and faster, and now the bike was tipping sideways as Jackson flung them around the corner. They had to fall. But then they were upright again, momentarily, then she was hurled the other way as they changed course on the bend. She had one fleeting thought through all the panic – she'd get him back for this. Then, the desperate instinct to survive kicked in and before she knew it she'd let go of the handlebars, grappling her the Lycra slide of Jackson's torso.

She felt the heat of his lower back as her cheek clamped against the solid sinew of his ribcage. Jackson's body like an anchor, holding her fast in the hell of the storm.

As she screwed her eyes closed again, she wrenched some air into her lungs from the hurtling wind that was choking her. Then, something shifted, deep in her core. It was like every emotion she'd ever had was erupting, venting, finding release. Something primal, something deep, some huge animal vibration. Reeling at the shock of the sound, before she even knew it was coming from her. It amplified, as she hurled back her head, threw her jaw wide.

A shrieking, howling scream.

# Chapter 5

A win for The Howler then.

Longer than Jackson cared to remember since that had happened. World event or charity gig, the taste was still sweet. Flipping the front wheel out of the tandem, he hoisted the frame up onto the roof rack and began to secure the fastenings. Wins all round in fact. Kudos for his Aunt and her charities; all his duties for the day looked after, the right hands shaken and enough of them, the right prizes presented, the right smiles smiled, the right egos massaged. A ton of goodwill for Jackson the good-boy, whose whitewash was getting a golden aura here today. And he gave the finger with a right and proper royal wave to the trashy papers waiting for him to mess up.

The upside of flying across the finish line in first place being slightly off-set by the downside of having a banshee along for the ride. Okay. He howled mildly when the adrenalin rush had nowhere else to go, that he'd concede – but the screeching wail that came out of the Cherry Bomb was barely human. Something else entirely. Although, overall he had to admit she'd surprised him, impressed him even, with the way she'd got a grip of her fear and hung on in there. She was obviously made of sterner stuff than that first candyfloss impression suggested.

And speaking of cherries.

'Jackson, you'll give me the heads-up when you're ready for our interview? A quick chat to camera won't take long, but sooner rather than later would be better. Like, now would be great.'

Bryony, seemingly transformed from the wreck of a woman who'd climbed off the tandem; she was still in the bubblegum shorts, though, striding across the car park waving her arms.

'Found your bossy self again, then?'

And her clipboard.

That oh-so-arrogant way she assumed people were going to go along with her every whim rubbed him the wrong way.

'No thanks to you.' Flicking her almost-perfect-again hair over her shoulder, she waggled a microphone in his direction and posted him an iron smile.

This was one lady who was very used to getting her own way. Super-efficient, super-composed. So long as she wasn't travelling by tandem.

He propped the bike wheel against the bumper. 'Now is as good a time as any.'

Playing it cool, he stifled a grin and rubbed his back. Still aware of where she had clung on to him, the imprint of her warmth sticking on his spine like a muscle memory that wouldn't shift. Hell, given those spiky nails of hers, he was lucky she hadn't shredded his whole stomach along the way, even if it was sending his blood rushing south as he recalled it.

'Dave, Tony.' A half-lift of one of her perfect eyebrows and a camera guy and a sound man materialised out of nowhere. 'Here will do, Jackson. Annie's gone, so I'm standing in to ask the questions. It's my first time, so please bear with me.'

*It's my first time...* He tried to ignore the way those words made his knees sag momentarily. For an interview virgin, she was showing no sign of nerves.

Palm on his chest, she slammed Jackson to lean against the car wing, then tucked in neatly next to him. So close he couldn't escape her woman-cloud; yet they were pointedly not touching.

Shoving the mike under his chin, she nodded at the camera guy and cleared her throat.

'A great win for you today, Jackson, wouldn't you say?' TV voice all pretty now, expecting him to play nice.

'So long as you overlook my perforated eardrums.' No harm in telling it like it was. 'That was one major scream you did back there.'

Contact alert. Nudging him with her shoulder as she stiffened. All huffy, then, with a shake of accusing.

'Which wouldn't have happened if you'd put on the brakes.' Judging by the shrill, he'd caught her by surprise there.

He returned her nudge, just for badness, and saw the whites of her eyes for his trouble. 'We won. Winning's what matters every time, even if it was just for fun today and hopefully we raised lots of money for good causes too. But asking a competition cyclist to brake on a final hill... Seriously, it's not going to happen.' Leaning back, he gave a low chuckle. 'It's like asking a tiger to turn vegetarian.'

Wow. Great view down her top from this angle. Trying to damp down his grin of appreciation for that and simultaneously ensure that his perving would not be discernible on camera. Good boys didn't gawp at boobs, full stop, even if the sight was unavoidable. And she was still wearing his jacket. He made an instant mental note to leave it that way.

'So Jackson, you've had huge success over the years – what's your secret? How come you're such a winner?'

A bit deep for a Saturday lunchtime in a car park. He blinked away the view of the tender skin at the top of her cleavage and focused on the mic instead as he searched for a suitably swift retort to shut up Ms Sure-of-herself.

'I always get inside my opponent's head, it's a great advantage to be a mind reader.' He tilted his head to see how she took that one, cocked a challenging eyebrow at her. For a first timer she was holding her own alarmingly well.

'On top of all your other gifts you're a mind reader too?' Her voice went up an octave and she sent him a disbelieving smirk.

'Yep.' He felt a grin spreading slowly across his face. It was rare to find an interviewer so delightfully...how could he put it... reactive. That had to be the rookie coming out and he couldn't resist the fun.

'Okay! Great! So prove it then, tell me what am I thinking now?'

She pursed her lips determinedly, and dragged in a huge breath that brought her boobs at least six inches closer to his face, making the view he couldn't resist returning to even better. Hmmm, soft flesh. Delicious, tantalising, even if it did belong to someone, who, now she'd recovered herself, obviously took pleasure in pushing him.

Half-closing his eyes, he slid out his reply. 'At a guess I'd say you're thinking I'm hot...' Holding back his smile, he waited in anticipation, and wondered how far as a good-boy he could push this. Interview boundaries were new territory for him – his whole career as a bad-boy he'd relished in saying exactly what he pleased and damn the consequences. Come to think of it, he wasn't sure he could recall an interview where there'd been underlying smoulder like this.

Whatever reaction he'd been hoping for, he hadn't counted on traffic-light-red cheeks, or the spluttering into her hair.

'Wwww...wh...what?'

He caught the panic in her eyes as she opened and closed her mouth, doing a pretty full-on impersonation of a goldfish.

Holy crap, he'd meant to needle, not cause the woman to do a total stall on camera. Who'd have thought the shiny armour plating of Ms Bossy would have been so quick to crack? He'd had his fun, but he wasn't completely heartless.

He swooped in to rescue her. 'Easy assumption, bit of a cheat, given most women find me irresistible.' As she was still picking her jaw up off the floor, he bashed on. 'Don't be too hard on yourself, I've yet to meet a woman who doesn't fancy the pants off me!'

'Not at all arrogant, are you?'

He breathed a sigh of relief as she came back at him and resumed staring down her top. Opponents were way more fun when they were fighting on all cylinders. And what he'd thought was smoulder between them was fast escalating into full blown fire.

'Hey, cheeky!' One swift smack on his arm from her sent his grin wild. That had to be for the inappropriate sight line, given the way she was dead-eyeing him.

'So Tiger, are they going to let you out of your cage any time soon? Any plans to return to racing?'

And all credit to her for the way she bounced back from the brink with that blinder of a question he had no intention of answering. Diversionary tactics were called for. He fired up the famous charm. He had no idea at what point exactly this interview had morphed from plain Q&A to out and out flirt, but somewhere along the line it had. And to hell with it; he was going in for the squeeze now, and good-boy was just going to have to suffer the consequences.

'Only if you promise to come with me.' Stretching an arm around her waist, he squished her hard against him, reeling at the way she smelled like heaven as he struggled to disentangle her hair strands from his chin stubble. However, she was weirdly delighted that she'd pushed him into grabbing her.

'Fabulous offer, Jackson. But you can dream on.' With a toss of her head, she shot him a wicked smile. 'Unless you discover the brake lever, that is.'

Nice retort. She'd had him for breakfast and now she was spitting him out. Not sure if the pain of being publicly humiliated by Candyfloss-on-a-stick was sweet or not. But regardless of the push of those delectable breasts against his chest, he was wrapping this up, and fast.

'Great, well thanks for the ride, Bryony. Screaming aside, you were awesome. We make a great team.' Giving her one last nudge with his hip, he tipped her a lazy wink. Stuck around long enough to watch the pink flow into her cheeks.

Then quick handshakes all round to the rest of the gawping crew.

And he was getting the hell out of here, before good-boy suffered any more collateral damage.

# Chapter 6

'Hey. Without the pink shorts, I almost didn't recognise you.'

Bryony knew it wasn't true. Jackson had clocked her as soon as she strode into the empty hotel bar three hours later, eleven miles up the coast. He'd watched every step of her high-heeled progress across the long room, almost as if he'd been expecting her.

'Pleased I've found you. Cressy remembered she'd booked you in here and your car was the final giveaway. I've brought your jacket.' She held it out to him as if to justify her arrival, now strangely reluctant to let it go. 'I'm the only one staying on tonight; the rest of the crew have gone back to London. I'm off to Northumberland in the morning, so I got the delivery job.'

Why the heck was she making the frantic excuses? Cressy and her 'go-geddim' cries obviously had her running scared. Running guilty more like, given she'd not exactly been mortified when he'd driven off leaving her wearing his top, and not minding at all that she had to leave the elegant streets of Scarborough and wind all the way to this isolated hotel that stood proud and lonely on the wind-raked cliff top. Just because he was the hunk of the century. For one more glimpse of his decorative awesomeness. Nothing to do with the way he'd sent white-hot shivers through her whole body when he'd grabbed her. And totally excused by the fact that she never dated, so she really couldn't be interested. *Could she?*

She shot him her best pro smile, just to prove this was work and nothing more.

'Miss Organization. Always last to finish. Why does that not surprise me?' Jackson climbed off his bar stool, and pulled out another for her. 'Might as well have a drink now you're here? Bit of a trek, but worth it for the seclusion. And best of all, no press – apart from you, that is.'

The lazy smile he slid her unleashed a single butterfly in her chest. Then another. Designer-threadbare jeans never looked so good on a guy. Impossible not to lock onto the bulge of his groin as he pushed up onto the bar stool again. Then the whole damn flock were loose. Five hundred butterflies. Choking her, with their frantic fluttering.

'The views here are awesome too.' Hauling her attention upwards, with that dark grin of his. 'Once you look out to sea that is.'

Loving the way his cheeks creased when he smiled, the crinkles at the corners of his eyes, that tan that was way deeper than any British summer gave. Just for a minute she soaked up the whole charisma of this super-athletic guy who was entirely at one with being head-and-shoulders above his nearest rivals. The whole superhuman quality was disturbingly familiar, reminding her an awful lot of her older and supremely successful brother, Brando. And, yes, Jackson had picked her up there. Again. But this time she wasn't playing.

'I'm sure the views are spectacular.' Determined to keep this professional, not risking an acknowledgement of where her eyes had landed, or that he'd caught her out. Again. 'So what can I get you to drink, Jackson?'

His eyebrows raised in surprise at the ease of her offer. 'Thanks, but it's my shout. The beer is good and cold, if you like that.'

'Beer it is then.'

A drink with the boys. No harm in that. She did it all the time. Didn't usually make her heart thump this badly though. As the barman pushed beer and a glass across the bar, she waved away the glass, picking up the bottle. They were two colleagues, sitting, with their elbows and their bottles on the bar. Nothing more.

'I admire you for what you did today.' He shot her a sideways glance. 'It took guts.'

She shrugged, knowing he didn't have to say this. 'I don't usually make that much fuss.'

'Even so – and before you jump on me, I'm not being patronising – you did really well.' The gravel in his voice sent a twang through her chest, his lips curving deliciously as he played mischievously. 'Backside sore?'

Not holding back, then, although there was something simultaneously charming and disarming about his directness.

'It could be worse.' She grimaced. Not that she should be discussing it with him, although talking like this made the drink more matter of fact. Somehow safer. Like she was simply one of the guys. Boy-talk was good.

He swirled his beer round in the bottle, angled his head and studied her through narrowed eyes.

Dragging in a breath, she stood up to his scrutiny.

'And I like that you aren't throwing yourself at me.'

Wow. That came out of left field. Tag-line for Jackson Gale: expect the unexpected.

'Throwing myself at you? As if.' Incredulity made her voice squeak. 'Spoken like someone who thinks they're irresistible.' She sniffed, definitely not about to reinforce his ego, whatever she thought privately. 'Or maybe I haven't got around to it yet?'

Another smile. All rugged jaw and the darkest twinkle. Many more of those, and she might have to rethink her hands-off policy.

'No. I'm confident that you won't. You're nothing like the women I usually come into contact with – or rather, fight off.' He drummed his fingers on the bar 'I like it. It's intriguing.'

Was she really hearing this? Not so much of the fighting off either, if you believed the official biography.

'Don't you get fed up of being so super-sure of yourself?'

That made him laugh. 'Spoken in person by Miss Uber-Confident herself.'

As he drained his beer, the hollow at the base of his neck played havoc with her insides.

'So…' He cleared his throat, swallowed again. 'Shall we take this outside? There's the beach, the terrace, or my log cabin. Your choice.'

What? Bryony's stomach officially left the building. A man who knows what he wants and goes all out to get it. Like a line from *The Official Biography*. Picking up her own beer, she took a like-I-even-give-a-damn swig. The past fifteen minutes had confirmed this as the weirdest weekend of her life to date, and it wasn't just the tandem fiasco.

Sadie, her last stoically-single friend, had just signed up for matrimony, she thought to herself, presuming that's what Friday's hold-the-date card meant. Okay, Cressy was still single, but Cressy was so far off the couples' radar she didn't figure. And Bryony was still reeling from her mum's approach last night; although to be fair to her mother, how did you sugarcoat an offer like that? It was bound to sound insulting. Suggesting someone was unlikely to meet a partner before it was too late was not the easiest line to spin. Then she'd been shoved in front of the camera for the first time ever, and that was definitely the wrong side, from the mess the interview with Jackson had turned into.

All going down in Scarborough of all places.

She allowed herself a latent shudder for what had gone on at the end-of-sixth-form weekend bash, at The Esplanade Hotel in Scarborough, when she was eighteen. Losing her virginity to Aphrodisiac-Alex – who really hadn't lived up to the name, even though he'd been everyone else's heart throb at the time – hadn't been her proudest moment. Drunk on the fire escape at six in the morning – it really had been a just a matter of her wanting to get that milestone out of the way and him being a) there, and b) ready, willing and able, which was more than could be said of the rest of the guys who were largely either spoken for or wasted. Last man standing, so to speak. It didn't take long and she hadn't seen him since. And granted that had been back in the day, before she took her teenage grab-all-the-man-you-can tendencies firmly in hand, and before she'd headed off from Lincolnshire to London and channelled her energy into a becoming a go-getting career-success instead. But it would always be there, an indelible shadow on the radar of her memory.

And as if the Scarborough shudders weren't enough for one girl to handle, this weekend was all being played out against the backdrop of the other biggie she'd promised herself not to think about, the biggie that had sent her fleeing up here in the first place. That would be the biggie she couldn't possibly dwell on for a whole weekend at home, because, let's face it, they didn't come much bigger than the love of your life getting married to someone else. Even if that love had remained completely unre-quited, unacknowledged, unreturned and unspoken for the best part of fourteen years, it still hurt like a hole in her side. Not forgetting that tomorrow she was about to start a month off work, and she didn't have the first idea what she was going to do with herself after she'd popped in on her married girlfriends.

And now this.

A drink with the worst womaniser, possibly in the history of the world, who thanks you for ignoring him, then asks you to his cabin. Presumably *not* to have sex with him whilst standing on her head, because, to be honest, this weekend the whole world was turning upside down and back to front.

And Cressy's words pirouetted around her brain. *We both know you need to lighten up. This could be your chance…* What exactly had that wild-girl teenager Bryony got out of becoming so serious? A successful career? Weekends when you worked because everyone in your social circle was married off? Being in control? Maybe she should have just carried on down Slut Street; at least then she'd have had some decent sex along the way. She cringed to think what a distant memory that was.

'So?' The most attractive hunk in the universe was looking at her expectantly as he climbed off his bar stool.

'Sorry?'

'If you've finished your beer shall we…go?' Inclining his head, raising his eyebrows, resting the lightest hand in the small of her back.

A convulsive shiver zithered up her spine. Why did he have to speak with that chocolate growl? Could she dare to try what she'd denied herself for so long? Take this outside, and see where it ended up?

Before she knew, she'd flashed him a dazzler of a smile that had nothing to do with professional. 'Why not?'

*Think of it as a gift.*

She slipped off her stool, and landed in the crook of his waist.

# Chapter 7

The sea was sparking blue in the late afternoon sun. Even though the wind was blowing a gale, no pun intended, Bryony had surprisingly plumped for the precipitous walk down the cliff path to the beach, maybe because she judged it to be the least high-risk sport on offer. Energetic sex back at the cabin or cliff-walking, and she'd opted for the latter. A wry grimace from Jackson to that one; although looking at the height of the heels on her boots, walking anywhere off piste in those could be considered crazy dangerous.

Leaning into the crosswind, those heels obviously weren't proving too much of a handicap as she picked her way between the wet rocks and the seaweed, hands rammed in her puffa-jacket pocket, hair whipping across her face. Almost like he could feel her heartbeat carried by the wind across the space between them. Those go-on-forever legs in those tight leggings made his mouth water. Something about the sheer strength and exuberance of her making his chest twang, not to mention…

'So, what drives you?' A gust snatched his words away as he spoke them, but he wanted to ask. Something to do with the gritty determination of the woman.

She whirled around to face him as he caught her up. Amazing how she still managed to look like a supermodel despite the Force Ten gale.

'I get a buzz from making things happen. Same as you, getting your rocks off by winning.'

'Succinct and insightful too. Sharp lady.'

'I do my best.' She twitched those delectable lips into a grin that showed her perfect teeth.

Funny how he'd missed that this morning. He'd been too busy watching for cracks in the gloss, to see through to the inside and kicking against the stone-wall of her determination. Je'd been aware of the whole explosion of chemistry, which he'd put down solely to his own need in that department, but he hadn't fully appreciated the long-limbed wow-factor of the whole package. Not that he was going there. She was seriously off limits, but for some reason he couldn't bear to let her go before he'd found out more about her. There was this inexplicable urge to keep her with him for as long as he could, just because the combination of her layers and her strength was fascinating; not like any woman he'd come across before.

'Getting your kicks from making people do what you want. That figures, from what I saw earlier.' Accidentally on purpose, he bumped his hip gently against hers. Gentle flirting was a contact sport, and there was definitely a buzz here. 'Used to getting your own way from an early age, A.K.A. being spoiled?'

'Not exactly.' She screwed up her face, as if weighing things up. 'It's complicated.'

And she claimed full marks for not dismissing the 'spoiled' taunt out of hand.

'Try me?'

'Don't worry, I'm not going to send you to sleep with my whole mixed-up childhood life story thing. But when I was eleven my older brother ended up inheriting a country estate. It's way less glamorous than it sounds. We didn't have a wealthy upbringing at all, we were a disaster as a family; my parents had spilt up, and it was just an accident that a couple of people died and unexpectedly left my brother, Brando, next in line. From quite a young age

44

I used to go to help with events there. In fact, it was lots of hard work, but it taught me how to handle people and that's where I got hooked on the satisfaction of pulling off the impossible.' She broke into a guilty smile. 'And you're right – I learned how to wind my brother round my little finger. Back in the day I used to commandeer his helicopter all the time, but I've pretty much grown out of that now. But isn't that what baby sisters are for?'

If she was hoping that would make his eyes widen, then she was in luck; but more strangely still, it appeared to have been a throwaway line. Eyes wider still at that thought. And a fellow survivor of a broken family too. He covered his surprise by blurting out the first thing about families that came into his head.

'I wouldn't know, I only have brothers.' A neat line that no way expressed the train wreck that was his family life, or the screwed up state of relationships with his father and brothers and as they stood now. Connor, a golden boy, who hadn't screwed up when it mattered like he had, who'd been snapping at his heels his whole life, who was still out there now, feeding their father's insatiable hunger for glory, providing him with the reflected limelight he loved. And Nic, a self-made success. As for his mother, well don't even go there. Who the hell started talking about families? 'Connor's a famous cyclist. You'll no doubt have heard of him.' The wind whipped away the bitter laugh he spat out with that last comment.

'Or maybe not.' She shot him a shamefaced grin. 'I don't know the first thing about cycling, I was blagging it this morning. The last time I went on a bike I was about six.'

'Why does that not surprise me?' Anything was better than discussing the Gale clan. Suppressing his mirth at her embarrassed discomfort, he gave her a shoulder nudge as he polished his next spinner. 'But bike-riding's like sex. Once you've learned how to do it, you don't forget.'

Only her eyebrows shooting up showed he'd surprised her. One-all in the surprise stakes then.

'*So* like a man to make that link. Or are you simply living up to your perennial reputation as a womanizer?' Tossing back her head, she let out a laugh. 'I read the biography, you know. What's your next line? Asking me if my favourite cocktail is "Sex on the beach?"'

'Let me think. Slimy rocks, the sea approaching… I don't think so.' He jumped to avoid the bubbles of tide running up the sand and steered her up the beach a little. 'Later maybe?'

And joking. Obviously.

'Dream on, Mister. I gave up on casual sex years ago because it was meaningless and empty, so I learned to say "No". Maybe you could learn that too.' She gave a shrug, but posted him a mischievous sideways glance. 'One tiny word, but it's powerful.'

And maybe she had a point. If the faceless sex was so great, how come he'd hardly missed it when he called a halt? Until today, of course, when his groin had been jumping like a jack-in-a box. Still was. Put it down to the adrenalin surge of a win, or more likely, the Cherry Bomb at his side and her explosive promise, which strangely hadn't lessened any since she swapped her silky pink wrapper for leggings and padded jacket. Still that same bewitching scent, screamingly strong, regardless of the salty, biting air.

'So I take it you're not propositioning me, then?' No idea why he needed to push it, but he did.

Now it was her turn to jump as the surf rushed towards her toes. 'We've already established that.'

A few more hand-in-pocket strides at his side, this human dynamo was walking so fast he could barely keep up, despite her precipitous heels.

She glanced back at him. 'To be honest I'm so far out of the couples game, my mother has offered to pay to freeze my eggs.'

Conversation stopper or what? Though judging by the way she was chewing her lip and furrowing her brow, she'd shocked herself as much as him with that one. Laying it on the line. Making it clear, her hurling herself at him wasn't going to happen.

Leaving the first move down to him. When had he ever had to

make the first move? Though that wasn't really happening either, even if he had taken every precaution to keep the press off his tail.

'So what do you do if you don't date? Are you implying that you work all the time?' And when did he become this big on interrogation?

She might be an organisational whizz, but what a waste of all that energy.

She smiled up at him, making the pit of his stomach fizz, making him ache to taste her. 'A professional cyclist should understand about non-stop work better than most, from what I read.'

So she'd been reading up, had she? When did he ever ache like this? 'Didn't you read about the extra-curricular bits?' Mind reverting automatically. Too bad he wasn't going to taste.

'There you go again. You and your one-track, extra-curricular mind.'

Grabbing her was his last intention, but he threw an easy arm around her shoulder anyway. No excuses, other than the caveman in him stepping up to stake his claim. One slight jolt from her. A strike before she organised her opposition may work to his advantage – if he didn't move in fast enough, he suspected she may well deck him.

Easy. Spinning around, heading for her lips, he pushed away the salty strands of her hair. Her gasp of surprise drew him straight into the luscious heat of her mouth as he traced his tongue along her lip, pushed beyond those perfect teeth. Soft, delicious, sweet as raspberry muffin. And hungry too. One second of hesitation, then she came to meet him, tangling, like he knew instinctively she would, her vitality surging into him. Forging her body against his, strong and arousingly urgent as he dragged her, crushed her against his pelvis. Embracing her exuberance, and doubting he'd ever held anyone this real, this human, her energy flooding through, making him amazingly, resoundingly alive. The ache in his groin thumping as she ground her hip against the thud of his erection. Barely pausing as he tugged past the soft wool of her cardigan, through the yielding cotton of her t-shirt to the hot skin beneath. The bang of his pulse, resounding in his ears, drowning out the wind, hearing that small groan of affirmation vibrating from her throat as he cupped her heavy breast in his hand. The full perk of her nipple strong enough to jut through the padded silk.

The thunder of desire galloped through his body as he slipped down the bra-cup, lightly scratching with his nail to bring her nipple to amazing standing attention. Then, as he rolled it between his fingers, her body sagged against him and the mewing from her throat told him that he'd hit the spot. Dragging the oxygen into his lungs to cope with the double speed pounding of the blood around his body, heart rate racked off the scale by the moans of the woman leaning heavy in his arms.

'Jackson!' With a squawk, she yanked away from him. 'The sea!'

The chill of water engulfed his feet as a wave rolled over his sneakers. Opening his eyes, he took a second to register the ocean fringe advancing towards them and another to decide he didn't even give a damn. Wanting to carry on pushing the Cherry Bomb past the point of no return, until she exploded and came apart in his arms.

'*Holy crap. We could drown here.*' His survival head coming late to the party, yanking down caveman's 'Do Not Disturb' notice. In a few minutes the tide rushing into the bay would be far enough up the beach to cut off their way back. Where the hell was protective caveman? Significantly AWOL apparently, whilst pillage-caveman got his rocks off.

Grabbing her wrist, he began to run. 'Come on, we need to get back to the cliff path. Fast.' Dragging her along the foaming edge of the sea, staying as far away from the mud cliffs as they could. A second super-charge of adrenalin surged through his limbs now as he hauled her into the headwind across the amphitheatre of the bay. Struggling, bumping, sliding, stumbling over the rocks, soupy water up to their ankles, looking up long enough to pinpoint the place on the cliffs they were heading for, where the diagonal line of the path stretched upwards to safety.

Her dead weight pulled on his arm, and he turned to see her, hair strewn across her mouth, hauling her breath in huge gasps. 'You go on.' Her panting words, torn away by the gale, as she bent, groaning, hands on her knees. 'I'll catch you up.'

'No way, we'll go together.' Catching her arm again, forging forward. 'Come on, you can make it – it's not far now.'

The familiar burn in his limbs. Unaware they'd walked this far, the length of the beach foreshortening, playing tricks, like the stones that were repeating beneath their feet in a continuous unending loop. Brine sticky on his face, his chest bursting as he hauled her on. The sun still glinting on the solid mass of the water beside them. Rocks and wind, wind and rocks, splashing, slithering. And then they were there, and he was heaving her up in front of him, shouldering her backside. With one lunge, he propelled her to the safety of the mud and grass on the cliffside path, and scrambled after her.

# Chapter 8

'Is my head too heavy?'

Bryony was lying on the ragged grass on the cliff top, limbs in a heap, staring at the sky, which, incidentally, was broad as any she'd seen lately. The heat of Jackson's chest was solid against her skull as she watched the cloud wisps and waited to get her wild jiving heartbeats back into line.

'Your hair's tangling in my stubble again. Does it hurt?' His gruff tones reverberated through his ribs.

*Hair caught in a guy's stubble? OMG. How far off-limits was she?*

'Nope'

And how darned okay it was. It was almost as if neither of them had wanted to break the moment by speaking, and then it had slipped into minutes and then a whole lot longer. The wind rushed over her ears, pushing the smell of damp ground up her nose and coating her lips with salt. She tried not to think how easy this felt, how she didn't want to move ever again.

'Here, have this, I picked it up on the beach before.' He shifted under her, pushed a small stone into the palm of her hand. 'It's a fossil, an ammonite. So you remember today. '

As if she'd ever forget it.

'Thanks.' She ran her index finger around the curl of the spiral. Still warm from the ride in his pocket. 'How old is it?'

'Possibly two hundred million years. Sorry, they don't make them any newer.'

A fossil from womanising Jackson Gale. Who'd have thought? 'It's perfect. Thanks.'

And then there was the tiny matter of that major snog down on the beach. Talking of perfect. Was that really her back there? Diving down his throat and loving it?

She shuddered at the thought of what he'd been doing to her nipples, shut her eyes and shook her head, just to check she was here. In person. Five minutes of ecstasy, then Jackson went on to save her life. Maybe the biography hadn't been exaggerating about his multi-faceted talents in all areas. Let's face it; some guys had it all.

Beneath her head his chest heaved in a comfortable sigh. 'Almost drowning kind of cements you together. Like we're lying under this sun as it slides down and, not wanting to be melodramatic, but it could have been the last sunset we saw.' His voice was gravelly, as one thumb grazed across the back of her hand and brought out the goosebumps in places she couldn't imagine. 'We might just have become a lost-at-sea statistic. When you get your breath back, we need to go and do something spectacular to celebrate.'

*Interesting… what might that be exactly.* This guy had charm by the shedload, and it was mighty hard to resist. *You only have to say 'no'.* One tiny word. Wasn't that what she'd told him? Whatever, she needed to make herself clear here.

'Back on the beach, the last thing I remember talking about was your one-track mind. I'm hoping we haven't gone there again.' She dragged in a breath, hating her sensible-self just for a moment. 'But, on the upside, a man who saves you from getting swept out to sea and then gives you a fossil has to be worth getting to know a little bit more. Possibly.' Grinning upwards, catching a glimpse of his chin. Capitulating, slightly. 'Dinner might be nice.'

'Dinner's a possibility.' He grinned back down at her, his teeth up close just as even and spectacular as her tongue already told her. 'Why don't we take it as it comes?' Bringing out those to-die-for wrinkles in his cheeks, he sent her on-the-ground stomach down to the basement.

'And to think, back there *I* was taking the flak for making people do what I want.' Laughing now, she gave him a soft poke in the ribs. 'It takes a manipulator to know a manipulator, wouldn't you agree?'

Easing her upwards, he got to his feet. 'I prefer to think of it as my incurable desire to win.'

Letting her gaze meander up the whole of his beautiful body, she locked him in a dead-eye gaze, lifting an eyebrow. Important to keep the man who knew he was best at everything in line, despite the fact that her head was whirling. *Especially* because her head was whirling.

He offered her a hand, 'C'mon then, Cherry Bomb, let's go.' One yank, and she flew to her feet. 'We'll get you into some dry clothes.'

More crazy talking that flipped her stomach into a triple somer-sault. Where the hell had her 'professional' gone when she needed it? *And definitely not reacting to the clothes comment.* Apart from with her racing pulse, obviously. Winning? Manipulating? Hot sex?

Whatever.

After a near-death experience anything was excusable.

She only had to say 'No'.

# Chapter 9

'Two bedrooms, two bathrooms. Made out of Swedish pinewood. It's a no-brainer. The TV company's paying, so strictly it's your place more than mine.'

So that was how Jackson had talked her into the log cabin, which apparently wasn't his at all anymore. Nice work. Thoughtfully, after this afternoon's near disaster, he'd omitted all mention of sea views from the list of facilities on offer. Add smooth talking and persuasive argument to his ever-growing list of attributes, and, no question, the guy was a killer opponent. Wheedling his way further into her good books, he propelled her straight in the direction of the en-suite with the spa bath and told her he'd be happy not to see her for the next hour or two, and inadvertently picked up more points when he didn't offer to throw in a personal massage service. Although, mentioning that thereafter the dress-code was relaxed. Bathrobes would do.

Nice try, Jackson. Dream on.

Pulling on some sweat pants and a slouchy top now, definitely the least sexy of the clothes she had here, she berated herself for only having thongs in her overnight bag. Somehow granny pants would have made her feel better equipped for the challenge ahead, because, regardless of what went on down on the beach, no matter how spectacular that kiss, now that she was back on the cliff top, her land-legs had taken over again – along with her common sense. So much easier to take refuge in the familiar persona of Bryony Marshall, workaholic man-avoider.

'How're the aching muscles?' Jackson was sprawled across the large corner sofa, entirely relaxed, half buried under a confusion of Sunday papers, as she emerged into the open-plan living area.

'Good.' Perching on the edge of the coffee table, she flashed him a smile. 'Considering what they've been through.'

Unnervingly, she felt as if she'd walked into her all-time favourite daydream. The one where she came down to Sunday breakfast to find her forever-fantasy-man sitting waiting for her… in their house… because they were married. Just this was the wrong man.

And yesterday the real man of her dreams had married someone else. Not that he'd ever noticed her, all the years she'd known him, even though he was her fallback man. Fall-back man? Who was she kidding? Matt had been her number-one choice, dammit, since she'd set eyes on him at the age of fourteen. Although close friends who knew her secret maintained he was nothing more than a vessel to place her affections in until the real guy came along, as and when she started to look for him, which she knew would be never. Good friend's brothers? Whoever said you were onto a loser with them was right. Gutting, all the same.

'You okay?' Jackson was scrutinising her through narrowed eyes. 'You look like someone walked on your grave?'

*Maybe they just did.* Who the hell said men couldn't be perceptive?

'Fine.' Lying through her teeth, for all the right reasons. She'd promised herself not to think about Matt, if not ever again, at least for this weekend. Although, strangely, that kiss on the beach had done a great job of dispatching all thoughts of him and his wedding tux, and his lovely new wife Tia, who, judging by the Facebook pics, was tiny and impossibly beautiful. But, thanks to the beach snog, there was a different man in her head now, which made a change, and he was occupying all of it. But something told her that wasn't healthy either.

'May seem better after a drink?' Jackson dipped into to an ice bucket on the table beside him, and pulled out a bottle. 'Sparkling white, the best way to smooth the race pains away, and I've started without you. Unless you'd prefer something else? Plenty of everything in the kitchen.'

'Sparkling white's cool.' Chilled. Like he was. 'Only a glass, though.'

He filled two glasses and handed her one. Funny how Jackson in the flesh was a hundred times more mesmerising than Matt had ever been, even though she'd spent the best part of ten years being hooked on him from afar. Although being here with Jackson didn't exactly feel real either, it was unusual enough to make her shivery in a dangerous kind of way. There was something compelling about the strangeness of the situation. She took a sip of wine, hoping the bubbles that spiked her nose would make it seem more concrete.

'Cutting back on the alcohol? I thought we were meant to be celebrating.' Jackson, totally edible in his slouch pants and white tee, smouldering like he was about to devour her.

And her central nervous system on crazy-time, making her whole body buzz every time his gaze traversed her boobs – which seemed to be a lot. Add in that the air felt like it had an electric charge, and she was in weird-city. He had to be mocking her as he studied her through narrowed eyes.

'One drink, and after that, I really should get going.' Doing a complete U-turn on what she'd implied earlier, but on reflection a whole night in the same cabin with Jackson and she couldn't guarantee that she wouldn't jump the guy and grind his bones to dust, however well-disciplined her good-girl act was.

'Going to where exactly?' His brow wrinkled into a frown. 'I thought we'd agreed you'd stay here? The two room guarantee and all that?' He tilted his head in query.

'You agreed. I didn't.'

One sniff, and he was onto her.

'I get it. Polar-bear feet. I can feel the ice from here.' He rubbed his chin, and slid her a sly grin. 'And talking of cold, I'm guessing a girl whose mother has given up all hope of a son-in-law is maybe a little out of practice on the one-to-one social front, which might explain why you're feeling jittery, but there's no need to be scared or run out on me. I've got quite enough experience for both of us, as you pointed out. Charm skills are the upside of having played the field.'

His grin split into a laugh. Bad move, because that exposed the column of his neck, and the hollow at the base, which made her toes go all wiggly. Oh my. Rumbled completely, by the guy with the confidence in bucket-loads. And second-guessing her like he really was a mind reader. Except he'd missed the bit about her not being able to keep her hands off him, or maybe he took that as a given, which would be where all that confidence came from.

'Super-sure of yourself aren't you?' She found herself laughing too. 'Like I said this afternoon.'

Leaning back on the sofa, he held both hands in the air.

'Okay, I get the message. Whatever you think, I'm not the cavemen you've got me down for. You have my word – I won't touch you. No action replays of what went down on the beach, I promise, if that's what it takes to make you comfortable. You come and sit on the sofa.' He jumped to his feet, steering her across the room, being extra careful to keep outside her personal-space zone. 'I'll grab the phone and we'll order some dinner, watch a movie. You have a look to see what's on.' He shot her another wicked smile. 'I'm exceptionally house-trained, I'll even let you hold the controls.' With a final satisfied grin, he flipped the TV controller in her direction, headed for the doorway to the kitchen, and disappeared.

Bemused, Bryony leaned to pick up the controller, dazed like an express train had just ran over her. What a man. Full-on didn't begin to cover it.

'Oh, and just to be clear…' his head reappeared around the door frame. 'I know you were just as turned on by that kiss as I was.'

Hanging in the air long enough to register her mouth drop open and hear the gulp that came when her heart leaped into fast-forward.

What?

All gravelly voice and hollow cheeks and stubble. Gone before she gathered her senses enough to reply. Rolling her eyes, snorting at the barefaced cheek of the man. Except he'd got it righter than she'd ever admit. Even to herself.

'And another thing…'

Back again, dammit. But this time she was ready.

'This had better be good.' She hit back with the don't-mess-with-me offensive, growled through gritted teeth. Always worked a treat on sound technicians who took the piss.

'Don't worry, it is.' He posted a beyond-satisfied smirk around the doorframe, tapped his fingers, playing for time and maximum impact. 'As I recall, you were the one who suggested dinner, so technically you're the one who asked me on this date. Thought it was worth a mention.'

Worth a mention? Worthy of a full-blown eye roll more like. Nothing else. Except a very weary sigh.

'Have you finished?' Firm, in control here, and letting him know it.

'Yes. Er, no, actually. Not yet.' And judging by the hesitation he was backing into line. Nicely.

'What now?' Exasperated was a definite put-down. Not that she meant to be nasty, but this guy took some handling. She couldn't afford to let him get one-over on her.

'I found the room service menu if you'd like to come and choose.'

Okay. Easy as. He just did.

#lookingstupid or what?

# Chapter 10

Dinner. Steak, chips and salad, on lap trays in front of the TV, with Jackson foregoing the chips. High-fat, bad carbs apparently. A body like a superman obviously didn't happen without a measure of deprivation and care. Enough fizzy wine to live up to its name, but not put her under the table. And two hours rolling around, howling with laughter, watching *Despicable Me* on DVD, which Jackson conjured from his room. Who'd have thought?

'Cartoon collection, never travel without it. Think yourself lucky I didn't make you sit through *Happy Feet.*'

She guessed that was his way of excusing himself for inflicting her with his childlike taste, not that she'd minded a Disneyfest at all. She could imagine, now she knew him better. Pin-up hottie of the century, morphed into one big kid. And trying not to think how engaging that was, and conveniently easy, as laughter diffused the sexual tension which crackled across the gap between them. Took her mind off the heat of the man, who'd moved next to her on the sofa, stretching those long sexy legs of his to rest tantalisingly on the coffee table. Making a deal with herself: *Look but don't touch.*

Made sure she didn't admit that after tonight *Despicable Me* had zoomed onto her list of favourite movies too, or give him the opportunity to seize on the fact they found the same things hilarious. It was important to play down how comfy she was in his company – give this guy any nugget he could vaguely interpret as a compliment, and he would be in danger of getting stuck in the building, given that his head would be too swollen to get through the door. His self-belief was not in short supply. Honing in now on his languid profile as he leaned by the open door to the terrace. Cressy would be disgusted at her for what she was throwing way. Sex on legs, think of it as a gift. Maybe she'd regret it too, tomorrow.

'So how did you get into cycling?' Suddenly reluctant for the evening to finish, she threw Jackson a carefully chosen, open-ended question.

'I've been at it for as long as I remember. When we showed some promise as lads, our dad seized on that, more for himself than for us. He got his kicks from our success, and he drove us pretty relentlessly.' He gave a pensive shrug. 'My old man's a bit of a fucked-up guy, I'm afraid.'

She assumed that last excuse had to be in response to her appalled expression. 'But didn't it make you want to rebel?'

Was a dad who was fucked-up and alive better or worse than one like hers, who'd broken her heart when he left, then died?

'My dad's regime didn't allow questions, let alone rebellion. His methods were harsh, but I guess we came through in the end. By the time we were old enough to stand up to him, we were hooked on winning. Signing up to a pro team was the fast way out, and I went when I was eighteen. Other young riders found the team life a shock, with the hard training, the discipline and being away from home, but for me it was like a holiday camp after my dad.'

'It all sounds rough.' Poor Jackson. Who'd have thought he'd had such a bad time. It made what she'd always thought of as her own raw deal seem easy.

'It toughened me up, made me what I am, and to be honest I don't often talk about it.' He gave a sigh and moved towards the open French doors. 'Coming out to see the moonshine on the sea?' A casual invitation, flipped over his shoulder as he sidled out, moving the conversation to somewhere safer for him, but less safe for her.

What a corny line! But innocuous all the same. They were both adults here; they both knew the score. Any moves that were going to happen would have been made hours ago. Since she laid down the unspoken rules, he'd backed right off, and now she'd got her own rampant woman back in the box, she was well out of the danger zone. Easing herself off the sofa, she padded across the polished boards. One last glimpse of the clouds scudding across the night sky before she went to bed slotted neatly into the low-risk category. Good-girl Bryony could manage that.

'It's breezy out here.' Keeping it light, the wind snatching her hair as she stepped into the small courtyard. 'And so bright. Amazing how the moon splashes across the water.' She moved across to where Jackson was leaning on the waist-high wall, scanning the horizon, t-shirt flapping.

'Hey, look.' She stooped to examine something moving on the ground at the edge of the planted area. 'I thought it was a leaf, but it's a frog.'

Two seconds, and Jackson was crouching beside her, hunky shoulder uncomfortably close to her cheek, extending a finger towards the ground. 'Ahhh, it's a toad.'

Trust Mr. Know-it-all.

'There's a difference?'

'Toads have more warty skin – and they don't hop, they crawl, although technically they're all frogs.' He tickled the top of its head gently with a leaf as it moved to take cover under a stone. 'We used to spend all summer collecting them on holidays in Cornwall when we were kids – when we weren't cycling that was.'

'Typical boy.' Smiling, she gave a shrug, 'Toad, frog, whatever, he's pretty.'

Jackson let out a snort. 'Typical contrarian woman. A frog and a prince to choose between, and you hone in on the damned frog.'

Laughing, she stood up, moving to take a last look at the sea over the wall.

'Not big-headed at all then, putting yourself in the prince category?'

'Prince of darkness maybe?' He raised his eyebrows, voice husky, sending prickles down her spine as he came to stand behind her. Not touching, but close enough for her to breathe in the scent of clean male, to sense the shadow of his warmth on her back. 'Cold?' His breath brushing her neck sent a skitter through her body.

'No.'

So close, she should be legging it. Except her legs were frozen, and nothing to do with the temperature. If she dragged her arms tight around her ribs she might get the juddering under control.

'Your teeth are chattering.' Not much of a warning from him, but the only one she got. Then the breath left her body as he folded his arms around her. 'I'll warm you up.'

*Nooooooooooooo.* Bracing herself to protest. Too late.

*Or, how about yes?* The sensuous slide of skin on skin as his muscled arms closed over hers… Reason flew out the window, and lust won hands down. She leaned into him, and as his lips traced an exploratory path below her ear, a silver avalanche began at her scalp, and tumbled over every inch of her skin to her toes.

'Jackson.' Standing rigid, she braced herself against the onslaught. Delicious, compelling. Wanting this frozen moment to last forever. And then his hands were strong on her shoulders, as he spun her to face him. One graze of stubble on her upper-lip and his mouth landed on hers like a heat-seeking missile, turning her legs to molten syrup with the taste of him. She sagged against him as he whipped the oxygen out of her. Sweet. Achingly sweet. Peaches and cream, raspberry cupcakes, white-chocolate cheese-cake. Feeding her the sugar-rush of her life, all wrapped up with the power of pure, unadulterated man.

The out-of-control brunt of his erection crushing up against her stomach, making the need pool between her legs. The aching pleasure of those strong male fingers as he slid his hand inside her top, and scraped his nails across her back. Dying as he moved around the front and teased a nail across her breast, then pulling down her bra cup, still kissing her as if his life depended on it, groaning his pleasure deep into her throat. Her knees sinking as he toyed with her nipple. Then, with his hand on her back, her bra clip twanged, and she gasped for air as he broke from the kiss. One yank and her t-shirt was up. She gave a small cry as his mouth landed on her nipple, shooting sharp judders of pleasure through her as his tongue tangled, sucking and circling, sending her cross-eyed, as his fingers deftly worked her other side.

'O my.' Back against the wall, lifting her leg, locking it over his hip, so she could thrust her pelvis and grind the heart of her pulsing wetness against the throbbing head of his erection. Meeting its heat through the fabric, every nudge forging a rocket of desire deep into her core. Searching, sliding her hand down the rock-hard muscle of his stomach, past the edge of his slouch pants, hearing him moan again as her hand closed around the length of his shaft.

Hot skin. Grappling with the elastic, tugging down his pants, and the dusky smell of male rising as she freed him. Closing her hand around his length, sliding up and down the hugeness of it, panting, aching for the whole beautiful rock-hard length of it.

'Can't wait.' Her mumbling was urgent. 'I need you. Now.'

Jackson, bleary, lifting his head. 'Here? Sure?'

Running her hand over the slippery arc, finding the tip, already sticky, a primeval force within her driving her to take what she had to have. 'Now Jackson.'

With one lift he'd swung her hips round to rest on the terrace table, a tug and he'd whipped down her sweat pants, flung her thong to who knows where.

'Protection.' A grunt, a fumble in his pocket, then he'd ripped the foil and rolled on, torn off his tee.

Bending her knees up, leaning back, feeling her eyes widen as she took in the size of him. Muscles shining in the shadows, and the massive thrust of his erection reaching for the sky.

Slick and wet and desperate to suck him inside her. He waited, just a second, a smile playing around his lips as he registered the ache in her. She lay back, shuddering, knowing that one touch was going to send her to heaven. Then she felt the glorious nudge of the tip of him. An inch was all it took. Pulsing on her, rocking into her, pushing her over the cliff edge, and she exploded around him, her whole body erupting in a volcano, pleasure throbbing and resonating through her.

Heart banging, dragging in her breath, and he was still, poised, shuddering a little, waiting.

'Hey…easy there…' His lips curled into a soft smile as he breathed into her ear. 'If that was anything like as awesome for you as it was for me…'

Leaning forward, burying her fingers in the muscle of his buttocks, she pulled him towards her, her first storm over, but knowing she wasn't done. The heat rising again inside her as she opened and he pushed into her. Slowly, screamingly slowly at first, then pulling back, teasing her, tangling with her, pushing and pulling as she gulped through the glorious agony of it. Then halfway in he stopped, cupped a breast in each hand and scraped his nails across her nipples. Scraping until she thought he was going to drive her crazy. Just at the point where she was sure she was going to go wild, he thrust deeper into her. One slide, and she had the whole damned length of him, no idea how she was going to breathe, no idea how she was going to exist. Then as he began to move, faster, faster, suddenly she knew she was going to go again, not able to help herself, throwing herself back, lying, arching herself to the sky, as he impaled her over and over again, driving her on. Then, suddenly, above her the sky split open, and as her climax erupted; her whole world disintegrated. Clamping onto him, and through her choking gasps, she felt the final thrust of his ejaculation, heard the howl of his orgasmic groan as he collapsed on top of her.

## Chapter 11

'What are you doing?'

Stuffing the last crumbs of a muffin into her mouth, knees up, feet on the sofa, Bryony looked up from her phone in response to Jackson's question.

'Tweeting. Why? I always tweet before bed, if I don't my friends will wonder what's happened.' Her defensive tone was no doubt a reaction to his eyebrows hitting the ceiling at that piece of news. 'And answering the text from my brother, who expends way too much energy trying to make sure I don't spend evenings like this with guys like you.'

Jackson grimaced. 'That's a bit crap. So what are you putting in your tweet?' He stifled a grin. 'Just had crazy terrace-sex with guess who? It was well worth the wait by the way. The wild, crazy sex, I mean.'

Not that he'd had a four minute table-ender on a terrace before, though he'd keep that bit to himself. Neither had he encountered anyone who insisted on fast-forward, then came apart twice in as many seconds. Polar bear feet not only coming in from the cold but getting super-heated on the way came as one big surprise – and fast as it was, the orgasm had blasted him out of this world. Wow to that one. Put it down to the sexual desert of the previous year.

'Fab moonlight on the sea hashtag east-coast-joys.' That'll cover it.' Looking up, she sent a flash of a smile over the top of her phone. 'Crazy's one way of describing it. I couldn't help noticing you had a condom at the ready out there.'

Nice tweet, then straight onto him. Nothing he wasn't prepared for though. Apology at the ready.

'Old habits. Nothing to do with my expectations about tonight, I promise.' Added hurriedly, in the vain hope she'd buy the truth, even if it did sound unlikely. 'With guys in cycling, carrying condoms is one way you look out for each other. That way no one's ever disappointed, and everyone stays healthy.'

'Hmmmm. Sounding a lot like an ad for an STD charity there. I believe you, thousands wouldn't.' She tapped her phone on her lip, thoughtfully. 'It was crazy, wasn't it? Why was it so wild?'

Good question. He'd never had sex that feral.

'No idea.' Shrugging, feigning ignorance, because he had an idea the blame lay entirely with her, but no way could he say that. 'Maybe it was the adrenalin hanging round from the ride or after running to beat the tide on the beach. Who knows? Maybe it's that basic human survival instinct that kicks in when there's danger around. The same way people shag like rabbits when there's a war on, and everyone bonks after funerals.'

'Like a celebration of being alive, you mean?'

'Exactly.'

'Maybe you should commemorate your survival by having a muffin. I brought them in from the car. No one should die before they've tasted one of these.' Sucking a finger of one hand, she shoved an open cake box towards him with the other. 'No arguments, I insist.'

Firm. Bossy. Or just plain domineering? He took a moment to adjust to the railroading.

'Diets are the norm for a pro-cyclist. You learn to live with the hunger. It's a way of life that takes a lot of sacrifice.'

'So for a pro it really is like it says in the books?'

'Depends on the books you read.' He jumped at the opportunity to derail her efforts to force feed him, and fill her in on his life instead. God knows, there was so much to say about it he could keep her quiet all evening. 'You get to travel, you train with the team for months on end in warm places, cycling hundreds of miles a week. It's usually somewhere in the mountain. Think hairpin bends and zigzag roads, heat beating off the tarmac, deep blue skies, Italy, France, Spain, Portugal or somewhere. You race with the team on races that last weeks at a time, and then when it's winter you do it all over again in the southern hemisphere. Your body is in an extreme and heightened state of fitness, you're at risk of injury from crashes every day of your life, your whole life is carefully controlled, from pretty much every calorie you eat to how long you sleep, and the more successful you get, the more the control. The team thing is incredible. Sometimes you're working for guys in the team, sometimes they're working for you, you're supporting each other, but at the same time it's hugely competitive. If you're successful, the pay is phenomenal, it's the roughest, toughest thing in the world to do, some days you love it, some you hate it, but the adrenalin rushes and the endorphin highs are totally addictive, so you never want to stop. And with all that at stake does it sound like I'd reach for the cookie jar?'

The life of a pro-cyclist in a nutshell. Missing out the bit about adoring women hurling themselves at him, obviously. And how much he'd missed it all since he'd been away from it since the accident. And how he didn't know what the hell he was going to replace it with if his damned knee didn't get the thumbs up from the surgeons and the physios soon. And what the crap he was going to do if the unthinkable happened and he had to give up. Given her gaping mouth, opening and closing, it had surely stopped her in her tracks. Hadn't it?

'Calorie-wise you have to have earned it today.' She shot him a wicked grin. 'One way or another. Can't the Prince of Darkness come over to the nutritional dark side just this once?'

Seemed like she was unstoppable. Nice reference to half an

hour ago when his claim to be the Prince of Darkness had got him straight into her pants. After a whole lifetime of deprivation one way and another, suddenly the novelty of submitting overcame his natural instinct to refuse.

'Go on then.' He plucked a muffin from the box, threw himself down on the sofa beside her. 'On one condition.'

'Which is?'

Loving the way her eyes, narrowing in suspicion, sent an unexpected shiver whistling down his spine as he slowly teased the paper away from the cake.

'You come to the dark side again too, when I've finished this.' Stretching across, he slid a finger under her top, traced a line across her side under the elastic of her waistband. Felt her squirm against him. Running his finger over the bumps of her ribs, slipping over the silky cup of her bra. A rush of blood hit his groin as he found her nipple already quivering on high alert. Sinking his teeth deep into the muffin, he let the raspberry sweetness zing his taste buds.

'I'll take that as a yes, then.'

The sugar-high hit him instantaneously, sent his pulse into overdrive, and his erection too – although that was already well established. No one could be immune, sitting next to nipples like those. Her workplace must have more hard-ons per square foot than most. Pity any red-blooded male who had to spend their days being tantalised by that view. And this time sex was going to be different. Long, and very slow.

Easing to his feet, he grasped her hand, spun her a smile. 'Coming?'

'Where?' The tension in her hand flashed up her resistance.

'I thought we might take advantage of the king-size bed?'

Or maybe not, judging from her appalled frown.

'Definitely not bed.'

Jumpy as hell then, and massive back-pedalling called for.

'Fine by me.' He let out a mental whistle of relief for the fact she hadn't ruled out the sex. 'You know what? I'm going to sit right on here, and we'll take it from there, okay? Anything goes, apart from bed.'

Easing down next to her. No sudden movements in case she ran. Happy to play it her way. Raising his arms, he stretched back on the sofa, feeling her gaze already locked onto the bulge of his erection. Leaving it up to her, the bang of his heart reverberating through the sofa. Waiting. Knowing, from the dark dilation of her pupils behind her faltering eyelashes, she wouldn't be resisting for long.

Too right.

One hand, inching across the sofa, winding under his t-shirt, sending his pulse rate off the scale in anticipation. One finger, achingly slow, tracing the line of hair down from his navel. Then the full-blown twang of her palm hitting his shaft, almost making him lift off.

Shifting a little, he snatched his breath at the agonising pleasure hit.

'All ready then...' More of a statement than a question, her voice all husky now.

His mouth was dry with anticipation. 'Whenever you are...'

His fingertips closed on the condom in his pocket. Taking his mind off the excruciating wait. Thinking slow, thinking moody, thinking maybe they should lower the lights to go with the smoulder.

So wrong.

Wham. One leap, she jumped to standing. A bob, and a kick, her joggers hit the coffee table, and he was staring at thighs, lush, tanned, taut. And the teensiest triangle of a thong. Midnight-blue silk. Made his mouth water. Those perfect russet nails feathering on the hem of her top. He swallowed. Bit his lip to stop himself grabbing hold of her, dragged in a breath to get control. Wham again.

One twist, and she was out of her top. Aware of his jaw hitting the floor as he locked onto her breasts, bursting over the silky balcony of her bra cups. He closed his sweating fingers around the edge of the sofa cushions, preparing for the white-knuckle ride of his life.

She flicked her hair out of her eyes, accidentally brushing his knee as she strode across him, to plant one leg either side of his calves. The deepening of her cleavage cranked his already bursting erection up another notch, as she bent to grasp his slouch pants. One excruciating tug from her, he was kicking his pants away and free to rise. His sudden view of the incredible size of what he had to offer knocked his arousal further into orbit.

'Oh, my.' Her breathy gasp of appreciation was low against the roaring of his blood through his ears.

Bryony, fist covering the sensuous pucker of her mouth, chest heaving, hesitated. Legs wide, eyes bleary, no doubt working on her next move. Shifting his pelvis, he tightened his grip on the cushions. Dying to touch her, exploding for her to touch him, he watched the hairs escaping where the thong cut into the delicious crease between her legs. Counting to ten. He got as far as eight. In one fluid movement she whipped off her thong, and snapped it around the end of him. Heaven. Sliding, teasing, tugging. Aching amazing heaven.

'Stop.' Releasing his fingers, he grasped her wrist.

'Not good?

He shook his head. 'Too good, too much.' Stone chips in his throat. 'I won't last if you do that.'

Lasting? That just went out the window. He watched her tongue slide over her lips.

'You could try sitting on me?' Just an idea, he tossed out.

'Maybe I will.' The trembling of her torso the only giveaway that she wasn't completely in control.

Climbing onto the sofa, placing one foot either side of him, the scent of hot sex engulfing him as she lowered herself to crouch over him. Natural blonde too. His stomach gyrated as her legs opened.

One moment to sheathe himself, then reaching up, he slipped her bra cups down, to leave her breasts jutting gloriously above his head.

69

'Hands away!' Shooting him a blurry half-smile, she pushed his wrist, pinned his hand back onto the sofa. 'No touching. It's more fun. Just this once.'

Not even minding she was bossing him around, as she nudged down onto the tip of him. One high-voltage zap. Wet, slick, sticky. Plunging deep, he groaned, as she impaled herself on his length. Then, as she dipped forward, her breast grazed his cheek. Opening his mouth, he captured the nipple she offered. Clamped it between his lips, ravaging with his tongue as she weakened against him, mewing. The throb of his penis excruciating as her muscles clamped onto him. Gently placing a hand each side of her hips to slide her up and down the tower of his erection.

Slowly at first. Aching to hang on here, vibrating to burst into her. Then building as she took over. Riding him, tearing at his shoulders, pounding as she thrashed above him, moaning as she writhed. Grinding him, milking him, extracting her pleasure, her eyes half closed, her half-smile merged onto a moan that sent him into orbit.

'Coming...'

One sharp cry as she rose, threw back her head, and screwed her pelvis hard down on him. The view of her breasts jutting above him, disintegrated as his final thrust came. One huge surge of ecstatic acceleration propelled him, and his world shattered as he shot into her with the force of a tidal wave.

# Chapter 12

So, there had been a sea change in Scarborough in Bryony's head, but it was taking some getting used to. The whole cringing memory of losing her virginity was now eclipsed by another. One scorching hot encounter with Jackson Gale. A decade's worth of sexual pleasure crammed into one crazy night. Her skin came out in white-hot goosebumps whenever she thought about it, not to mention the tender bit between her legs – knickers sticky wet every time she remembered. Knees buckling a bit even now, as she pushed open the door of her flat to hear the landline ring off.

It was good to be back. The creak of the floorboard just inside the door, the single scuff mark on the white wall where Cressy fell over when they were moving the new TV in, were all reassuringly concrete and familiar. Hopefully, she'd left all things Jackson Gale right back in Yorkshire.

She suppressed a shudder.

Crazy was the only word for it.

Bryony Marshall. Getting down and dirty? And oh, how dirty! A one-night stand, with arguably the most arrogant man on the planet. *And the most sexually gifted.* Sexually gifted? What was she thinking? Still reeling at the shock, obviously, if her brain was throwing up phrases like that.

Eight hours of personality transplant... How else did you

explain a night that began with an explosive clinch on a terrace, ended with a sizzling coupling in the shower just before he left, and visited all places ecstasy in between? For a woman who didn't do dating, it was off the wall. For a woman who rarely had any sex at all, let alone sizzling hot, raw, rip-the-roof-off sex, it was unbelievable. Inexcusable. She shuddered every time yet another graphic image flipped into her brain. Had she really…? Unfortunately, yes. She had. And with every flickering image she was simultaneously horrified, shocked and appalled all over again. Embarrassing didn't begin to cover it. In fact, nothing much was covered. That was the whole trouble. Lucky then that she hadn't been working this week because no way would her mind have been on the job.

As it was, a few days visiting girl-friends had provided the space for reflection, even if it did mean she was mentally absent from the catch-up conversation a lot of the time. Frankly, a little jarring too to see mental flashes of a naked Jackson in all his animal glory whilst she moseyed around kitchens, playgroups, and school gates with first Claire, then Cat, then Jess, her three settled best friends, busily absorbed in their happy-ever-afters.

She was always slightly ambivalent about visiting her settled friends. One by one, they'd all got their grown up lives together, leaving her lagging, woefully far behind. She often mused over why this was, wondering if the lack of stability and upheaval in her home life when she was small meant she'd somehow missed out on some vital stage of her development. She always tried to avoid telling people, about the way her dad had left home so abruptly and then died a few years later; and his alcohol problems were something she rarely mentioned even to her closest friends. Although her mum remarried and had more children, somehow her second family never inspired her to build a family unit of her own. The yearning-for-a-baby thing was a different matter altogether – that part of her development was not impaired at all, as she knew to her cost.

Despite the fact that all traces of gloss and adult fun seemed to have disappeared down her friends domestic plug-holes as their homes filled up with offspring, she might have had more than a pang of regret for the cosy domesticity they had and she didn't, had she not been preoccupied with playbacks of Jackson's extraordinary assets. The only plus was that she and Jackson hadn't actually ended up in bed. She'd made damned sure of that. Bed was just too intimate of a place to go. Too dangerous. One night in bed with any guy might set a girl thinking about what she was missing. A night in bed with a guy like Jackson might be enough to blow your mind. Folly, when relationships were right off your personal agenda, and wouldn't be on there any time soon.

The one saving grace was that it was secret. No one knew. No one was ever going to know. No one that was apart from her and Jackson and she was one-hundred percent confident that he wouldn't be telling. And she damn well knew she wouldn't. There was no earthly reason why she'd ever see Jackson again. And she promised herself as of now not to think about him at all, especially not the crinkles in his cheeks when his face cracked into one of those aching smiles. So, that was all good. All over. A week ago now, so it was almost as good as ancient history. She threw her bags down in the bedroom, and began to check her answer phone messages. Six from Brando, filling in the non-urgent gaps between the texts he'd sent. Three bits of news from Edgerton Manor, his place in the Cotswolds, one tip about a work contact at his London company, a warning that their mum was on the lookout for someone to look after her retrievers – and the rest were from Cressy sounding more and more irate with each call. The landline began to ring again the minute she put the phone down.

'At last. I've been desperate for you to come back.' Cressy, bursting with energy. 'Did you get the bad boy into bed then?'

*Shit, going straight in for the jugular, then.* Bryony took a mental deep breath and sprang to her own defense. No way could she afford to let Cressy pounce on a hesitation here.

'Nope.' And definitely telling the truth there – sofa, floor, terrace, shower, but definitely not bed.

'Jackson Gale on a plate and you didn't end up in the sack with him?'

Bryony held her phone against her shoulder, masking Cressy's shrieks. 'I resisted. Like I told you I would.' Dicing, with that last bit.

Trying not to think about falling asleep on the floor of the cabin, head clamped in the delicious crook of Jackson's neck, waking to find he'd covered them with a quilt, because she'd promised herself she wasn't going to go there again, and – way more pertinent – in case Cressy managed to pick up on her daydreaming.

She braced herself for Cressy's 'I'm disgusted with how you've letting down womankind by passing up a chance like that' tirade. Surprised a little, when it didn't roll down the phone.

'So, lots of great news for you…' Cressy's voice was uncharacteristically restrained. 'You're going to love it.'

'Yes?' Having to wheedle it out of Cressy now. Like Cressy'd had a personality transplant too while Bryony had been away.

'First, fab news about your interview with Jackson.'

That? She'd almost forgotten about it. Bryony wished her stomach would stop leap-frogging over her shoulder every time Cressy mentioned him. Guilt about the deception making her nervous.

'That interview was such a mess; talk about newbie falling at the first hurdle. The arrogance of the guy totally rubbed me up the wrong way.'

'Or the right way, depending who you are.' *What the?* Cressy was purring now. 'You should see it – you're amazing in front of the camera. Management can't think why they haven't put you there before. And the chemistry between you and Jackson is something else.'

'You're kidding?'

'Nope. It's fantastic. So fantastic that they want you to do some presenting.'

'Wow.' Bryony taking a minute to let that sink in.

'Presenting's such a great career hike for you. I wasn't sure about your plans…' Cressy, hesitated, then blurted. 'But I blagged it and told them you'd be available to work right away. I knew you wouldn't mind?'

So that explained the holding back.

'You know me, I don't exactly have a lot of plans to ruin.' Sad or what? Whatever happened to the world tour she hadn't had the enthusiasm to book? When she was doing eighteen-hour days working on a reality show, a month off when she finished had sounded like bliss, but now it was here she didn't know what to do with herself. Other than a bit of tweaking around her flat, the three weeks Bryony had scheduled as free time were looking horribly empty. As for presenting, Cressy was right that it would be fab for her career.

'Phew. It's great to hear that.' Down the phone, she heard Cressy exhaling with relief. 'You've no idea how hard we've worked this last week to pull this thing together. It's the mega-coup *Sporting Chances* has been trying to line up for ages.'

'Sorry, what thing's this?' Cressy was losing her now.

'Nabbing Jackson Gale.'

*Jackson?*

Eeeek. Jaw on the floor. Trying not to hyperventilate.

'What's he got to do with this?' Bryony's stomach had given up leaping, and was on its way, slowly, but surely, to somewhere around her ankles.

'He's been so difficult to pin down. Then, on Tuesday, his management rang and agreed that in addition to us following his return to racing, Jackson would film a feature ride for every programme in the series from different places. It's phenomenal – that guy is such a star.'

'Sorry to sound dense, but where do I come in?'

Was that Cressy sucking in a huge breath? As if she were bracing herself?

'Seems it's his manager, Dan's idea. He wants Jackson to do

tandem rides, and Dan's insisting it's you on the back. And Dan's rock-solid firm that he wants you to do the research with Jackson too. It's the only way they'll consider it.' As Cressy's words tumbled out, Bryony's brain began to spin.

'What?' That would explain the huge intake of breath on Cressy's part, and her own involuntary shriek.

'Chill, babe. It's cool. You don't need to start until next week. It's all sorted, you'll have a ball. He's got a camper van lined up and everything.'

Bryony gulped. 'A camper van…?' Heart thumping. Hands clammy. Adrenalin coursing through her system, her body instinctively leaping into action, all on its own, on red alert for the Jackson Gale one-man danger zone. Bryony opened and shut her mouth. What could she say? No way could she spill her secret, but no way either could she mosey round the countryside with Jackson blasted Gale. Not after… She'd only survived since that night because she knew she'd never have to face him again.

'I'm sorry, it's out of the question.' Bryony racked her brain for a sensible reason to put forward. Because he'd shagged her senseless and she never wanted to see him again wasn't going to cut it here. 'I barely survived the last time. That tandem was terrifying. Plus I'd murder the man for being so cocky.' Ouch to that word choice and the images it conjured. 'If he didn't kill me first that is. He hated me because I wasn't sporty.'

'Seems like he's changed his tune. Big time. You know I'd swap places with you in a heartbeat, but sadly it isn't me they're asking for. '

Bryony jumped in before Cressy could begin to speculate further.

'I'm happy to try some stuff in front of the camera.' Bryony desperately trying to appease Cressy here. 'I just don't think I can work with Gale.'

When Bryony held her ground firmly enough, Cressy knew to back off. It was an unspoken agreement. One more moment of silence, and Bryony knew Cressy would retreat, gracefully, like she always did in their stand-offs. Except this time Cressy wasn't retreating.

'Okay, I'll lay it on the line. It's important or I wouldn't be pushing you.' Cressy, not backing down. What the heck? 'We need Jackson, Bry. He'll raise the profile, and pump up the ratings. Without him *Sporting Chances* is going to struggle, so the whole team is counting on you here.'

No pressure there, then?

'What's in it for Gale?'

'Cash, and the exposure will be good for him too. The company will pay for a name like his and I think his manager liked what he saw of the two of you on the rushes.'

'What? He saw the film of the interview?' And she'd thought it couldn't be any worse.

'One of his conditions – he vets every scrap of film we take. But I guess he saw how great you were together, and realised it wouldn't harm Jackson's profile to grab some of that. There was something about the two of you on screen, Bry. Talk about sparks. Believe me, you two sizzled, the public will lap it up. It's a no-brainer. Gale's man is astute, and he's onto it.'

'Give me a day to think about it?'

As if twenty-four hours would make any difference.

'Pleeeeeeeeease, Bry. Do it for me. It's my first big programme – I'd hate to lose it. You can't leave me hanging, say "yes" now.'

Emotional blackmail wasn't Cressy's style. Nor was begging. This had to be important.

'You might like Jackson better when you see more of him...' Cressy hesitated. No idea how deeply she was putting her foot in things. As she began again her voice deepened with concern. 'He didn't push you to do anything you didn't want to, did he?'

Oh, no. Everything she'd done was with complete, unencumbered abandon, a hundred percent willingly. Her choice all the way. Hey, she might even have been the one doing the asking, and, what's more, she'd wanted everything he had to give. No doubts there. Shivers zipping up her spine at that thought. Strange that afterwards she hadn't been able to work out who pushed who, who instigated what. Details lost in the sex-fuelled heat haze, all definitely on the understanding that it was a once-in-a-lifetime blowout. So, right now she had to man up, put it behind her, and stop being such a drama-queen about it. But how the hell could she face the guy again after that?

'Bry? What happened with Gale that you can't work with him?'

Cressy's insistent tone dragged her back to reality. Her London flat, polished and pimped to within an inch of its life. An excess of styled perfection and interest. Vintage pieces, perfectly amassed to look like they had happened by accident, because that's all she had to do outside of work. Maybe that was why she was making such an issue out of what was technically one night of lust, which was definitely over and done.

'Bry, I won't give in 'til you tell me.' Cressy with her terrier-with-a-bone voice? There was only one sure way to shut Cressy up.

'Okay. You win. I'll work with Jackson.'

Knowing, as she said it, she was letting herself in for the nightmare of her life. Just not knowing how to avert it.

Lord knows how she was going to pull this off.

# Chapter 13

'So, Jackson…'

Jackson braced himself. Two weeks since he'd seen Bryony. That final image of her, eyes closed, face upturned to the shower jets, rivulets of water flooding down her curves, as he'd pulled out of her to run off to his early meeting, had been burned onto his retinas ever since. And now she was here, in the flesh, those long, delectable thighs he'd dreamed about incessantly pushing taut against the denim of her jeans. Playing havoc with his peripheral vision as she crossed one high-heeled foot across the other in the front seat of his camper van. And given the determined jut of her chin, poised to give him a hard time. Of entirely the wrong sort.

'Bryony…?' Catching the five hundred-watt publicity smile she flashed at him, he made sure he returned it twofold. No idea how the hell a guy was expected to drive from London to Brighton next to distraction like that, and cursing Dan a) for having the idea in the first place, and b) for forcing him to go through with it. So well-meaning Dan, with all his good ideas and flair for grabbing opportunities by the balls, had somehow decided that he should come along on this trip rather than heading back to the team, arguing that it would be great to capitalise on any opening in TV. Jackson suspected it was as much about keeping him occupied, whilst his injuries healed further, but Dan wasn't coming clean on that one.

And Dan also knew that as much as Jackson was protesting about having Ms Dominatrix come along for the ride, he wouldn't have entertained taking anyone else. This was both the up side and the down side of having his best mate working on your management team – Dan knew Jackson almost as well as he knew himself, or sometimes even more scarily, he seemed to know him better than he knew himself. It wasn't that Jackson minded the idea of being close to Bryony's scorching body, which, if he was honest, had been playing on his mind a lot the last couple of weeks. Pretty much non-stop since that night of white hot meltdown, in fact. But the down side was, that from what he'd seen in Scarborough, Bryony might be physically and sexually delectable, but she was also hell bent on doing things *her* way. He'd had enough of doing as he was told, and bending to his dad's will when he was a kid. He forced himself to work within the team discipline simply because it was a means to an end. But no way was he, as an adult, being ordered around by some jumped up TV woman. Call her strong-willed, call her spoiled, call her driven and talented – however you looked at it, she would be a pain in the arse to spend two weeks working with. Make that two weeks of non-stop contact in a camper van, and he'd be vapourising on all fronts.

'A few things we need to get straight before we set off.' Her tone couldn't have been any more snippy or bossy.

Which underlined his point entirely.

That tone backed up every howling protest he'd made to Dan about this trip, but it was too late now, dammit. Although, given they were already well on their way, this put him at an immediate advantage. Anyone who took the best part of an hour stuck in traffic to get around to making their point was not half as sure of themselves as they were pretending.

'Namely?' He smoothed her a compliant smile.

'You need to know I don't mix work and pleasure.'

Taking every illicit fantasy he'd had in the last two weeks and stamping on it. Firmly. Trying to ignore that his stomach had hit the road with immediate disappointment. How had he expected anything different?

'Fine by me.' He reined in an escaping grin. 'I wasn't expecting you to do both at the same time.'

Beyond her fingers rearranging all that shiny hair on top of her head, he caught an OMG eye-roll.

'The point I'm making is I'm not here to provide sex on tap.' Her nostrils flared. 'That's definitely not what this trip's about.'

'Did I say it was?' No harm in playing innocent here, but he wasn't going to let on that he was only here because Dan had held a metaphorical gun to his head.

'So why did you insist on bringing me then? Surely there was someone else? Anyone.'

And Jackson definitely wasn't about to tell her how annoyed he was that he was having to come at all.

'Maybe because we share the same taste in cartoons.' That, she was not expecting, judging by her jumping eyebrows. He flashed her a triumphant grin. 'You've no idea how the cycling roomies complain when I ask them to sit through *Happy Feet*. You, on the other hand, seemed more than pleased to watch it if I remember rightly.' Naked on the sofa at one a.m., recovering between bouts. He'd been very appreciative at the time. 'Stuff like that counts for a lot when you have to spend time with someone. No point making something difficult when it can be easy.'

And given the way she was chewing her nail frantically she remembered just as well as he did. But she was up and running again faster than he expected.

'I thought I made it clear I don't date.' And sounding razzy, despite that front of a smile she was hiding behind. 'And I don't put out.' He was starting to notice that a lot. The smile mask, not that he was going to mention it now.

As for the rest…

'Excuse me for being dense, and let's be clear, I'm definitely not expecting a re-run, but how exactly does the other evening fit in with the not-putting-out bit?' Not just the once either. Five times wasn't it? With numbers as big as that a guy could be excused for losing count and *no* woman could claim *that* was an accident.

She cleared her throat, no doubt playing for time. From the corner of his eye he caught her brow, furrowed. Not even she could wriggle out of this one.

'You know damned well that was a heat of the moment thing. An aberration. It won't be happening again.'

The hottest night of his life dismissed as an aberration? But she was playing right into his hands, anyway.

'All good. If you read my biography like you said you did, you'd know *I* don't date either.' One more wicked grin. 'See, there's another thing we have in common.'

She gave a snort. 'Now you're being ridiculous.'

Talking down to him was not going to shut him up.

'As you helpfully said, it's important we get this straight. It's not something I try to hide, but I only do one-night stands. I guarantee great sex for one night only and I never do repeats. The whole world knows that.' Up for sex, but never anything more. His mantra since his mother walked when he was seventeen, ripping his heart out and leaving him with a hole in his chest the size of Africa. One night ensured things never ran on. He was reminding himself here as well as Bryony. He wasn't willing to put himself out there and risk the burn of another woman leaving him. 'So whatever you might be hoping, it's not going to happen again. As far as sex with me goes, you've had your allocation, Ms Marshall.'

And looking like he talked himself right out of it too. He'd conveniently overlooked that the sex with Cherry he'd been fantasizing about non-stop since he left her in the shower totally contravened his own dating rules. He was strictly a one night only guy. How the hell had that detail passed him by?

Leaning back she sucked in a breath, almost taking his eye out with the jut of her breasts as she readjusted her shirt, tucking it into her waistband. Inadvertently re-organised a major cleavage exposure. Talk about blood surging southwards. He forced his eyes back onto the road, and the crawling stream of traffic. Jackson winced as his tightening jeans clamped on a hard-on the size of the Empire State.

Who exactly was doing the bullshitting here? Once it became clear he couldn't get out of this, he'd given into fantasies of some sex-fest road trip. What the hell had he been thinking? What the hell had possessed him to abandon his own lifetime-survival guide? All credit to the Cherry Bomb for bringing him back to earth here, with a crash hard enough to remind him of his own rules and bump some sense into him. Whatever sexual diversion from the norms his ball-breaking libido had been planning in secret, his sensible head knew it was out of the question. Out of bounds. Talk about being dragged off course, ambushed by your own lust-craving.

From somewhere on her side he heard the beep of a mobile.

She dipped to the floor, delved into her bag dragged out her phone, cursing as she looked at it. 'Damn, damn, damn.'

'Something wrong?'

She pushed on her sunglasses and let out an exasperated breath. 'Not really. Just my brother, Brando, checking where I am. I'd kind of implied I was working from home for the next couple of weeks and didn't want to be disturbed, but he called the office and discovered I'm not there.' She gave a sigh. 'He worries about me, he can't help it…'

'And if he knew you were heading towards Brighton on a two week jaunt with me?' He hardly needed to ask.

'He wouldn't exactly be ecstatic.' She texted madly, put her phone back in her bag, unbent, then pushed on some dark glasses and rubbed on some lip-gloss from a tiny tin. 'To put it mildly.'

Great news. Not. Add in that as far as Brando Marshall was concerned it looked like he was abducting the guy's sister, and the day just got better and better.

'Good thinking on the shades, Bry. Could you grab me my

sunnies please? They're in the front glove box.'

'In here?' She leaned forwards and rummaged in the compartment. Then her furious squawk pierced his eardrums. 'Jackson Gale. You are so full of shit!'

'What now?' Nothing good, obviously.

'Only a mile of condoms, that's what.' Enough decibels to shatter the sunshine roof. One yank of her hand and a multi-coloured condom strip zig-zagged through the air. 'Nice to see you've packed for all eventualities. In bulk.'

True, it trailed pretty much to the floor. Hugely incriminating. No place to hide.

*Holy crap.*

'It's not how it looks.' He was already resigned to the fact that she'd never believe him, even though he was telling the truth here.

'So how is it then?' As her stare bored into him, he jumped as she prodded his elbow accusingly.

Dammit that he'd even asked for the shades in the first place.

'I'm guessing those are a "Happy Holiday" present from Rik and the boys from Vintage VW's in Manchester. Their little joke. I hadn't even noticed the damn condoms were there.'

'Have reputation, will travel?' She was almost spluttering here. 'I have to be crazy heading off with the womaniser of the century who lays in condoms by the gross. I really don't know why I agreed to this.'

How the hell could he have pissed her off so fast without doing anything? Probably not helpful here to point out they weren't even his size. Colourful though they might be, that brand wouldn't go anywhere near. Major grovelling called for, and oxygen.

He dragged in a breath. 'You agreed to come because you're super-efficient, organised and talented, and you're the best person to work with me to make some great TV. And with any luck it'll haul both our careers to a better place than where they are right now. End of.'

All thanks to Dan's shrewd manoeuvring. Jackson had to admit that Dan worked wonders on his behalf. Here's hoping his own grimace was contrite enough. 'We already agreed to be civilised about this. However many condoms are stashed in the dash it's definitely hands off. On both sides. Okay?'

Her nostrils still twitched but no steam was coming out. Phew to that. Maybe he'd got away with it.

'So what about the itinerary, Jackson?' Straight in. Ms Bossy, back to replace Ms Incensed then. 'That's what we need to discuss next. I've got everything worked out. The details are all on my iPad.'

Or, how about not discussing it? There was no rush as far as he was concerned.

He had Bryony down as a strong woman. Her strength was part of what had him hooked. Hooked? Bad word choice. He'd never be hooked by a woman, not now, or ever. But there was a fine line between feisty and domineering. And he had to keep her the right side of the line, for both their sakes.

An hour of ceasefire would give him time to regroup. Recover the ground the condom fiasco had cost him.

'No special hurry on the itinerary front. We'll get onto that later.' He slipped his phone out of his pocket, slid it across the seat to her. 'Why not choose something to listen to in the meantime?'

An olive branch of mega proportions. No one was allowed to touch his phone. Ever.

He just hoped she appreciated it.

Everyone knew hungry women were impossible.

He hoped a nice lunch would soften Bryony up, though he suspected the fact she'd been in charge of selecting the restaurant and had phoned ahead to make the booking had already taken care of a large chunk of the much-needed mellowing. Control freaks were so much more manageable when they thought that they were getting their own way.

'What a lovely terrace.' Bryony's bright tone now they'd arrived suggested he was going to reap the benefits of that arrangement.

'So lucky I found out about the restaurant before we'd gone too far past. What a combination – thatched roof, beamed barn conversions *and* award-winning food. I can't think how I missed it when I was planning or I'd definitely have included it as a lunch stop.' Tucking into the seat the waiter held out for her, flicking back her hair, she wowed first the waiter, then Jackson, with that full-on smile.

Zap. His pulse rate kicked up. Bryony, alarmingly, even more disarming face-to-face as opposed to side-by-side, in the front of the van. He hadn't been able to help noticing that, as he walked through the restaurant with Bryony, she held the gaze of staff and customers alike. There was something about her that they couldn't bear to look away from. Just like for him.

And she'd worked her magic earlier too, when, as a late arrival, they'd been shown to a tiny table in a dark corner of the restaurant. She'd simply powered up her smile, and the next moment they were being whisked out to the special reservation-only, outdoor tables. One more beam, and the tables were being shifted around so they could eat in the shade of a clematis-covered bower as per her enthusiastic request, whilst Jackson looked on, shaking his head in disbelief, at both her gall and the lengths the staff were prepared to go to in order to make her happy.

'You almost sound like you have every detail of the trip worked out already.' That would be with no consultation with him at all. Regardless of the wow factor, he couldn't let this pass without comment. 'Slightly ridiculous seeing as I'm the one calling the shots here.'

She put down the linen napkin she was shaking out and eyeballed him.

'Er, excuse me?' For a split-second her mouth fell open, and he basked in the luxury of shocked silence. Then she kicked into overdrive. 'As production manager here, any shots to be called are technically mine.'

'Hang on.' He wasn't letting her get away with that. 'I thought

86

you were a production assistant?'

'Which translates to manager in the absence of a superior team member.' Her elbows arrived on the table now, her chin resting on neatly-woven fingers. 'Whereas you're simply a featured celebrity, which may count for gazillions in terms of fans, but when it comes to organizational decisions out in TV production land, it counts for zilch.'

One uninterrupted view of those perfect teeth of hers as she posted him another inscrutable beam, putting him instantly in mind of how easily his tongue slipped past those teeth back in Scarborough, dammit. He wasn't fighting with his usual unerring full-strength concentration here. His mind was on the job, just the wrong job, and if he didn't watch out it was going to cost him dearly. Still she could be bullshitting here, and two could play at that game.

'Featured celebrity with a possible executive producer's interest.' He watched through narrowed eyes as her expression slid.

'You're coming in as a backer?' Her mouth and eyes popped to perfect O's.

Result. She'd swallowed it.

'Possibly.' Backtracking now on every front except the power one and not exactly lying either. Financial involvement had been mentioned in passing. 'But I already have the final say on input and content, so I'm guessing those shots are mine to call after all.'

Race won. Mentally, he let go of the handlebars, punched the air with a fist, and he was whooshing across the finish line ahead of her when he noticed that she was still smiling. Benignly.

'That's what the backers always like to think.' Was that the tiniest hint of a mocking wink she was sending him? A full-blown satisfied gloat more likely. 'In practice everyone knows it's all in the hands of the production assistants. Has to be. We're the ones who do all the work. Talking of which, I'd better go and shake up that waiter and his menus.'

# Chapter 14

'So you're sure you don't want a sweet? Now I feel guilty for ordering three, and eating them in front of you.' Bryony tucked away her phone, after yet another Brando induced text-fest, and eyed Jackson thoughtfully over her pudding mountain as he stirred his coffee. 'Don't you miss chocolate?'

He watched her devour another spoonful, simply for the spectacle of her lips closing around the spoon, and the glimpses of her tongue sliding across those perfect teeth.

'I've avoided it for so long it doesn't bother me at all anymore. Like the traveling, the physical punishment, the endless hotel rooms; it's just part of the package.'

Raising her eyebrows, she posted a passing beam of appreciation to their waiter as he sped past across the broad stone flags. Amazing, the way she had the staff eating out of her hand. As he was beginning to realise, only Bryony Marshall, with her dynamite blend of enthusiasm, charm and force could end up in the kitchen ordering the Chef around in a five-star establishment, as she had done earlier. Funny how he saw her as bossy and domineering, yet other people thought she was irresistible. In the face of that persuasive smile, people were happy to roll over and give her exactly what she wanted. Ecstatic even. Or, would that be in the face of that full-on sex appeal? Not that she seemed aware of that. She definitely didn't flaunt it. It just seemed to radiate off her, leaving casualties knocked helpless in her wake.

'This amaretti ice-cream is delish – here try a tiny bit.' She pushed a spoonful towards him.

Giving a half shake of his head, he slid her a playful grin.

'There's only one way I ever eat ice-cream.' He knew he was pushing it, but what the hell. 'And we've both agreed that's off the menu.' Probably inflicting more pain on himself than her. Blocking the image of nipples peaking as a melt trail of ice-cream trickled down her cleavage. 'And probably too sticky anyway for when we're out in the wilds camping in the van.'

Something about that last thought cut her off in mid eye-roll and stopped her spoon halfway to her mouth.

'Excuse me. Who said anything about camping?' Her eyes narrowed in query. 'Cressy gave me an idea of where you wanted to go, so I made a week of hotel bookings to fit and we can take it from there.' She bathed him in another of her smiles. 'I hope that's good?'

He took a minute to absorb this. Let his eyes wander over the big stone planters cascading with purple flowers. *Holy crap, this was going from bad to…* He had to stand his ground here.

'No, it's not good. Couldn't be worse in fact. Sorry, but that's not what I signed up for.' Who said anything about hotels? Cressy said you'd come in the camper, or there's a tent if you'd prefer. The whole idea is that we're independent and we can get to out-of-the-way places.'

'What?' She stared at him, brow furrowed in disbelief. 'I assumed the camper was transport, not accommodation.'

'I was going on a road trip to try out the van, and Cressy suggested we could combine it with the programme research. Seemed certain you'd be up for it.'

'Tell me honestly, Jackson.' Beam turned up another hundred watts now. 'Do I look like a girl who camps?'

'I spend my whole life in hotels. They're soulless, I want a change.' Realising his muttered tirade wasn't going to cut it, he upped his game. 'What's wrong with camping anyway?'

She shot him a wide-eyed glance of disbelief.

'It takes a lot more than a quick rub with a wet-wipe to get me ready to face the world. I can't work the festival grunge look.' She pulled a face, leaning forward to emphasise her point. 'My kind of polish doesn't just happen, Jackson, it takes a lot of time and hard work to look this good, not to mention facilities. Besides, look at my shoes. Jimmy Choos aren't exactly outdoor equipment.'

'Facilities?' He tried to look less bemused than he felt.

True, he mixed with and appreciated attractive, well-groomed women, but quite how they got that way was outside his immediate experience. As for the hooker heels, no hidden messages there. They made his mouth water every time he caught a glimpse.

'Hot water, baths, showers, hair dryers, straighteners, endless supplies of fluffy towels. A shower-block in a field won't cut it, and I always iron all my clothes too.' She snapped her mouth shut, with a case-closed head toss.

'What, everything?' She had to be joking. 'Even your…?'

'Yes, Jackson.' She flashed him a trust-you-to-push-it eye-roll. 'Even my underwear.'

A woman who ironed her knickers *and* had a double-dose of camping phobia? This had to be his unlucky day, and that was before he got to the bit about her iron will.

'Fine.' He spat out the word only as a way to buy time, because it wasn't fine at all and there was no way he was backing down on this. Bryony wafting round acting regal was bad enough but taking the spoiled princess act to extremes was not on. He leaned back in his chair tapping the table with his spoon handle. 'So what do *you* suggest?'

'Maybe we could start by acting like adults.' If the withering look she shot him made his blood boil, the follow up placatory smile vaporised it. 'This isn't exactly my idea of fun either. Ever heard of the word compromise, Jackson?'

Compromise? Only every second of his adult life, and most of his adolescence too, not to mention the way his bully of a dad trampled all over his childhood. Making yourself best in the world didn't happen without sacrifice. Decades of it. Which was why now he was temporarily removed from the fray he was damned well going to do as he pleased, regardless of the intervention of Team Royal Cherry Bomb.

'You seem hell-bent on talking down to the world, so let's hear your solution.' He knew the venom in that delivery had a lot to do with this morning's brush-off, and the miniscule flinch of her cheek in response made his gut churn. But he couldn't turn soft here *and* win.

'Easy.' She pursed her lips, a smile playing around the corners of her mouth, obviously pleased with herself. 'I stay in the hotel as planned while you sleep in your camper – wherever – and we'll meet up again in the morning. Nothing so hard about that is there? That way we both win.'

Smoothly put. Persuasive. Neat and tidy. And the clattering in the background? That would be his dreams of a proper road trip crashing down.

It was the camper van that had got him through, when he'd been in hospital after the bike crash. Like so many of the good suggestions in his life, it was Dan who dreamed it up, putting him touch with Rik and the guys from Vintage VW's, who, it turned out, they'd been at school with. It was so like Dan to keep in touch with Rik across the years, so like Dan to go to great lengths to travel around the country on Jackson's behalf, while he was laid up, helping him choose the perfect vehicle to restore. It turned out that the details and the interest of the restoration were just the distraction Jackson had needed to get him through the multiple operations and endless physio sessions that followed.

There was something optimistic and satisfyingly parallel about dreaming of future trips in the van which was being rebuilt, at the same time as the doctors were trying to put his broken body back in working order again. He was the first to admit that he had too much riding on this first camper van trip, given the emotional input poured into it was way out of proportion to a mere van refit – too much emotion for one aged vehicle to hold, *way* too much expectation on his part. It was bound to fail. And he was the one whose mountain of hugely unrealistic hopes was about to come crashing down.

The disappointment gnawing at his gut suddenly took control of his tongue and next thing he knew he was lashing out. 'You go to your damned rabbit hutch of a hotel then, Bryony. Only a control-freak like you could make this about winning and losing.'

Her nostrils flared, but he noted the surprise in the widening of her eyes as she shot him a sideways glance. 'Excuse me? You're the one insisting on imposing your taste for traipsing round the countryside like an itinerant. That sounds fairly controlling to me.'

He chose to ignore that she might have a point there. 'Are you scared that if you climbed down off your high heels and your high horse and let go for once, you might accidentally enjoy yourself then?'

'Actually, I'm not scared of anything of the sort. And I'm not scared of speaking my mind and standing up for my right to my own opinion either.' This time her eyes flashed angrily. 'It strikes me that for the first time in your life you've met someone who isn't going to roll over and give you your own way, and you can't handle it.'

For a fleeting moment he was distracted by the image of her doing just that. *Rolling over and giving him his own way.* And again the fact she might have a point. Holy crap. What the hell was he doing arguing with Ms Starchy Pants anyway? He should be ecstatic she was going to get her pain-in-the-arse presence out of his blasted camper and give him an evening on his own.

He gritted his teeth. How the hell had he expected anything different? More to the point, why the hell had he wanted anything that ridiculous? More fool him, and great that he'd finally come to his senses.

'You know, you can give me an invitation to these arguments that you so obviously get your kicks from, but I don't *have* to come.' Fighting fire with fire wasn't getting him anywhere. He was done with fire. From now on he was going to fight with ice cool irony. 'Well done, Cherry Bomb. I guess we'll call that a win-win situation after all, if you insist. You go and enjoy your ironing board. And make sure you get all the creases out of your life whilst you're there.' Biting back that too familiar taste of disappointment, he gave her one sardonic smile. 'And next time I mentally undress you, remind me to fold your clothes neatly.'

Whatever Ms Control-fest-neat-freak thought, he was still on top.

And that was where he was going to stay.

# *Chapter 15*

Forty minutes of stony silence later, back on the road, Bryony gritted her teeth. Someone was going to have to make the first move here if they were going to get any work done today.

'If you pull over here Jackson, I'll explain what we need to do for the programme plan… I mean, that's what we're here for, isn't it?' She braced herself for his resistance.

'Fine.' His snort was disinterested, but at least he pulled over.

'This is the first ride I've worked out. It's a twenty-mile circular route.' She shoved her iPad towards him.

He studied it then gave a disparaging grunt. 'Where did you get this from?'

She winced. 'I found it on google, then changed it a bit.'

He gave another snort. 'It's a pretty standard route round the area. I've ridden most of it before. You might want to re-do the bit where you've re-routed it along that dual carriageway.'

Ooops. Rooky mistake. She grabbed her iPad, and began to change the line on the map where his finger rested. The way he leaned towards her and watched in silence made her fumble.

'That's better.' His voice was almost a growl.

She knew he was the expert here, but did he have to sound so condescending? She grappled to sound cool and authoritative. 'So what we'll do now is drive the route slowly, and look out for the places where we might get some good camera shots of us riding the route when the time comes. If we see anywhere suitable, we'll stop and take photos, and note the exact location, okay?'

'Okay.'

Put the flags out, he just agreed with her.

'And then if there are any villages, or specific places of interest we can stop and have a look around for anything that might be good for pieces to camera. I'll make notes on it all as we go and add more when I write it up later. Okay? Have you got that?'

'It's not rocket science, Cherry.'

She searched for the most acidic smile she could find. 'Whenever you're ready then…'


An afternoon pottering along the Sussex country lanes, past patchworks of fields and pretty, higgledy-piggledy villages left Bryony in a much better mood. Better still, they were three quarters of the way through the first ride and hadn't had any major disagreements. In fact, Jackson had become surprisingly compliant, which left her feeling generous.

'Condom Rik certainly did a good job with this van, even if his taste in going-away presents sucks.' She ran her palm across the smooth walnut dashboard appreciatively as she pushed a packet of toffees into the glove compartment for handy access. Despite her hearty lunch all the brainwork meant she was in need of a late afternoon sugar-boost.

Now she'd found keeping the man-whore of the century in his place wasn't going to be so hard as she'd thought, she could afford to throw out a few compliments.

'Rik and I go way back – hence the gift. We were at school together in Manchester when we were eight.' Taking one hand off the wheel, he ran his thumb across the stubble on his chin. 'Getting involved in the van rebuild helped fill the time when I was laid up recently. It's the first vehicle I've ever owned, all the rest have been on loan from sponsors.'

95

Strong hands. She allowed her gaze to linger on those long fingers. *But only for a nanosecond.* Just the tip of a very attractive package that she was definitely ignoring, along with the secret butterfly rush in her chest. And also shutting out that the thought of an eight year old Jackson made her stomach squish ever so slightly. Why the hell did her already overactive maternal instinct jump out and go crazy whenever she was around him? Not to mention her altogether less wholesome instincts.

'The contrast of the distressed grey paint on the outside of the camper, and the fifties colours in the inside work well. Blue, brown and orange. Very cool. And this bench seat in the front is fab too.' Getting down and dirty with Jackson was so not where she meant her head to be, so definitely needing not to think where those fingers had got to last time they met. 'Although, it's obvious it's been masterminded by guys. Some bunting and flowery fabric would make it more homely.'

'The paint finish is known in the trade as rat-look. It's a special blend of distressed and tatty that takes a lot of time and skill to perfect.' His cheeks creased into a wry smile that played havoc with the butterfly situation. 'And girly wasn't what we were after, nor was homely, even though this is probably the nearest I've come to a home in years.'

'Really?' Trying not to let the shock leak into her voice at that revelation. 'Although looking at the size of the sink, it's way too small for any meaningful washing up.' Now she was talking gibberish. 'I can't imagine not having a home. When I'm not working, I'm home-obsessed, always have been – that's what comes of not dating. I've done well out of it though, making my way up the so-called property ladder.' Somehow, once she'd got a home of her own, pouring all her energy into it made her feel more secure.

'So that explains your swanky flat. Sorry, but I couldn't help noticing when I picked you up.' He shot her an apologetic grimace. 'Underground car-park, river views. Whereas I've seen a lot of the world since I was a teenager but mostly the blur of foreign tarmac and the inside of dingy hotel rooms. True some of the guys with families do establish strong home bases, but I never saw the point myself. And you're right, I'm not big on washing up.'

'Must be a weird way of life.'

'It's pretty dysfunctional, but it has its rewards.'

She laughed. 'What – shedloads of cash, recognition, and hot-and-cold running podium-girls?' There was an unexpected twang in her chest at that last thought. One dig at him that bounced right back to bite her.

'Something like that.' Drumming his fingers on the steering wheel, he gave a dismissive shrug, a half-grin. 'Although, podium girls are strictly off-limits.'

She laughed. 'Even for you?' That slipped out before she could stop it.

No point biting her tongue now. But why her sudden anxiety about podium girls? It wasn't as if she was jealous. *Was it?*

'Especially for me.' He shot her an almost wicked grin. 'With my reputation.'

Trying not to bounce with relief at that. *Trying not to be so ridiculous. Fighting with podium girls? Over Jackson Gale?* When the hell did her world get that upside down? Easy answer. When she slept with him. One wild, ill-considered decision, with repercussions which were turning out like giant waves at sea. She flailed to find a change of subject quickly.

'S-so what about your accident?'

Bad move. His chin shot upwards as his back stiffened. Talk about a hole in the conversation big enough to lose Brighton.

'I'd rather not discuss it.' Short. Terse. The muscles at the base of his cheek twitched as his jaw clenched and his knuckles shone white as he gripped the steering wheel.

Oh my. 'Sorry, I had no…'

'I'm fine.'

She winced at that expression. Instantly proving that he was anything but fine. He was almost shouting. Jumping down her throat. Ooooh. She'd definitely hit a nerve there.

He recovered fast enough to bat a question back at her. 'So what have you been doing since we last – er – met?'

Nice hesitation; ditto the euphemism. But damn to her having to answer the question.

'I was on leave, although I did some prep for the trip too.'

'And when you weren't planning my every last move?' He was screwing her down here.

'I caught up with some girlfriends.' She missed out how she'd chickened out of her world tour, and the bits about happy-ever-after-land.

'And did you have wild times?'

'Hardly.' She sniffed. 'My old friends are mostly settled.' No need to cover the whole domestic bliss thing, or the empty way it left her feeling when she drove away.

'Settled as in two cars on the drive, two-point-four children?'

'That's the one.'

His grimace made her laugh.

'Highly overrated from what I've seen. Why anyone would choose that kind of prison is beyond me. The racing has been limiting, and I've had to make sacrifices; but from what I've seen, a family grabs you by the balls and squeezes you dry. That's one full-on trip I won't be going on.'

Bad boy Jackson doing a 'don't fence me in' rap! No surprise there.

'My friends seem pretty happy.' Something about the vitriol in his remark made her jump in to defend them. 'And kids can be quite squishy and cute.' Underplaying the last bit, and definitely forgetting all those moments when the smell of clean toddler had made her want one for herself. And definitely not going into how broody it made her when she saw Brando and Shea's babies. And her niece Emily, with all her ginger curls, was so cute now she was two, it made Bryony's insides melt every time she saw her. Anyone who said nieces and nephews worked as substitute children was talking rubbish. Hers only served to make her long for some of her own.

'You're a woman, you would say that.' he rapped straight back. 'At your age your biological clock is a ticking time-bomb. One mention of the "B" for "baby", and the want is all over your face. If you're still set on your dating ban, Cherry, you need to take your mother up on her offer and fast. No point risking disappointment later.'

*Really?* Picking her jaw up off the floor on all counts. Squirming inside that he'd not only remembered the damned egg freezing, but that it was fresh enough in his mind to bring it back out for another airing. Embarrassing or what? And was he implying that she was old? The sheer impudence of the guy made her blood fizz. Not to mention the unsettling accuracy of his observation. No way was she going to admit he'd scored a direct hit, honed right in, like he knew all about the private panic about being on her own forever that plagued her in the wakeful early hours.

'Whatever.' She moved on swiftly. 'The rest of the time I was doing grown up-things. I'd set the time aside for a bedroom make-over.' And ouch to the way that sounded now it was out there. She really didn't want him to pounce on the way one night of action, albeit out of the bedroom, had jump-started her sort-out.

'Upgrading the princess bed, then?'

Not that she was planning on having visitors in that holy-of-holies any time soon. Far from it.

'Meaning?'

He let out a snort. 'Your tiara attitude hasn't gone completely unnoticed.'

*What?* He had to be joking. Gritting her teeth, she clenched her fists. No way was she rising to that, but she wasn't letting it go either.

'Neither has your arrogance, or your need to win every point.' She rammed a handful of hair firmly behind her ear, preparing to fight.

'Who just did the compromising back there? Errr, that would have been me. You're only in a good mood now because I gave in about tonight's accommodation. Isn't that right, Princess Cherry Bomb?'

'Excuse me!' Hard not to sound like a harpy here, with her voice all high and incensed. 'That had nothing to do with me winning, it was simply the most sensible decision.'

'From your point of view maybe.' Still all cool and collected as he flipped her a sideways glance but the gravelly depth of his voice and the set of his jaw told her how deadly serious he was. 'But it's not attractive only being happy when you get your own way, and even if most people do cave in the face of your full-on persuasion tactics, that Princess strut of yours gets right up their noses.'

Oh, my. Was that really how people saw her? Or was this a bad case of sour grapes from a guy who was world champion of arrogance?

'Thank you for sharing, Jackson. Nothing like a few home truths.' She dragged in a breath, crossed one leg over the other, grasped hold of her knee – hopefully not too regally. Staring out of the window to take in a fleeting glimpse of the passing white-washed cottages, she realised how much scenery she was missing by arguing with this impossible guy. Okay. She'd got his number here. 'This wouldn't be because you're a bad loser, would it? Only you could make this into a competition, then go on the attack because I won and you didn't. Maybe it takes one to know one, Jackson...'

'Not at all, I'm simply trying to make a valid suggestion.' Sounded like he was backing down here. 'That it might be better for you to back-pedal with the spoiled daddy's girl bit.'

Crash, and he'd fallen. Come slamming down at the finish line. Ridden straight into his own trip wire.

She didn't mean it to, but her chin was jutting forward anyway. 'Well I wouldn't know about that, given that my father left when I was six, and died before I got to find him again.' Couldn't say Jackson hadn't asked for it. Except if she'd had any inkling that was coming she'd have headed him off. Keeping her voice level, she let him have the full blast of her disgust through gritted teeth. 'Being a spoiled daddy's girl isn't something I was lucky enough to experience.'

Not that she made a habit of pulling the sympathy card. She didn't. Her dad leaving wasn't something she talked about. It was in the past. He was gone. She'd closed the door on that one long ago.

'Oh, shit, I'm sorry.' One arrogant guy folding, hammering his head with his fist. 'I'm dying here.'

And she wasn't rushing in to save him either.

'You weren't to know.' She gave a shrug. 'It's a long time ago.'

'Doesn't mean it hurts any less.' Looking away from the road, he snagged her eyes with his held them for a second more than she expected – long enough to make her stomach drop. Then steering the van around a left-hand bend, narrowly avoiding the hedgerow, the follow-up grimace he sent her put her stomach on full spin.

Something about the soulful muddy brown of those eyes made her think it was only fair to come clean. 'I've got Harry. He's a very caring stepfather.'

'Not quite the same thing though, is it?'

Stretching past the gear stick, his hand found hers and she flinched as the grainy roughness of his thumb grazed her skin. Damn to the way the tan on his knuckles whitened as he squeezed. She turned to him expecting to meet a self-deprecating grin or maybe a glint of flirt, but instead the eyes she met were grave as his concern flooded across the space between them.

*Oh my.* 'You understand, don't you?'

One nod from him. Enough to say there was no need to explain about all the nights she'd wailed. Six years old, and thumping her pillow, not understanding why her dad wasn't there. As Jackson pursed his lips and withdrew his hand to ease the van around another bend, she caught her gaze lingering on those knuckles again. Pushing back against the seat, she let out a sigh at the sheer unexpected relief of being with someone who understood. Jackson

Gale, there for her. No words, yet making her feel comfy as an old cardigan. Who'd have thought?

Another hundred yards before he eased out that smile. 'I guess after this I'll have to buy you dinner, once you're hungry again that is.'

'You know me, Jackson, I'm always hungry.' Flipping back her hair, she fought the way that lazy growl turned her insides to hot toffee. 'But shouldn't we be doing some work first?'

A message flashed onto her iPad screen. Dammit. Yet another text from Brando.

**Where the hell are you?**

He was so persistent, and she didn't want to lie to him. Maybe if she ignored him he'd give up.

Jackson's shout cut into her thoughts. 'Village coming up. Cue shots to camera.'

If she hadn't known better, she'd have thought he was enjoying himself.

# Chapter 16

'Whatever you say, you are bossy.'

Jackson had parked up along a quiet patch by the beach edge to catch the evening sun and now as he crouched by the campfire barbie he poked at the sausages, wrinkled his nose at the smoke and hoped this particular princess appreciated crispy.

'Or, you might say I'm dynamic and highly efficient, depending on where you stand.' She pursed her lips, and sent him a take-no-prisoners dead-eye over the top of her mirror as she made more adjustments to her make-up.

'Whatever.' He raised an ironic eyebrow to that one after the Bryony Marshall whirlwind he'd suffered this afternoon. 'And what exactly are you doing to your face there?' Not that he was nosy, but he had to ask.

'Running repairs.' There was a mocking twinkle of amusement in her eye as she wound up some kind of lipstick. 'It's a girl thing. You wouldn't understand.'

'Don't be so sure, we have team cars to look after that stuff out on the road. We could've done with a team car this afternoon, the rate you were driving us.'

At least by wrestling control of the cooking he'd finally managed to bring her to a standstill; although, the way she was stretched out on the rug now, chin propped on one hand, shirt buttons being tested to destruction where they pulled across her chest, wasn't doing anything for the cramped conditions in his groin area. Not as if he hadn't seen it all before. The shower image flashed past again followed by a whole stream of others, each more explicit than the one before. As a strictly one-time-only guy not up for revisits he'd assumed the excitement would have waned but somehow knowing what was underneath those clothes and how fricking amazing it was made it all the worse.

She turned and gave him the benefit of her newly-applied smile. 'I don't see you complaining that we worked out the route and the best camera shots in record time, although all those pretty villages made the job easy. You have to admit the choice of area was spot on, even if it was my choice not yours.' Perfectly slicked lips, maybe, but that smirk was way too superior. 'I'll get the script ideas drafted as soon as I get back to the hotel, and that's the first programme sorted.' Bringing him back to earth with a bang – or more to the point, without a bang – as she eased off her shoes and wiggled her toes.

'I can think of better ways to spend an evening.' Taking a swig of beer, he grabbed the bread rolls and stifled the accompanying grin before it escaped. No way was he going to be accused of innuendo.

'No doubt.'

Given the disgusted-of-Brighton eye-roll she shot him, he might as well have let the grin go, and chucked in a quip about those bright-pink toe-nails for good measure. But the way she let her beer bottle rest on her lips, all rosy and newly glossed, then moved it to nestle in the hollow between her breasts... Now that was just plain mean.

Seems like she'd got over him crashing in with both feet about her dead father. He shuddered to think how that had happened. So much hurt in her eyes back there, all he'd wanted to do was wrap her in his arms, shield her from the world. Instead, she'd thrown herself into more work, dragging him with her, consenting or otherwise. Understandable. He'd done the same with his training when his mother walked.

'The sausages smell amazing by the way. Fab to see you're so relaxed with the cooking, although men never can resist a fire; I reckon you're all latent pyromaniacs.' She waggled her beer bottle idly. 'I'm useless in the kitchen. Three-ingredient easy chocolate brownies are the one culinary trick this pony does. You make them with chocolate spread, but even that's a bit hit and miss.'

Obviously unaware that resisting her brand of flame was taking every ounce of his self-control.

'Good to hear you aren't entirely perfect then.' And disappointing to think he'd only got to cook because she didn't want to. Splitting open a roll, he added a sausage, then picked up the frying pan. 'Onions?'

'My favourite. Lots please.'

He shovelled in as many as he could, grabbed a plate and a serviette, then handed it to her. 'There you go, brown bread, grilled low-fat sausages, nice and healthy. Watch you don't get grease on your Jimmy Wangs.'

'My what?'

'Your shoes.'

Her mouth twitched. 'You mean Choos.'

'Do I?'

A smile spread across her face. 'Jimmy Choos are the shoes, Vera Wang does wedding dresses.'

'Whatever.' He wasn't sure it was *that* funny.

'You must've heard of them or you wouldn't have got mixed up. Stacks of my friends walked down the aisle wearing Vera Wang.' Bryony stopped, hot dog halfway to her mouth. 'Her dresses are amazing.' Drifting into silence, she stared dreamily into the middle distance.

A big expanse of sea, albeit blue and glittering in the evening sun, some sky, the occasional seagull. Nothing to hold her attention for that long as far as he could see.

'What's this? Ms Decidedly-Single mooning at the memory of

wedding trains? And how many mates make a stack? Sounds like at least the population of Guilford. Do I take it your friends have been signing up for a lifetime of compromise and misery en-masse?'

He bit into a sausage.

'Pretty much. Soon I'll be the only single one around, apart from Cressy, obviously, who's so wild she doesn't count.' Bryony gave a shrug. 'All my own fault though. I introduced most of them to their partners. Even Helen from admin chose Vera Wang when she married Phil from sound.'

'So you get off on playing the matchmaker?' Why did it not surprise him? He didn't mean to let the accompanying guffaw of disgust escape. 'That has to be the ultimate in controlling behaviour, even for you. Couldn't you have trusted your friends to make their own choices?'

He was aware of her eyes widening in displeasure, but this time he didn't give a damn.

'What? Most people benefit from a nudge in the right direction, and I can't help intuitively knowing who goes well with who.'

'If you say so.' It wasn't worth an argument, but he tossed in a last warning. 'So long as you don't start playing your manipulation games with me.' Though privately he railed at the thought that right now she was the one woman he did want to play games with.

'Excuse me?' Spluttering, she choked on a mouthful. 'As it happens, I don't have any free friends left, but if I did I'd hardly advise them to hook up with anyone as arrogant and domineering as you, who is entirely incapable of compromise.'

He wrinkled his nose. Took a moment before he bowled the slow return, along with a knowing smile. 'You do realise you could be describing yourself there.' He gritted his teeth, watched her swallow the last of her food and crumple up her serviette. 'Another hot dog?'

'No thanks.' She got up, smoothed down her jeans, glanced at her watch. 'It's later than I realised, I should be heading to the hotel.' Bending down she whipped up the rug she'd been lying on and

106

began to fold it into meticulous squares. 'If that's okay with you?'

That snippy tone showing he'd overstepped the mark, big-time.

'No need to iron it.' And he was only stooping to sarcasm because he was kicking himself here. Stupid of him, anyway, to imagine they'd be having an easy evening, watching the sun go down.

She reached into the van to stow away the rug, then scooping up her shoes, she perched on the edge of the van floor to put them on. Seeing her there, framed by the open side doorway, with only the odd crumple in her jeans to show for a whole day on the road, her gloss and polish made a jarring contrast against the faded backdrop of the van. No idea how the hell he'd ever thought this trip was going to work out. He silently cursed his personal manager Dan for bludgeoning him into it in the first place. No doubt Dan had his own ulterior motives for keeping Jackson occupied, a.k.a. out of the way. Dan knowing how Jackson was desperate to get back to training with the team again, thinking it would take his mind off the whole question of his long-term fitness, and give his body another few weeks to recover before he threw it back into the rigors of full-time training. Right now, Jackson was completely blocking the twinges of pain in his knee he knew he shouldn't be getting.

Better get on and clear up. He'd take the royalty back to her hotel in town then come back along the coast and find a quiet place to park up for the night. He crouched down to sort out the barbie.

'Ouch.' He picked up the tray, and dropped it again swiftly when it burned him.

Aware from the denim-clad legs beside his chin that Bryony had arrived. No doubt here to supervise.

'You'll probably need to pour water on that.'

'Thanks for stating the bleeding obvious.' He sucked the side of his finger, and counted to ten.

She was brandishing a plastic bag of dirty plates and utensils.

'Anything else over here need collecting?' Towering over him, she looked down on him imperiously, sounding snappy. 'The washing

107

up…not your department but it still needs doing.'

*Holy crap.* Eye roll. Count to ten. He took in the close-up detail of her shoes.

Scarlet suede? With beads? *For a camping expedition?* That pretty much said it all.

This was going to be a hell of a long trip.

## Chapter 17

As Bryony emerged from the hotel next morning, pulling her bag on wheels behind her, the startling sun made her already banging head thump harder. So much for going to a hotel for a good night's sleep. Shading her eyes against the glare with her hand, she scanned the car park. Her gaze skimmed across the row of sleek cars and jolted to a halt at the dull bulk of Jackson's van, bike on the rack on the back, and Jackson. Legs long and oh-so-sexy in frayed denims that had to be almost as old as the vehicle, shoulder resting nonchalantly against the van side, arms and feet crossed, and tanned face pointed to the sky. Even with his eyes closed, his huge attitude radiated across the car park. Had thinking about *that man* kept her awake all night?

'Oh my.' She ignored the echoing jolt in her stomach and shook her head, then wished she hadn't when it reverberated. She dragged herself together as she crossed the gravel, forcing her mouth into what she hoped was a breezy smile. 'Morning, you!'

'Morning.' He turned, eased his shoulder away from the van, his face breaking into a lazy grin. 'What happened? You might have ironed your knickers, but what about the rest of you?'

She started slightly at the greeting. So like Jackson not to pull his punches, but she'd make him go all the way with his explanation, just to see what insults he would come out with here. 'I'm sorry?'

'I'm the one who slept in a van, went for an early morning bike ride, then got washed in the sea, yet you're the one who looks rough. Have you seen the dark circles under your eyes? You look like you haven't slept a wink.'

*What the…?* A girl could do without that kind of honesty first thing in the morning. 'When I next need a compliment remind me not to come to you.' Arrogant *and* observant? The guy was beyond a pain. And she'd been hoping to keep her sleepless night a secret. 'I wound up in the room next to the rugby team, who by the sound of it were taking on anyone and everyone in an all-night bonk-fest.' True enough, and there had been some noise along the corridor, but that wasn't why she'd been awake.

'You weren't in there with them, were you?' He all but dived down her throat, an anxious furrow hewn between his eyebrows, then, seeing her dismissive eye roll, he backed off with an almost embarrassed shrug. 'I can tell you haven't slept.'

Thanks again, Jackson.

'I might as well have been in there, the amount of sleep I got. Plus they were still partying downstairs this morning, so I gave breakfast a miss.' Hoping he'd buy the excuse and not assume *he* was the main reason for the bags under her eyes, although with a guy as arrogant as this you never could tell.

'Why risk a night in a comfy hotel that might turn you into your grandmother when you can sleep in a camper and stay youthful?' One flash of an extra cheeky grin. 'It's bad to skip meals, by the way – you'll get a headache.' His x-ray stare bored straight into her skull, as if he had personally examined her pulsing, painful brain. 'Just goes to show you can't rely on luxurious hotels for peace and quiet and a good night. Whereas in my van, which you shunned, I enjoyed all of those.'

And got the smug-man-of-the-morning award too.

'Yes, but you do have sea-weed in your hair…' She leaned in, being extra careful not to nudge his body, and twisted a piece out of his curls, just to make her point. '…and salt rime on your cheeks, and I don't mind betting your iPad's all out of power.' She sent him a jubilant smirk. If he was hell-bent on playing top-trumps, she'd get him every time.

'If you must know, my iPad gave up twenty minutes into *Finding Nemo*.' He gave a sniff of disgust. 'The van battery isn't its strongest point, so I didn't want to plug the charger in.'

She hesitated for a moment. A dodgy battery on the van? One huge inward groan to that, but it would have to wait for later. The rest she could do something about immediately. Turning, she put a hand on his arm.

'Come on. Grab your iPad and charger, we're going in.'

'In where?'

'Into the hotel, of course. I know I checked out, but the room's officially mine 'til ten.' She glanced at her watch. 'That means we've got an hour. I'll sweet-talk the guy on the front desk, and we'll get the room back.'

'The hotel won't like it.' He frowned, and gave a shrug. 'Thanks for the thought, but I can live without my iPad.'

'I'm sure you can. What *I* can't live *with* is sitting next to you all day when you smell like the beach.' One glance to measure his resistance, and his frown told her she needed to up the pressure, so she shortened her tone. 'Either use my room, or I'll rent you one by the hour. I'm sure a stunt like that would have the Jackson Gale scandal-reporters flocking.'

He narrowed his eyes thoughtfully, drummed his fingers on the van door as he weighed up the options, then slowly a smile spread right across his face.

'You're inviting me up to your room then? For breakfast and more. Who'd have thought?' His voice, low and velvety resonated across the space between them. 'I knew you would. I just didn't think you'd crack this soon.'

Something about the laid-back confidence of the guy drove her wild. The way he tilted his head then raised one eyebrow pushed Bryony's interior temperature gauge straight into the red zone, and out the other side. How could anyone make you this angry and yet make you ache for them at the same time? Aching? What the hell was she thinking?

She snorted in a breath, and tossed her head. No way was she going to play into his hands by acting like he was serious. She shut out the pneumatic drill in her head, and sent him the most condescending smirk she could muster.

'Nice try, Jackson.'

The sarcasm brought her the satisfaction of seeing his other eyebrow jump skywards in surprise to join the first, and gave her the boost she needed to smooth ahead. She spun around, and, dragging her case behind her, set off back towards the hotel. 'Come on, Tiger. Let's go and see what we can sort out at reception.'

The excitement of heading up to a hotel room with Ms Starchy wasn't lost on Jackson, even if it was ten in the morning and completely unfounded. Although Bryony was apparently wilting from sleep deprivation, the electricity zapping between them in the confines of the lift was as undeniable as it was uncomfortable. He stood in silence beside her, eyes tight shut to close out the view of her bra-strap inside the open neck of her shirt, trying desperately not to breathe in the clean scent of morning woman. Even so, by the time they reached the first floor, the pictures flashing through his brain were disconcerting enough to make him wish he'd taken the stairs. Nothing clean about those. It was a great relief when the lift doors slid open.

'Room 313, it's just along here.' Even her brusque, no-nonsense instructions sounded sexy.

She had to be feeling it too, given the way her chin was in right the air and she was fixedly avoiding eye contact as they made their way along the corridor. And 'yay!' to the way those heels made her bum wiggle when she strode out like that, dragging her case on wheels behind her. Holy crap, he was having to run to keep up here.

By the time he pushed into the room she was already unzipping her case.

'So here we are then.' As he dropped his iPad onto the bed, he took in the dark blue silky bedspread, the bed neatly remade by Bryony, and the expensive wallpaper. It would be waste of a room, not to sleep. Waste of a room not to… 'I'm guessing you're stretching the expenses claim with this place?'

Still bending over her case, that accusation yanked her gaze up to his face. One more accidental view of cream satin bra-cups that sent blood rushing to his groin. Budgets weren't the only things that were stretching here.

Drawing her laptop out of her case, she slid it onto the desk. 'Not all budget hotels are dives, Jackson; you just need to know what you're booking that's all.' Her lips were dark-pink this morning, and she was gently biting the lower one.

'And you nabbed a room with your own ironing board?' He tried to keep the incredulity out of his voice as he assessed his surroundings. There it was, propped neatly against the voluminous wardrobe, beside a big shiny iron.

'I had housekeeping bring it up. They usually will if you ask them nicely.' One small, yet smug smile from her, acknowledging the triumph this was, as she ran her palms over her those perfectly smooth jeans of hers.

She jumped slightly as a muffled crash resonated from the room next door, then someone started singing on the other side of the wall. Slurry, male, with a bad memory for words by the sound of it.

'Rugby club?' *Crap.* The thought of drunken guys partying in the room right next to her had the back of his neck prickling.

She nodded. 'Now do you understand why I look like death?'

'That reminds me…paracetamol.' He dropped his hand in his pocket and flipped a pack of tablets onto the table. 'Two, straight away, with water will help your head.' Keeping his mind right away from the other packets his fingers had been toying with in his pocket. Nothing to do with condom Rik's present, these were definitely his size. God knows why he'd brought them, other than

113

his eternal optimism.

'Thanks for that.' She poured herself a glass of water, and the column of her throat bumped as she swallowed the tablets. Then she swung around to face him. 'Right, well, the bathroom's that way…' One glossy pink nail pointed to a panelled door, but her eyes had somehow slipped downwards and were now firmly locked onto his groin.

Talk about superglue.

Okay. Nice view, but still it left him helpless. Nothing he could do here under scrutiny like this but rise to the occasion. Big style.

And there she was, standing like she'd turned to stone, except she was still biting her lip. And there he was standing like he'd turned to stone too, but in quite a different way.

How the hell was he going to get out of this? Thinking about it, there was only *one* logical way out of this, for both of them. And in that case the first move was down to him and it involved clamping his mouth over hers. Maybe his optimism with the condoms was less ridiculous than he'd thought. High risk strategy, but what the hell, he was going to go for it. He took a deep breath…

A sudden clatter made them both jump.

'Holy crap…'

'Damn…' Bryony lurched across the room and grabbed the door handle. 'That'll be my breakfast.'

What a time for room service to arrive. Why the hell had the sodding guy at reception insisted on pressing a complimentary breakfast onto Bryony, just because she smiled at him? Damn, damn, damn, to the whole damned morning.

Jackson, clamping the burst of his erection with the heel of his hand, made a dive for the en suite.

'Great. I'll grab my shower whilst you eat. Enjoy your Full English!'

By the time Bryony had taken delivery of the breakfast trolley from the waiter and wheeled it into the room, Jackson had disappeared

114

into the shower, and taken his jaw-droppingly edible erection with him. 'Lucky escape or what?' her sensible head was telling her, whereas the aching need between her legs was saying something entirely different. If he'd actually made a move there she'd have been straight onto him. That was the kind of moment it had been. Pure, concentrated, unadulterated lust. Two more minutes and she'd probably have jumped him herself.

Damn, damn, damn. Talk about lost opportunities.

She downed three cups of coffee in swift succession, devoured the sausage, bacon, eggs, beans and mushrooms, and she was still kicking herself for letting that one get away. She listened to the drone of the power shower and the water splashing in the en suite as she buttered a slice of toast, spread a thick layer of chunky marmalade, and took a bite. He was actually standing naked under a hammering spray of water a mere two yards away from her. A mouth-watering thought, but how the hell could she concentrate on eating her toast, knowing that?

Instead, she pulled her laptop towards her, flipped it open and switched it on. There was a sudden silence as the shower stopped. Phew. That was better. Now all she had to think about was him drying himself. Not really better at all then. She sent a silent prayer to the God of sex-starved women to send Jackson out of the bathroom draped only in a towel. How sad was that? Coming up to her room with him had been *such* a bad idea. And her own reaction was so far away from her original intentions for the trip. She needed to take herself in hand, firmly. Now.

She'd just opened a file on her computer as the en suite door opened, letting through a cloud of steam from the bathroom, followed by a wet haired Jackson, looking slightly damp, but definitely fully dressed in jeans and tee.

So much for the power of prayer.

'Leaving your toast, then?' He was hovering beside her now.

'Help yourself. There's coffee too.' She reached for the pot and began to pour him a cup. 'I was too full after the rest.'

He swooped on the piece of toast without marmalade. 'Is that yesterday's route?'

'Yes, I put this together last night.' She scrolled slowly through so he could see the annotated map, followed by the pictures and the pages of notes. I've already sent it through to Cressy. A lot of this will eventually go on the website so viewers can find out about the ride in more detail, and it might even get put out as a book if there's enough interest.'

Leaning forward, and his arm was already pushing against hers. Even though he'd been in the shower, he hadn't lost his distinctive scent.

'That's awesome Bry.' He flashed her a grin. 'And it's good to see what we're aiming for too.'

She gulped, and pushed herself up to stand. There was way too much stomach flipping going on for her liking here.

'Right, well if you're ready, maybe we'd better…' Her sensible head told her she needed to evacuate the area and fast.

'Good idea. You're right. Another eleven rides to sort. We *definitely* need to get on.' Jackson jumped up too, downing his coffee in one. 'If you've nothing left you want to iron, let's go.'

# Chapter 18

This time when she pushed her way through the hotel door, Bryony had a spring in her step and not just thanks to shoes by Mr Louboutin. Blinking in the zingy sun that bounced off the tarmac, she almost fell off her heels as she skidded to a halt. One tall denim-clad guy leaning up against the camper van… Except Jackson was behind her, so it couldn't be him. Then her heart sank as her gaze slid to the next car along – a smooth sleek Aston Martin that looked horribly familiar.

Of all the car parks in all the world, Brando's car had to rock up in this one. Talk about interfering brothers. She stomped across the car park as the man in question glanced over his shoulder, and hit her with a glare. With superhuman effort she forced herself to sound upbeat.

'Brando, *what* are *you* doing here?' As if she didn't know.

'Cressy from *Sporting Chances* told me where you were, and when you appeared to be permanently blocking my calls I thought I'd better check things out.'

Well thanks a bunch, Cressy. She had skirted round telling Shea and Brando the details of her trip because it was just easier that way.

'Okay, so you've found me. I'm on a work assignment, what's the problem?' She stuck out her chin defiantly.

'The problem is the guy who's crossing the car park now. What the hell are you thinking, going off in a camper van with Jackson bloody Gale?'

It sounded like she wasn't the only furious one around here.

'Did someone mention my name?'

And, suddenly, Jackson was there, his broad chest hovering six inches behind her spine, an instant grin on his face, proffering his hand to Brando. 'Jackson Gale, exceptionally pleased to meet you, you must be Brando Marshall?'

Smooth talker or what? Bryony picked up her sagging jaw in time to see Brando grasp Jackson's hand.

'Hi Jackson, great to meet you too.'

What? Would it be mean to point out Brando was being a total hypocrite here?

But Jackson was already in there. 'As Bryony will have told you…'

*Thanks for that one Jackson…*

'…we're touring the south coast sorting rides for *Sporting Chances*. Bryony's staying in hotels making the most of the spa facilities and the fluffy towels, and I'm staying in the van. It's the first trip since restoration.'

Bryony held her breath.

Brando nodded towards the camper. 'I've heard they're hard to get hold of now. What are you running in the back?'

Jackson sprang across and flipped up the engine lid. 'It's a two-point-one type four…'

'Are those Webers you've got on there?' Brando was beside him in a second, leaning in for a closer inspection. 'Ah, fuel injection, that's interesting…'

Jackson bent in beside him.

Bryony's eyes widened in surprise. What was it with guys and engines? She retired to sit on a nearby wall. By the time the bonnet on the Aston went up she knew that from the guys' point of view time had ceased to exist.

'You know what, guys, I'm going for a coffee – call me when

you're done.'

She swung off back to the hotel, safe in the knowledge they hadn't even heard her.

# Chapter 19

'So Brando's a bit of a petrol head?'

Back on the road again, back with her itinerary, albeit a couple of hours late, and Bryony shook her head at Jackson's level of understatement. 'You could say that.'

Jackson gave a shrug. 'Funny, at first I got the feeling he was about to deck me. Does he often wade in like that then?'

How about all the time – not that she was going to spill to Jackson about that. 'Now and again. People always assume I only get where I do because of his intervention, but actually I try to do things on my own, entirely without his help. Thanks for reassuring him, anyway.' Not that Brando had ever really needed to warn a *guy* off before. It was usually Brando jumping in to help with just about everything else she could think of. Career, homes, cars. If he ever got wind of her making a job application, his style of helping was to buy the company. And whereas lots of her friends found it totally awesome, in reality she found it tiresome at best, and at worst, undermining.

Jackson gave a laugh. 'Funny, by the end there I got the feeling we were getting on okay.'

And strange as it seemed, she'd had that impression too. Something to do with the way Brando took his leave of Jackson saying 'Bry's awesome at her job, but don't let her bully you!' *That* she could have done without, although Jackson had got Brando right off her back, and that could only be good.

'He's just a bit protective of his little sister, always with the best of intentions. He's always done it, ever since he took on the role when I was small…after my dad left and everything.' She squished her lip sideways as she remembered the time Brando wasn't there to protect her. How bereft she'd been when he'd been sent away to school because he was getting on so badly with their stepdad. She'd howled and howled, clinging on to him so tightly she'd scratched his hand and drawn blood. It had seemed like she was very much alone for a long time after that – they only became close again once he inherited Edgerton. By then she was old enough to go and stay with him, and it was as though he'd been making up for leaving her ever since. 'Actually, we both interfere in each other's lives big time now. I drive him around the bend too, just in a different way.'

'Why does that not surprise me?' Jackson grinned at her over the gear stick.

She gave a sheepish sniff. 'And it's not just that I hijack his helicopter. One time I thought he needed a wife, so I flew one in to Edgerton Manor for him.'

That sent Jackson's eyebrows shooting upwards. 'And was he cross?'

'He was livid, obviously, except I'd chosen her very carefully, and it took them all of five minutes to fall madly in love. He and Shea are married with two children now.' She gave him a triumphant smile. Of everything she'd done in life, getting Shea and Brando together was one of her proudest moments, because it had made Brando so happy, Shea was wife of the century, and he and Shea were so good for each other.

'You and your matchmaking again. You and Brando must be close if you can pull that off.'

'He's always been there for me as long as I can remember, and our family situation made us cling together. When our mum remarried he didn't get on with our stepfather and in the end he went away to school. It's a long time ago now, but at the time it was hard.' Oh, shit. She was at it again. Talking about stuff she never usually mentioned to anyone.

'Hey...'

And there was his hand on her arm again. And here was she leaning into him as he swung the camper around onto the sea front.

'The pier's behind us. Look back now and you'll see it.' They were speeding along now. Jackson had been pointing out Brighton's places of note as they passed them since they set off. 'We're missing the Royal Pavilion this way, but I'll show you that another time. We don't want to get snarled up in the traffic.'

Bryony screwed around, then turned back again, and looked out across the beach to the ocean and the flocks of starlings circling above it, as the elegant Georgian buildings flashed past on their right. 'Talking of royal, I'd just like to point out it was my so-called princess behavior, which you complained so loudly about yesterday, that got us back into my room at the hotel just now.' Bryony paused for breath for a minute. Sensible Bryony was already filing the hotel room experience in the "let's count our blessings and move on" box. 'Acting regal has its advantages when it opens doors. When you're on the same side as me you'll be pleased about it.' She flipped him a grin. 'Just not when we're in opposition.'

'I'll take your word for it.'

'And it got us the washing-up done too. I popped that bagful of dirty crockery in at the kitchens after you dropped me off, and a nice boy brought it up to my room later looking like it had had a sparkle clean.'

'You're incorrigible, do you know that?'

'I gave him a tip obviously, but at least I got the dishes done.' She twitched her mouth. 'I admit it's better when we're on the same side.'

'Too right.' He sent her a grimace. 'Did you call me "Tiger"

122

back there in the car park?

One swift change of subject that put her on her guard. 'I might have. Why?'

'That's what you called me in the film clip, isn't it? It's all due to that clip that we're here.'

'Tiger suits you.' She'd leave out the bit about feeling way more in control when she called him that. 'Cressy mentioned the clip.' She deliberately left it vague.

'Dan, the guy who sorts out my stuff, was watching the tandem race tapes back, and spotted that we sparked.'

'Sparked?' Picking up the word and repeating it blindly in a high pitched voice. *So* not a good idea. And totally not thinking about that one incendiary night when she hadn't been able to keep her hands off Jackson. Damn to the way that hearing him in the shower this morning dragged that out from where she'd buried it, deep as it would go, but obviously not deep enough.

'No need to get those hand-pressed granny-knickers of yours in a twist.' He slid her one wicked grin. 'He was talking about on screen, not in the…'

'You have a guy to *sort your stuff*?' Another repeat. And worth sounding dumb if only to steer Jackson away from wherever he was heading with that one.

'I have a few. My trainer, my agent, my PA. I'm damned lucky to have got away without them in tow.' The shrug her gave was almost shamefaced. 'All the top sports people have them. Dan sweats the business details and leaves me free to concentrate on the training and the racing – not that there's been much of that lately.' He spat that last bit out.

'But you're going back to the team soon, aren't you?' She made a floundering attempt to chat about cycling. Anything was better than discussing sparks.

'Who knows what I'll be doing.' A bitter statement, not a question. Then he turned on her, jaw set, eyes steel-hard. 'Not that it's anything to do with you.'

She'd hit a nerve there then. Rolling her eyes in silence, she drew in a long breath, and bit her tongue. And he was the one accusing her of getting her knickers in a twist? Another outburst from Jackson, a warning to back off from where he didn't want to go. Did he think she hadn't heard of people going on the attack at times of weakness? Out of the corner of her eye she clocked him delving in his pocket. A moment later his phone landed in her lap.

'Put some music on will you.' *And shut up.*

The anger in his voice had dulled, but she could read the subtext. Message received loud and clear. Jackson Gale didn't want to discuss his cycling career. Or his accident. She'd add that to the list.

# Chapter 20

'Are you a natural blonde then?'

Five in the afternoon, and Jackson was feeling particularly pleased with himself. He'd made it his mission today to derail Princess Cherry Bomb and her plans, to knock her off her control-freak perch, and this far it was working like a dream.

'What is it with you and your random questions?' She'd noticed his tactic then, for keeping her mind occupied elsewhere whilst he went right on and hijacked her schedule. Helpful for him he had a mind with grasshopper tendencies. 'Why do you want to know anyway?'

Good question. He'd been asking himself the same. But somehow, since he'd banned himself from his mission to get her into bed again, instead of the loss of interest he'd expected, he'd developed an unnerving full-blown fascination for every detail of her life. As perturbing for him as it was for her, if not more. Yes, he'd always been a guy who asked a lot of questions, who had a healthy curiosity about life, yet usually this meant challenging his coach, pushing his mates, plaguing the team mechanics for answers. As far as he could remember he'd never had the remotest interest in the workings of a woman. Whereas now, here he was, rapt to discover she had a hundred and forty two pairs of shoes – used to be one more before she wrecked her boots in the sea

– did Pilates three times a week before work if she could fit it in, hated orange lilies, owned four pairs of hair straighteners, and had a hypo if she didn't get cupcakes by four.

'No reason. Just a way of passing the time.' He put it down to a measure of how dull his life had become this last year that he'd been driven to this. That in the absence of anything more intellectually important, his overactive brain had seized on the nearest available material to dissect.

'It isn't going to take all the way to Bournemouth to tell you my hair colour's all my own.'

'Even the streaks?' Surely all women dyed their hair. As for Bournemouth, he hadn't broached that part yet.

'The lighter bits are where I've been in the sun. And one tip for the future, Jackson, hair dyeing is like cosmetic surgery. It's rude to ask.'

'And have you…' He paused, enjoying the push. 'Had surgery?' He ignored that the word sent a twang through his gut for his own scars, and the knee that still wasn't right. He pushed that thought right out of his head.

'Bloody hell, Jackson, no I haven't had surgery; and don't you take any notice of what I say? I said it was rude to ask.'

He flipped her his best grin, feeling the smallest twinge of guilt for the exasperation in her voice. 'I'd have thought you'd have known the answer to that by now.' He clocked the flare of her nostrils, the dismissive eye closing. 'I hear you, but unlike the rest of the world, I'm not necessarily going to roll over and do everything you say, especially if my suggestions are better.'

'You relocating today's ride route to the New Forest instead of the Isle of White at the last minute was a complete one-off, which we did because I agreed.' Her jaw jutted defiantly as she flicked her hair back. 'As you pointed out it's a popular area for cycling, it gave some great opportunities for good camera shots, and saved us a boat trip.'

'You don't have the monopoly on good ideas. Other people

have them too.' It was true. And learning to listen to other people would be no bad lesson for her to learn.

'Hey, too much talking. You're in the wrong lane here.'

'Are you sure?' Playing for time. But what the hell, he was the one driving. He was amazed he'd made it this far without detection.

'I'm following the route on my phone, and the hotel I booked is definitely left.'

Taking his life in his hands here. 'How about if I tell you I've made other arrangements?' Out of the corner of his eye he saw her tense. He braced himself for the fall-out.

'What exactly do you mean by that, Jackson?'

A weaker guy would have shrivelled under her searing sideways look. 'I sorted something better.'

'I don't believe this! Better for who?' Her crescendo of complaint bounced off the van roof and ricocheted round the walls. She puffed out her chest as she drew in a breath, presumably preparing for battle.

'You'll see when we get there, think of it as a surprise.' The smile he dared to lob across hit an invisible wall of acrimony.

'I hate surprises.' She clapped her fists together in frustration.

'Only because you're a control freak, and because it's way past time for your four o'clock cupcake. Sugar is addictive, you know, and it's bad for you. If you didn't have so much of it you wouldn't be getting the blood sugar highs and lows.' Going for broke now.

Her reply came through gritted teeth. 'This isn't about sugar, and you know it.'

'So what is it about?' Why the hell couldn't she drop the attitude, go with the flow and enjoy the ride?

'It's about control, about you wanting to wrestle the power away from me.' She jabbed the air repeatedly with one bronze finger-nail.

Difficult, or just plain difficult? Anyone else, and he'd have been out of here. He tried to blank all thoughts of her nails scraping down his backbone as she…

'Interesting interpretation.' And a shame to spoil the secret

127

he'd spent the best part of the day pulling strings to set up, but he was going to have to spill the beans before Princess Cherry Bomb exploded completely. He gave a shrug, tapped his fingers nonchalantly on the steering wheel, and dropped the bombshell of his own, casual as you like. 'And here's me thinking that having run of a luxury mansion at Dartmouth, with hot-and-cold running butlers and an uninterrupted view of the sea was a better bet than a run-of-the-mill hotel in the centre of Bournemouth, complete with bonking rugby teams.'

He basked in satisfaction as he saw her jaw drop.

'That's the surprise?' She looked at him disbelievingly.

'Yup.'

'Why didn't you tell me earlier?'

'Because I wanted it to be a...' His words ground to a halt. Why *did* he care so much about making it a surprise? When had he *ever* tried to please a woman, especially one as downright awkward as this one? 'Never mind. It's not important.' He scratched his head, let out a sigh. Tried to concentrate on the car in front.

'Jackson?' Her hand arrived on his forearm.

His stomach clenched as her fingers slid around the bare skin. 'What?'

'Dartmouth sounds fab.' As she squeezed his arm, one nail caught. 'Thank you. For sorting it I mean.'

As a shiver of expectation zipped through his body, he stamped on it. Hard. Then he swallowed, shot her a swift sideways glance as he exhaled. 'No problem.'

Except the way her tentative smile zapped straight down to his groin, there was every problem in the world as far as he was concerned. In terms of their power struggle, he'd just won the day, dammit. Better than that. He'd won every battle, every step of the way. He'd been prepared, he'd worked out a strategy, come out all guns blazing today, and he'd wiped the floor with Bryony. So why the hell did he feel like a guy in the deepest of trouble?

# Chapter 21

'So how did you blag your way into this place, Jackson?'

Bryony wandered out of the tall glass kitchen doors, sidled across the decking, and rested her hands on the stainless steel rail on the precipitous balcony edge. All through the lovely seafood dinner they'd had in the restaurant down on the buzzing harbour side, on the clanking ferry that carried them across the river, and even on the narrow road that wound its way along here, she'd had no idea of what was to come. They'd spent the rest of the evening lounging out on the deck, but even now she was in the middle of making her bedtime cocoa, something about the jaw-dropping panoramic view drew her out for one last look. Across the estuary the scattered lights and illumination of houses on the opposite hillside shone out of the darkness, and the sound of rigging clinking on the masts of the yachts anchored in the river mouth below carried on the warm night air.

As Jackson sauntered across the decking and came to a halt next to her, she eyed the space between them. He was close yet maintained a distance which was fiercely, annoyingly respectable, and damn to the fact she was wishing he'd close the gap. She'd made it totally clear they were keeping things strictly hands-off, especially after her wobble in the hotel room this morning. So why the hell was she so disappointed he was respecting her wishes so meticulously? He'd lost no time switching to sailing resort casual. There was something disgustingly raw about his bleached low-slung jeans, rolled up. His bare feet. And she could so do without him bringing his delicious man-scent with him to engulf her.

'Let's just say, us being here is a friend returning a favour.' He clasped his hands, leaned on his forearms, slipped her one of those lazy-boy smiles that flipped her stomach. 'He doesn't need the house right now because he's away racing. Pretty amazing isn't it.' He turned, leaned with his back against the rail.

Still just as far away. Two feet, which might just as well be two miles. Her gaze followed his, as he looked up at the house that towered above them, the huge vertical windows illuminated against the interlocking planes of the walls. Her eyes slid back onto the column of his neck. Bad idea. As she watched him swallow, a shiver dithered down her back, and her own mouth watered. So much more dangerous here than a hotel, given the way Jackson Gale brought her hormones out to play. Bonking rugby players were way less trouble.

A sudden thought struck her. 'You don't have to try to impress me you know.'

'I'm not.' He shrugged, as if he didn't quite get where she was coming from. 'It's a cool place, better than a hotel in my book. It'll make a good base.'

'I told you before, my brother has a stately home, so I'm kind of over being wowed by flashy places.'

'I'm pleased to hear it.' Jackson tilted his head, as if he was suppressing a smile.

'What I'm trying to say is…' She snatched a breath, jutted her chin to screw up her courage to make the crucial point. 'Impressing me won't make me sleep with you.' She eyeballed him, straight on. Damn to how those dirty brown irises made her knees sag. Sure of what she wanted to say, yet somehow feeling like she was digging herself into a huge hole at the same time. 'Bringing me to this jaw-dropping, amazing place is not going to make me change my mind.'

There. That told him. She'd set her stall out fair and square here. No mistake.

'Who said anything about me *wanting* to make you change your mind?' A full-blown grin escaped and spread across his face. 'I really wasn't planning to do this.' One step, he'd flipped around behind her. His hands clasped her shoulders and his warm breath hit her neck as his growl reverberated in her ear. 'This has to be on your mind, or you wouldn't be talking about it incessantly, and if this is what it takes to shut you up…' he spun her around.

Eyes wide, she opened her mouth to protest but his lips crashed onto hers, and he slid right on in. Rough, hot, tasting like salted heaven. So not what she wanted. One moan of protest whipped away as his tongue tangled, and she was closing her eyes, throwing her weight against the thrust of his body, hearing the roar of blood through her ears as her heart went into overdrive. Feeling his fingers coursing through her hair, the sting on her scalp as he grasped a handful, dragged her head back, bending her backwards over the balcony rail. His hips grinding against hers, her waist sliding against the steel as she arched into him, his erection hard against her pelvic bone. She dragged in a breath, gasped as a triple shot of desire zapped between her legs, and she shifted her feet to rearrange, clamping herself against the whole muscular heat of him.

A sudden high-pitched bleeping pierced the air, and she caught the blur of the cloudy night sky as she opened her eyes and they pulled into focus. Her mouth suddenly empty as Jackson pulled out of the kiss, his stubble stinging as his chin brushed against her cheek.

'What the hell is that?' He dragged the back of his thumb across his mouth, sniffing the air. 'Is something burning?'

'Shit! My cocoa!' She shot off towards the open door, high heels skittering as she hit the polished granite floor and launched herself across the kitchen.

She lunged at the smoking hob, turned off the heat, grabbed the frothing pan and whipped it across to the sink, but the beeping carried on.

'Nothing worse than milk boiling over.' Jackson appeared, padded across to a bank of switches, flicked one and an industrial-size extractor fan whirred into action. Moments later the smoke alarm fell silent.

'I'm sorry. I wasn't thinking out there.' Understatement of the decade. What the hell was she doing snogging him again? After everything she'd said and all her best intentions. It was difficult enough sitting beside the guy in the van all day long with his smoking body and easy laugh. Leaving the pan in the sink, she took refuge behind a monumental kitchen island, wrapping her arms around her chest to steady her hammering heartbeat. Coming to an empty house was always a dangerous move but she'd hoped she'd last longer than an hour before she succumbed to the Jackson Gale effect. That would be the Jackson Gale who had assured her he would be keeping his hands off, the same one who was eyeballing her now with a quizzical stare that cut right though to her solar plexus.

'My fault as much as yours.' His face creased into a grimace, but above his shrug his eyes were smouldering. 'I know you said you were no Nigella in the kitchen, but burning cocoa? Here, I'll make you some, show you how it's done.'

'No, it's fine, I really don't want any.'

He was already opening the towering stainless fridge. 'No bother, Cherry Bomb.' In one easy movement he'd filled a cup with milk and slipped it into a microwave. Punched some buttons on the control panel. 'Two minutes, you'll have your cocoa, and no need for firemen.' He flashed her an inscrutable grin.

Without that grin she might have let it go, but something about the look on his face made her chest tighten and she turned on him. 'Never mind the cocoa, what the hell just happened out there Jackson? I thought you said you wouldn't be making any moves?'

He drummed his fingers on the stainless steel work surface. 'That wasn't a move, Cherry Bomb.' Only the slightest furrow on his brow giving any indication that he gave a damn at all. 'That was simply me making a point.'

Trust him to try to wriggle out of it like this. She gritted her teeth. 'And what point would that be?'

'You implied I was trying to get into your perfectly ironed knickers by bringing you to somewhere flashy.' He narrowed his eyes. 'Whereas if I was serious about getting access, I'd be relying on other methods entirely. With raw natural talent like mine who needs bricks and mortar? I was simply giving you a taster of how I'd be doing my persuading, and, given your reaction, I'd say you're much more up for it than you've been pretending.' The knowing grin he slid her sent her heart-rate into overdrive again.

Something to do with the adrenalin kick that went with being found out crossed with pure lust for the guy who just turned her insides molten, even if he did have an ego the size of Cornwall.

'That's ridiculous.' Knowing her protest was phony, but she had to make it anyway. She really couldn't have him knowing how up for it her body had been.

'Some things even a princess can't hide.' The wattage of his grin just doubled. 'And a hint, something for you to work on – next time you might want to throw out the control and embrace the spontaneity.' One ping, and he was whipping her hot milk out of the microwave.

Cocksure didn't begin to cover it. She blinked, grappled with being speechless, and forced out a reply through gritted teeth. 'There isn't going to be a next time, Jackson.'

Unmoved, he carried on whisking the cocoa.

'Not with me, obviously, given my one-night-only rule, but there might be with someone else.' Breezy as a force four wind. Then his thousand-watt grin faded. 'Contrary to what you think, good sex can't be scheduled on your damned itinerary. Intercourse for the princess at 4.30, scheduled between list writing at 3 o'clock and underwear folding at 4.45? No way will that work. You need to loosen up, let go, then maybe you'd enjoy yourself more.'

Arrrrrrrgggghhh. How many times had she heard this speech before? Except it was usually Cressy giving the lecture. And more to the point, what the heck gave Jackson the right to dish out Dr Love advice to her?

'Thanks for that.' She throttled her mental scream, and aimed for low and ironic. 'Great to get heartfelt advice from someone who is obviously *such* a relationship expert.' Not.

'Any time.' He placed her mug in front of her with a flourish. 'Enjoy your cocoa, sleep tight, I'll see you in the morning.' He backed out of the kitchen with an airy wave, giving one last quip as he turned. 'The laundry room's on the second floor. Help yourself there if you need the iron.' Then he sidled away, nonchalant as you like.

'Thanks.' Calling down the corridor after him, she swore the flat feeling in the pit of her stomach wasn't because she was hoping for a backwards glance. At least now her heart-rate could get back to normal.

She picked up her cocoa, and cursed that he made her so mad. Damn to that perfect butt of his. Damn to those to-die-for cheekbones, that oh-so mocking smile. Damn to the crazy part of her that had been hoping he'd suggest a movie fest. But the biggest damn of all was due to that huge lust-starved part of her, which was aching for more of Jackson Gale.

# Chapter 22

When Jackson wandered out onto the deck next morning after his early bike ride, Bryony was already hard at work, stretched out on a lounger, poring over her laptop.

'Coffee, juice, muesli, toast?' He slid a laden tray onto the table, and began to unload it. 'I take it you haven't had breakfast, seeing as there are no firemen in the area.' He mentally cursed that she was wearing a short dress and hardened himself against the view of those lightly tanned thighs which immediately sent his blood rushing south.

Way more disturbing than he'd bargained for, given that he'd just ridden the best part of fifty miles, promising himself every inch of the way that he'd show no further interest in the Cherry Bomb, or any part of her oh-so-lush body. That had been one ill-advised kiss last night. He'd tried to justify to himself that it was the only way to shut her up at the time, but it had been blistering enough to fuel his body with an adrenalin flood that kept him up all night.

'Cheeky – fireman quips are below the belt, though seeing you've brought coffee I'll forgive you.' She flipped back her hair, uncrossed those problematic legs and pushed herself up to stand, wrinkling her nose as she squinted into the sun.

'Help yourself; dig in.' How could he sound so unperturbed?

More flicking of that hair. He was determined not to notice how the sharp morning light turned it to gold, or that the way she bit down on that full bottom lip as she piled toast onto a plate made the pit of his stomach ache. Bad luck for him her dress turned out to be some kind of flimsy wrap-around thing that looked like it might unwrap at any moment.

Pulling up a chair, she sat, adjusted her top to hide her cleavage, took one deep breath that undid all her good work, then set about buttering her toast mountain. 'Have you been bike riding again?'

He ignored the pucker of her lips, as she sucked a jam smear off her fingertip.

'Yep, just a quick one.' No matter how delicious she'd tasted last night, no matter how she'd made his head spin, this morning on his ride he'd finally decided she belonged on his list of banned substances. He'd placed her firmly between chocolate éclairs and coconut ice. Despite the short-term enjoyment to be had from an immediate taste sensation, there were some things in life it was wise to forgo. He'd long since worked out that coconut ice wasn't worth the bother, and his early-morning sensible-head told him that any more tangling with Bryony Marshall wasn't either.

'This professional cycling sounds like a weird thing to be involved in.' She wrinkled her brow, gave him a quizzical stare. 'There was a book in my room, I was reading about it last night.'

Bryony reading about cycling? Someone else who couldn't sleep, then.

'Ah, you fell over the piles of signed autobiographies? Another hazard of crashing in a pro-cyclist's house I'm afraid. All of them ghost-written in case you were wondering, most of them bad, all saying the same thing.' He gave a grimace. 'But you're right. Pro-cycling swallows you up; it demands total dedication, it's harder than almost anything else a person could choose to do, it wrecks your body. But there's something about it. Once you win you can't stop.'

'You really ride over a hundred miles a day on the road, then go

136

to the gym? Then do the physio, and promotional stuff? Haven't you ever wanted a normal life, without all the hardship?'

So she'd been reading. And thinking about it.

He gave a shrug designed to look diffident. 'I never really thought about it.' He was lying through his teeth here. This last year as he struggled to recover from his injuries he'd barely thought of anything else, but the thought of trying to adjust to a life that was in any way normal scared the shit out of him.

'And you're how old?'

'Thirty-five.'

'And you've been doing it since you were…'

'Nine. Maybe younger.' He watched her nod her head, saw her nostrils flare in silent surprise. Or was it horror.

'Wow. You really are institutionalised.' She chewed on her toast, thoughtfully.

'That's one way of putting it.' Something about her earnest concern diluted the insult, and had his lips twisting into a wry smile.

'And when do people stop?'

A casual question, requiring a simple answer. No need for his heart to drop two feet into his gut and start panic-jumping.

'Most cyclists carry on as long as possible and when they've achieved all they can, they make the choice to retire.' Saying it like this, like he was talking about other people made it sound a breeze. He missed out the bit about the fear that gnawed at his gut in the wakeful early hours when he remembered that the choice of when to retire might yet be wrestled away from him, that he was going to need a whole load of luck and more to even get back into racing at all. He took a large gulp of coffee to hide the fact his palms were sweating at that thought and clocked Bryony's eye-roll across the top of his cup. Some trouble was better pre-empted.

'Okay, what now?'

'Nothing.' She twitched her lips. 'It's just funny that you were the one telling me to lighten up, when it seems like you're the one who needs to.' Her twitch spread into a full blown grin. 'Plus, I'm wondering how you ever found time to earn that dreadful reputation of yours...'

Bang. She'd nailed him to the spot, simply by raising one querying eyebrow. For a second he wriggled under the scrutiny, then he bounced free.

'I'm truly dedicated to whatever I set my mind to, and there were times I was hell-bent on going wild.' And then some. Not that he was going into that now. He let out a chuckle, partly at the way her mind was working, but mostly at the brainwave that just came crashing into his head. 'And right now I've decided to dedicate myself to relieving you of your administrative duties. That way you get to learn to chill and at least one of us comes out of this thing better off.'

And he got to keep Princess Bossy-Pants off his case. Pure poetry. Granted, it had taken him a couple of days to get the measure of her, but now he had, he was winning all the way.

'Excuse me?'

There was something astonishing about how wide she opened her eyes when she'd been knocked off her game. He ignored that it made his pulse gallop.

'We're only organising a few routes for your programme. I can handle it from here, leaving you free to concentrate on enjoying yourself.'

One silent coup from him, and he braced himself for the explosion. And waited. He narrowed his eyes, scoured her face for a clue. No reaction at all. Not even the give-away flare of a nostril. Should that worry him?

'Okay Jackson. That's fine by me, if you're sure?' If anything, her mouth was lilting, almost as if she were trying not to laugh. 'So, it's over to you then. What are you suggesting?'

She tilted her head expectantly. Was she enjoying *his* eyes popping in surprise?

He floundered for a moment. Not often that he was at a loss

for words.

'As I see it, we've got two weeks to sort out some rides. There's a lot to go at here on the south coast; I know the area so I can wing it. I'll sort where we stay as we go. Only three rules. No hotels, no camper vans. And we have to have a hell of a good time.'

'Wing it?'

He wasn't sure if that squeak was scepticism, excitement, or Princess Cherry having a full-blown seizure.

'In two weeks we should have enough material to pitch and that'll still give us time to film before I go back to full-time training.' If he said it fast enough he could almost convince himself the last bit was going to happen. 'All good?'

He made a grab for the low-fat muesli and rattled some into a bowl. Concentrated the power of positive thinking in as many places as it was needed.

'Sounds perfect.'

Not a hint of mockery in that cherry-lipped smile she turned on him. And, more surprising still, no argument. Yet from some-where he got the feeling she was only stepping back to measure out enough rope for him to hang himself.

# Chapter 23

'So today worked out okay, didn't it? A ride on Dartmoor sorted, a drive down the coast, a serious shopping opportunity, water-side dinner, and now a wander round a picture-postcard Cornish village?'

They were picking their way along beside the pretty white-washed shops and houses in the last splashes of the evening sun, dodging the sunburnt tourists in surf-shorts, very carefully not bumping shoulders with each other. And why the hell he was hell-bent on seeking her approval, he had no idea.

'Mmmm, fab day Jackson. And later I can sit and finalise my notes for the route.' She bit into the chocolate flake of her ice-cream cone, then tidied up the chocolate crumbs. She was still obsessed with work then, even when he'd wrestled the decision-making away from her.

'So, how do your sneakers feel, now you're walking in them?' He was almost gazing over her head now she was a good five inches shorter. Increasing his height advantage might seem like a marginal gain, but when you were tussling an opponent like Cherry Bomb every little counted.

'Flat.' She surveyed her rolled-up jean bottoms dismally, squinted at her new Converse with a critical eye, as she chased an escaping dribble of ice-cream. 'Scarily flat, and difficult to walk in after heels, although now they're on they are a very classy shade of grey.'

Now he'd heard it all. 'We're in Cornwall, surf paradise. Jimmy Wangs are hardly practical for the beach, are they?'

'Today's were Christian Louboutins.' She shot him a disparaging eye roll, as if he should know the difference. 'And I'm not really a practical girl, in case you hadn't noticed. Although, like Ginger Rogers, I can manage most things in heels, backwards if need be. But you're right – the salt on the beach would have spoiled them, so thanks. But don't forget the deal. I'm only wearing sensible shoes if your van gets glammed up – as soon as we see a shop with bunting, I'm buying some. And next time, by the way, I'm going to insist you have an ice cream when I do, and a cupcake.'

He took a deep breath, listened to the chink of the rigging banging on the masts of the boats moored along the harbour edge in an effort to give his eardrums a rest, and made a superhuman effort not to wilt under the onslaught. Out of the corner of his eye he caught sight of a shop doorway, festooned with flapping fabric. He shuddered and quickened his pace. Why the hell was he wasting time on marginal gains when it was obvious he needed something way more major?

A sudden iron-grip thrusting on his forearm made his legs veer across the cobbles like they belonged to someone else. 'Steady on. Where are we going now?'

'Don't act like you don't know.' She stared up at him indignantly.

Now she'd lost those heels their eyes were nowhere near level. Her looking *up* at him was a whole new experience which, in theory, *should* give him the advantage. This he could get used to. Up was good. Although, it wasn't proving that effective as a Bryony-blocking tool. She was still on his case.

'If you take off your flashy cycling sunnies, Jackson, you'll see we just walked right past a bunting shop. Come on. Judging from all the pretty stuff that's hanging outside, your van is one transaction away from *the* most fabulous make-over ever. No eating in the shop, though, so I need to finish this.' She rammed what remained of her cone into her mouth, rubbed the crumbs off her lips, and brushed her hands together.

And what if he happened *not* to want a make-over? What then? For a second he raked his fingers through his hair, contemplated resisting. Then a sharp thrust in the small of his back propelled him forwards, and a yard later he landed in ditsy-print-central, in a space so confined he had to clamp his arms hard against his body to fit. Then two seconds later Cherry Bomb arrived right beside him, and filled his personal exclusion zone with woman scent so reminiscent of that *other* night by the sea that it made his head go fuzzy.

'So. Did we have a deal?' Jackson pushed his shades up onto his head and forced his face into a grin. Some things weren't worth fighting; you simply had to work with them, woozy head and all.

'We certainly did.' The smile she swished up to him was pure pleasure, and not in the least triumphant. But something about her clear, unguarded enthusiasm set his alarm bells ringing. Open, honest women were part of why he had his one night only policy. Open and honest went with high expectations, an immediate ability to empathise and the tendency to bond – although not in a good way. Clingy women who stuck like glue were his nightmare scenario. To be avoided at all costs.

'Come on, Jackson. Let's shop!'

Her excited cry bounced off the ceiling, despite the damping effect of a thousand quilts and cushions, stacked high, waiting to be bought. Unnervingly uncomfortable, the way it made his stomach clench, and nothing to do with retail excitement either. He gritted his teeth, hardened his resolve, and blocked the fleeting thought that she'd bent to his will all day. Maybe he'd misread her bossy domineering side. Definitely dismissing that one. She was ahead of him now, dipping, delving, whooping like a child. His credit card may be in for a meltdown, but he had to be sure to keep his libido on ice and stay far away from Cherry Bomb. For the sake of both their sanities.

'You know I can't see a damn thing out of the windows with these flags hanging everywhere. I know it's only heather and more heather, but a view would be good.'

Bryony let out a sigh as Jackson slung himself into his seat, slammed the door and peered into the rear-view mirror. They were back in the middle of moorland nowhere again and it was her fault for stuffing up earlier, and failing to get all the pictures they needed.

'You don't think you're overreacting? It'll be dark soon, then you won't be able to see anyway.' She was determined to jolly him along, rather than argue. In retrospect, she had overbought on the bunting – the stripes and flowers were so pretty she hadn't been able to resist – but no way was she going to admit that. Admission of anything was a sign of weakness that Jackson would pounce on and take advantage of, and if it meant her getting her way when Jackson didn't, well, so much the better. She wasn't quite sure how he was doing it, but this far he was making a good job of doing just what he pleased at her expense. And what was worse, the louder she complained, the better he seemed to get at outwitting her. Shutting up and fighting him by any means other than head-on had seemed like her only hope. And even though she wasn't naturally an antagonistic person, she was ashamed to admit to herself that the bunting driving Jackson around the bend was a huge incentive for her to big it up. Desperate times and all that.

'A guy has a right to see out of his own van windows without being obstructed by daisy print.' His fingers hammered on the steering wheel. 'As for these…' He threw a disparaging snort at the flower garlands hanging in the windscreen. 'We're not in Hawaii.'

'No, Jackson, and to quote someone not a million miles away, "We're in Cornwall, surf paradise". Where you're supposed to hang loose? That's what the garlands are about. And seeing how you're the one who's always telling me to lighten up, you might like to take your own advice on that, because from where I'm sitting you're the one who needs to.'

By way of reply he shot her a look, one long smouldering disapproving stare that made her take a mental grip on her panties. She dragged on her own seatbelt and made herself look anywhere but at his lean tanned hands. Insides melting over some guy's sexy thumbs was not a good place to be.

'Thanks for doing the detour anyway. We were lucky to get the shots before the rain started, but I can't think how I missed those crucial pictures this afternoon.' Except she could. Totally unable to keep her mind on the job because snogging Jackson last night had blown her concentration skywards. She added blatant lying to the ever-growing list of today's bad deeds and tore her eyes away from Jackson's hands as he took his phone out of his pocket and tossed it onto the dashboard. 'Who'd have thought it would get dark so fast?'

'Just bad luck we had to come back to the remotest part. Not to worry, we all screw up sometimes.' He flashed her a grin through the dusk. 'These little moorland roads are slow to drive on. It feels wild and remote. There's no phone signal, but we're probably not much more than an hour from the house.'

And phew to that. Sixty short minutes, then she could get some distance.

'Great.' Her eyes snagged on his T-shirt as he reached forward to the ignition key, slid to catch the slice of bare skin at the base of his back. She gave herself a mental jolt as her mouth watered. Dribbling over a guy? Really not so great.

She watched him turn the key, waited for the engine to roar into life. She heard one small click. Nothing more.

Jackson cursed. 'Damn thing.' He tried again. Nothing. 'What the hell…?'

He flung open the door, jumped down, then she heard him open the engine bay at the back of the van. He banged about for a few minutes, then jumped back into the driver's seat.

'Everything okay?' She breathed in the smell of wet man.

'It's the ignition.'

'Right.' As if that told her anything, but he didn't sound too concerned.

'Probably linked to the battery.' He gave a sniff, swiped the rain off his forehead. 'Common problem, happens all the time, goes with the territory. It's why you see so many of these vans on the back of recovery vehicles.'

'What?' She tried to keep her voice level. 'We're on a tiny lane in the middle of nowhere, it's almost dark, I can't remember when we last saw a house, or even a car, and there's no phone signal. What are we going to do?'

'No need to panic. I'll give her another try.'

'Great.' She tried for sincere, not ironic, held her breath as he went for the key again.

One click instead of the roar of the engine sent her heart into free fall. The next click it went plummeting past her knees.

'Nope. It's completely dead. That's not going anywhere. ' He leaned back in his seat, grabbed a handful of hair.

Oh, shit, this couldn't be happening. 'So?'

He blew out a long sigh. 'Good thing you bought those covers. I'm sorry, Cherry Bomb. I'm going to have to go back on the no camping promise, just for tonight. On the upside, you get to try the rock and roll bed.' He gave a wry grimace. 'Probably best to go for help when it gets light – don't you think?'

She sat, listening to the rain drumming on the roof. A night in a van, with a guy who was driving her crazy on all fronts? A rock and roll bed? Shudders on all fronts for those things. On the other hand, why was Jackson asking what she thought? That had to be the silver lining to this cloud.

She flipped off her shoes, drew her legs up underneath her, and counted how many hours until dawn.

# Chapter 24

'Oh, my.' Bryony wriggled a stiff shoulder, pulled on a corner of quilt, and eased one eye open. Registered the blinds at the van windows were pale with light.

Top to tail. Last night it had sounded like a fool-proof method. And back to back. The best arrangement to fit two tall people into the space available, and more importantly, to ensure a contact-free night's sleep for both of them. Safe as houses, seeing as she'd planned to stay awake anyway and wrap herself in a ton of quilts to make a job of it. But if she was waking up now, that meant she must've been asleep, and it had to be morning because there was enough light for her to see exactly what she was using as a pillow. Inky blue denim, just like Jackson's...

Crap! She was lying on him! And where she was lying couldn't be worse.

*Cheek crushed onto his crotch?*

As her stomach disintegrated, she snapped her airways shut. If she stopped breathing she would move less, and maybe his man-scent wouldn't make her head spin so much. Man-scent. That's what she could smell. Soap and musk. And even though she'd been here all night it was still registering. Playing havoc with her hormones too if her sticky pants were anything to go by.

'Oh, crap, again.' It was going to take a damn good plan to

get her out of this one. Judging by the gentle snoring, Jackson was still dead to the world. With luck and a following wind, if she only moved her eyes, she could assess the awful geography of the situation, then extricate herself whilst he slept, as long as her thumping heart didn't wake him first.

She shifted the tiniest bit to get a better view. Jackson was lying flat out on his back, one bent arm thrown out above his head at the other end of the bed. Her heart skipped a beat when she watched him lying all vulnerable. And she was oh-so-cosily curled, knees by his ribs, elbow wedged in the valley between his thighs, face gently resting on the oh-so-comfy cushion of his genitals. How the heck that had happened, she had no idea. Achingly, deliciously comfy? She banished that thought before she'd even had it. Listening to the slow, regular rhythm of his breathing, she began to push herself up on her elbow. Slowly, slowly.

'Cherry Bomb?' Jackson's voice was deeper than usual.

She jerked as his hand landed on the side of her head. At first the weight locked her down, then, as she stopped fighting against the pressure, the touch merged into a caress that sent shivers down her spine.

'Jackson.' The denim bulge under her chin was hardening, as his erection rocketed into life. Not that it was his fault. He hadn't asked to be woken up by a harpy head-banging his privates. Her gaze slid across the tanned skin of his stomach, the gap below his T-shirt, followed the trail of hair that started at his navel, and descended. The waistband of his jeans hung slack across the hollow between his hip bones. What the hell kind of an excuse could a girl make for this? Clever and witty fell by the wayside, as all she could find was lame. 'This is not what it looks like.'

He gave a throaty laugh, shifted his spare arm higher, yanking his T shirt up a notch. More exposed skin that brought her own out in a rush of goose bumps. Not a good look.

'Whatever. No worries.' Disentangling his fingers from her hair, he rubbed his thumb across her cheek. Snaked a nail down her neck. 'Sixty-nine's good by me any day.'

Trust him to make something out of this that it wasn't. Sixty bloody nine? So not the idea. So not on the schedule. So... She didn't even care. Couldn't have moved if she had to. All she could do was to lie and let his fingers work their teasing way across her skin and let her bones melt. She held her breath as his fingers moved on down, followed the centre of her chest, stopping only for a moment to undo a button. As he snagged a nipple she let out a small cry, felt her insides turn to syrup and her panties get wetter still.

'Jackson?' She shifted her head, twisted. One inadvertent tweak of his waistband, and the tip of his penis thrust into view. Thick and sculpted and beautiful. She swallowed hard. Bit her lip. Her hand was itching to touch, her mouth was already open, ready to swallow as much of him as she could take. All she wanted to do was to rip off his jeans, release him and ride him for all he was worth. Except she wasn't going to do that, was she?

She placed one fingernail in the hollow by his hip bone. Heard his guttural groan of anticipation as she dragged it inch by teasing inch, arcing around the top of his penis, and easing across to his other hip. Then she walked her fingers across his jeans, heading straight for the fly button.

The very thing she'd promised herself she wasn't going to do. The very thing she'd been aching to do since the moment she stepped into the van four days ago. Sizzling Jackson Gale. There for the taking. Just like he had been that first shameful night. And knowing it was a bad idea wasn't helping her at all. One glimpse of that sexiest tip of him sent aching contractions of need shuddering through her. She held her breath as she fiddled with the first button of his flies. Then the next. Stopped to run a finger along the skin of his shaft, his low groan making her insides dissolve, his penis thrusting further with each undone button. Three more, and it made a break for freedom, arched toward the roof, and blow the thought of the arrogant guy it was attached to, wild horses

148

wouldn't stop her now.

She scrambled to her knees, tore off her own jeans. Straddled his thighs, ran one long nail up and down the awesome length of him. Looked up to meet his gaze.

'Condom?' She shivered at the expectant tension quivering in the hollows of his cheekbones, and the smoky arousal in his eyes made her insides go molten.

'Damn it. I don't have any.'

'But you always…?'

'Not this time.'

'What about the condom string?'

'I chucked them.'

'What?' This she could not believe.

'You were giving me a hard time about them.' He gave a snort. 'They were too small anyway.'

That much was believable, looking down at the towering height of him. He shifted, put his hands on her hips, pushing her away. 'Sorry, Cherry Bomb, looks like the fun is over.'

'No, it's okay.' A sniff hid her cringe. 'I might have one.' Might? This was not the time to cringe with embarrassment for having come prepared – for the unlikely emergency, when she couldn't keep her hands off him. Unlikely? She gave a hollow laugh at that, slid off him, and made a grab for her bag.

'So, obsessively organised does have an upside.' Jackson eased back against the cushions with a grin twice the width of the bed. 'Throw it over, and take a seat.'

'Fruit flavour, okay?' She tossed the packet to him with a guilty smile, hurriedly undid her shirt and shrugged out of it. As he looked up again, she was kneeling beside him, arching her chest towards him, and thanking the God of lingerie for her aquamarine silk balcony bra. She bit her lip. Something about providing the condom made her suddenly shy in the face of Jackson's narrow eyed scrutiny. No way could she do this looking at him.

She flipped a knee over him, twisted and landed on his stomach, facing his feet, anchored in place by the tower of his erection. Something about the self-service aspect of this position made her more at ease. Her clit throbbed as she opened her legs wide, slid herself against the rippling muscles of his stomach. Much more comfortable, now all she had to worry about was the huge penis, standing massively to attention, straining in front of her. The thought of it had been keeping her awake for almost three weeks. She was beyond ready to put it to good use, so ready she was almost coming here and now. She shifted to stifle the orgasmic flickers already threatening to take hold. This time she wanted to save it all for the big one. Dragging in his musky scent, all mixed up with strawberry fruit sweetness, pushing herself upwards, she eased herself over him. Behind her, she heard Jackson's grunt as she nudged the tip of him into position.

'Easy, Cherry…'

Opening herself, her gasps juddered through her body as she captured the length of him, inch by achingly slow inch.

'Oh, my.' The colours of the bunting blurred out of focus through her half closed lashes, and the whole world was falling away, leaving her, and her need to ride on Jackson, to thrash on him until her insides exploded. Leaning forwards, she grasped his thighs, gouging the hard muscle with her nails through the denim. Grinding her pelvis, gasping for oxygen, as her heartbeat banged in her ears. Then one last push and she had it all. Cliffs, mountains, rainbows, waterfalls, thundering hooves. One huge gigantic ecstatic release. She heard her own cry echoing a long way off, then Jackson's animal roar rose behind her and blotted everything else out.

She came to, skin damp with sweat, finding her face crushed into his jeans for the second time that morning. Feet by his head. Top to tail again, but this time the uncensored version. Whoever said top to tail was a safe bet needed their head examining.

'Oh, my, that was worth waiting for.' She mumbled more to herself than him, then remembered her manners. 'Thanks, Jackson.'

His hand landed flat on her butt, as he let out a low laugh. 'You're welcome, Cherry Bomb. Any time.'

All casual and sated now. He would say that wouldn't he, given his strict one time only rule went right out of the van window somewhere along the line? To borrow a phrase from Jackson, that could have been the upside of jumping a guy when he was half asleep. Not that she was complaining. A noise in the distance made her lift her head. An engine. Chugging. Getting louder. She froze as it drew alongside the van, but instead of going on past, it juddered to a halt outside. Then a door slammed, and the next moment the whole van reverberated as someone banged on the side.

'What the hell?' Jackson pushed up on his elbows. 'Watch the paintwork…'

Then the bangs subsided and a man shouted, 'Hello in there, you having problems? Saw your engine bay open, do you need help?'

'Great, with you in a sec.' Jackson sent Bryony a rueful grimace as he rolled her sideways. 'Well what do you know, Cherry Bomb? Looks like we're being rescued.'

# Chapter 25

Early evening, three hours up the motorway, Jackson was sitting at a table in a Service Station opposite his manager, Dan, swilling coffee around a plastic cup. And whatever Dan's accusations suggested, meeting halfway to pick up his car was the most practical solution in the situation. It had nothing at all to do with running away from Cherry Bomb because he couldn't handle seeing her after her dawn-raid this morning. But having said that, it was damned comfortable being in this godforsaken transitory place where no one knew you and there was no explaining to do, and best of all, no post-mortems.

'So, how is the awesome Bryony panning out?' Dan opened his sugar tube and tapped it into his drink.

Jackson had momentarily forgotten that Dan would be giving him a grilling, but whatever Dan threw at him had to be minor compared to Bryony's exacting stare.

'Pain in the ass.' Jackson gave a grimace. 'As expected, only a hundred times worse. Think control-freak with tiara aspirations, add in a complete inability to enjoy herself, and you'll have it in one.' He ignored a niggling feeling that he was betraying her here. He wasn't saying anything other than the truth. More to the point, loud complaints would hopefully provide a smoke screen. No way did he want Dan to know the reality of his plight. That when she was there, she sucked all the oxygen out of the air, that sex with her was the best he'd ever had even when he still had his jeans on, that when he was with her he felt more alive than he'd ever felt, or, that as women went, she was the biggest challenge he'd come across in his life.

'Bit of a ball-breaker then?'

'She won't be breaking mine.' Jackson gave a hollow laugh, though in reality he wasn't so sure. 'She's a handful – kind of larger than life, like a human steam-roller on fast forward. Took me a couple of days, but I've got her worked out now.' Until she wrestled the reins back off him again, and no knowing when that would be. Something told him any advantage he had was strictly short term.

'And the camping?'

Jackson gave a snort. 'Total non-starter. Would you believe the woman actually…' Jackson swallowed his words. Sharing what Cherry did with her knickers was a bad idea, especially given he'd been inside them only this morning. He took a gulp of coffee, and blinked away the image he'd been seeing all day – her bare ass, bouncing as she rode him. What a turn on, although holy crap, he needed to get a grip. 'Let's just say she's high-maintenance. Not her fault the camper broke down, but I reckon the Range Rover will be faster and more reliable.'

No idea how had he got this far through life and not tried reverse cowboy before. But despite the fact he'd been rock-hard ever since with the mental re-visits, he wouldn't be going there again with Cherry Bomb. Rules were rules, and this morning was one slip up he wouldn't be repeating. His survival instincts were well enough honed to know to stay well out of this one.

'So the trip isn't bringing you two closer?' Dan's tone was nonchalant, but the flinty glint in his eyes told Jackson the question was fully loaded.

'Closer?' After all the years he'd known Dan, Jackson knew how to bluff him.

Dan gave a shrug, clearly faking diffidence. 'The sparks I saw on that interview clip, I thought she might be...'

Jackson rounded on him. 'Be what?'

'Suitable, significant maybe?'

'You mean "The One" don't you?' He gave an indignant splutter. 'Bloody hell, Dan, this isn't Dating in the effing Dark. You need to back off.'

'I'd hoped she might bring a bit of happy your way, that's all.' Dan tapped his spoon on the table idly. 'You do know who she is?'

'Obviously.' Jackson jutted his chin belligerently. 'And?'

'Bryony is Brando Marshall's sister. Brando, as in billionaire magnate, and TV production company backer, amongst other things.'

'What exactly are you getting at, Dan?' Definitely for the best he'd kept quiet about meeting Brando.

Dan hesitated. Spoke slowly, as if he was not only choosing each word very carefully, but walking on eggshells too. 'Well, taking a view of the longer term picture here, taking everything into consideration for you career-wise, dating Bryony Marshall might be no bad move.'

Jackson opened his mouth to reply, then closed it again. Where the heck was Dan coming from? With phrases like 'long-term', 'career-wise'? Dan was usually down-the-line, but this time the guy was talking out of his ass. They both knew in a couple of weeks Jackson would be back to full-time training again. It might take a while, and a heck of a lot of work, but he'd get back to where he was when he had the accident. Hell, he had to. Not making it wasn't an option. As for the rest...

'So you're suggesting I date Bryony to clinch a TV contract?' Jackson's voice rose, was Dan really implying what he thought he was implying? He knew he was about business deals but this was something else.

'Not at all.' Dan was doing a fast reverse here, using that soothing, matter-of-fact voice that drove Jackson round the bend.

'She's stunning, you've obviously got the hots for her, plus she's one of the few women I've come across who looked like they had any chance of handling you. You know me, I'm thorough, cool and analytical – that's why you employ me. I can't help that I see a situation from every angle. What I'm saying here is that the TV advantage would be the icing on an already fabulous cake, that's all.'

So even if that wasn't *exactly* why Dan was suggesting this, the Brando link had certainly come up on his radar. Jackson grimaced. Bryony had mentioned people thinking she only got where she did because of Brando. Him using Bryony to gain a similar advantage had never occurred to him, but now the idea was there, it was just another solid reason to stay well away. And dammit, because he shouldn't be feeling like he just got a kick in the guts when he never intended to go there anyway. He let out a long sigh. Talk about ulterior motives. So many reasons why Dan had been so insistent on bundling him off on a road-trip with Bryony. Unbelievable. Out of line. But no doubt done with his own best interests close to Dan's completely misguided heart. He and Dan went way back, but even though they'd known each other since junior school, looked out for each other all along the way, were more comfortable in lots of ways than he was with his own brothers, Dan wasn't always right about what he needed.

'Getting your rocks off by matchmaking?' Jackson flung a defiant grin across the table. The guy was so far off course he had no idea. 'Sorry, Dan. Me and Bryony are not gonna happen. As for TV contracts, I'll get them on my own merits, although there won't be time for TV when I'm racing again.'

'Life isn't only about winning races.' Dan spoke slowly, without meeting his eye.

For a moment Jackson baulked. 'We're here to win, Dan.'

Then Dan's affirming punch smacked Jackson hard on the arm, and whooshed any doubt away. 'Too right, Jackson. Let's go geddem.'

Halfway into Jackson's cycle ride next morning, and his groin was aching. Nothing to do with hours in the saddle, everything to do with the view he'd snatched of Cherry Bomb padding out onto the decking at dawn in skimpy pyjama shorts – and him knowing he wasn't going to go there. Yesterday had been an aberration, the only time in his life he'd gone back for more, and that'd only happened because she'd pretty much ambushed him when he was asleep. Not that he was complaining… Yep, he'd had the ride of his life yet again – the woman was superhuman, the way she turned him on.

Emotionally and physically he was fully equipped to give one night of pleasure, but anything more than that, and he was lost at sea. Something to do with the depth of those bright-blue eyes set his alarm bells ringing every time, because now she was less uptight, what he saw when he looked into those princess eyes was all soft and warm and squishy, and horribly complicated. The woman was full of need. Need for a guy, need for babies, need for what the hell else, he didn't know. It couldn't have been clearer if she'd had it tattooed all over her forehead. He'd never seen eyes so full of complication.

Now he came to think of it he couldn't remember looking that deep into any woman's eyes ever before. There was usually some invisible barrier that bounced you back out again before you got far enough in to look around, let alone notice anything. But what he did know was that he was in no position to go any way to meeting any of those needs. He had no earthly idea how a man would go about the job. He was good for riding bikes and winning races, full stop. It was what he'd spent his whole life doing. Winning races was easy. There was a finish line; you crossed it, end of. So long as you got there before anyone else, it was a cinch. That was his specialty, whereas this other stuff – who knew how any guy began to start with all of that? It was in the too-hard box, the don't-even-go-there box, the risks-this-guy-is-never-going-to-take box. And he was well out of all of them.

Ahead of him the road kicked up, steep and punishing. If he thrashed himself, by the time he reached the top his heart would be exploding and his chest would be on fire. He grappled the handlebars, stood up on the pedals, and prepared for the pain. This pain he could deal with.

## Chapter 26

'Shit.' Jackson rounded the corner onto the decking, helmet and cycle shoes in the crook of his arm, to find Bryony lounging against the balcony rail coffee mug in hand, the sun behind her shining all the way through her gauzy slip. Might as well not have bothered getting dressed at all the way her legs were outlined, all the way up to that delicious point where they met. He tugged down the zip of his top, gave his flattened, sweat-soaked hair a tug, and cursed that the release of the last three hours had been undone in two short seconds. Cursed again as the hard-on of the century began to thrust against the Lycra of his shorts.

'Jackson. You're back sooner than I thought.' Bryony spun round to face him, with a bright smile he picked up in his peripheral vision given his sight-line was locked onto her crotch. 'Good ride?'

Damn that the see-through situation was just as bad this way round. And damn that now she'd turned, her eyes had zeroed straight onto his groin, where her gaze acted like a massage vibrator and hiked the size of him up another couple of notches. And damn to the exhibitionist in him that wanted to show off everything he had, lapping up her gaze like she was licking him when he had no intention of following through. The show-off in him was getting off on her not being able to look away, whilst the primal, come-and-bed-me-and-sod-the-consequences guy in him was revelling in wherever this was heading, despite his efforts to keep his sensible brain engaged.

'Great ride, thanks. Sweaty.' He gritted his teeth. Civilised-guy gave caveman a swift kick on the shins and got him into line as he casually slid his helmet in front of the offending bulge.

'Right. Okay.' Her eyes climbed to his meet his. Was that disappointment?

'I need to jump in the shower.' If only to deal with what was never going to subside on its own. 'Catch you in ten. Will you be ready?'

'Ready?' She sounded a million miles away.

Spelling it out in words of one syllable here. 'To go out? To do some work?' One mention of the 'W' word, she was back in the room.

'Yes, sure, just got a couple of things to iron. I'll go.' She began to head towards the house, hips swaying as she strode. Bare feet today then.

Best scenario of all. He got to watch her leave.

Bryony grabbed her dress and headed for the stairs, where the polished wood was smooth under the soles of her feet. She was relieved to grab the first excuse to leave, because it let her off the hook. Since she slid off Jackson yesterday morning in the camper, they'd had no time alone together. Jackson had shot away with the farmer to get help, then they'd been bundled into the cab of a recovery vehicle, and once they'd got home Jackson had rushed off to pick up some car. She'd gone to bed early so she didn't have to face him when he came back, then woke at dawn. Sex-on-the-brain was one bad reason not to sleep. Seeing him out on the deck just now, she still wasn't sure how he was going to play it, or how to play it herself. Was there even any protocol on how to pick up and carry on after you'd jumped a guy when he was half asleep, simply because he'd sent your hormones out-of-control crazy and you couldn't stop yourself? If he did decide to

159

make a move now, would she be gagging for it against her better judgement? Or would her sensible head win through and let her give him her best frosty-knickers knock-back. Confused.com didn't begin to cover it. His tree-trunk of an erection making an escape bid from his shorts this morning suggested a certain level of interest. She swallowed the saliva that filled her mouth at that thought. Him, his unzipped jacket flapping around the sculpted tan of that delicious six pack. As for the rest... She hadn't been able to take her eyes off it, but hopefully he hadn't picked up on that. His head was big enough as it was without him thinking he was completely irresistible. But even though the body language of certain parts had been screaming his intentions loud and clear, and his eyes had been all dark and soft, there had been contradictions. She'd been on full-alert, ready to deal with an advance, yet he'd been definitely standoffish in his attitude. Cool even. Like he was the one giving her the icy-boxer brush off, not the other way around. And mixed messages were not what she'd expect from Hot Stud, Jackson Gale.

She'd found her way to the ironing room the previous evening, so she knew the route up to the airy top-floor laundry space criss-crossed through the dramatic modern house, giving constant views from landings and walkways, through to the cavernous spaces below. When she reached the top this morning, she realised there was a high level deck she hadn't noticed yesterday in the dark. She tried the door handle, found it was open, and pushing out, she arrived on a dizzying second floor platform.

'Wow, amazing view.' She leaned over the balcony rail, peering down to the decking below. Beyond the river mouth, the sea glinted turquoise. Closer in, she could look down on the roofs and jutting angles of the house.

She snatched a breath. A movement lower down, behind a long narrow window, caught her attention. 'Oh, my.' Embarrassing or what? Only a birds-eye view straight into what had to be Jackson's en-suite. A wet room, given the fact that in the shadows below she could make out water jets coming from all angles and a figure which had to be Jackson.

Dammit. She should leave. Immediately.

Mesmerised, she strained to see more. Jackson. Naked. Monochrome in the shadows beyond the glass, soaping and scrubbing himself, angling his body into the spray. He turned, unaware he was being watched, and her stomach slipped away as she made out the arc of his erection his hand somewhere round the base of it. She bit her lip sharply, desperate to move yet somehow frozen. Her limbs locked completely as his hand began to move, slowly, up and down the length.

'Jackson jerking off? What the...?' She shut her eyes tightly, as her heart thumped. Then she opened them again. Wide. Not because she wanted to, but because she had to. She took a gulp of air, screwed up her eyes to focus.

His hand was moving faster now. As she watched, a flutter of need between her legs, grew to a pulsing ache. This was so wrong, yet it was so damned hot. He was moving in a steady deliberate rhythm now, and, as he tugged faster, more roughly, she sagged against the rail, crossed her legs, clenched her thighs. Then he leaned back, thrust his penis upwards into the air, and let go. Awesome. Dragging in a breath, she rammed a hand between her legs, found the pulsing heat of her clit, and pressed. A second later her body clenched, then a rippling explosion of pleasure spread through her. She clung onto the rail, head thudding, body spinning. When she finally opened her eyes again Jackson had collapsed too, shoulder against the wall. Less than a minute since she arrived, and it was all over.

'Okay. So much for pressing that dress...' She blew a sweat-dampened strand of hair off her forehead and smoothed down her shirt. Ten minutes, Jackson had said. If she was going to be ready she needed to get a move on.

Ten minutes later Jackson had settled himself on the terrace table, feet on a chair, elbows on his knees, prepared for a very long wait. No way would Cherry Bomb appear within the hour, given all the woman things she had to do. At least it would give him time to decide why what Dan had said yesterday was disturbing him, and, more importantly, to work out how he was going to handle what was turning into some kind of meltdown in the lust area. Revisits were not his bag, and the last thing he expected was seconds turning out hotter than firsts. He was used to one explosive night which left you feeling happy and fulfilled, whereas Cherry made more feel like he'd had less. Rather than satisfying his need, the more he got, the more he wanted, like some exponential dependency. As if someone had turned up his libido onto high, then carried on off the scale. He'd heard the guys talk about needing to burn out the heat. So what if Cherry Bomb was a woman who was going to need total burn-out before he got her out of his system? Her complexity didn't sit easily with him. No way was he going to get embroiled with someone who wasn't going to let go once he was ready to leave, just because his sex-drive was temporarily out of hand. The trouble with Cherry was the way she kept wrong-footing him, taking him by surprise.

'Aren't you ready, Jackson?' Her voice behind him made him jolt.

Dammit. She'd just done it again. Standing there in her white linen dress, tight in all the right places – or should that be the wrong places? – with the scariest high heels yet. His guts disintegrated.

'I'm ready.' She tapped her watch. Jackson eased off the table, tried to take his mind off her dress pulling taut across her ass as he followed her around to the car. From the absence of a panty-line, he could've sworn that she wasn't wearing any knickers. One time he'd have queried this out-right, no second thought, just for the shock-value, but today he wasn't going there. He opted for something less challenging. 'What's in the bag, princess?'

'That's my alternative shoe store – converse and flip flops.' She flashed him a dazzler of a smile. 'In case we go skinny dipping…'

Holy crap. He might be backing down, but there was no way

she was.

How the hell he was going to survive today?

## Chapter 27

Bryony prided herself on being able to get the best out of people. She was renowned at work for being able to coax anyone, from the most bloody-minded celeb to the grouchiest cameraman, but today Jackson was proving impossible. Getting the better of her by sheer power of personality was one thing, but following up by grinding her down being completely uncommunicative and moody was something else entirely. Carefree Jackson had disappeared along with his camper and been replaced by a Range Rover driver with a face like thunder and a personality to match the blacked-out windows. They'd sorted another ride, albeit communicating in monosyllables and grunts, but it hadn't been the easiest day. Afterwards they'd eaten lobster at a quayside restaurant in total silence. By nine in the evening, Bryony finally decided that for this thoroughly awkward patient, shock treatment was the only option.

'Here you go, Jackson.' She plonked herself down beside him, on the wall where he was sitting, prised the top off the large ice-cream tub she'd just bought from the quayside store, and rammed a plastic spoon into his hand. 'Sorry about the plastic spoon, but this works like a dream for me when I'm in a mood.'

'I'm not in a…' One squawk of protest from him that proved her point completely.

'My favourite chocolate cookie-dough flavour, usually reserved for spoil-myself nights in front of the TV. They had a frozen yogurt version, but to hell with that, I got the creamy stuff.' She sucked a smear off her finger. 'Put it in your mouth – for me, for one time only. It's so bad for you and so sugar-laden, it has to make you feel better.'

'I'm not…'

'Jackson, just shut up, try it, and don't speak again until you're halfway down the tub.' She splashed a grin at him. 'Then you better pass it over, or else…'

Jackson all tangled up but he was finally doing what she asked him. One last protesting eye-roll, one last clench of those hollow cheeks that were more tightly drawn than ever today, then he lifted the spoon, sucked in a slick. And then another.

'Not bad.' He scrutinised the horizon as he swirled the contents around his mouth.

Shit Jackson, it's an ice-cream fest, not a wine-tasting. She bit her tongue. 'Cool?'

'Mmmm, I guess.' The most positive he'd been since morning.

After the run around he'd given her today, it was enough to make her bounce. A strange day given how it began, and when you've started by inadvertently – yet unavoidably – crashing a guy's most private activity ever. Even if he doesn't know it, the guilt you feel is going to make you cut him some slack. She should never have watched but at the same time that was a moment of double realisation. Firstly, because she finally decided that hands-off was no longer an option for her with Jackson. He was too hot, the things he did to her insides were too major for her to stay away. To hell with it. In that moment she decided to do what everyone always told her to do – to let go. She was going to grab her good time. He was around for a short while, and then he was leaving. The situation couldn't be more perfect for someone like her, who refused to receive commitment, or to give it. And having come to that decision, the consequences became suddenly clear. All along Jackson was adamant that he was backing away from any more

165

than the night of physical involvement she'd already had. What she'd snatched yesterday had been a departure from the norm for him. If she made him change his mind now, she immediately got back the power he'd whooshed away from her when he grabbed control of the itinerary. Easy.

Except first she had to make that happen, which was why she'd come out fighting in her tightest dress and her sexiest shoes. And, because a girl has to do what a girl has to do – a measure of her desperation, or her determination, not sure which – she'd come out without her underwear, which, now she was sitting on a wall, bottom button gaping, passers-by gawping, was feeling like rash bad judgement.

'All good?' She slipped an ice-cream-sharing, co-conspirator smile to Jackson.

'Your turn now.' He gave his spoon a last lick, and pushed the tub into her hands. 'About before...'

At last. She took it gratefully, dug in, and let the chocolate melt on her tongue. 'Mmmmmm...'

'Dan implied my racing days are over, when we were chatting yesterday.' He gave a shrug. 'It's been on my mind.'

Was this him explaining away the bad mood?

'And would that be so bad?' Musing here, given most of her mind was on cookie dough.

'Obviously.'

Despite the hard time he'd given her all day, something about his downcast reticence made her chest twang.

'Jackson, you're sitting here, and for the first time since you were seven you're the one actually making the decisions about what you do, minute by minute. You're eating your first ice cream for twenty years. I see that as good. '

'Life as a racer is dysfunctional. But it's all I know.'

'Maybe you need to move on, build some different dreams. There's a whole glorious world out there just waiting for you to find it.' One easy thought in the slanting evening sun. She'd give him that one for free. From his grimace she guessed he'd dismissed it, except a moment later he turned on her.

'So, what about you and your dreams? The Jimmy Wang dress, the house in the suburbs, the school run? It's obvious you're desperate for kids.'

She opened her mouth and closed it again. Inadvertently her brain flipped to the picture of her everlasting-dream, the one where she came down for Sunday breakfast with the now completely unavailable, Matt. It was weird – the kitchen was still there, she could still smell the toast and the coffee, but it wasn't Matt standing by the island unit. There was a guy, definitely, but it wasn't him. If this week had finally erased Matt from her unrequited-dream-guy spot, then it had to be a good thing.

She re-engaged her speech cogs to stamp on Jackson's wild claim. 'I can't think where you got that idea.'

'Probably you going gooey-eyed when you talk about your friends' kids was the giveaway. You're telling me to move on, but how about you move on from organising all your friends into happy coupledom, and sort out your own life? Forget about egg-freezing and find a real live fertile guy.'

'What?' She was doing her high-pitched shriek. Again. 'I can't believe you said that.' He was playing hard ball now and he wasn't backing off.

'You started this, Princess. And let's be honest, sometimes the truth is hard to face. Sounds like everyone went on to the next stage and left you behind, but it's time for you to go there too. You can't sit home-alone, eating ice cream forever.'

His straight talking might be stinging, but she wasn't taking it lying down. 'And you *can* sit watching kiddie cartoons?'

He gave a snort. 'That's different.'

She wasn't letting him get away with that. 'How?'

He narrowed his eyes as he thought, then shot her a triumphant grin 'They're ironic.'

*Bollocks to that.* She blew, shook her head, but stayed silent.

Damn him for always having an answer, and damn him for nailing her with some darned awkward questions. How did he always do that?

He got up from the wall, ran his fingers through his hair, 'Come on, you can finish your ice cream in the car. Let's go and find that beach.'

As he turned, his gaze snagged on her thighs. The perfect opportunity to get her own back, and to relaunch her take-over bid. Eyeing him closely, she slowly crossed one leg over the other. From the way his jaw dropped she guessed he'd clocked the panty-free situation, and as he yanked up his jeans, she caught his lips curling into a private grin, stretching pretty much the width of the bay.

# Chapter 28

'There's a quiet cove up along the coast I thought we might check out.'

Beside him in the front of the car she slid off her shoes and tucked her feet up underneath her. 'Fab.'

Not so fab that her dress was riding up, a couple of buttons undone, top *and* bottom, taut tanned thighs slanting towards him. Not to mention the erection-stoking expanse of cleavage that popped in and out of view as she shifted in her seat. And that was before he got to thinking about that one eye-searing flash of confirmation he'd snatched earlier. His early-morning no-knicker theory had been right, God help him. He'd had a physically punishing life, but what he'd lived through today had to be his idea of torture.

'We're heading for Pascoe Cove. Do you want to check we're going the right way?' If she concentrated on navigating it might put a stop to those wriggles. He knew the smile he posted her wouldn't go halfway to making up for how he'd been today.

'Give me a minute.' She grabbed her phone, and her airy mix of eager enthusiasm and startling efficiency sent another shot of guilt through his gut. 'Okay, got it.'

No excuses on his part. Having her body paraded in front of him and knowing it was off-limits had wound him up beyond the point of explosion. Not that it was her fault, although there were times today when it seemed like she was almost taunting him.

'We'll need to turn off somewhere soon.'

'Fine.'

Cherry was a lot of things, but no way would she push a guy's buttons to deliberately tip him over the edge; it wasn't her style. She couldn't help being off-the-scale hot and it was his fault he hadn't got his libido in line, but who'd have thought sexual frustration would be this excruciating.

'Next left after this one, Jackson.'

Back there he'd tossed out a line about his racing career being washed up because the last thing he wanted was her suspecting the real reason he was biting her head off every two minutes. No guy wanted a woman – who he'd decided was too hot to handle – to know she was driving him wild. Running scared was not a good look.

And who knows why he was heading out to some isolated beach when the sensible course of action was to head back home, where at least he could hide behind the safety of a closed door. Somehow everything he'd decided yesterday, about staying away because he didn't want to capitalise on the Brando link, had already gone out the window too. And something told him that sticking to his hand's-off-Cherry policy was about to get a whole lot harder.

'That's as flat as I can get it.' Bryony battling with the breeze, finally flung the rug down on the sand. 'And the beach to ourselves. How good is that?'

Not good at all, from where Jackson was standing. And tomorrow he'd definitely come up with a different way of handling the situation. Only a couple more hours to endure tonight and he'd be clear.

'Fantastic.'

Or it would be if she wasn't walking straight towards him. He flinched as her hand dropped onto his arm. Precisely why he'd loaded her up with the rug and the cool box to bring down from the car, so she couldn't do the random touching thing and turn his pulse rate crazy.

'Thanks for bringing me here, it's beautiful.' She kicked off her flip-flops, buried her feet in the soft sand and put her hands on her hips. Suddenly the vamp was gone, and she was there, a whole lot shorter, hair whipping in the wind, linen all crumpled, eyes shining up at him.

'Coming in the water, then?' Not being able to resist goading her. Payback for what she'd put him through all day.

'Nice thought, but we don't have our swimmers.' She chewed her lip doubtfully, put her hand to her brow, and squinted wistfully at the sun sinking over the sea.

He was determined to brazen it out here, see how far he could push her. 'Who cares about swimmers, underwear will do.'

'Shit, Jackson.' She took a deep breath, gave a tilt of her head and wrinkled her nose. 'You may as well know, I haven't got any on.'

'What…?' Feigning surprise was cheap.

'Don't ask why.' She gave sniff, and rolled her eyes. 'But I'm definitely without knickers.'

He allowed himself a minute to enjoy the shivers those words sent zinging through his body. 'So you'll be skinny dipping after all, then?' He hung onto his grave expression. 'When you mentioned it this morning I thought that was a bluff.' His stomach lurched as he watched her face drop.

'What a shame. I'm so sorry, Jackson.' She turned her face up to him, crestfallen. 'All this way, and I've wrecked it – I haven't even got any knickers in my bag.'

Hot was what she'd been all day, all arch smiles and confidence, glossy and sexy, perfectly buffed, with her killer heels, her raunchy butt, and her carefully slicked lips. Sizzling, scorching blistering. All day and he'd been aching to touch her, and all day he'd held back, held off. But now she was here, pale lipped and creased, tangled by the wind, her sudden vulnerability flipping his guts, she was completely irresistible. Then his own grin broke free.

The way those bare lips parted, if she didn't shut them soon he would have to… He took a step forward.

Dammit. He bent to meet her mouth, but she'd already whisked around and was away, running down the beach.

'Come on, we can still paddle.' She yelled to him, as she stamped up a storm of surf in the shallows, and for the second time that day, as he broke into a run, he found himself obeying without question. As he arrived at her side she was thigh-deep, wading, dress hitched high, skin already flushed with the chill. Putting his faith in the strength of his Calvin Klein's, he threw off his jeans, and splashed in after her. Bumping hips, and he had the advantage given she was clutching her dress with both hands. One step, he'd grasped a handful of hair, yanked back her head.

'What the…' Her mumbled protest melted away as he crashed his mouth over hers. He caught the lingering taste of cookie dough sweet on her lips, then her tongue met his. No holding back, she was already out there, whipping his breath away, turning his pulse onto fast forward. Achingly sweet, yet hungry, demanding, thrusting her breasts against him, grinding against the thick heat of his erection, hands still on her hem. Dizzying, as the waves sucked and swirled around their legs, then the fleeting feeling of coming home, was overtaken by the mindless desire to bury his whole self in her.

'Come on you.' He staggered backwards, dragging himself out of the kiss. Bent to put a hand under her knees, another under her arm, then one swoop, and he'd lifted her high, and was striding out of the water.

'Grab my jeans before the tide takes them.' He paused to dip her shoulder, and she whisked them up. Then he marched back up the beach, half threw her down on the rug, and landed beside her, propping himself on one elbow.

'Jackson.' She lay, hair splashed across the wool, eyes smudgy and imploring, lips parted expectantly. The wet clingy fabric of her dress ruched high, the buttons pulling as her legs splayed. She jumped as his hand landed on her thigh, shuddered as he edged it upwards, unbuttoning as he went, his own shudder echoing back, as his hand slid. The soft skin of her inside leg was salty-wet against his fingertips, as he wound all the way to her pubes. He hesitated a second to take in the colour of her there. Still heart-stoppingly blonde. Then he went to work, scouring the horizon of the cliffs, as he sorted the rest of the buttons. Great. Looked like they were alone, but he left her belt done up as a precaution. Her dress gaped, to expose full breasts, bursting against white lace.

'Nice bra.' His voice grated with need.

'Front opening.' She slipped him a knowing smile. 'Let me.' One twist from her, and her breasts were all his.

How the heck he didn't come on the spot, he wasn't sure, as he took in the most aroused nipples in the history of the world. He took a second to regain control, then scraped a thumb lightly across each, heard her quiet moan as they peaked in response. Dipping his head, he bent, teased with his tongue, sucked, grazed with his teeth as her moans rose, working the other side between his finger and thumb.

'Ahhh, Jackson.' She was writhing beneath him as he swapped sides, raking her fingers, first through his hair, then sliding her hand, under his T-shirt, scraping his spine with her nails. Sending high voltage shocks through his ribcage as she dug into his flesh in response to his rougher bites. Sliding his other hand down, slithering across the soft warmth of her stomach, and feeling her ribs collapse as his fingers slithered downwards, and he honed on her throbbing clit.

'Yes.'

Stroking, he slid one finger, then two inside her, feeling the whole hot wet heat of her clamping on to him. Then he moved downwards, tracing his lips over the soft curves of her stomach, as the heady scent of her engulfed him. Delving with his tongue, hearing her loud moan as he found her clit. If today had been torture, this was the sweetest torture of all – tangling, sucking, licking, sending her softly wild, her feral groans rising and falling, sending him off the scale. Then suddenly, she disintegrated under him, thrashing onto his mouth, tearing at his hair as she screamed, panted, howled, ripping at the skin on his back, then thumping her fist onto the sand.

'Jackson.' She was gulping, choking, 'That was totally....' She paused, gasping for breath, '....amazing. There's a condom in my bag, shall I get it?' It was a plea, not a question.

'A girl who carries condoms, but not knickers is *my* kind of girl.' It slid out without a thought, along with his grin of appreciation. 'Although...' What the hell was he thinking? No woman was *his*, or ever would be. Plus they were on a public beach. 'It might be best to wait, seeing as it's still light – unless you've got a better idea.' He could already imagine the headlines. He might be close to bursting here, but a rain-check was the sensible option.

'I have, as it happens.' She was already sitting up.

He groaned loudly as her hand made sudden, unexpected contact, grasping his erection through the fully-stretched fabric of his pants. One tug, another groan and he sprang free. One nudge, and he landed on his back, his erection towering towards the sky. The next moment her hand was pushing at his T-shirt, and a curtain of hair brushed his hip. What the...? He choked as Cherry's hot mouth slid right over the end of him.

'Holy shit.' Desperate. He clung onto reality, threw out the anchors to stop the vortex that was sucking him in. He couldn't come, not right... She might not even want him to. 'This might... not...take...' The words ground to a halt in his throat, tumbled away by a full scale roar as an avalanche of pure pleasure thundered into him, and the volley of his ejaculation surged. He thrust with a rocket force, straight down her throat, then the after-tow picked him up, and carried him a million miles to who the hell knew where.

'I can't believe you carried me out of the sea' He had no idea how long they'd been lying there, when her head, heavy on his flank, finally shifted slightly.

As the clouds pulled into focus, scudding across a fading sky, she rubbed her nose, absently, already moving on. 'I'm quite heavy.'

'Sorry?'

'You must be quite strong, to lift me I mean.'

'Are you trying to make me dig a hole for myself? Well, the considered version is – I work out, you were light as a feather. Okay?' He gave a chuckle, brushed her hair off her cheek, let his voice drop. 'I value my life too much to say I do weight training.'

'You…'

'What?' He rolled out of the range of her slap, dragged his boxers back into place, sprung to his feet.

A minute later she was chasing him down the beach.

# Chapter 29

'Do you want cocoa?'

Back home again, and Jackson followed her into the kitchen, a breath behind her, his growl reverberating against her neck. Bryony hesitated. Two hours sitting next to him in the car, watching those oh-so-capable hands sliding over the steering wheel, biting her lip every time she thought about how he'd exploded into her throat just before. After the way he'd turned her inside out on the beach, her ache for him should be satisfied not amped off the scale.

One lazy finger arrived on the nape of her neck. Ran slowly, yet deliberately down the length of her spine, sending shivers sparking through her thorax. She leaned back into him as her knees faltered.

'Cocoa?' She snatched another close-up of his delicious man-scent, and caught the brunt of his erection on her butt. 'Later maybe.' Enough to make a girl disintegrate.

'Good answer.' He twisted her around to face him.

She kicked off her shoes, dragged in a deep breath and angled her head expectantly. Already hooked on looking up at him then. He came down to meet her, feathered her lower lip with his tongue. Then he cradled her scalp with one open hand, wound the other arm around her and clamped her against the rippling heat of his body. And as if that wasn't enough to take her breath away, he came in and kissed her like she'd never been kissed. Deep, velvety, powerful, dizzying. Going on forever. When she finally opened her eyes and pulled away, she felt like she'd been to heaven and back at least.

A sudden pang of guilt sprang into her chest. Now it came to it, she didn't want to push Jackson where he didn't want to go. 'Are you sure you want to do this?'

She watched the corners of his eyes crinkle as a wave of amusement passed across his face.

'You don't think I'm grown up enough to make my own decisions?'

'You seemed reluctant. All that one night stuff?'

The humour left his face, his voice deepened, and he rubbed a thumb across her jaw. 'Trying to save you trouble, I'm not around for long.' He shrugged. 'I'm here, then I'll be gone, that's how it is.'

'Grab the fun, live in the moment, isn't that what you said?' No need to tell him if he'd wanted it any other way that she'd have legged it long ago. 'Sounds good to me.' Smiling up at him – and oh, wasn't up good – a flicker of concern in those melting brown eyes of his told her Jackson Gale was running more scared than he was letting on.

Best to set him straight now rather than later.

'Are you thinking I'm going to get all clingy?' She registered his hesitation, scoured his face for clues.

'Clingy?' His voice broke.

She'd got it in one. 'You just assume I'm going to want more don't you?' She pounced, then eased off. 'Don't worry, my body's coming to this party but my emotions are elsewhere.' Not quite the truth, but a foolproof way to say she was not up for involvement.

'And where would that be?' And so like him to jump on it, except then his eyes softened. 'An ex?'

'Kind of…' Thinking of Matt here, and unrequited love central. Being hooked on him had kept her conveniently out of the game, and no need to say it was a game she was too scared to join.

'Still in love with him?'

Another typical, Jackson-has-to-know-everything question, which she wasn't going to deign with an answer.

'It's complicated.' How the heck had they got onto this? She gave a sigh. 'But the good news is, I won't want any more than your hot body, for a couple of nights.'

'So that's a deal then, we're both here for the fun. Speaking of heat…' He flipped her a grin, nestled a finger in the hollow at the base of her throat, then dragged it slowly downwards. 'Your room or mine?'

'Erm…' She swallowed a shiver. Bed with Jackson? That was something else. So scary, but *so* what she ached to do. So different from that night in Scarborough, which seemed so long ago now, when she wanted to avoid bed with Jackson at all costs, and now she couldn't think of anything that sounded better.

'Executive decision. Mine's got the best TV, and the biggest bed, and a whopping spa-bath. Not that we'll be watching TV, or sleeping much.' He broke away, went to the fridge, rammed an ice bucket under the ice dispenser, grabbed a bottle of champagne from the fridge as the ice chips flew, grinning across at her as he clattered the bottle into the ice. Then he took her hand and gently, but firmly pulled her in the direction of his bedroom. 'Come on Cherry, let's go and play with bubbles.'

There were two things Bryony noticed about going to bed with an athlete: 1. Positions. 2. Stamina – and both were incredible. Which was the reason why Jackson woke her at eleven o'clock the next morning, and why she was opening her eyes, raking her gaze over the flexing muscles in his forearms, mentally shaking her head in disbelief at what she'd got up to the night before.

'Scrambled eggs, smoked salmon and bagels okay for you, Cherry?'

'Wow, you cooked this? That coffee smells amazing.' She pushed up to sitting, and blinked at Jackson, who was deliciously morning-crumpled, in a faded T, and low-slung cotton pants. 'I'm ravenous.'

'I thought you might be.' He slid the tray onto the bed, sat down beside it, and began to pour coffee. 'All part of the service.'

'What time is it? What about work?'

'Don't panic, I checked the itinerary.' He gave her a wink. 'You have exactly eight minutes to eat, because it says hot sex at eleven-ten.'

He grinned wickedly and she bit back a smile, took a slurp of coffee, then dug a fork into the eggs.

'And who wrote that?'

'I did, as I'm taking full responsibility for the schedule now. I don't think I'm doing badly this far.'

'So hot sex, then.' She tried not to laugh and failed. 'Will that be all day long?'

'Not quite. There was my bike ride, but I've already done that, and I included meals, a film or two, and an after breakfast shower.'

'Right.' Not in the vast spa-tub in front of the window, but in the wet room where she'd had a birds-eye view of him yesterday. 'Great... Fab... Brilliant...' Not. How the hell was she going to face him in the very place where he'd been when she'd watched him pleasuring himself? Her stomach crunched up with guilt, not only for having intruded on him, but for the way she'd come so easily as she'd watched him.

'Everything okay?' His brows furrowed, as he screwed up his face in a quizzical stare.

'Mmmm.' What was it with Jackson? Sometimes she had the feeling he was able to read her mind. 'Couldn't be better.'

A less perceptive man would be so much easier.


'This has to be one of the world's best showers.' Jackson grinned at her through a mist of steam, as he adjusted the controls.

'It's quite a boyish place, isn't it? Brown tiles, and power jets.' She let her towel fall to the floor, as she stepped past the glass screen into the horizontal arcs of spray. Heard his growl of approval as the pummelling water stung her skin to goose bumps and rapped

179

her nipples to instant attention.

'Come here.' His voice was low and hungry. Swiping away the rivulets that ran down his face, he found her mouth with his and swept her into a long, hot kiss that sent her head spinning.

As she resurfaced, breathless, heart banging, her eyes slid upwards to the high level window she'd been looking through yesterday. Chin against his chest, she rubbed her eye with a fist, scraped away the water to see more clearly. She could make out the balcony rail high above.

'What are you looking at?' His nail dug into her neck, scraped across her shoulder.

'Nothing special.'

'That's the balcony you were on yesterday.' Matter of fact. Straight up. Simultaneously nailing her, with his stare, and his erection, which slid against her stomach.

Her banging heart went into over-drive. 'You saw me?'

Those creases in his cheeks were a killer when he smiled.

'I might have done.' His fingers walked down her backbone as his questions tumbled lazily. 'Why? Did you see me?'

She gulped, drew in a long breath. How the heck was she going to answer that?

He pounced. 'You did see me, didn't you?' His face split and his low laugh exploded into her ear. 'What a turn-on. You know what we do to voyeurs?' His hand slipped between her legs, and she let out a yelp of surprise as he bent, caught a nipple between his teeth, and began to torture her with his tongue.

'What?' Her reply descended into a moan as he began to rub her clit. Talk about technique. She was throbbing onto him, her knees buckling within seconds. 'Jackson… Jackson… Oh God, Jackson…'

'Voyeurs have to pay.'

One thumb, one lazy graze of her other nipple, pushed her straight over the cliff-edge, and launched her into orgasmic free-fall. As her insides exploded, she threw back her head, felt his arms slide around her waist, grasping her as her legs gave way. She fought to get her breath back as she came slowly back to earth.

'Oh crap, Jackson, you make me do it every time.'

'That's the idea, Cherry.' She could feel his low laugh, reverberating through his ribs against her cheek. 'So what about yesterday? Did watching me come make you come too?'

How the heck did he know? She clung onto him tightly, dug her fingers into his arms. No way would she admit that.

'Cherry? Cherry?' His voice was teasing now, verging on delight. 'Blow me down, you did.'

She clamped her eyes shut. Felt him turn her, place her back firmly against the tiles, hook up her left knee with his arm. When she opened her eyes he was still looking at her, his eyes laughing yet dark, smudged with desire. Ten seconds he'd grabbed a packet from the shower hanger, and he was sheathed and huge. He bent his knees, nudged against her. Wet, open and oh-so-ready for him, she gasped as he slid into her.

'Steady. You're so tight, I'll go gently.' Three thrusts. 'There we go, you are so damned hot.' His voice grazed her cheek, but the words washed away as he dug in and out of her, with slow, deliberate movements that sent thrusts of pure pleasure jolting through her, sending her closer to heaven with each excruciatingly amazing pulse. And then he began to move faster, building, pounding, driving. Nothing she could do, she was there.

'Jackson…' She heard her own voice in the distance, howling as the pleasure erupted through her, choked as she struggled to drag in her breath. Through blurry lashes she saw him throw back his head, as she contracted onto him in a series of convulsions. He gave a final push, then the force of his release blasted into her, and his guttural groan echoed off the tiles.

An hour, and a whole heap of mind-blowing orgasms later, Jackson finally turned off the water. He'd had Cherry down as hot, now he'd revised that to super-heated. The way she turned him on she needed to come with a health warning. Something about her honesty and enthusiasm was so different from anything he'd encountered before. Put together with her own explosive sexuality, a need that seemed to border on desperate, and that oh-so-curvy body, she pushed him over the edge and beyond every time.

'Towel, Jackson?' She came towards him.

'Thanks.' Just for a moment the shine in her eyes made his stomach falter. Then, she draped the towel across his back and rested a hand on his shoulder. He shivered as she gently ran her finger, hardly touching, over his scars.

'Some of these look so sore, you're like a human patchwork. Did we stay in the shower too long?'

'I'm pretty much one enormous scar. I've got so many pins and plates I lost count, and that's before you get to the gravel-rash.' He gave a laugh. 'I'm a surgeon's nightmare – my scars stay red for ages.'

'So the red ones are recent? But there are so many!'

'Yep, they're all from the last crash.'

'It must have been bad.'

Not mentioning the scars on the inside. That those were the worst ones. The ones that turned his insides sour every time he thought about the damned accident.

He gave a shrug. 'Crashes happen, they're part of the sport. Mostly you bounce, this time I was unlucky. It cost me the London Games. I've won medals before, but these ones would have been special. A home Games comes once in a lifetime.' One soft woman, her warm breath on his chest, her touch feather-light, making it all seem far away. 'Worst of all, it was my brother, Connor, who took me out. The bad man in me thinks he did it deliberately. He's always been snapping at my heels, now he's the one winning.'

'Poor boy.' She began to spread a line of light kisses along each scar. 'So that's why you wouldn't talk about it.' She carried on, descended to his hip, then slid along his thigh to his knee. 'It's eating you up, isn't it?'

182

'You might be right there, Cherry.' And why the heck had he cracked and told her?

'I read that you and Connor didn't speak. Do you really think it was deliberate?'

'In my sane moments I know it wasn't.' Alone and angry and hurting in the night was something else entirely.

'Didn't you used to be close?' She was pushing him, and just for once he didn't even care.

'When my mother left, we were thrown together.' No way was he opening that can of worms. Three brothers, and the battering hurricane that was his dad. All the sweet, feathery kisses in the world couldn't heal that hurt. 'But that's another story.'

'Maybe you need to talk to Connor.' She was squatting in front of him now, face upturned, all eager and optimistic and hopeful. Way too good for a bad guy like him. 'Clearing the air would make you feel better.'

'We'll see, Cherry Bomb. I'll think about it.'

'I think it would make you feel better.' She stretched to pick up the discarded condoms which were lying at the shower edge. 'I may as well take these.' She sauntered out across the bedroom, dropped them into a tissue, and tossed them in the bin.

'Hang on, I didn't check them.'

'Check as in?' She sent him a blank stare.

'For rips – always a good idea.'

'You do that? Sorry I didn't know…'

And why would she? Something about the hunger in her told him she hadn't seen a condom in years. And something else in him told him he liked that. A lot. Not that he had any right at all to feel that way. But hang on. He pulled himself up short. When she was bigging herself up as the ideal short-term bet, hadn't she mentioned an ex? Inexplicably, that thought sent an unscheduled stab of jealousy through his chest. She'd neatly dodged his probing at the time, which was why he was in the dark now. But far from being hang-out-the-flags good news it should have been, the thought that she might still be emotionally attached to someone else, made his blood run cold. He was in the process of awarding himself the hypocrite of the century award when an image floated by, of another morning, another shower. Another condom he'd walked out on, just north of Scarborough, leaving Cherry Bomb to do the checking. Dammit. He gave a sigh, and pushed it out of his mind. Too late to do anything about that one now. As he looked up his gaze landed on Cherry, across the bedroom, climbing into what had to be the sexiest knickers on the planet.

He knotted the towel around his waist. No point getting dressed. From the way things were rising, he wouldn't be needing clothes again for quite some time.

# Chapter 30

Early on Sunday morning, Bryony pushed her way into the kitchen, hit the fridge, sloshed juice into a glass, and hurriedly filled up the coffee maker, ready for when Jackson came back from his ride.

She'd fallen into a deep after-sex slumber when he'd slipped away round five o'clock. In fact, after-sex sleep was the only kind she'd had the last few days, which was possibly why she was so bleary now; but she'd forced herself out of bed, knowing there was a long day ahead, with a two hour drive across to Padstowe, where they were going to sort out a ride feature on the famous Camel Trail. Eighteen miles of off-road track, perfect for cyclists. And more fool her for agreeing to do it whilst riding on a tandem.

When the alarm had roused her earlier, despite the fact she rarely dreamed, she'd been in the middle of a particularly vivid dream she was still shaking her head about. Even as she reached for her laptop now, thinking to check her mail before Jackson came back, the images had her shivering. She'd dreamed she was on a tropical beach, dressed as a mermaid, being a bridesmaid for Matt and Tia, who were dressed as Captain Hook and Snow White. She kept telling people she was the wrong person for the job, but no one would listen. Then the ceremony started and Tia was there looking all elfin and petite and beautiful, just like she had on the engagement pictures on Facebook. But when the happy couple turned round to face her, it wasn't Matt at all – it was Jackson with Tia, and Bryony had woken up shouting. Although, maybe she'd just been shouting at the alarm.

No wonder her head was thumping. That would teach her to watch Disney movies in bed. She took a swig of juice, opened her email, and began flipping through her in box. She looked at some cute pictures of the kids that Shea had sent. Brando was still keeping in touch daily, but at least he was using more subtle means. She flipped through a few more, and did a double-take when she came to an email from Matt's sister, her best friend Claire. How weird was that? Okay, not so weird, given they'd been emailing regularly since she'd visited Claire recently, but still. She clicked it open.

**Bry, I know you said you were off to work along the south coast. Just found out Matt is down in Cornwall for the weekend. It's a big place, but I thought I'd flag it up, just in case. Hugs, Claire xx**

Bryony let out a sigh, and mused on how unnerving it was when dreams pre-empted real life. Typically thoughtful of Claire, trying to save her the shock of stumbling unprepared, across the unrequited love of her life, and his lovely new wife, given she was still reeling at the shock of Matt getting together with anyone at all. Bryony had no idea which was worse – was it tougher that Matt and Tia had met, fallen in love, got engaged, and married, all within a mere three months, or would a long drawn out courtship and engagement have been harder to bear, more difficult for her to watch? As it was, Bryony knew it had hurt a lot. At the time she'd felt as if the bottom had fallen out of her world, which was slightly unjustified as Matt hadn't been a substantial part of it anyway. He'd never reached any more than vague hope status really. And she had to admit that the past few days here had blasted a lot of things off her radar, not just the Matt and Tia issue. She still didn't want to run slap bang into them though. At least now she could keep a look out, and take avoiding action if necessary – not that it was likely to happen. As Claire said, Cornwall was vast, and even if Matt was the outdoor sporty type, hell would freeze over before a girl like Tia would even be seen dead on a bike on the Camel Trail, which was where Bryony was destined to spend her whole day.

Great to get the heads up from Claire, but Bryony really had no spare time to worry about this – she was far too busy worrying about how she was going to get on, back on a hire tandem with Jackson.

Bryony thought she knew what today's plans were, but it turned out that Jackson had added a few extra details. When they arrived at Bodmin there was already a tandem waiting, courtesy of the local Jackson Gale Cycling shop.

'One of my stores is nearby, we might as well have a nice bike to ride. Those hire bikes are pretty heavy.' Jackson was full of excuses for his takeover of arrangements. 'It's got nice flat pedals so you can ride in your Converse, and it's even got panniers, so you can stash your iPad and your lippy.' He sent her a grin as he wheeled the tandem across the car park. 'It's a good bike, but I promise, we'll take it slowly, and the trail is pretty level; it's mostly along disused railway line.'

'It was supposed to be level last time.' Bryony gave a groan, as she stowed her things in the side bags and climbed on. 'Okay, I've got enough pictures of the start here, so I guess we're good to go.'

'We're going from Bodmin to Padstowe, rather than the way you'd planned because that way we'll get the surprise view of the sea, and we get to ride across the old railway bridge that crosses Petherick Creek, then along the estuary towards the town at the end. It's all very picturesque, lots of great shots. It's about ten miles; we can stop for lunch half-way in Wadebridge.'

'Great.' She'd had no idea Jackson was going to change the day like this. 'What about the ride back?' He seemed to know what he was talking about, but this was diverting a long way from what they'd discussed yesterday, which…well it hardly mattered what she thought any more.

He fiddled with his saddle, then got on. 'I decided by the time we've stopped to take pictures and make notes, ten miles might take all day, so I've arranged for us to be picked up in Padstowe.' He cocked a glance over his shoulder at her. 'All ready? One two three go…'

No time to argue, the next thing she knew they were away, and the breeze was brushing gently past her face as they swerved to avoid a bike pulling a trailer full of squealing children.

She pushed an escaping strand of hair behind her helmet strap. 'It's quite busy isn't it?'

'Lots of families use the trail.' He steered past a zig-zagging youngster. 'It's important that we include rides for everyone on the *Sporting Chances* features. In fact, when we shoot this we should definitely ride with one of those kiddy trailers on the back to emphasise the family angle.' He tossed a grin at her over his shoulder. 'Any of your settled mates got some kids we could borrow?'

'What? I draw the line at rent-a-child.' The thought of her and Jackson pretending to be a family had her stomach disappearing. 'But I take your point. Many more ideas like that, you'll be taking over my job.'

'Well now you mention it, it might be good to schedule so we film here mid-week when it's quieter. Plus, the sky and the sea turn azure-blue when it's sunny, so we need to organise that we film on a good day too.' One more full-blown smile delivered from him in the nick of time stopped her hitting him on the backside for being a know-all. 'We used to come here all the time for holidays as kids. That's why I'm such a mine of information.'

'Really?'

'My mother used to come here as a child.' But that was all he'd volunteer. Despite her concerted efforts, he wouldn't be drawn further on anything to do with his mother.

As the day progressed it seemed Jackson was more than living up to her earlier joke. He was so familiar with the trail, he warned her in advance of every potential shot, and provided a running commentary of information for her to note down whenever they stopped. So much so, that they made brilliant progress. He'd even booked a table for lunch at an old pub in Wadebridge. As Jackson pulled over without any prompt from her later that afternoon, at yet another perfect vantage point Bryony couldn't help protesting mildly.

'I feel pretty superfluous today.'

'Not at all, you've done way more than me other days; this is just me doing my share when we're somewhere I know. I reckon overall we're a pretty good team...unlike these people coming.' He raised an eyebrow and nodded towards an approaching tandem. Even from fifty yards away the squawks of the couple on board, who appeared to be having a full-blown argument, carried on the wind.

'Oh dear.' Bryony wrinkled her nose. 'How awful to be yelling at each other like that when you're supposed to be enjoying your-selves. At least I only howled.' As the tandem came closer she clocked something strangely familiar about the forehead of the guy on the front, who was bowing over the handle bars. As the tandem wobbled past them they were blasted with a mix of strong perfume, bright flowery dress and loud complaint. Beneath the cycle helmet of the woman on the back Bryony clocked a very elfin, yet very unhappy face. Surely not... 'Tia...?' What the heck? It was too... 'Matt...?'

But a gust whipped her words away, and before she had time to shout again, they'd passed and were gone.

'Somebody isn't happy.' Jackson shook his head and gave a laugh, his T-shirt flapping against his body. 'Did you say something?'

For a moment she was concentrating on the glimpse of Jackson's tanned toned torso. She pulled herself together, sounding doubtful, not quite believing what she'd seen going by. 'Oh no, I think I might know those people who were shouting ...'

She'd so wanted Matt for herself, loved him conveniently from afar for so long, been so shocked when he was getting married, yet she really didn't want him to end up unhappy.

'Probably best to leave them to their argument.' Jackson gave a laugh. 'Some people just aren't made to ride tandems together, are they?'

'Getting on together on a tandem isn't always easy though, is it, Jackson? If anyone knows that, we do.'

Jackson didn't seem to hear that comment. He simply looked at his watch. 'We're running behind schedule. Come on Cherry. Get pedalling. I'll race you into Padstowe.'

# Chapter 31

As promised, the van emblazoned with Jackson Gale Cycling shop signage was waiting for them in the car park at the trail end.

'I thought you'd organised a lift, not a publicity event,' Bryony teased as they approached it. 'Only joking. My bum's aching so much I'd gladly hitch a ride on a rubbish cart if necessary.'

Jackson noticed the dark circles under her eyes, and hoped the ride hadn't been too much for her. He did a double-take as the driver of the van jumped out as they approached and he recognised his brother Nic.

'Nic, great to see you. What are you doing here?' Jackson wasn't sure he'd have *chosen* to expose Bryony to *any* of his family, although, of all of them, Nic was the best.

'I was down for a meeting tomorrow and the guys at the store mentioned you needed a lift, so I grabbed the van. I thought I'd do the honours.'

'Cherry, this is my brother, Nic. He's the business brain of the family.' He cringed at lumping good old Nic in with that collective noun, given the disaster area that the rest of his family was. 'Unfortunately, the athletic genes passed Nic by... Nic, meet Bryony. Bryony is in charge of everything to do with *Sporting Chances*, and I'm included in that remit too.'

Nic cocked one eyebrow in disbelief at that last statement. 'Hi

Bryony, great to meet you. Jackson's a dark horse. If he'd only said, we could have met up for lunch.' He gave an easy laugh, patted his belly as if to emphasise his lack of fitness and extended his hand towards Bryony. 'Connor and Jackson are the sporty guys, who look like our dad, and I'm the non-athlete, who looks like our mum.'

The mention of their mother made Jackson start. He'd shut her so completely out of his life after she'd left; it was a shock to hear her spoken about so nonchalantly. He assumed Nic, being more easygoing and more forgiving, must be in touch if he was mentioning her so casually. As far as Jackson was concerned, his mother had chosen to abandon the family and she deserved to be cut off.

'Throw the tandem in the back, jump in and we'll get going.' Nic might be laid back, but he could get things moving when he wanted. Five minutes later they were bouncing across the car park.

'This so-called dark horse had no idea you were coming down. If only you'd said......' Jackson gave a guffaw, to cover that he probably wouldn't have arranged anything, anyway. Right now he wanted to keep Cherry all to himself. He stretched an arm out along the back of the bench seat, dropped it onto her shoulder and pulled her towards him a little. They didn't have that long, and the days were flying by.

'Well, the least you can do is stop by the store now you're here. I'll run you down there now on the way back to your car; it's only ten minutes away.' Nic was onto him, and what's more, he was in the driving seat, so he was in charge for now. 'It's our flagship, and you haven't seen it since we opened the upper floors, have you? Apart from in the video clips I sent you, that is.'

'True...' Jackson was hoping Nic wouldn't twig that he hadn't actually watched the clips. He liked to know the shops were there, doing well, but he was more than happy to leave the details to Nic. But if an unscheduled shop-visit was what was needed to keep Nic happy, he would go along with that.

Nic turned to Bryony with a hopeless shrug. 'Ten fabulous

shops he's got now, and I don't think I've managed to get him into more than a couple. As for the bikes and clothing lines, turnover's fantastic, but I can't get him interested in the hands-on stuff.'

Jackson gave a shame-faced grimace. 'That's where you come in, Nic. It's your forté, and admit it, you'd hate it if I did start to interfere. And let's face it, so long as what we sell is high quality and good value, the only cycling clothes and bikes I'm interested in are the ones I'm wearing and riding. I turn up for your photo shoots, but that's all I'm good for. Like all the best teams, we each play to our strengths; everyone's happy and hopefully we all do well out of it. I know this side of the business was my idea, or rather Dan's, but it's your baby. You take the credit for it.'

Nic rolled his eyes at Bryony. 'He's got a multi-national company, and he's dismissing it as a baby.'

Jackson gave a sigh. 'I've always wanted to treat every shop as individual and do well by our employees, but apart from that, I don't have the knowledge *or* the inclination to handle this side of the business.'

'There's always room for you though, I was hoping you might…' Nic tailed off.

'Might what?' Jackson was onto him, jumping straight down his throat. If this was Nic's way of telling Jackson there was room for him in the business because Nic didn't think Jackson was going to cut it when he returned to racing, well, Jackson could do without it. 'I'd appreciate your support for what I'm doing, rather than your assumption that I'm going to fail.' He tried to keep the annoyance out of his voice for Cherry's sake. No way should she be witnessing this.

'I'm not assuming anything, Jackson, and I know it's a tricky area.' Nic blew out his cheeks as he crashed through the gears. 'But even if it's a safety net you don't use, I wanted you to know it's there, and that's all I'll say about it.' He turned to Bryony again with an eye-roll. 'Sorry we've veered onto family stuff, but I'm sure Bryony knows how hard you are to pin down. The thing is

193

you threw yourself into racing when we were young. No one could come out of a childhood like ours unscathed, and I think racing was a way for you to blot out the past. Dad, with his rages, the hammering we took… You probably never dealt with your issues. If you get help with that, you might find it easier to move on to something else. Have you considered therapy?'

'Spoken like a man who's married to a psychologist.' Jackson gave a hollow laugh and wished Cherry wasn't hearing this. 'Therapy's for wusses, Nic.'

Nic tapped the steering wheel impatiently. 'Two more questions for you, Jackson, then I promise we can get back to discussing the weather. Okay?'

'If you must.' Jackson agreed grudgingly.

'So, what are the docs saying? And any news about when you're going back to race training with the team?'

'Very little, and very little.' Jackson gritted his teeth defiantly. 'So if you're finished, perhaps we can visit this flagship store of ours?' He hoped Nic would back off now.

'And finally.' Nic grinned across at Bryony as he swung into a wide and perfectly gravelled car park behind a large quay-front warehouse. 'You have no idea how long I've waited to hear him say those words.'

Bryony grinned back at Nic and shot a mischievous glance at Jackson. 'Oh, knowing how stubborn Jackson is, I think I *can* imagine.'

'Stainless steel, grey paint, lots of glass, acres of space and a view through four floors up to the sky.' Jackson stood in the centre of the store at the end of their tour, nodding his approval. 'Fabulous stock, amazing presentation, friendly staff, stacks of customers. As always, you think of everything and you've done amazing things, Nic.' Jackson gave him a hearty thump on the back.

Bryony nodded in agreement. 'It's wonderful, Nic.'

'It's a shame you can't stay on for dinner, but I know you've got lots on.' Nic rubbed his hands. 'So, come on, one last thing – let's get Bryony kitted out before you go. Some cycling shorts will save you a lot of pain next time you go out, and you might as well take a couple of touring bikes too. Ten miles on the trail, Bryony, I'm sensing you're going to take to this.'

'He's right, Cherry – everyone should have a bike. We could try some leisure rides together.'

He watched her chew her finger hesitantly.

'I don't know…'

'Come on. I won't take no for an answer.' Nic was nothing if not persuasive. He tipped her a wink. 'I thought women never said no to shopping.'

And as Cherry gave in to charm from a different Gale, Jackson was suddenly very pleased that Nic had a settled wife and family at home.


The Sunday evening traffic was quite heavy as they made their way back home again. Bryony kicked off her Converse, tucked her feet up underneath her and gave a yawn.

'Your bike shop was fabulous.' She was musing on a long and rather strange day. Almost bumping into Matt and Tia, then meeting Nic. 'You didn't mention you had a chain of bike shops before?'

Jackson kept his eyes on the road ahead. 'Maybe I didn't tell you because you didn't ask.'

She wasn't sure he'd been comfortable with her hearing everything Nic had said. Jackson had mentioned his screwed up home life before, but she felt it was more to empathise with her than because he wanted to share the information.

'If ever you want to talk about…' She hesitated. She wanted him to know she was here if he needed help, without sounding pushy. '…you know, if you want to use me as a sounding board, I'm always happy to listen.'

As he drummed his fingers on the steering wheel, she saw his jaw clench.

After a few moments thought, he replied. 'You know, Cherry, the great thing about us is that we're in the moment.' He ran his fingers through his hair. 'We don't need to think about the past, and as we're short term, we definitely won't be thinking about the future. Let's keep it like that, shall we? Go for broke, and make the most of the next few days.'

Bryony opened her mouth to answer, then closed it again. Damn it if she felt disappointed by that. He was right of course, and there really was very little to say to that.

'Fine. Good thinking.' She bundled her jumper on her shoulder, rested her head against it and closed her eyes.

# Chapter 32

'Including a lighthouse was such a brainwave, Jackson. We'll get some great shots of this when we come to film.'

Their last afternoon of work before heading back to London, they wound their way up the stone spiral staircase and emerged into the glare of the lantern room.

Jackson blinked in the brightness. 'It doesn't have much to do with cycling.'

'Who even cares about that?'

He nudged Cherry's hip, and grinned down at her. 'Whatever happened to Ms Work-her-socks-off?' A rhetorical question. They both knew the non-stop sex had taken Cherry's mind clean off the job in hand. His too.

'Good thing we got stacks done the first few days, and we've managed to fit in everything we needed to, working around the clock.' She shot him a wink. 'Especially since we stopped arguing so much.'

Good point; well made.

'We've made a pretty good team these last few days.' He sucked back a smile and braced himself for the protest. 'Once you let me take charge, we never looked back.'

'I learned a lot by stepping away. Thanks for that.'

Who'd have thought, instead of the squawk he anticipated, that she would be quietly reflective?

'Although, you are kidding yourself. Once things get physical, I'd say it's always the woman who's in charge, wouldn't you?' She slid him a smile with a whole lot of smoulder, which sent his blood rushing to one place, proving her point entirely.

'Giving me a come-and-get-it look in a public viewing area is below the belt.' He grappled to find a fast change of subject. 'It's a great view from here on a clear day like today, isn't it?'

'Neatly handled, Jackson.' She sliced him a grin to acknowledge that she'd just beaten him hollow. 'How far away do you think the horizon is, then?'

'There's a formula, depending on how high up you are. If you're on the ground, it's about three miles away, more if you're higher.'

'I love trying to decide the exact point where the sky meets the sea.' She pursed her lips and scoured the distance enthusiastically.

He squirmed. The shiny eye thing had happened again, and it felt a lot like an antelope got loose in his gut.

'So, what's on your horizon, Cherry Bomb? Are you going to go and find yourself that family guy?' It slipped out easy as, but once he'd said the words the thought of her bumping shoulders, not to mention other parts, with another guy left him suddenly cold. And he really hadn't meant to get onto this.

She bunched up her mouth, uncertainly. 'It's not that easy. The nice guys usually only come up to my knees and I'm not that sold on the hobbit look, and even tall guys seem to find me intimidating.'

'And no idea why that is.' He gave an ironic laugh and cursed how jubilant that answer made him feel. 'Although your impersonation of a human steamroller might have something to do with that.'

She narrowed her eyes at him. If she thought about hitting him, she must've thought better of it. 'So, how about you? What's on your horizon?'

He gave a grimace. 'A couple of weeks and I'll be back to racing.

I'll take that as far as I can.'

She was straight onto him. 'And you think your injuries will hold up?'

Damn that the only woman in the world who ever made his guts flip could nail him down so hard.

'They should.' He gave a dismissive shrug, sounding a lot more confident than he should, given the way his knee had pulled every day this week. Her deep-blue gaze bored into him like a truth drug, making him change his mind. 'Who knows, might be a better answer?'

'So, how are you going to cope if you can't race?' More of the hard blue treatment coming out here. She'd obviously picked up on what Nic had said too.

'To be honest I don't have a goddam clue what I'll do. I've always been a winner and if that goes I'm left with nothing.'

'Right.' She hesitated. Rubbed her nose as she thought. 'You'll always have the past to look back on; no one can take away what you've won already.'

'Up to the accident all I've ever known is winning races. If that's permanently taken away, what the hell's left?' He thought he could keep the bitterness out of his voice, but it leeched in, big-time.

'Plenty, I'd say.' Her hands were shoved deep in her jean pockets. Her feet were together, and she rolled backwards and forwards in her sneakers. 'You could begin by playing around with your freedom?'

'I'd have to start at the bottom and be someone else; for the first time in my life I'd be vulnerable not powerful.' He dragged in a breath. 'Too much time to think. It scares the shit out of me.' He listened to the sound of the truth hitting the deck. Now he'd said it, there was some kind of relief.

She rounded on him. 'But you're brave, you've been brave every day of your life on your bike.'

'That was easy.'

She gave a snort. 'The times when we're vulnerable can be

199

when we learn most.'

'Well let's hope I don't need to find out. I'm not sure I'm ready for my career to end yet. Who the hell wanted to talk about horizons anyway? Let's get back to the job in hand.' Planning TV shoots was so much easier than real life. 'Shall I make notes on the voiceover for this, or have you got it covered?'

She made a grab for her bag. 'Nope, I'm fine.'

He blew out a silent breath of relief. Princess Cherry was as much a Queen when it came to documenting information as she was with getting him to spill his innermost fears. He was confident she'd never let him get his hands on her iPad. It was maybe a bit of a cheap trick to get her off his back, but right now the future was definitely not what he wanted to think about.

# Chapter 33

'Thanks for....'

Back at her flat after dropping her off, standing in her echoing white living room with the acres of shiny floor boards, Jackson broke off, suddenly lost for words. This place spoke volumes about Cherry and her control issues. And sunny Devon seemed a long way away.

Bryony jutted her chin, gave her hair a swish. 'Thanks for what? The sex-fest, the home truths, or the fun? Most of all I'm pleased you finally got to eat ice cream.'

So much for his fears about her becoming a limpet. Now they were back she was anything but. In-your-face brittle, but definitely not grabbing onto him. For one disturbing second, he was the one who felt like doing the holding. The thought of driving all the way north tomorrow for Team Doctor's appointment without her in the passenger seat was a dismal one. She might be an argumentative pain in the ass, who was stubborn as a mule and twice the trouble, but her guts and spark more than made up for the shortcomings.

'Thanks for all of it. I had a great time.' Understatement of the decade there from him.

'You turned out to be very different from my first impressions.' She was leaning against the kitchen bar, curves perfectly defined in that soft dress, tapping one towering heel on the floor. Not a cupcake in sight.

He tried to prise his gaze away, and failed. Not fishing for compliments, but he had to ask. 'Different in a good or a bad way?'

'Let's just say, if I had a friend in need of a great guy, I'd give you a recommendation.'

'Right.' He felt his eyebrows shoot upwards. Not quite what he was expecting in the way of a compliment. His stomach had gone flat with disappointment because it hadn't been something more personal to her.

'There couldn't be higher praise, Jackson.'

'Cool. I appreciate it.' Damn that she'd noted his dismay enough to need to jump in with reassurance.

'Right then. I'll let you get back to that bedroom you're going to make-over.' What the hell? Mentioning bedrooms, like he was angling for an invitation to stay. Rookie mistake. 'You'll be needing to polish that princess crown of yours. Iron some knickers in time for work tomorrow.' Sounded like a good parting line, as he screwed himself up to leave.

The trouble was, the princess was back in her castle and she was already pulling up the drawbridge, pushing him onto the wrong side. Now that he had to walk away, he was rooted to the spot. Damn that the heat was still there, welding him to her. One step forwards brought him close enough to sense her quivering. Maybe she was less decided than she was pretending. He took hold of her arm, rubbed his thumb across the tender skin on the inside of her wrist and registered her intake of breath. To hell with driving north tonight. It could wait until the morning.

'We could make one last night of it?' He watched her bite her lip, listened to his own heart, hammering against his chest wall. When had he ever laid himself on the line like this? And when had he been so sure of how a woman was going to react, what she wanted? 'I'd like that.'

Fixing his eyes on hers, he held his breath and waited.

'Mmmm.' Behind her flickering lashes, her pupils darkened.

'Me too.'

Right answer. He exhaled with relief, ran his thumb across her jaw, then cupped her face in his hands. As he dropped the lightest kiss on her lips, her thigh moved to meet his, and just for a moment he felt like his chest was going to burst. When had winning ever felt this sweet? He took her hand and as she smiled up at him his heart gave the kind of twang he'd never had before. Lust that strong? Who'd have thought?

'C'mon, Cherry. Show me where'

Just this once, given they were at hers, he was ready to back off. Let her lead the way.

# Chapter 34

'Hello stranger. Thank Monday you've turned your phone on again, and come back to the office. Finally.' Cressy gave a dramatic groan and took a swig from a can of energy drink. 'Oh my, what a night. Hot guy, no sleep.'

For once Bryony knew just where she was coming from.

'Nice to see you too. Any more energy drink around?' Bryony caught the lurid blue can that Cressy flipped in her direction. She couldn't remember a morning when she'd arrived at work this disorganised. 'My phone hasn't been turned off, it's just there isn't much signal out in the wilds. Such a pain.' One guilty afterthought added in to cover that staying off the radar had been blissful, not to mention imperative. Much less chance of being found out that way.

'Well, the good news is the stuff you've been sending through is ace.' Cressy posted her a grin. 'You've done an awesome job as usual, superwoman. Everything you sent has got the go-ahead, and Jackson Gale's guy, Dan, has been hassling for film dates, because apparently Jackson won't be around for long. He's flying out to Spain in a couple of weeks for a training camp apparently. Dan wants us to wait a while before we pick up on filming his comeback.'

Bryony breathed a sigh of relief. At least Jackson had been good as his word on that one. He really had been perfect fling material, with no complications. Jackson was like a box of luxury chocolates – naughty, delicious, but once they were gone, they were gone. Having him at hers last night had been a shock. All that hunky maleness draped around the place had tipped her cool upside down and shaken it. Hard. And when he'd headed off at the crack of dawn, he'd left an aching, gaping void that she preferred to blank out.

'I take it you didn't…?' Cressy sent her an airy glance, which morphed to a grimace. 'I knew you'd have spilled the beans the minute you did. Not sure what we're going to do with you – how anyone could keep their hands off a dime like Jackson Gale, I have no idea.'

'Dime?' Too little sleep to work out Cressy's man-slang, but Bryony couldn't believe she was getting away with it this easily.

'Dime as in ten… Ten out of ten, geddit?' She gave a wicked chortle. 'Anyway, that was the good news, the not-so-good stuff had to wait 'til we were face to face.' Cressy banged her knuckles together, narrowed her eyes. 'Brace yourself, turn up your sense of humour and I'm sure it won't seem so bad.'

'What are you talking about, Cressy?' Had energy drink overdose finally turned Cressy's brain to mush?

'You and Jackson – there's a film clip that's gone viral.' Cressy tossed it out onto the table like a grenade, and left it to explode all on its own.

Film clip? As the words ricocheted around Bryony's head, she felt the blood drain from her face as her intestines disintegrated. 'Holy crap.' She gulped wildly. Her going down on Jackson on that empty beach. How would either of them ever live that down?

'Hey, "holy crap" is Jackson's saying.' Cressy's whoop somehow didn't match the gravity of the situation. 'Ten days together, and you're talking like him! Don't worry, the clip's not that big a deal; in fact, if you can find it in your heart to overlook the humiliation, it's awesome publicity for the show.'

So that ruled out the beach scene. As the banging in her chest subsided, Bryony began to breathe again. 'What is it then?'

'It's a phenomenal clip featuring you and JG.' Cressy sent her a rueful grin. 'And it's already had three million views.'

Bryony's voice soared. 'You have to be joking?'

'Nope. You screaming your head off, flying downhill on the tandem. Classic YouTube. The motorbike cameraman was alongside you all the way down, filming. It's hysterical.'

'Phew. That could have been a whole lot worse.' And *how* much worse. Bryony shuddered at the thought, simultaneously realising she shouldn't have let those particular words go. Hopefully, Cressy wouldn't pick up on it. 'But how did it get out? Jackson's the only one to have had access to the film of the race, so anything up there on YouTube has to have come from there.' Bryony's chest tightened. 'I'll kill him when I get my hands on him.'

'To be fair, I think Dan and Jackson were playing it back, and some other guy who was round took a clip of the TV on his phone. Jackson probably didn't even know.'

'Even so, they had responsibilities, and they've failed to measure up to them.' As the relief was replaced by indignation Bryony stiffened.

'Try not to be too offended.' Cressy patted her shoulder. 'You'll laugh when you see it, and it'll send the ratings through the roof. It'll be a great career hike for your presenting.'

'Oh my. I need a sugar boost.' Bryony pushed away a pile of papers, sank onto the desk. Took a swig of drink, and shuddered as the liquid hit her stomach. 'I don't know how you drink this stuff, it makes me feel green.'

'Don't move. Five minutes, and I'll be back with cupcake supplies.'

'Cupcakes?' Brrrrr. She shivered, made an effort to yank her cringe into a grin. 'Great. Perfect. Brilliant.' For the first time in her life it felt like cupcakes weren't going to hit the spot.

'Well, what have we here? Flowers for Ms Marshall. Could this be Mr Gale, grovelling?'

Bryony looked up from her computer screen the next afternoon to see Cressy staggering across the office peering out from behind an explosion of cellophane and ribbon.

'It'll take more than a few roses, after the way he just dismissed it on the phone.'

It had taken her until lunchtime today to finally nail Jackson, by which time she was hopping mad. But the way he'd quietly taken full responsibility, apologised quietly, then left the line, had caught her right off guard.

'There's a card, look at the card.' Cressy balanced the massive display carefully on the desk, then began jumping from foot to foot.

'Wow.' Bryony sat back in her seat, and gritted her teeth. 'They're gorgeous, even though I don't want them to be. I'm still cross though.' And all white to go with her white apartment. Unnerving how Jackson knew her favourite colour flowers.

'Yeah, sure.' Cressy wiggled her eyebrows. 'But you're not half so cross as you were two minutes ago. Right? That's how flowers work as every tuned-in guy knows.' She flipped the envelope in front of Bryony. 'Okay, see what he has to say for himself.'

'Probably one of his assistants who sent them.' If it did happen to be Jackson, and he'd written anything relating to the last two weeks, she was dead in the water. She'd brazen that one out when it happened, and dammit that her heart was pounding in anticipation. She slid her finger along the envelope edge, pulled out the card. 'There, what did I tell you? "Sincerest apologies, Jackson".' She slipped it down on the desk with a sigh. Why the heck did she want it to say any more? Totally ridiculous that she had the urge to pick it up and drink in the smell of it, simply to see if she could get one last blast of Jackson's scent, when he hadn't even touched the damned thing.

'Sea-shells and sand. Ubiquitous.' Cressy propped the card on the desk, had the envelope halfway to the bin. 'Holy crap, as Jackson would say, there's something else in here. Woohooo, lucky we didn't miss this.' Her face lit up jubilantly, as she flapped a flat card through the air. 'Ms Marshall, I think you just hit lucky. He *must* be feeling guilty. He's only inviting you as his plus-one to the Lottery Sports Awards Gala Celebration in Manchester. Haven't we all been dying to get in on that one?'

'I'll be far too busy to go.' Bryony gave a disinterested shrug. The thought of going anywhere as Jackson's plus-one was out of the question, let alone to an event as prestigious as this one. In fact, given how jittery she'd been feeling being home alone, the less she saw of him the better. She'd spent the whole of yesterday evening curled up on her bed, drinking cocoa, feeling like her apartment was way too large for one person. Her metaphorical box of chocolates was empty, and she needed to get used to life without. As an independent woman who didn't ever intend relying on a guy, she was completely disgusted with herself. Served her right for going there in the first place.

'Bryony Marshall, cut the crap. If I have to personally drag you to this function by your hair, I shall.' Cressy was wagging a finger at her now.

Bryony stood, drew herself up to her full height and glowered down at the diminutive Cressy. 'Good luck with that one.' Her insides twisted with guilt. No way should Cressy be getting it in the neck, just because she herself was all screwed up about missing a guy. 'I've spent the last couple of weeks placating Jackson Gale. I refuse point blank to do it any more.'

'We'll see about that.' Cressy gave a snort. 'You may be taller than me Bryony but remember, the strongest poison comes in little bottles. We'll talk about this later.'

'Fine.' Bryony tossed her head just to show she meant it, but it wasn't fine. Nothing at all was fine. It used to be fine, but now she'd messed up, big time, and from the stony feeling in her stomach, she doubted if anything would ever be okay again.

'Cherry!'

Two evening's later, Bryony, snoozing on her bed, made a grab

208

for her vibrating mobile, and almost dropped it again when she heard Jackson's dark-chocolate voice.

'Jackson.' She pushed up on her elbow and rubbed her eyes, drew a deep breath to steady her voice. 'What can I do for you?'

There was a long pause. No need for him to say anything, they both knew what he was thinking. His voice in her head, all laid-back and sexy, said it all on its own. 'I can think of a few things...' And damn that she walked into that one.

She jumped in to fill the gap. 'I hope your secretary passed on my message thanking you for the flowers.'

'That wasn't my secretary, that was Phoebe – Dan's wife.' He sniffed, hesitated. 'You still cross, princess?'

She pursed her lips. No way was she going there.

'I'll take that as a big fat "yes" then.' She heard the lazy half smile stretch across his face, gritted her teeth at the thought of the creases she knew would be slicing down his cheeks. 'Are you busy, Cherry?'

Damn the way his quietly spoken hope made her insides twist. 'Up to my eyes.' True, she had a mountain of work to catch up on in the office. At home, despite the fact she'd been crashed out on the bed, she hadn't even unpacked properly yet. She stared at the pile of washing on the floor, and gave an inward grimace. What the hell was wrong with her? Since she got back all she'd done was wander around aimlessly or sleep.

'Cherry...' Another long pause.

She rolled her eyes. 'What?'

'Would you...do you have time...to talk, maybe?'

She tried to ignore that her chest was tightening.

'I told you I'm busy, Jackson.' She tried to keep her tone distant, yet firm. She was already aching because he wasn't here. No way was she going to make things worse by prolonging the agony. There was something about aching twist in her chest that flipped her all the way back to when she was six, and her dad had left.

'I'm sorry...' His voice drifted off again. 'Cherry?' One more silence, then his voice, low and grating sent her heart into free-fall. 'I miss you...'

Oh my. She dragged air into her lungs. He couldn't be saying this. Much less with so much need in his voice. Then her heart gave a kick and began to beat double speed. 'I really do have to go...' She hated herself for cutting him off, but she'd already veered way out of her comfort zone. It was time to claw herself back on course. Self-preservation was making her slam the door on him. If she hadn't cared, she could have chatted for England. As it was she couldn't say a thing.

'Sorry, Jackson.' The last word she almost whispered. 'Bye.'

## Chapter 35

When it came to time to filming, the first class preparation Bryony had done paid dividends, and when word had come through from Dan that Jackson had two free days, Bryony had pulled out all the stops. On the day she had a cracking crew on the ground, and like a true pro, she'd even managed to get Jackson's camper along for added atmosphere, although when it came to it she had to work double hard to block out the images of the morning after they'd broken down. As for facing Jackson, she'd done everything in her power to make sure she kept her distance, and it seemed to be working. However gut-wrenching it was.

'What the heck did you do to Jackson?' Cressy gave Bryony's cycle helmet a nudge and gave her hair a flick, as they finally had a minute to themselves in the late afternoon. 'His grin's gone AWOL, you're acting like an ice machine on fast, doing double-snarky, and he's not even fighting back.'

'I haven't done anything to Jackson.' So not true. Bryony gave a covering snort, tried to seem indignant. 'Maybe my new Lycra doesn't make me look like I'm bursting out of a double-G cup, so there's less for him to perv on?' And oh, what a bitch she felt saying that, when Jackson's behaviour was nothing short of impeccable. He'd come towards her, all tentative and gentle, and she'd blasted him with one dry-ice smile that was out before she knew and froze him to the spot. As for the slash of puzzled hurt in his eyes – best for her not to go there. She had to remember this wasn't about power any more, nor about winners and losers; it was simply about self-protection. After that he'd taken his lead from her. She wrinkled her nose as Cressy brushed a last stroke of blusher across her cheeks. 'Although, the jacket seems much tighter than it did when I bought it last week.'

'That's Lycra for you.' Cressy sent her a sympathetic smirk. 'From where I'm standing, he's still looking at you like he wants to eat you.'

'Rubbish.' No idea when Cressy had found her chance to see that, given Bryony was doing her damnedest to stay as far away from Jackson as she could. She'd worked late into the night to be sure she'd rearranged all the interview locations to make good use of props, to keep maximum distance between herself and Jackson. Him sitting on the bike, her sitting on a wall. Jackson driving the camper van with the window down, her standing outside. And for the shots on the tandem, she arrived right at the last moment, bundled herself onto the bike once he was in position, so all she had to contend with was a view of his back.

'You should so get in there.' Cressy on repeat again.

'For the last time, I wouldn't touch him with a bargepole.' Bryony winced at her own blurted protest. Maybe she was being excessive, but she needed to keep Cressy in check somehow, and a tiny part of her knew this was her sensible-self trying to make a point to the part of her that was hurting like hell. Been there, done that, got the scars, and a heart that ached like it had been trampled by an army. How could she have been so stupid to think she could handle even a short term taste? 'Plus there's the small matter of the three million views of the viral film, which should never have been leaked. That's down to him, I'm the one who comes out of that looking like a fool, and I flatly refuse to overlook it.' And thank Christmas for that excuse.

'Five million, not three; it goes up every day.' Cressy's eyes lit up momentarily, the she went back to chewing her lip. 'Well, at least try to cut him some slack, Bry. The producers were sold on the heat between you two. Now every time there's a spark you extinguish it faster than the New York Fire Brigade and that isn't making for great TV. If you want to pursue the presenter thing, you're going to have to do better than this.'

A whole crew to hide behind, a schedule without a minute to spare. No idea seeing Jackson face-to-face would be this hard, even if every time he looked her way now he was glowering. She'd thrown up her barricades, but every time she saw his jaw clench she felt like she was going to cry.

'Okay. Point taken.' Bryony gritted her teeth, dug deep to find a compliant smile. 'I'll promise to try for fun and flirty.' *Fun and flirty? She had to be mad.* She gave a shiver as she thought exactly where that had landed her before.

Friday, two weeks later, and Bryony couldn't help remembering that this was the day of the Sports Gala Night, even though she'd spent all day stuck on a hillside, battling in the wind, filming a rock-climbing feature. All carefully scheduled, as far away from Manchester as she could be.

'Who'd have thought it could be this cold in July?' She shivered inside her parka hood, as she stumbled along the track to the car park at the end of a long afternoon, weighed down by the last of the bags.

'Who'd have thought we'd ever see you throwing off your heels, and opting to do a shoot of people dangling on ropes in the middle of a moor?' Cressy, in front, threw a glance over her shoulder. 'Or that I'd get dragged along too.'

'You didn't have to come.' This was *her* way of coping with *her* problem. Why Cressy had insisted on tagging along too, she had no idea.

'But I did have to come. Who else was going to make sure you made it to Manchester in time for tonight's Gala bash?'

'Which I'm patently not going to, given that we're hours away.' Bryony flipped out a triumphant smile. 'I'm totally safe.'

Cressy threw her bags down beside the van, checked her watch, then looked up, and scoured the sky. 'I know you've technically given up hijacking Brando's helicopter, but he was happy to oblige and help his little sister today, given the importance of the occasion. Bryony Marshall *will* go to the ball, and if I'm not mistaken her transport is about to arrive!'

Jackson had no idea why Cressy was hell-bent on delivering Bryony in time for the Gala, but who was he to grumble. Though what the hell was going on there was beyond him. Putting Bryony down as clingy? He couldn't have been more wrong. Her walls had gone up, and there was no way in for him. He suspected the viral clip was a red herring, not that he'd got close enough to discuss it. He'd taken full responsibility for the clip, even though he hadn't even been there when it was taken, but insisting on the truth risked looking like he was trying to wriggle out of it, and no way did he want to give Bryony that impression.

Every time he'd tried to phone her she answered but then strangled the call, and in some ways her distant, clipped politeness was worse than no reply at all. His hopes for breaking through at the filming had been dashed immediately when it became obvious she'd planned her avoidance with military precision, and he'd headed off to train with nothing resolved, with his mind anywhere but on the job. For the whole of his life, cycling had been his escape, his obsession, his whole existence, and suddenly finding that he wasn't able to concentrate on it was as shocking as it was unnerving. A woman under his skin? This one was had taken over his whole being, and he couldn't get her out. Meanwhile, in the background, for some unknown reason, Cressy had been working her butt off to get Princess Cherry to the Gala Ball, and it had to be for more than the free press pass that he'd managed to wrangle for her.

And now he was back in Manchester, but as for how tonight was going to pan out, that was anyone's guess. One thing though was certain – you couldn't leave a fire half-burned. As far as he and Cherry were concerned, business was very much unfinished, and he was going to go all out to make her see that.

He'd flown back in from training at the team base in Portugal in the late afternoon, only to find a full photo-shoot waiting for him at the main house. Black lingerie central. A posse of women, draped around the elegant bannisters, wearing – ahem – very little. Once he'd have been delighted with the overdose of stocking tops; today he was less than. Thank you, Dan. Not.

'How is this going to help my image?' Sometimes he doubted Dan's judgement, big time.

'Lads' mag charity calendar. Note the word "charity". All in the best taste, which is why we're using your gracious Georgian home as the backdrop.'

'This is yours and Phoebe's home, not mine, Dan.' Jackson, irritated, felt compelled to point this out. 'I live in the flat over the garage.' Not wanting to be pedantic, but it was true.

'You're the owner, it's not my fault you'd rather camp out in the handyman's quarters.' Dan stuffed his hands into his pockets. 'For God's sake, Jackson, what the hell got into you? Just think of the women as ironic, get your kit off and play nice.'

Five-thirty on a Friday; nowhere he wanted to be less. Naked except for his Calvin's, ten women clambering all over his body, taking instructions from a photographer who made camp sound mainstream. Jackson drew in a breath and shuddered as Ricardo's shrill set the chandelier jangling. Again.

'Okay. I want a forest-of-limbs shot!' Ricardo clapped his hands. 'Girls, legs wide and interlocking, spread those arms, Jackson, dart through those branches darling!'

'Holy crap.' Jackson cursed under his breath. He'd worked with Ricardo before, and the results were usually spectacular, but a man

215

had his limits and he was pretty close to his.

'Fabuloso. And relax.'

Not that you could relax, when a Nikon was being pointed at your groin by a guy from Bolton, who used words like 'fabuloso'. Jackson gritted his teeth.

Ricardo shook away a waterfall of fringe, spiralled a finger in the air. 'Okay, let's get down and dirty. Jackson on the stairs, girls coming at you from all sides, all hands on the guy.' Ricardo clattered by, ruffling Jackson's hair as he passed. 'Nice and rough, Sweetie, okay?'

Twenty hands. Twenty pointy strapped up boobs. Not to mention someone's thigh slapped under his chin. The perfect moment for Cherry to walk right on in, led by Dan, who should have had more sense. What the hell was wrong with the back door?

'Bryony's just flown in with Cressy. Did you hear the helicopter?' Dan's cover-all announcement made Jackson grimace. Obvious that Dan wasn't here because of his PR skills.

Bryony took two steps across the tiled hallway and skidded to a halt. Windswept, wrapped up, muddy. Real, exuberant, delicious. Forget the twenty models with their limbs variously draped over him, one glimpse of Cherry, and Jackson wanted to rush down the staircase and sweep her into his arms. His heart hammered on his chest, and his blood surged south. Instant. Immediate. *Anywhere but there.* Caveman on a mission, and a hard-on that seriously challenged the flimsy fabric of his boxers. He registered her startle as she took in the scene and her eyes widened. Not what she'd expected, then, but for the first time in his life the element of surprise was putting him at a disadvantage.

Her nostrils flared, as she regained her composure. 'Ten out of ten for the impressive location.' She spun a mocking smile towards Jackson. 'Although, it seems I'm overdressed for this particular party.'

'It's a photo-shoot.' He shoved out an explanation, then remembered who he was talking to. 'But you'll have gathered that.' His eyes followed hers, as they locked onto his erection. How the hell she'd found that in the forest of female limbs was anyone's guess. And now she was going to draw the wrong conclusion, dammit.

She gave one don't-give-a-damn head toss, but her brows, descending like a thunder-cloud told a different story.

Dan butted in. 'We've got a fast turnaround, the cars will be here to pick us up in thirty minutes. Phoebe's upstairs, she'll show you your rooms, ladies.'

Passing on the stairs was not the best of ideas, despite the stately-home dimensions. The group of bodies collectively inhaled to let Dan and Cressy past, then Cherry followed. Her scent hit Jackson when she was still two steps down, turning his legs weak. As she drew level, he raised one eyebrow, meeting her deep-blue gaze. Pure ice-fire. A nanosecond was all it took to read the wrath, and clock that he was in deep shit here. His insides were torched, but he had to look again. She was here, and he couldn't take her eyes off her. If looks could kill... Except now it wasn't him she was dead-eyeing, it was the women draped over him, who were getting the slayer treatment. Looked like Bryony could happily rip them apart, limb from limb. Her jaw clenched as she swallowed, and his heart soared.

She was wild. Yes. Wildly jealous. Which meant she did give a damn after all. His veins filled with hot syrup as she sniffed, bowled him the scowl of the decade, then bolted up the stairs.

'Catch you later, Cherry.' One gruff statement of intent, and damn that he wanted to hurl his Calvin's in the air and throw himself after her in one joy-fuelled leap.

## Chapter 36

It had taken an age for the limo to negotiate the Friday evening traffic and deposit them at the end of the red carpet under the imposing arched windows and monumental stone facade of the city centre's most salubrious hotel. Only now, as they wove their way across the marble floor of the immense entrance hall and Cressy peeled away into the crowd of other guests, did Jackson find the chance to slide up close enough to growl into Cherry's ear.

'Impressive enough for you, Cherry?'

'Not bad.' She cocked her chin, looked up at the lights that spangled the lofty stairwell. 'I like the way the old front of the building changes to new, and suddenly it's all floor-to-ceiling glass and stainless steel.'

Okay. Sounding like an architecture correspondent, but the talking had to be an improvement on her arctic silence. His mouth watered as he clocked the column of her neck, vulnerable and exposed now her hair was swept up, and he wished he didn't want to bite it quite so much. And damn that the only way he could imagine that shimmering grey silk sheath of a dress was pooled on the floor at her feet. 'So, I take it you did your undie-ironing, Cherry, given the importance of the evening?' He drew close behind her now, brought a guiding hand close enough to the small of her back to feel her heat on his palm.

She twisted round to deliver her retort. 'As if I'd ruin a dress like this with a panty line.'

'Right.' Point to Cherry. He made an effort to pick his jaw up off the floor, and tried to unglue his eyes from those full lips of hers, tried to stop twisting the foil pack in his jacket pocket. 'What colour do you call that lipstick then?'

'Raspberry pie, or plum crush. I forget which.' She screwed him a narrow-eyed glance. 'Although after this afternoon, I'd have thought you'd be the expert on panty lines.'

Just the right amount of huffy to show she cared. He gave a low laugh. 'You wouldn't be jealous would you? Sexy women with their hands on my body, when you want a piece all for yourself?'

'Jealous?' Her yelp followed her chin towards the ceiling, and the woman next to them jumped to stare at them, then looked away again. 'Not in a million years, Jackson.'

'I love the way your shoulders go up when you're annoyed.' He lowered his voice and splashed a grin through her fury. 'So worth the tease.' The sooner he cleared the air with Cherry, the better. Just a question of where, given the bustling throng of guests around them, and the transparent lift. 'Come on, we'll go up by the fire escape stairs.' He slid his fingers through hers, and tugged her down a side corridor.

'Still hiding out from the press, then.' She gave a sniff, but held his hand tightly. 'Not the most logical place to come if you're press-shy.'

'There are plenty more interesting targets here than me.' He gave a shrug, came to a halt outside an open door, then bundled her through it. Managers' Rest Room? Just the place. He spun her into the half-light, and backed her against the wall next to a filing cabinet, wincing as her hip grazed his hard-on. 'There are things we need to sort out.'

'What? Like your exciting afternoon?' She thrust her chin upwards again, the tension in her body holding him at bay.

Whoa. Not exactly what he'd been thinking, but given the

venom she was spitting, it might be a good place to begin. She'd brought it up again, so it must have riled her. He stifled the smile of pure gratification that was threatening to split across his face. He couldn't help but like Cherry's fierce possessiveness.

'That was work, and if you must know, it left me cold.' A shock to him too, that he hadn't felt so much as a flicker of lust until she walked through the door.

She gave a derisive snort. 'You looked aroused enough from where I was standing. Calvin Klein's and tent poles spring to mind.'

Nothing like being put on the spot. He dragged in a breath. Making excuses for virals on YouTube would have been so much easier.

'That happened as you walked in the door. I saw you, and zap.' He gave a shamefaced grimace. 'You're going to have to trust me on this one. I promise, whatever you saw, it was all yours.'

Her nostrils twitched. 'Nice try. I believe you, thousands wouldn't.' She didn't meet his eye, but from the secret smile that was playing around her lips he'd guess she liked what she heard. 'So, you said you want to talk?' Her eyes slid upwards, locked onto his and sent his gut into free fall.

'Talk, and…' His voice caught in his throat, as he drank in her scent, took one step forward, rubbed a thumb along her jaw. Aching to hold her here. 'It might be good to reconnect.'

'Aha…'

Sensing a thaw here. Slowly, he wove his fingers between the folds of her pinned up hair and she juddered towards him. One silky breast rubbed his lapel, he dragged in the warmth rising from the shadow of her cleavage. Snaking an arm behind her back, he pulled her towards him. Warm, firm, vibrant and so damned alive. Tugging on her hair, he dragged her head back, until that perfect raspberry-crush pout parted. Desperate to crash his mouth over hers, but he had to make himself wait. He teased the corner of her lip with his tongue, to measure her resistance. Heard the shudder as she hauled in a breath, felt her breasts heave towards him as she filled her lungs, then her pelvis ground forward, hit his erection and rocketed him to who knows where.

'God, I've missed you, Cherry.' The only thing he'd promised himself he wouldn't say, spilled out against her neck.

He watched her mouth twitch, then her fingers closed on his hair, prised into his scalp and sent an ice-shower down his spine. Then he was crashing his lips onto hers, and she came right out to meet him. All cherry sweetness, and plum warmth, tumbling his body, making his head spin as she sucked him in. The heat of her body pulsed under the slippery silk of her dress, her breasts arching towards him, hungry, desperate, demanding, making what went down before look like kindergarten. The snog of his life made his guts churn, set his heart banging like a jack-hammer and rocketed his already-burning libido into the stratosphere.

He pulled away to drag in some air. 'You've no idea how much I needed that.' Took in one thigh, slicing through the split of her dress, one high-heeled strappy sandal. Sexy as hell. Delicious pink toe nails.

She already had the heel of her hand hard against the end of him, tugging at his fly. He put a hand over hers to restrain her. 'Not here.' One kiss to clear the air, and she already had him on his knees. 'And we're due upstairs.' Hurling out every sane reason in the book, knowing he didn't mean a single one, he dipped in for another hot deep kiss.

Knowing as their mouths locked that he was aching to devour her here and now, but hesitating. No way did he want her to walk out of here feeling cheap – Cherry was worth so much more than a quick shag in a back office.

'No…' He put his hand down to restrain hers, as her fingers closed around him and squeezed him to the first stage of heaven. 'I want to wait, do it properly.'

'But I need you.' She groaned against him. 'Like, now.' His heart slammed into overdrive she thrust her hand into his jacket pocket. Pulled out one foil packet, biting her lip as she held it up, her low voice slurred with need. 'Jackson Gale, never without.'

They needed to go, he should be strong, should say 'no', but the word jammed in his throat.

'Undo me. Please.' She spun around, her eyes pleading. 'It won't take long.' From the urgent grating of her voice, she was as desperate as him.

Grey silk. Spilled over an office chair, not pooling on the floor. Even as it happened he knew it would stay with him forever. Cherry, half closing her eyes, lips parted. Leaning back, bending up those achingly perfect legs as he rested her ass on the desk. Watching him, her pupils hazy with desire as he unzipped all the way. That blurry half smile as she knew he was going to give her just what she was aching for. The way she was hot and sticky, oh-so-ready to suck him in, the way she snatched her breath as he parted her, clamped onto him as he slid inside her. And the way when he was up to the hilt, and she gave that familiar groan of pleasure, a strange and deep satisfaction swept over him, because it felt like he was coming home. Then pulling slowly in and out, her insides closing around him like hot velvet, her sticky scent driving him way past wild. Turning him further on than he'd ever been. Loving the way she disintegrated. She threw her head backwards in slow motion, her face contorting into one long ecstatic cry. And her frenzied contractions milking him, until he poured himself into her in one crazy orgasmic explosion.

'You're sure my hair's okay?' Bryony fiddled with the clips, emerging into the foyer, feeling like everyone was staring at her.

'Hair looks fine to me but then I'm not an expert, and given what your dress is highlighting, there's no way I'm going to be looking at your hair.' Jackson straightened his tie, nipped his shirt behind his belt, the creases slicing down his cheeks as he grinned making her heart lurch. Not helpful at all.

'I'd rather not look like I've just been snogged senseless against the wall.' That was a glaring euphemism too, but somehow she couldn't bring herself to say shagged witless on the desk. Right now she had no idea what just came over her back there.

'You should have thought of that before you threw yourself at me.' He whisked out of the way of her swipe. 'Sorry, but those pink cheeks are a total giveaway – that and the way you're looking at me like you want to eat me. Then there's your smile the width of the hotel entrance hall; talking of which, maybe we'll take the lift after all, now it's quieter.' He slid an arm around her hip, filling her air with his scent all over again, as he steered her through the foyer. Clean, raw man. A hint of body spray. He raised his eyebrows pensively. 'I'm pleased you're talking to me again, at least.'

Talking? Ever the man for an understatement. It wasn't the talking that was the problem, it was the way she'd dived straight down his throat. How the hell did she get sucked back in so fast, when she'd promised herself she'd keep her distance? She'd spent the last two weeks weaning herself off him, aching because of the gaping chasm that opened up in her life when he left, desperate not to open herself up to hurt again. Five minutes alone with him – if you counted being at an event with five hundred guests as being alone – and she was already a goner. So, what the heck happened?

Beside her Jackson ran a finger along his collar, where his tan met the sharp white of his shirt. Readjusted the lapels of his tux. And there she had her answer. One look at how this guy scrubbed up and her best resolutions had gone into meltdown. As for her self-preservation instincts, they'd been overruled by something much more powerful. In the face of competition from those other women, she'd been driven by an undiluted fever to possess him for herself, mark him as hers, which, given the way she ran scared of attachment, was beyond ridiculous.

'Damn.' As they moved out into the crowd Jackson jived.

'What's wrong?'

'It's my brother, Connor, and my Dad. Over there, behind the woman in yellow.' He inclined his head. 'Grey haired guy waving his arms, and that's Connor, looking the other way.

One snatched glance past his shoulder confirmed a profile disturbingly like Jackson's. 'He's much smaller than you, isn't he?' A lightning appraisal. 'Way less pretty.'

Jackson's brow furrowed. 'I've spoken to him, I phoned, like you suggested…when we were in the…'

'Great.' She cut him short. That time in the shower was still etched on her brain, some morning that was. She was taken aback he'd remembered, more surprised still he'd acted on what she'd suggested. 'And how did that go?' The mental image of those raw scars sent a shiver through her chest even now.

He gave a grimace. 'Things are better than they were. We almost made our peace. I wasn't sure they were coming tonight.' His voice trailed off reticently.

'Are you going to say hello?' It was a tentative query, not a push.

'Maybe, if I can catch Connor's eye.' Jackson squinted across the foyer, peering at the pair, then as Connor looked across at them he gave a nod of greeting. 'He's seen us; we're in for an audience, take a deep breath. I'll apologise in advance for my father. However he behaves, it won't be good.'

As they threaded their way through the crowd Bryony noted that Connor was slighter than Jackson, with a tan several shades deeper. But as with Nic, although he was different, the family resemblance was undeniable. He looked more wired and nervous than Jackson, and the narrowing of his eyes as they approached hinted at his apprehension.

Jackson threw a mock punch at Connor's arm. 'Hey, how's it going, Con?'

'Jackson, hi, can't complain, how about you?' His tense expression eased a little as his gaze landed one Bryony and he rolled back on his heels. 'Scrub that question, I can see from your date you're more than fine. All that happy on the phone a couple of weeks back, now I see why.' He tipped a slightly forced wink in Bryony's direction. 'Am I going to get an introduction, or do I have to wait?'

Despite the striking physical similarities, Connor had none of

Jackson's easy charm.

'Maybe not, until you get your manners into line…' Jackson's stony expression suggested his quip was serious, but he obliged anyway. 'Cherry, this is Connor; Connor this is er…Bryony. And just to lay out the ground rules, stay right away, she's all mine.' Jackson glowered at Connor.

Bryony had no idea that brotherly competition went this far, but at the same time, being claimed by Jackson sent a strange thrill running down her spine, even though she would never let it happen in reality.

Their dad, meanwhile, was oblivious, scouring the horizon of the crowd. Connor tapped his him on the shoulder to get his attention.

'Dad, Jackson and Bryony are here.'

Jackson's father did a half turn to face them. 'Right, great, Ted Norton's over there, need a word, I'll catch you later.' His snappy voice was almost a bark. 'We're together upstairs, Con, I'll see you up there. Don't be late.' And he shot off as fast as the crowd would allow.

Bryony reeled. What the hell…on every count. Jackson had mentioned his awful dad, but ordering Connor about like he was a kid, and as if that wasn't enough he'd practically cut Jackson dead. Not that Bryony was desperate to be introduced, but she hadn't expected this.

'Charming as ever.' Jackson muttered. 'Don't mind him, Cherry. I'm afraid you only register on dad's radar if you're going to be useful to him in the next thirty seconds.'

'He doesn't get any better.' Connor's forehead wrinkled in a frown. 'I've only had the dubious pleasure of his full-blown attention lately. When you were the one winning and I wasn't, as far as he was concerned I didn't exist.'

'He's a pain in the ass whatever side you're on.' Jackson gave a shrug.

Connor blew out his cheeks. 'I used to be jealous of the

attention, but now I've had a taste of it I don't know how you stuck it all those years. He's such a parasite.'

Jackson shrugged. 'No idea what we did to deserve a father like him. He craves limelight and he'll do whatever he can to grab a piece of it, and it's never his own.'

'Listen to us. United complaining about our nightmare of a father.'

'Nothing new there – suffering together pretty much welded us until, well...' Jackson broke off. '...until I crashed.'

Connor let out a bitter laugh. 'Ridden off the road by your own brother.' His cheeks hollowed as his jaw tensed. 'You know I didn't mean it to happen?'

'Yes, I do.' Jackson rested a hand on Connor's shoulder. 'At the time I was so screwed up by the pain it fucked up my judgement, but I can see straighter now.'

Connor looked up at him. 'So we're good?'

'We are.' Jackson nodded. 'Gales sticking together in the face of the common enemy. Speaking of which, hadn't you better go or you'll be getting your ass whipped?'

'Too true. We'll catch up later.' Connor clasped Bryony's hand. 'Lovely to meet you, Bryony. Make sure you look after this guy well.' And then he was gone, dashing towards the staircase, and they watched in silence as he jumped up them two at a time.

'My family's such a screw up. It's a very long story, now's not the time to tell it. Were we on our way to the lift?'

'You're not on your own, Jackson.' Meaning to imply that hers was a mess too, but ending up sounding like she was there for him, which was no bad thing. She had a sudden urge to wrap her arms around his head and rock him. *And never let him go.* Where the heck did that last bit come from? Instead, she rested a hand on his arm, not that that would help. 'At least you and Connor have moved on now. That can only be good.'

She looked up, watched the lift sliding down towards them in its transparent shaft. Tonight was promising to be hugely illuminating, and nothing to do with the spangly lighting.

# Chapter 37

'Tonight's not a bundle of laughs, is it?' Phoebe leaned across the table towards Bryony. 'Band playing through dinner is a great idea, but no one gets to talk. Plus, this year's speech writers must've had a collective sense of humour bypass.

'At least there's lots of champagne.' Bryony sent Phoebe a look to acknowledge their mutual pain, her eyes skimming across the remains of her chocolate mud cake. After a day in the open without much food, overdosing on the champagne maybe hadn't been the best idea. When had she ever been queasy enough to fail to finish a sweet? She scoured the horizon to see if she could locate Cressy to provide some light relief, but failed.

Phoebe leaned towards her again. 'I'm so pleased you're here, so at least we can exchange eye-rolls.' She looked over her shoulder, gave a vague wave to someone in the distance, pulling a face as she turned back to Bryony. 'That's Jackson's father over there.'

'Mmm, we kind of met earlier.' Bryony supposed that covered the uncomfortable encounter in the entrance hall.

'Not a very nice man, I'm afraid.' Phoebe lowered her voice. 'From what Dan says, he gave Jackson a really rough time as a kid, and it got way worse when his mother left. Jackson totally freaked out after that. Late teens is the worst time for something like that to happen; his father was totally out of control once the family split, and so cycling was Jackson's escape from a dreadful home life.'

'It must have been hard.' Bryony's heart ached for Jackson. He'd never talked about his mother and although it was good to know what had happened, she wasn't sure she was comfortable finding out from Phoebe.

'Dan's very concerned about him now. He's sure Jackson's knee isn't going to hold up to the strain of racing. Jackson's refusing to even to consider jacking it in, and he doesn't know how Jackson will cope if he has to retire. He's put everything into racing, and if that goes, he'll have a huge void in his life. That's why Dan's so pleased his plans for the TV side are blossoming, in more ways than one.'

One look at Phoebe's knowing smile told Bryony she was somehow included in this. Not good. She had to divert the conversation fast.

'So, what do cyclists do after they retire then?' Bryony hoped this would shift the emphasis away from herself, and the answer would be interesting too, given that she could never get Jackson to talk about it.

Phoebe fiddled with her nail as she considered. 'Some of them stay in the sport, as team directors and coaches with the pro teams or the national teams; some go into business. Jackson's got a whole lot of business interests, but they already run like clockwork and he's not that interested in being involved further. He already does a lot of charity work. I know he's had his wild moments, but there's so much more to him than the bad press makes out. He's a great guy, which is why Dan is so anxious for him to be seen in the right light. Less of a bad boy, more of an angel, kind of thing.'

'I see.' Bryony wasn't sure how Dan would fare on the angel front. She hadn't expected the retirement answer to be quite so Jackson-orientated.

Phoebe picked up the theme again. 'Some of the guys go to TV as commentators or presenters – Dan's pinning his hopes on that for Jackson. And some of them just enjoy a normal family life, which would be nice for Jackson too.' Another of Phoebe's smiles winged its way across the table. 'You're a very honoured guest by the way, Bryony – Jackson usually comes on his own. He seems pretty smitten. Where is he anyway?'

Family life? Smitten? Bryony's heart hit her knees.

'He said he had to see someone.' Bryony wanted to set Phoebe straight here. 'And Jackson and I aren't that close – in fact, we hardly know each other.' That just about covered it.

'Sure.' Phoebe's smile broadened, and her eyes glistened. 'Whatever, it's lovely to see him looking so relaxed and happy.'

Ker-ching. Bryony felt her chest tighten. Looking relaxed and happy? Just the kind of thing she used to say when she was on a matchmaking case big time.

'I'd better grab this chance and nip to the Ladies.' Bryony pushed back her chair, blustered an excuse as she stood up. Phoebe might be lovely, but Bryony needed to escape before the proverbial water got any hotter. 'I've got a bit of a chill on my kidneys, we've done a lot of outdoor shoots this week.' Not exactly lying either, given the way she'd been dashing off to the loo lately.

'Out of the main doors, then left at the top of the stairs. You can't miss it.'

At least Phoebe wasn't coming along too. Bryony doubted she'd personally have let her quarry go so easily. As she slipped out of the doors onto the landing she ran straight into Cressy.

'Hey, I was just about to come looking for you.' Cressy dashed up to Bryony, smoothing down her dazzling red dress. 'Fab evening isn't it, aren't you pleased I kidnapped you? Looks like you and Jackson are getting on better too.'

Cressy always looked amazing but Bryony couldn't help noticing that her eyes were extra-sparkly tonight.

'It's brilliant to be here and I'm sorry if I resisted too much.' Bryony sent her a sheepish grin, hoping to avoid details about her and Jackson. 'I'll make it up to you when we get back to Jackson

Gale Towers – apparently Jackson has a fridge full of champagne!'

'Right, that's what I came to tell you. Thanks all the same, but I won't be coming back with you...' Cressy's smile had a smug twitch to it. '...let's say something's come up.'

'For "something", read one hot guy... Fast work there, even for you!' Bryony gave her a mock scowl. 'Cressy, you're incorrigible!'

'I try my best!' Cressy grinned up at Bryony.

After what Bryony and Jackson had got up to earlier, Bryony wasn't going to speculate about the flush in Cressy's cheeks, which was somehow heightened by the scarlet of her dress.

'I'll catch you later then!' Cressy wiggled her eyebrows, then stretching onto her ultimate tiptoes she managed to pop a kiss on Bryony's cheek.

'See you Monday then!' Despite Bryony's airy goodbye wave, she made a mental note to look out for the guy later...'Don't do anything I wouldn't do.' Although, even as she said it Bryony realised this was way less of a limitation than it used to be.

The sumptuous Ladies' was worth a visit, regardless of need. Bryony was enthroned, admiring the frosted glass partitions, wondering where these twinkliest of lights came from, because, oh my, she had to have some, when she heard a familiar voice ringing outside the cubicle. Annie Brookes? Sports presenter/celebrity... albeit last seen in the Ladies' in Scarborough, when she should have been on a tandem with Jackson Gale...Sporting Gala. No reason why she wouldn't be here.

'Bryony! What are *you* doing here?' Annie swooped and kissed her on both cheeks the second she emerged from her cubicle, almost as if she'd been waiting for her.

Good question. I was kidnapped and brought here by helicopter sounded way too dramatic of an answer. Bryony tried for low-key. 'Oh, a bit of promo for the show. We're doing a couple of pieces with Jackson.' Throw it out, and see how it landed.

Annie seemingly ignored Bryony's reply and bashed on. 'And

guess what, Bryony, I'm pregnant.' One triumphant announcement, as Annie flapped her hands in front of Bryony's face. 'All those queasy afternoons, going off chocolate, throwing up in Scarborough, dashing off to pee every twenty seconds. Who'd have thought?' Annie's ecstasy bounced off the polished glass and ricocheted back off the mirror wall.

'Wow, a baby. Congratulations.' Bryony flung her arms around Annie. 'Oooo, just think – outfits, from baby Gap.'

'Already bought. I couldn't resist. And I went crazy over the teensy stuff in Agnès B. It is GORGEOUS.'

Bryony struggled to make her expression bright, digging deep to sound suitably enthusiastic. 'Oooo, you'll have to get some teensy Nike trainers. We'll be able to do a piece on sport for babies. Fantastic.' And damn that someone else's wonderful baby news always made Bryony's heart squish, because there was no way she was ever going to let herself get into a position where it could happen to her. It made her feel so mean. By way of penance, she drove herself to ask *all* the prerequisite questions and more. 'So, when's it due? How's the father taking it? Where are you having it? Have you had a scan?' All duly asked as Bryony tried desperately to concentrate on every answer. They'd been standing by the hand driers for ten minutes and more, Annie seemingly oblivious to the other women coming and going. Surely they'd covered everything there was to cover by now.

'But do you know what's best of all?' They were about to push their way back onto the outside world when Annie gave a whoop and hugged her chest, cupping a tiny breast in each hand. 'I already gained two inches round my boobs. Happened instantly. Roger's over the moon, although they are a bit tender.'

Bryony looked down at her own cleavage. Thought about how she'd been bursting out of her bra this morning, remembering that morning six weeks ago when she'd had to pour herself into Annie's pink lycra. How long ago that seemed now.

And then they were out at the top of the stairs and Annie rushed off, leaving Bryony, head spinning, blinking. Reeling. Two minutes and she'd get herself together to go back to the Gala.

'Bryony Marshall, what the hell are *you* doing here?' A tap on her shoulder, a drawly voice unsettlingly close to her ear, and the feeling of being stuck on a loop. 'Or did the world's least athletic girl become a sporting legend whilst I wasn't looking?'

She lurched, spun around, and her stomach left the building. Holy crap. (Thank you Jackson, for the perfect expletive.) She was not prepared for the familiar raggedy blonde hair, jaw like a rock, that toothpaste-perfect smile and those same blue eyes that had haunted every dream, night and day, since she didn't know when, until… With a vague unease she realised that somewhere along the line some of her Matt-obsession had silently leeched away. Who'd have thought that would *ever* be possible? It had to be somewhere this side of Scarborough, because she'd gone *there* because she couldn't think of anything else, with the sole intention of keeping him out of her head for the duration of his wedding weekend.

'Matt?'

That would be newly-married Matt, journalist, and brother of best-friend-forever Claire. No surprise meeting him here then. The surprise was that she hadn't anticipated it, hadn't given the possibility a second thought, when once she'd have thought of nothing else.

She grabbed hold of her voice and yanked it down an octave. 'Me? I got thrown into a bit of presenting, and I'm here with some of the *Sporting Chances* guys.'

'Well, who'd have thought?' And sounding like they were all working with the same script here. 'Whatever happened to the *Antiques Road Show*?'

She locked onto those lilting lips as they curved. Still built like a rugby player, always like a God in his tux. Still taking her breath away, still making her heart race. She screwed herself up to get hold of her pulse-rate and steady it.

'You mean *Country House Crisis*?' She gave a shrug. No surprise he didn't even know the name. 'It led to other things.'

Hang on. What the heck? Her heart wasn't racing unduly. Cheeks not hot. Her blood wasn't rushing through her ears. And the single gasp? Well, maybe she could put that down to the shock of being accosted from behind. Looking again more closely now, Matt didn't have that all-over glow any more, and she could even make out a rash around his neck. How the *hell* could Matt Clifton *ever* look like a mere mortal? Had six short weeks of married life robbed him of every atom of enchantment and hunkiness? Bracing herself, she allowed her eyes to sidle down to his left hand. *What?* No ring?

'How's Tia?' Once the words would have lodged in her throat, now they floated out, airily.

He gave a grimace. 'Actually not so good. We separated a couple of weeks back.'

'Already?' Definitely the wrong thing to say, especially with that much shrill. Not a good advert for fast-forward romance then, given how those two had rushed into matrimony, or for tandem riding.

'Seems she was more interested in the wedding than the marriage.' He gave a shrug. 'C'est la vie and all that. It became obvious halfway through the honeymoon it wasn't going to work.'

'Oh dear, what a bitch queen.' Could she even say that? And why the hell wasn't she whooping and bouncing off the ceiling? The forever man of her dreams just came crashing back onto the market. She should be feeling more than…nothing. 'I'm sorry.' She gave what she hoped was a sympathetic grimace, and slid her eyes upwards to lock onto his to-die-for baby-blue ones. Jeez. Nothing at all. All cold. Somewhere along the line she'd turned to stone.

'I don't suppose…?' One half-constructed thought from him that bounced off the balcony rail, and hung in the air between them.

'Sorry?' Puzzled, she scoured his eyes, trying to read the sentiment, but only found blue like dead denim, instead of the anticipated summer-sky.

'Well, let's face it, you're here, I'm here, we're both singularly unattached, maybe we should give it a go? Don't know why I never thought of it before.'

Oh my. It certainly wasn't down to the lack of downright flagrant efforts on her part. How many times had she dressed up, sparkled, gyrated, trying to make him notice her? She'd tried every trick in the book, short of physically throwing herself at him, and come to think of it, she might even have done that on a couple of extremely misguided occasions. She gave a mental shudder.

'You know what, it's a lovely thought, but I don't think so.' Her voice was coming out, but it was as if someone else was operating her mouth. For the best part of fifteen years she'd ached to hear him say those words – well, not those ones exactly, the ones in her head had been way better – but something along those lines. And now, they left her frozen.

'But why not? Claire always said we should be each other's back-up plan. I know it sounds a lot more last resort than I mean it to…' He gave a grimace that turned into the kind of a hopeful grin that would have had her melting helpless into a pool not long back. 'But friends to lovers is a great basis for a relationship.'

Anything had to be better than the three-month whirlwind romance Matt just had, that crashed and burned three weeks past the altar. Bryony chided herself for that mean thought.

'I think that might have been Claire's joke, Matt.' Except she never had until now. 'Put it down to bad timing.' She slid him a conciliatory smile, although if anyone was in shock here, it was her. 'As for the last resort bit, I'm not sure I'm quite there yet.' Was this really coming out of her mouth?

'Well, if you change your mind, give me a bell.' He slid a card into her hand. 'I'll be waiting.'

'Thanks, but I don't think so.' Burning her boats here too. What the hell had got into her? 'Sorry, but I really need to go now.' She moved to go past him.

'Cherry?'

As Matt melted away into the crowd, Jackson, springing up the stairs three at a time, arrived at her elbow, face blacker than a summer storm.

'Who the hell was that?'

This guy smelled good. Every time.

'Just the brother of a friend.' She sighed. Really not ready to expand on this. 'He's a journo.'

'Was he hitting on you? His tongue was hanging so far out it was practically down your cleavage.' Jackson's growl came through gritted teeth, his body rigid, his hands thrust into his pockets. 'I can have him thrown out.'

Testosterone fest or what.

'Chill, Jackson. That really won't be necessary. Let's go back in.'

'If you're sure you're good?' He rubbed his hand across the dark stubble on his chin. Cocked his head, and stared deep into her eyes, like he was looking into her soul.

'I'm fine. Everything's fine. Absolutely fine.'

Except from the way her heart was clattering in her chest suddenly, she knew she was anything but.

# Chapter 38

Close up, this evening, she had been finding it hard to keep her hands off Jackson. The scent of him, the push of his leg against hers under the table, every flash of his profile. Near enough to focus on the pores of his skin, make out the individual spikes of his stubble, the buzz of his proximity had been driving her wild. Now that he was up on the stage, about to make a presentation, she was expecting a temporary respite. From her place at the table with the lights dimmed, she took in his skin glistening slightly under the bright lights as he approached the microphone, noticed that half-rub of his chin with his thumb that was so familiar. He was far away yet somehow he seemed larger and more impressive than ever, as if the benefit of distance had sharpened her focus and she was suddenly zapped by the full blast of his charisma. The rest of the audience were also hanging on every gravelly word, eyes glued to every lilt of his lips, every ironic lift of his eyebrows, every wry aside, quite simply awed by his bad-boy charm.

All the way here in the helicopter she'd been so determined not to succumb, but somehow the moment she was with him she had no choice. All her hard-nosed resolve dissolved, wiped out by the buzz and fluttering that zipped through her. But now she had caved and given in, was it really so bad? His voice burred through the speakers, drawing everyone in the room up close to him. She had five minutes at most to think about this rationally whilst she was out of range of his power charged pheromones. She was here; he was hot, sexy, and irresistible, and he was hers for the taking. And on Monday he'd be flying off to get on with rest of his life.

What could be safer than that?

She really hadn't meant to come back for more. Coming back for more made her so much more vulnerable, but now it had accidentally happened, she could surely make the most of it. Hadn't Jackson always insisted she needed to lighten up, and what had Cressy said all those weeks ago?

As Jackson pulled his speech to an end, the applause thundered around the room, and she watched him winding his way back towards her, his dark gaze locking onto her like a heat-seeking missile.

She shivered, braced herself. Maybe she should look at this weekend as her final gift from Jackson, give herself the green light for forty-eight glorious hours of debauchery. And then she could go away and deal with the fall-out afterwards, on her own.

'Okay, Cherry? How was the speech?' His voice reverberated against her neck as he slid back into his seat.

Her blood began to fuzz in her veins. 'Life affirming?' Not quite a lie.

'I bet you didn't even listen.' He nudged her arm and bent towards her, his warm breath on her ear sending goose bumps pebbling down her spine. 'By the way, I booked us a suite – I need you, sooner rather than later.'

She slid him a smile. 'Me too.'


'I haven't got many clothes with me for a weekend away.' Cherry sent him a grimace.

Midday Saturday, arriving back at his place, and how like Princess Cherry to be bothering about what she was going to wear. He was happy to work with her slinky grey silk left over from last night, given that he planned to take it off her again as

238

soon as; although, whether she'd still be up for that once she saw the full glory of his rudimentary flat, he had no idea.

'I was hoping you wouldn't be needing clothes.' He grinned, as he unlocked the door, ushered her up the stairs. 'Didn't you ever hear of boyfriend jeans? You can borrow some of mine.'

Damn. The B word sent her eyebrows shooting skywards as she stepped out into the wide space. He should be more careful, knowing how touchy she was. No point getting her this far into a reunion burn-out-the-heat weekend, then ruining it. He watched her eyes widen to saucers as they swept around the bare room, then narrow quickly, and for the first time in his life, he felt compelled to cobble together some explanation for the emptiness.

'I'm rocking the man-cave thing here. Bare essentials, bike on rollers, TV, fridge, sofa, bed, in order of importance.' A throwaway comment, and aware that he was holding his breath, anxious for her approval.

'Wow, Jackson. You've got a great outlook across the gardens and over-the-garage translates perfectly to the loft-look.'

He knew she was being generous here. The flat he hadn't given a second thought to for years seemed achingly stark now it was being exposed to female scrutiny for the first time. 'So,,you aren't going to berate me for my lack of designer pieces?'

'I've got a feeling there's more designer here than you realise.'

He gave a shrug. 'I wouldn't know, I asked for a sofa and someone delivered it. And the lack of comfort?'

'It's just nice to see you in your own place at last.' Her voice was soft as her touch on his arm. 'At home, I mean.'

His turn to flinch now, this time at the H word. 'It's mine, but it's not exactly home.' No need to tell her nowhere had felt like home since the day his mother walked out when he was seventeen.

'Whereas you seemed very much at home in the five star hotel this morning, comfortable enough to order condoms from room service, along with breakfast.' Despite her chiding tone, the corners of her lips were twitching with amusement.

'And a measure of the establishment that they delivered them along with the Full English on their own silver platter.' He flashed her a wry grin and wondered how the tiniest movement of some-one's mouth could make his insides go molten. Had to be the lust. And with Cherry as edible as she looked this morning a guy couldn't have enough condoms.

He watched as she casually flicked off one high-heeled shoe, slid onto the sofa and tucked one foot underneath her. Perhaps he was misreading her body-language, but from the way she draped that arm along the back of the couch, stretched to maximise the thrust of her breasts, the way she was chewing her lip, he was guessing she might just be as out-of-control-amped as him. With any luck this weekend they could finish this thing once and for all. As she turned her gaze on him, he caught the haze of desire in her eyes, saw the heat from her skin radiating into the air. Strange how the whole emptiness of his flat was instantly warmed by her presence. Cherry sitting on his couch, and the whole world taking on a fuzzy glow? High fives to the power of lust. Where the hell he was going to find the heat to warm his home when he gave up racing, he had no idea. And damn that his mind had slipped to that slap-in-the-face shock realisation he'd come to during the last two weeks of training, when he'd sworn that he wouldn't even go there until after the weekend.

'Talking of silver platters, where are all your trophies?'

Cherry's question inadvertently reinforcing the ice-shower already cascading down his spine. True, individually the trophies had long since lost their shine, simply because he had so many. But if he went through with his decision to quit, the thought that there wouldn't be any more turned his gut to permafrost. And the way the training camp had panned out this last two weeks, quit-ting was where he was heading. Seemed like Dan had been right all along with his view of the future.

'All the tinware is either in storage or in a room below here. Except for my first major medal, which is on the wall over there.'

An unscheduled grimace escaped as he cocked his head in the direction of the bike anchored on a turbo-trainer.

'I couldn't hold it, could I?'

Cherry asking same question everyone always asked, except his chest hadn't ever constricted before in quite the way it was doing now.

'Sure.' Striding across the room, he plucked the ribbon off the wall and swung the heavy gold disc into her hand.

'Thanks Jackson.' Balancing it carefully on her palm, she scrutinised it then she raised her eyes to lock onto his. 'It kind of takes my breath away when I touch it.'

'I know exactly what you mean.' Different reason, same result. For him, it was the shine in her eyes that had squeezed every ounce of oxygen out of his lungs. He took the ribbon from her, ignoring the thousand volt jolt as their fingers brushed, then he slid the medal into the pocket of his tux and raked his hand through his hair.

Bryony watched the hollows of his cheeks flex, took in the clenching of his jaw and made a dive for a swift change of subject.

'So, why do you choose to live here and not in the main house, Jackson?' She had no idea what she'd done, but the way he'd changed from smouldering to broken in a blink left her feeling somehow responsible.

'Dan's here all the time. He has the family and the life to fill the place and I don't. I bought the house as an investment, he enjoys it – it's win-win. Meanwhile, the man-cave gives me everything I need.'

'I'm sure it does.'

Great line, but no way she was buying that. Anyone with eyes that sad wasn't even beginning to get what they wanted. His formal, black leather shoes clicked as he paced across the painted floorboards, and the stripped-back volumes of the apartment seemed to echo Jackson's emptiness. She scanned the unadorned expanse of pale grey walls, the windows with their black slatted blinds. The only trace of anything personal relating to Jackson were some bike wheels propped in the corner, a couple of pairs of cycling shoes and a Lycra top draped across the saddle of the stationary bike. Strange then, that she'd had an immediate sense of coming home as soon as she stepped through the door, felt almost too comfortable as she sat here now. Maybe it was something to do with the power of smell, because although there was very little of Jackson here in terms of possessions, the whole place smelled good, as if the air was loaded with his achingly familiar scent. She wiggled her toes, readjusted her legs beneath her. Deliciously at ease pretty much summed it up. If she hadn't been so relaxed, the realisation might have unnerved her, but as it was she was leaning into it, breathing it in, given it would be over in no time. Coming home? Easy? If a teensy alarm bell was ringing in her head she was choosing to ignore it. Just for now.

She watched his thumb scrape absently across the stubble on his upper lip, thanked God for making Jackson look so edible in his tux, even the morning after. Not so long ago, his strength had driven her to distraction. He had been such a pain in the butt, and dealing with him had been like battering her head against a wall, but that was before things between them had shifted. Somewhere along the line she'd given up her struggle to stay in total charge, and she'd inadvertently trusted him to take control. But the surprise for her was that it didn't feel bad. On the contrary, it felt strangely easy and comfortable. Relaxing. Enjoyable even. His strength, which once seemed like a wall to kick against, now felt more like a shelter. Just for now it was good not to be out there in the storm, fighting every battle on her own. Just for this short time she'd let herself enjoy the novelty of the protection that wall was offering, not that she'd allow the independent woman in her to hear that thought. Strange how she and Jackson were similar in so many ways – both perhaps too headstrong and stubborn for their own good. She stifled a smile as she clocked the jut of his chin. How many times had she stuck her chin skywards as she struggled to come to terms with something?

'You do know that clenching your teeth isn't going to make things better, Jackson?'

'Sorry?' He spun on his heel, arrived to face her.

'If you grind your teeth you'll just get jaw-ache.' She drew in a breath, knowing that when she was like this she needed to be challenged head-on.

'I don't know what you…'

She rounded on him. 'There's no point acting all insouciant and airy. I know something's wrong.' Harsh, but confrontation was the only way.

'Whatever.' He thrust his hands deep into the pockets of his jacket and rolled his eyes.

'I'm not going to ask what it is.' Pulling out her trump card she saw his eyes widen in surprise. Great. The last thing he expected was for her to back off here. 'All I want to say is that when you're ready to talk about whatever it is, I'm here for you Jackson, and I might even understand.'

The click of his footsteps moved around behind her, and then his thumb was on her cheek, rubbing, sending shivers to deep, delicious, oh-so-familiar places. A fleeting twist of guilt twanged in her chest, as she remembered all the times he'd phoned her, when she'd cut him short.

'Thanks, I'll remember that Cherry.' His deep voice resonated and her shiver situation got a whole load worse as his lips landed at the base of her throat. 'Hey, what's this?' His tone lightened as the words hit her skin, and his arm slid past her elbow towards a colourful carrier bag lying further along the sofa.

Seizing it, he gave a low laugh. 'Marge from the photo-shoot kept her promise then.'

'A promise of what?'

'Lingerie left over from the shoot. She said she'd look out a few things in your size.' He peered into the bag, with a grin that stretched the width of the room. 'I think this solves your wardrobe problem for the weekend; there's loads to wear here.'

So like a guy to say that. 'How did she know my size?'

He thrust the bag towards her. 'One look, and Margie knows. It's her job.'

Bryony fumbled in the bag, pulled out something black and sheer, and flipped out the label. 'Very pretty if you like dominatrix style, fabulous designer, but she's got my cup size way too big.'

'Marge doesn't make mistakes. Try them on, and see.' His eyes darkened, 'I'll give you my expert opinion.'

Bryony ran one silky ribbon between her fingers as she hesitated. 'You did look very sexy with those women yesterday.' No need to admit she'd felt like clawing the faces off them, how it had made her want to shag the pants off him. The desperate need she'd had to claim him for hers.

And now he was here for the taking, what the heck was she waiting for?

One slight tilt of his head. 'The bedroom's that way, if you want to change.'

His Adam's apple flexed in the open neck of his shirt as he swallowed, making her tummy flip, and the deepening shudder of his voice sent a flurry of goose bumps down her arms. Her eyes slid, snagged on his trouser zip, which was level with her face, and the shadow of his erection sent a stream of hot syrup to pool at the base of her stomach.

'Cool, I won't be a minute.' She grasped the bag of lingerie, pushed herself to her feet, and slipped towards the bedroom. Though if this was request time, she had one of her own. 'Sit down, and stay just as you are. I want you in your tux.'

The smile she shot over her shoulder collided with his grin.

'Anything you say, Cherry.' His cheek creased into a wink. 'Happy Saturday, I think this flat's about to get a whole lot more decorative.'

# Chapter 39

Jackson was as good as his word. When she clicked back into the room five minutes later, wobbling slightly on the precipitous heels, the way she found him, on the sofa, jacket open, long legs pushed out in front of him, all laid back and relaxed, made her want to eat him.

'Nice one, Cherry.'

Taking it from his growl that he liked what he saw.

'You were right – everything fits.' She'd been surprised to find she'd gone up a cup size, but designer-wear was notorious for being undersized. Taking a deep breath, she slowed her walk, fiddled with a stocking top, as the unnerving sense of her own sexuality pulled her up short. The Calendar Girl look was working wonders for her ego, and today her guy was here, begging to be claimed. When had she ever felt this alluring, or empowered? And so damned turned-on.

Three strides and she'd be kneeling over him, unzipping him, straddling him, as she dipped onto the tower of his erection. And the same as every time before, she'd be in charge, because that was how she liked it, how she had to be. She'd watch his eyes blur at the moment that he abandoned himself to her, hear the grate in his throat as she lowered herself to take him deep inside her. A shudder of need jived between her legs.

'Hey, I love those black straps on the bra cups.' His lips twitched his as he surveyed her. 'And those patent heels are phenomenal. As for the pants...'

He'd find out soon enough about the lack of crotch. One more step towards him. She paused, shivered at her own touch, as she realigned a ribbon, took in Jackson, lounging like a cover model with his morning after stubble. Cover model? Make that a Sex God.

'They're definitely a new take on control briefs.' She slid her hands over shiny satin, stretched across her butt, peered down at the mesh panels that streamlined her stomach to a board.

'Control briefs? They're certainly controlling me.' His low laugh resounded across the space between them. He leaned back, shifted his hips, then his eyes turned to smoke.

One twang, deep in her chest, and her legs turned molten. What the heck? His lips curled into the softest smile, which sent her stomach descending to her knees and left a hollow in her gut like she'd never felt before.

'Cherry?' His querying grate scraped across the floor, as his eyes narrowed, between sooty lashes.

Butterflies crowded into the space in her chest. They'd been there before, just never this bad. Now their furious flapping was making her throat ache, her heart...

Oh crap. She couldn't say what was happening to her heart. One smile that had acted like an incendiary in her chest. Men with flamethrower grins should not be allowed out. Except it wasn't men, it was Jackson. And that smile wasn't making her feel like she wanted to shag the pants off him. That would have been acceptable, this was so much worse. It was making her feel like she wanted him to wrap his arms around her and never let go. What the hell was that about?

He stretched out his hand, inclined his head, as his lips parted in anticipation. 'Come here, I need to touch.'

Come here? He might as well have asked her to fly to the moon. She swayed on her heels, on the spot. Feet superglued to the floor? An ache in her chest like someone just cleaved it open with an axe? Craving to be swallowed up? She was getting in far too deep here. Thank the God of accidents on Saturdays that this was one weekend only, which would come to a natural and satisfyingly abrupt end when Jackson flew back to Spain and his racing life on Monday.

His eyes locked onto hers as he inclined his head, rubbed his thumb across his chin. Slowly, he pushed himself up from the sofa. She dragged in a breath, her body juddering crazily, as he took what seemed forever to cross the space between them. And then he was in front of her, his eyes just a little above hers.

'You're killing me here, Cherry.'

She winced as his knuckle brushed across the jut of her nipple through the silk. 'Am I?'

She tried not to bite her lip and slid him the smallest smile instead.

'You know you are.'

Her scalp tingled as he stretched out his hand, combed his fingers upwards through the strands of her hair. Then he stretched his fingers around her head, drawing her towards him and into a slow, warm, velvet kiss that made her body hum. As his strong, hot body closed around hers, she knew she was ready to give him anything he asked for. One last sane thought flashed through her mind; she hoped he was in the mood for light and flirty, because if he asked for anything more, she wasn't sure she'd be able to say no.

# Chapter 40

'So, this is where you grew up?'

Late that afternoon, sitting on a park bench, squinting at the sun seeping under the chestnut tree branches, Jackson blinked as Bryony's hand slid onto his knee. No idea why he'd let her talk him into visiting his old childhood haunts, although the way he was stiffening as her fingers closed around his thigh might have something to do with it. What she'd done to him repeatedly last night and again this morning had torched him. Talk about explosive satisfaction. Let's face it, these days, when Cherry Bomb asked for something – anything – he was pretty much powerless to deny it. But what was worse by far was that he didn't even mind. Somewhere along the line he'd fallen under her spell and right now, thanks to the smoking hot sex, she'd got him wrapped right round her little finger. And then some.

'Yep. This is the park I told you about and the Harry Potter house where we lived is across the other side. We'll drive by there later.' Kids on bikes were whizzing around in front of them. He stared straight ahead fixing his gaze on one boy undulating over the ramps. 'This cycling area wasn't here then, though. I organised this a few years ago.'

'You did?' Her grip on his leg shifted as her eyes widened.

'It keeps the kids out of trouble.' He shrugged off her surprised gaze, trying to downplay it. 'The kids' trust I set up is set to roll them out nationwide.'

'That's fabulous. I had no idea.'

'Must be a million miles away from the kind of place you grew up. I imagine you probably had a park all to yourself.' Not that he felt inferior but it was important to acknowledge their different backgrounds.

'Not quite.' She pursed her lips, and shook her head.

'Your brother inherited a stately home.' He rounded on her – this one she couldn't get out of. 'That suggests a certain level of wealth and comfort.'

'Not really.' She gave a sigh. 'Edgerton only came to Brando when an uncle we'd never met fell off his yacht. We rarely saw that side of the family when dad was with us, and even less when he left. I guess he'd alienated them as much as my mother with his drinking.'

'Drinking?' He had a sudden feeling she was about to wipe the floor with him here.

'That's why my parents split up. He died of liver failure, so that charmed upbringing you're implying didn't exist. I'd have thought of everyone, Jackson, you would know that money is no guarantee of happiness.' Her voice cracked. 'I had material things, but I'd have swapped that in a heartbeat for a life with more emotional security.'

His chest constricted as he met her impassioned gaze. Dammit for jumping in with his size tens again.

'Your dad, I'm sorry; I didn't know the details.'

'Why should you? Everyone did their best to make up for it. Brando was a very protective big brother, my step-dad and my mum tried really hard. I have two lovely step-sisters who are both at uni now. It was pretty rough when Brando was a teenager, but in the end he went away to school. Despite everyone trying so hard, sometimes all a child wants is two parents that belong to them.'

If the helicopters and interference were anything to go by, from

249

where Jackson stood it seemed like Brando was still fulfilling that role.

But one flash of the hurt in those deep-blue eyes had Jackson digging deeper into his own past than he could believe. 'It wasn't all roses in Harry Potter-land, you know. My mother walked when I was seventeen. My brothers and I stayed with our dad, but it wasn't easy, and it definitely wasn't comfortable.'

Understatement of the year there, but he couldn't begin to tell her how he went off the rails when his mother left, or how when there was no one left to control him his dad went ape.

'I didn't know that, Jackson.' Now it was her turn to sound all guilty and sympathetic. 'Why didn't you say?'

How about because he didn't talk about it with anyone. Ever. He gave a grimace. 'You didn't ask.' And moving swiftly on. 'Anyway, enough about that, how are the borrowed jeans shaping up?'

Worked like a charm. She immediately turned her attention to her legs.

'They're fab. Cressy chose the clothes for my weekend case from my old stuff, so I wouldn't realise they were missing and guess what she was up to, but they have to be two sizes too small now. There was no way that zip was going up.' She rubbed her hands over her hips giving a doubtful grimace. 'My recent hot chocolate addiction has gone straight to my bum.'

'I'm not complaining.' He shot her a grin. 'That jacket of mine looks great on you too.'

She pushed her hands deep into the pockets, returned his smile. 'The leather's so soft, I'm not sure I'll be giving this back in a hurry.'

And just to drive the conversation right away from danger and keep her sweet. 'Not wanting to talk about putting on weight, but isn't it time you had your sugar fix?' He glanced at his watch. 'How about coffee and cupcakes?'

Her anticipated whoop of delight didn't come. Instead she hesitated, gave a gulp. No idea her hangover was that bad. She almost looked green for a moment there.

Whatever, she recovered quickly, sent him a reassuring smile. 'Tea and toast would be lovely. Thanks.'

'Okay, Cherry, tea and ibuprofen coming up.'

Sitting at a pavement bistro table in afternoon sun, which slanted over the rooftops of the wide pedestrian area and bounced off the flinty stone setts, Jackson watched closely as Bryony swirled her spoon in the froth on top of the hot chocolate that she'd finally decided on. When exactly did he lose the ability to take his eyes off her? Finally, she propped the spoon against the cup side and raised her gaze to meet his. Given the way she nailed him with that stare, he sensed something big was coming.

'So, last night when I asked how the training was going you said ask tomorrow.' Her lips moved into a determined pucker that told him there was no place to hide. 'How is it?'

'Hard.' He couldn't avoid the question any longer. Maybe he'd been putting off admitting the truth to himself. 'Okay, if I'm honest, sometimes it feels like it's damn near impossible.'

There. Out in the open. At last he'd said it.

'I thought it might be.' She inclined her head, gave a sniff. 'I've been reading about it.'

He felt his eyes widen. Cherry, reading about cycling again? Whatever next?

He might as well level with her. 'Last night I felt like a total fraud up there in the spotlight acting like a big hero when in training I haven't even been keeping up with the young guys who are starting out.' Somehow it was a relief to share it.

'It might get better.'

He gave a shrug. 'And it might not.'

She gave her drink one last stir, put her spoon on the saucer and tapped her thumbnail on her teeth pensively. 'You don't *have* to do it. You do know that?'

'I've been programmed to race for as long as I can remember. When I was young, my dad drove us hard. Winning was the only

251

way to get his approval.' He wanted to offer some kind of explanation, without revealing how punishing and relentless his father's drive had been.

Jackson could still make out the blue of her irises, through the narrowed lines of her lashes.

'However hard the training is now, it's going to take a lot more guts for you to give up than for you to carry on.' She stared at him again, this time piercing straight through to his inner being.

Still no idea how she did that. He gritted his teeth and exhaled slowly. She had him on the ropes here. How the hell did she read him so well? Almost better than he knew himself.

'There's nothing scarier than the unknown, Jackson.' Her hand reached towards him, and he felt her fingers close around his. 'You might have to be brave here.'

He glanced down at their hands clasped on the shiny table, and felt a bizarre warmth seeping right through his body. Cherry was right. And what's more, the knot of tension that had been in his chest for as long as he could remember had eased. It was so damned obvious that he needed to give up. He should have seen the truth months ago, and perhaps he would have done, if he hadn't had that cavern of fear about the future in his gut.

'I know you're strong enough to do it.' The smile she spun him was simultaneously confident and reassuring. 'And talking about important things, I'm so hungry and this looks wonderful.' She sank her teeth into her toasted teacake and brushed a crumb off her lips as she chewed.

Okay. It looked like she'd let him off the hook now, but he had to admit he was better for having been strung up there in the first place. And Cherry was the only person in the world who knew how to make him face things, and find answers all at the same time. No one else, not even the highly trained team psychologists, had her knack.

'So, what do you fancy eating tonight?' He steered the conversation to a more neutral place. 'We could go into Manchester, or there are some good places round here.'

'Sounds exciting.' Her smile was way more enthusiastic than her voice, but that had to be down to her hangover.

Undeterred, he flipped out his phone and scrolled down a list of restaurants.

'If you're going for atmosphere you can choose anything from Victorian cottages, to office blocks, converted warehouses, interior gardens with real trees, or decadent opulence complete with retro lampshades.'

'Okay…'

'And you can have traditional English, or you can go Japanese, Chinese, Indian, French with everything cooked at exactly 63 degrees, which might appeal to your exacting nature…' He watched her pull a face at him for that one. '…Thai fusion, or Pacific Rim…'

She eyed him levelly.

'You know you could travel to all those places for real now, don't you? If you gave up racing, you'd be free.' Her direct gaze pulled him up short. Again.

'Hey, you're imposing your dreams on me here – a world tour is what *you* never got around to,' he was compelled to protest.

'And you could eat whatever you wanted too if you gave up.' Her mischievous grin told him she was winding him up and enjoying it. 'Think about the joys of all-you-can-eat carveries with the bottomless ice-cream option.'

And then some.

'*If* I give up. It's a big "if".' It was important that he was keeping his options open as far as Cherry was concerned, at least until he'd spoken to Dan.

But right now, sitting next to this vibrant woman who sent his pleasure gauge to levels he'd never imagined possible, he couldn't think of anything better. World trip with Cherry. Life together, with Cherry. He ran the words through his mind. How the hell had he missed this before? It was a no-brainer. But it was about much more than the pleasure. It was about the fact that when he was with Cherry, he felt secure and fulfilled and whole and pretty much deliriously happy. Like the endorphin-buzzed high of a win, but on-going. And with Cherry, the thought of the future wasn't scary at all, in fact it was mind-blowingly awesome.

The curtain of her hair brushed across his wrist as she leaned towards him, and his insides shifted like a tidal wave just hit them.

Holy crap. Did he just think that?

Her warm scent filled his nostrils as her cheek rubbed against his.

'I wouldn't mind a takeaway and a night in.' Her hoarse whisper and the way she teased his earlobe between her teeth had his crotch jolting to instant attention.

'You want to get your hands on my DVD collection?' He slipped his hand under her jacket. 'You really are up for watching *Lassie Come Home*?'

'Sounds good to me.' She gave a soft intake of breath as he ran his thumb along the gap at the back of her jeans. 'Plus, I've nothing suitable to wear to go out in.'

'Whereas there's a whole pile of photo-shoot stuff you haven't even tried on yet.' His attempts to keep the lust out of his growl failed.

'Exactly.' Her purr in his ear sent his heartbeat into overdrive, then she gently leaned away from him.

'Well that's this evening's plans settled then.' He screwed the top off his smoothie bottle and emptied the apple-green contents into the frosted glass in front of him.

Her eyes shone as she caught his eye over the rim of her cup. 'I loved what you did to me just before by the way.'

'Which bit?' Knowing darned well that she was talking about the silk scarves, and the teasing, but making her say it herself was so much more exciting. He watched her push away the gingham tablecloth, cross her legs, then uncross them again.

'The restraining bit.' She squirmed. Aluminium café chairs never looked so sexy.

'What? The part where I tied you to the bed?' His voice was low and grating, but not low enough given the way the woman at the next table jerked upright, open-mouthed, clattering her tea cup onto her saucer.

'That's the bit.' Her hand arrived in his groin, pressured the bump of his erection, and then she began to scrape the tip of him through the denim. 'And what went after.'

'What you're doing with your nail is below the belt.' Now he was the one with the gaping mouth, and thank God for overhanging bistro tablecloths. 'And talking of scarves, you could always return the favour?'

'Sorry?' The glance she shot him was insouciant.

'You could tie me up?' And damn the way that thought made his pulse race even faster.

'Maybe.' Her eyes blurred. 'But I think I like it as it was this morning.'

What? The sudden seismic shifts in his universe left him reeling. Do-as-I-say-Cherry passing up a chance to boss him around? Him looking forward to quitting racing? Finally finding someone who he felt comfortable enough to watch *Lassie Come Home* with?

His world had turned upside down.

And no question at all who was responsible.

# Chapter 41

'Dan! How considerate of you to drop in at eleven on a Sunday morning.' Jackson hovered by the closed door ignoring the loud knocking, gesticulating wildly across the room at Bryony.

Bryony meanwhile skittered around, scooping up a thong and bra from the floor, stuffing a rogue suspender belt under a sofa cushion, then hitched Jackson's wool socks as high up her bare legs as she could and yanked down the tail of the shirt she was wearing.

'All good!' She waved a hurried thumbs up to Jackson and flopped down on the sofa as he threw open the door.

If Jackson sounded less than pleased about Dan's interruption, for her it was a welcome distraction. She'd come out of the bedroom, and unintentionally plunged headlong into her Sunday morning forever fantasy. Again. The one where she came downstairs, into a kitchen, for a cosy Sunday morning, with the newspapers and her imaginary guy. The same fantasy she'd had for years and years about being married to Matt, which had got progressively more and more mashed up ever since that night in the log cabin in Scarborough with Jackson. Obviously it had been kicked off today by the Sunday morning thing here, and the absence of stairs between the bedroom and the kitchen in Jackson's flat didn't seem to matter a jot. What did matter was the faceless guy in her dream-vision. Since time began it had been Matt who turned around and grinned at her in her fantasy, and she was totally used to seeing him. But today when he turned around, the fantasy man in who was grinning at her wasn't Matt at all, it was someone who looked just like Jackson. And it totally threw her off kilter. Holy shit! Where the hell had that come from? Her daydream head had to be playing tricks on her here. She couldn't cope with stuff like this. Jackson was a temporary fixture, who was about to jet off into the blue yonder. He had no business crashing into her day-dreams. The only saving grace was that after tomorrow Jackson would be safely out of reach for good, and then she could put all her efforts into blotting him out of her head and getting on with her life again. She knew she should have stayed well away from this weekend. Cressy was going to have so much making up to do when she got hold of her, for landing her in this mess.

'We haven't even had breakfast yet, Dan.' Jackson's protest was loud and rueful as he ushered Dan into the room. 'Coffee, Cherry?'

'I'd prefer tea.' She'd intended to help but no way was she venturing into the kitchen area in her knicker-free state now Dan was here. And no idea why her lifetime habit of strong coffee at breakfast had suddenly dematerialised. 'Weak and milky please.'

'So, there's some great news I knew you'd want to hear.' Dan dropped an armful of newspapers onto the long table. 'I gave you guys some space yesterday but it's back to work today, especially given what's in here.'

Jackson's forehead wrinkled as he stood by the sink filling the kettle. 'This had better be good.'

'Believe me it is, and congratulations are in order.' Dan scooped up a tabloid, rustled through the pages and slammed it down triumphantly, open on the table. 'Pictures from Friday evening on every gossip page, and everyone has you two nailed as an item.'

Bryony's stomach lurched.

'And you call that good?' Jackson's astonished tone suggested that he was as shocked as her.

Dan gave Jackson a stare that suggested he was gone out for

missing the point. 'Get real, Jackson. The papers acknowledging you have a steady date on your arm catapults your reputation skywards. A steady date, who – did you know they're calling you single catch of the year –' he bowled a beam in Bryony's direction. 'You've been high up on their list of eligible women refusing to be tied down. And frankly, Jackson hooking up with, and I'm quoting here, "Brando Marshall's uber-respectable sister", is pure gold. It's the coup I've been working my butt off for all year, and more. Thanks to you, Bryony, Jackson's been fast-forwarded from bad-boy extraordinaire to respectable citizen. I'd hoped for good things when I sent you two off together in the camper, but this is beyond my wildest dreams. Look, here's a lovely picture of you both. You're looking as if butter wouldn't melt Jackson – "Smiling all the way to the Marshall dynasty". Just more icing on that fabulous cake I was talking about a few weeks back.'

'Holy crap, Dan.' Jackson sent an apologetic grimace across to her. 'Don't take any notice of him Cherry, he's just been working so hard to improve my public image and the fact he's succeeded has gone to his head.'

Bryony opened her mouth to reply, and shut it again when nothing came out. Being shouted about publicly as if she was in a relationship with Jackson was bad enough, when it so obviously wasn't the case, but it was looking more and more as if Dan had a whole host of motives for sending her and Jackson away together. The way Brando's name kept coming up was unsettling, but worse still, it sounded as if Jackson was in on it too. Her head throbbed as the cogs of her brain chewed through what she'd just heard, until she finally scraped a protest together.

'You two talked about this before?'

Dan and Jackson exchanged nervous grimaces, but it was Jackson who came clean with a desperate sigh.

'Yes, we did. A while back Dan admitted to me he sent us away together because he thought we might…er…get on.' Jackson screwed up his face and shook his head sadly. 'He meant well, it was his idea of matchmaking, carried out with all the finesse of a lumberjack in size ten boots.'

At least Jackson wasn't trying to hide it.

'You've got to admit my hunch was spot on – you did get on.' Dan gave a guilty sniff.

Jackson gave Dan a warning stare. 'That's enough, Dan...'

'And the cake? What the hell did he mean about icing?' Bryony spoke directly to Jackson, her mouth almost too dry to form words.

Jackson's nostrils flared, and his brow furrowed deeply. 'I'm not making excuses, and I swear that what I'm about to say had nothing to do with anything that happened between us.' He rolled his eyes, the resonance in his voice faltering slightly. 'But from somewhere Dan had the misguided and ridiculous idea that if *we* got together, the link with Brando would be beneficial to me.'

Bryony's stomach turned to stone.

The fact that he'd come clean here and admitted it was small comfort. The one time she had the feeling she was doing something, finally for herself, and it was all just an illusion. Yet again, she'd ended up here because she was Brando's sister, and not because of who she really was. In sheer hot, frustration, she dug her fingers into the cushions on the sofa. Across the room, the black slats of the window blinds began to wiggle, and she swallowed down a mouthful of sour saliva. As the room began to slip in and out of focus, and her head began to spin, she closed her fingers onto the sofa, clung on harder, in an effort to keep the room from turning. Then, as the knot in her gut erupted, she clamped her hand over her mouth and made a desperate dash for the bathroom.

If Dan just lost a whole load of credibility points with his revelations, Jackson was desperately clawing his own way back into her good books with his quiet yet attentive reaction to her sudden throwing up. Or maybe he was just a good guy.

'It's nothing, honestly.' She gave a shudder as Jackson tweaked the rug he'd insisted she put over her knees when she'd returned to the sofa and handed her a tray of tea and toast, but somehow she couldn't bring herself to smile.

'My tummy's been a bit weird ever since I took an accidental swig of Cressy's vile energy drink the other day. I feel much better now.' Just one more thing Cressy had to answer for, although thinking about it, that was a couple of weeks ago now.

'That's good to hear.' Dan was still here, propped against the far wall with a large mug of coffee in his hand. 'I've got some things lined up for Jackson for this afternoon, which are pretty non-negotiable.'

Jackson dropped onto the sofa beside her, flopped a hand onto her leg and grimaced apologetically. 'So long as it's nothing too energetic then, Dan.'

'I've already had a local guy getting some photographs together for a retrospective exhibition, an artistic look back at your career. I thought we could drop by and make some final selections, and we'll use that as a platform to launch you into retirement.'

Bryony clattered her cup down, and turned to Jackson. 'What retirement? I thought you were flying back to Spain for training tomorrow?' She tried to keep her voice steady, despite the tension rising in her chest.

Jackson flying far away to his racing life after their weekend of debauchery, she could cope with. That was simple, easy, a neat and tidy end. Jackson at home, with a glaring big hole where his racing used to be was a whole lot different. She hadn't signed up for that, she wasn't prepared for that and Jackson happily waving at her out of her fantasy made it all the worse. She'd promised herself one last weekend of fun to burn out the heat, although if last night was anything to go by, that hadn't worked at all either, because the heat was still like a furnace. But him being around didn't figure anywhere in her plan, and for some reason, the thought that he might be around was making her feel like a vice was closing around her head.

'I told Dan yesterday, but I didn't want the news to dominate our evening.' Jackson gave a sheepish shrug. 'It's been pretty impossible ever since I went back to Spain. The repairs to the knee I injured in the crash aren't holding up. It was probably always hopeless, but I didn't want to face up to it. It took me a while to come to terms with it. But I'm still flying back to Spain tomorrow to tie up the loose ends.'

'Right. Fine. Fab to know you've decided at last.' She tried to sound airy. No reason why he should have discussed it with her, even if he had made a total turn-around on the impression he'd given her yesterday in the café.

'Great, good that one's settled then.' Dan swooped into the awkward space in the conversation, brow wrinkled into a frown, which was somewhat at odds with his upbeat delivery. 'So after the gallery, we've got a quick piece to the news guys, to get some footage of you riding locally to send out with your retirement announcement. We'll spin it that you'll be spending time on charity work. All good? I'm sorry if it seems like I'm putting a hatchet through what's left of your weekend but time is of the essence here. And you guys have got forever, after all.'

Forever? Bryony couldn't explain why the word made her feel like bolting down the stairs.

'Great.' Jackson's grim tone said otherwise, and he sent a Bryony another grimace.

'I'll leave you two to it then.' Three strides, Dan had crossed the room, and was half way out of the door. 'Enjoy your breakfast, I'll pick you up at one.'

So much for putting a hatchet through the rest of the weekend – Bryony felt like someone just dropped a hand-grenade on her secure, and perfectly ordered life.

# Chapter 42

As Jackson pushed through the monumental glass doors into the photographer's gallery later that afternoon, Cherry brushed past him with a scowl that unequivocally froze him out. He just wished that instead of stone-walling him she'd tell him which part of this morning's undeniable catalogue of disasters was bothering her most. Cherry shouting he could cope with, Cherry ordering him around was no problem, but a silent, uncommunicative, evasive Cherry was impossible.

Since Dan arrived with his publicity bombshell this morning her walls had gone up, and she'd morphed into Ms Strong and Silent. They'd had separate showers, then she'd spent an inordinate amount of time fiddling with her hair straighteners even for her, then she'd sat in the back of the car in silence as Dan drove them to the gallery. True, it was hard to get a word in edgeways when Dan was in full flow, but she'd simply stared out of the window in the opposite direction, as if she wasn't listening at all. Not that he could blame her for being upset, but he still hadn't worked out if her dashing off to be ill was due to the shock of Dan's gossip pages or her dicky stomach. And her mumbled excuses of hangover slash high energy drink she drank last week somehow didn't ring true, given she'd hardly drunk anything the previous evening. And he couldn't get away from the feeling that she hated the whole idea of being linked to him in any way at all, which pretty much rubbished his rose-tinted mental picture of spending his retirement with her. The way she'd backed off suggested the whole idea of them as an item left her completely cold. Whatever, he had had a hell of a lot of catching up to do simply to stay standing still.

'I'm sorry we can't fit in our wander round the retro shops, but I promise I won't let Dan ruin our dinner plans.' He attempted to make up ground as they followed Dan towards the stairwell. 'So long as you're up to it, I've booked us a surprise table in town tonight and Phoebe's friend with the boutique is dropping off a whole lot of dresses for you to choose from.'

'Fine. Great. Brilliant.'

Great. The same snippy reply she always used when things were anything but. She still didn't meet his eye as they set off together between the faux rusted balustrades. He threw out a line in a desperate attempt to reach more neutral ground.

'How is your bedroom makeover going, anyway?' He caught himself hoping her new bed was king-sized, with some sort of slatted bed head, and gave himself a sharp mental kick. The way things were going he'd be lucky if he even got to see it again.

'Fine. Great…' She registered his eye-roll expression, and broke off with a sigh. 'It's not going that well as it happens but it's always interesting to browse round shops in a different area. I'm always looking out for something quirky and original.'

Sensing he'd caught her interest, given that she'd momentarily suspended the sub-zero treatment, he moved to capitalise on his gain.

'Why not hang some retro bikes on the wall?' A wild line, thrown out in desperation. Interiors were a long way out of his comfort zone.

'You would say that, wouldn't you?' She gave a half shrug. 'Not sure bikes would work for me though.'

He racked his brains to keep this going, and remembered a wooden couch at a team doctor's house in Switzerland. 'What about a period doctor's couch to play on the clinical theme?'

'I've actually been looking for a vintage dentist's chair to use as a clothes-dump for ages.' She flicked her hair behind her ear, but still didn't smile as they reached the first floor and her heels clicked across the industrial metal landing in front of them.

One vertigo-inducing view down to the foyer and another set of huge glass doors and they arrived in the studio.

'Come on in and meet Phil.' Dan led them across a cavernous space towards a small guy in denim, who came towards them holding out a broad hand. 'Bryony, Jackson, meet Phil, photographer and resident exhibition wizard.'

'Hi Phil.' As Jackson's hand met Phil's he felt his jaw gape as he stared around the high, white-walled space, and took in the images of himself on every surface. 'Quite a collection you have here.'

'Great to meet you properly on this side of the camera, Jackson, I feel like I already know you well, given this lot, and how often I've pointed a camera at you.' Phil nodded towards the photographs, and shook Jackson's hand vigorously. 'So, you've decided to hang up your racing bike and go on to better things then?'

Jackson wavered, took a deep breath. What the heck, he was going to have to get used to this question.

'Someone told me the Pacific Rim's worth a visit, add in the promise of bucket-loads of ice-cream, and it was a no-brainer.' He looked deliberately at Cherry but she was fiddling with her cuff. Catching Dan's non-plussed expression he grasped for a better soundbite. 'The biggest lure is the freedom.'

The sound of his own hollow laugh echoing off the ceiling was joined by a mobile ring tone, and Cherry dived into her bag.

'Sorry to disturb you all, I should have put my phone off.'

Jackson watched her as she tapped the keys frantically. 'Everything okay there, Cherry?'

'It will be, in a bit.' She pursed her lips, doubtfully. 'It's only Brando, going postal about the reports in the papers.'

Brando on the war path was all Jackson needed. 'He's not

coming on another flying visit is he?'

'Who knows…' Cherry gave a past caring shrug, but didn't look up from her phone.

Still giving him the North Face of the Eiger treatment, dammit.

'Brando's coming?' Dan sidled over.

'Of course Brando won't come.' Cherry took the words right out of Jackson's mouth, and dismissed Dan with one snap.

Jackson kicked himself for not getting in first. There were times when he could have cheerfully strangled Dan.

'So, we're here to look at the pictures.' Jackson was aware of the weariness in his own voice. He needed to move this on, firmly, and fast. 'What do you want us to do?'

'We've hung our initial choices here.' Phil gave a rueful grin. 'If you could confirm that you're in agreement that would be good. I've got some other pictures in the back and on the laptop, so you can look through those too and add any more you'd like. I've put them in chronological order. They start over here, if you'd like to come this way, Bryony.'

Jackson felt his jaw sag as short, balding Phil honed in on Cherry, with open arms and a five hundred watt beam. In seconds he'd waltzed her to the other end of the gallery. Jackson tried to ignore the immediate impulse to wring Phil's neck.

Dan raised his eyebrows at Jackson and blew. 'Sounds like she's got it in for me, big-time.'

'We're both in the firing line.' Jackson couldn't believe Dan sounded surprised. 'None of us like being set up, Dan.' He hoped he made it clear to Dan from his pointed glare that he included himself in this statement.

'When she sees the pictures of you as a boy she'll soften.' Dan gave Jackson a pat on the back.

'Somehow I doubt it.' Jackson swallowed back a mouthful of bitter saliva, and ground his teeth as he watched Cherry and Phil chatting, working their way around the gallery. How the hell could they find so much to talk about?

Jackson looked at his watch, then at Dan, still next to him, rolling on his heels. 'How the hell has it taken them forty five minutes?'

'I'd think of it as useful cooling off time.' Dan took his hands out of his pockets and flashed him a grin. 'They're almost done now.'

The scent of Cherry's perfume pulled Jackson's senses into focus.

'Totally amazing.' Cherry had come to a halt a couple of yards away, and was quietly gazing at a four-feet high blow-up of Jackson's face. 'Well, they're all amazing, but there's something extraordinary about this last one. Don't you think, Jackson?'

Jackson lurched, taken aback by her first direct question since breakfast. At least she was speaking to him again, even if she still was looking at him stonily.

'That one's at the world championships. My last win.' Jackson's footsteps echoed over his mutter, as he crossed the wooden floor, arrived at her elbow. 'And?'

When she turned her gaze onto him it was sharp and clear. Piercing even. 'Well, don't you see it?'

'Sorry, but to me it's the same as all the others.' He gave a grimace. 'So many pictures, all of me, to be honest I try not to look too closely.' And more honest still, he was relieved to have her attention again.

She shook her head, and sighed. 'Okay, Jackson, let me explain – it's as if the whole of your personality is encapsulated here in this one picture. Your fearsome determination is there, and your deep reliability, yet there's a sense of your lilting sense of humour too. But most of all I can feel your vulnerability.'

Her usual smile had been replaced by a grave stare, but her hand landing lightly on his bare forearm sent a thousand shivers exploding through his body.

'If you say so, Cherry.'

Phil shot Bryony a glance filled with admiration. 'She's totally right, guys. Brilliant insight. Of all of them, this is my personal favourite too.'

Jackson took in Phil's blunt chin on a level with Cherry's breast,

266

and swallowed a grunt of disgust.

'Thank you, Phil.' Bryony acknowledged Phil over her shoulder, gave the smallest toss of her hair, and then she sauntered away to examine a cluster of smaller photographs, leaving Jackson blinking.

'Impressive observation there.' Dan shuffled up to Jackson, and lowered his voice. 'Although to me it looks a lot more like love than insight. Instead of blasting me for setting you up Jackson, I think you should be thanking me.'

'You have to be joking, Dan; Cherry's been like a proverbial ice queen ever since you blundered in this morning. If she ever *was* interested, she's backing off big-time now.'

Dan gave a grunt, and gave Jackson a slap on the back that left him reeling.

'Lovers' tiff, you'll get over it. I know these are all firsts for you, Jackson, but believe me, the make-up sex will more than make up for the pain.' He shot Jackson a sheepish grin as he consulted his Rolex. 'And sorry to break up the party here, but we need to be moving on. There's a camera crew waiting.'

Jackson gave a sigh. With Cherry in this mood, who knew what was going to happen there.

# Chapter 43

Two hours later, arriving in an empty car park ten miles across the city, and as they were getting out of the car, Jackson pulled Bryony to one side.

'How are you feeling, Cherry?'

She pulled a face. 'I've been better.'

'I'm so sorry about the mess up over the papers. There are times when Dan needs a pillow putting over his face and this morning was one of them, but overall he's worth his weight. And neither of us meant to plot things behind your back, least of all advantages from Brando. Dan's been such a good friend to me, he just gets over enthusiastic at times. He doesn't mean to be half the pain he is.'

'Whatever.' Maybe this wasn't down to Jackson, but feeling used wasn't pleasant.

'If you knew how he's slogged to heave my name out of the gutter, you'd understand why he was so excited this morning. He's already got a lot of work for both of us in the pipeline apparently.'

'How come?' She wasn't about to sound enthusiastic. She didn't want to be bought off with offers of work.

'He's a human whirlwind, he rarely sleeps, and he's got phenomenal contacts, but mostly it's down to your raw presenting talent. No one's going to think you got there by anything other than your own efforts when they see you at work. Dan will help you prove yourself in your own right, if you just let him. Hard to believe, but Dan is a managerial genius. He'll make it up to you I promise. And I'm sorry about what happened, okay?' Jackson gave her hand a squeeze.

'Thanks for apologising.' She met his eye fleetingly, then dropped her gaze. That was the best she could offer right now.

Jackson gave a deflated sigh. 'If you're sure you're up to it, shall we go and get this ride done?'

Ten minutes later, Bryony decided it was time to dig her heels in. And those would be her metaphorical heels, given she'd once again been talked out of her five-inch high Christian Louboutins, and into toes-in-the-air cycling shoes. No idea how she kept allowing this to happen, but now it had, she needed to take a stand. Not that she was feeling stroppy exactly, but today's events hadn't left her at her most cooperative. She turned her back to the bikes leaning against the wall, put her hands on her hips and faced the crowd of guys in front of her.

'If you lot think I'm getting on the back of a tandem with Jackson again after the whole YouTube fiasco, you're mistaken. I'm very sorry, but you can forget it.'

A sea of hopeful male expressions sagged in front of her.

'No problem, we'll ride separate bikes – it's only one minor shot after all.' Jackson stepped in immediately, to smooth the situation. 'It's very helpful of Cherry – I mean Bryony – to agree to join in at all.'

'We are all very grateful to you, Bryony.' Dan carried on. 'And we're only suggesting the tandem because it will be great for both of you, career wise.'

Something told her she was getting the kid glove treatment here.

It was hardly Jackson's fault that she had her lifelong struggle trying to prove herself without falling back on Brando's influential name and reputation. But she was also confused herself. True, it hurt to know she'd been thrown into the camper van with Jackson, yet again, simply because of her name. But in the dappled light of the summer afternoon, after what Jackson had said today, it seemed like that was the least of her problems. This weekend she'd thrown caution to the wind, and let herself go for the first time ever, and she'd landed in the strangest of places, under Jackson Gale's wing. And despite the unexpected nature of the place, she loved the way it felt. But the whole point was, it was all a fantasy, and it was only wonderful because of the certainty it wasn't going to last.

His bit part in her all-time dream had thrown her completely, but she could have taken that in her stride if he'd been heading off at top speed on his racing bike, never to be seen again. Whereas, as things were, she couldn't handle any of it. And she could barely admit it to herself, let alone talk about it to Jackson. It was making her short-tempered and cranky, which was why everyone was acting like she needed careful handling, when really all she needed was for the weekend to end so she could shoot off back home and hide.

And here were Jackson and Dan, not just pouring oil on troubled waters, but hosing it on by the tanker-load. The last thing she wanted was to be difficult. She'd dealt with too many prima donnas to become one. She needed to take a lead here, to be strong, independent and pro-active. She took one deep breath.

'I'm fine to ride the tandem, so long as I'm on the front and in control.'

Her words came out in a rush, and Dan took all of a nanosecond to seize on her offer.

'Fabulous. Why we didn't think of that before?'

'I'm not sure.' Jackson's brow furrowed. 'The tandem isn't that easy.'

'I'll be fine.' It was a flat, quiet stretch of road, and at least this way she got to operate the brakes.

Dan backed her up. 'How hard can it be? We're talking fifty yards, max.'

'No, Cherry, I'm sorry, I'd rather not risk it.'

All these guys, too much testosterone, and Jackson was reluctant to hand over power. After this morning, she needed to prove, at least to herself, that she still had a grip on the situation. This way too, on the film, she would look like she was decisive, in control, and calling the shots. That might shut Brando up too, given that her phone was practically on meltdown with the texts he'd been sending – and she'd been ignoring – since he'd seen this morning's papers. One little bike ride that looked like it might solve a whole lot of problems, and all she had to do was to hold her nerve, steer and pedal. For once she was with Dan on this one.

'I've let you be in charge all weekend, Jackson.' She flashed him a loaded glare. 'It's my turn now.'

From the smoulder in Jackson's eyes, she guessed her silk scarves and total submission point had hit home.

'Good point, well made.' Dan was in again, although she had to hope he had no idea what the heck he was talking about.

'You've got me there, Cherry.' Jackson gave a grimace, then taking the tandem by the handlebars he wheeled it around. He took a moment to adjust the front seat. 'Come on, climb aboard, Captain. Looks like I'm taking a back seat today.'

'Okay, great, one last time along the road.' The camera guy's shout followed them as they did yet another lap around the car park.

'Not so bad handing over control, is it Jackson?' Bryony resisted the urge to send him a smirk over her shoulder. Despite her hands shaking so much she could hardly hold the handlebars at the start, thanks to Jackson's calm, reassuring instructions, posted straight into her ear, her confidence had grown and she'd nailed this one. As she headed towards the road, her heart was soaring.

'All clear, keep on going, keep the curve wide.'

Jackson's measured instructions were keeping her on track, and as she steered onto the carriageway her mouth stretched into a huge smile.

'Great, now wave as you come past, Jackson.' Another shout

from the cameraman, and she was waving too.

'No, not you, Cherry.' Jackson's shout was urgent. 'Holy crap, get hold of the bars.'

'Whoops. Shit.' She'd lost her line. The front wheel clanged off the kerb.

Then the world tipped, and the last thing she knew was the ground whizzing towards her and an almighty thump as her head smashed into the tarmac.

# Chapter 44

'Really, apart from my wrist and a bit of a headache, I'm sure I'm fine.' An ambulance ride, and what seemed like an age later, Bryony screwed up her eyes, and yet again caught a glimpse of tubes and screens, and the pink painted plaster of the wall behind her head. 'I was woozy before, but that was the pain and the smell of antiseptic and lying so flat.'

A woman, this one wearing a pale-blue smock, smiled down at her. 'We'll get you off this board as soon as we can, I promise.'

'Thanks, that would be great.' Bryony attempted to return the smile, and winced as she rearranged her wrist. She needed to get out of here before Brando got wind of it.

'In the meantime, I'm your radiologist and I'll be looking after any scans and X-rays you need.' The woman smiled again, and adjusted her clipboard. 'So, Bryony, we ask all young women – any possibility you're pregnant?'

'No, definitely not.' Categorical 'no' to that one.

Beside her Jackson leaned back, and let out a long, low sigh.

'So, date of last period?'

'They tend to be irregular.' Bryony racked her brains. She'd finished just before the weekend in Scarborough. 'Six weeks ago. Seven maybe.' Out loud, it didn't sound so good.

Jackson shifted on his chair next to her.

'Okay. Just to check. Have you experienced any nausea, or vomiting recently? Morning sickness?' The nurse sent her an apologetic grimace. 'Sorry, but we have to ask.'

Morning sickness? 'No way.'

Jackson leaned in and rested an elbow on the stretcher edge. 'You were sick earlier on.'

'Thanks a bunch for that, Jackson.' Whose side was he on? And how the hell had this spun so fast into an inquisition? 'That was different. It wasn't morning sickness, it was almost afternoon.'

'Okay.' The nurse raised her eyebrows, and sighed as she made a note. 'Anything else, are your breasts swollen or tender?'

Bryony opened her mouth, then shut it again. Was this really happening?

'Maybe. A bit. But it's probably just my period coming on.'

'They definitely have got bigger, Cherry.' Jackson tapped his chin with his thumb. 'Two cup sizes wasn't it?'

The nurse stepped back. 'Fine, I'll just check with the Doctor. Give you two a minute.'

'These people are so ridiculous sometimes.' Bryony tried to toss her head, but given the restraint, she had to make do with grinding her teeth.

'You don't think…?' Jackson began, then trailed off.

'I've fallen off a tandem.' If she said it firmly enough she could stop her mind from racing, stop it putting one and one together and making three. 'I'm an RTA, not an ante-natal case. I came here to get my wrist in plaster, not to get pregnant.'

It was mind-blowing, scary and crazy, all at the same time. She didn't need to look at the flickering figures on the monitor to know her pulse was racing.

'She might be right?' Jackson stood up, sat down again, then fumbled with the sheet they'd draped over her, found her good hand and rubbed her knuckles. 'How wild would that be?'

Wild? What kind of word was that? 'She can't be right, I'm not…' She couldn't even make herself say the 'p' word in relation to herself. 'End of.' And when did her voice become a strangled shriek? Strapped down, flat on her back, was no way to fight this.

'Okay, don't get your sling in a twist.' As his face broke into an anxious grin, his cheeks sliced, and sent the butterflies from her stomach to her thorax. 'Look on the bright side. If you are, at least your mom won't have to freeze your eggs.'

Despite his low laugh, his fingers had locked around hers, and he was holding on. Holding on so tightly, that by the time the nurse in blue came back with a doctor, Bryony's whole hand had turned numb.

## Chapter 45

'Thanks for bringing the takeaway.' Jackson, bum propped on the bonnet of Dan's car, opened the box, stared down at the burger and decided to leave it where it was for now. Somehow the monumental slab of a hospital building that overshadowed them took his appetite away.

'No worries. It's lean steak. I wasn't sure about the fries.' Dan gave him a punch on the arm then slid in to sit beside him. 'How's Bryony?'

'Pregnant.' Jackson tested saying the word out loud. If it bounced back off the tarmac and hit him in the face, he couldn't have been more gobsmacked than he was when they found out.

Dan raised his eyebrows. 'I know that, but I meant generally, more immediately…?' At least Dan hadn't said the word back to him.

'She's in theatre now, they're knocking her out to realign her wrist.' Jackson let out a sigh. 'Thanks for coming back again, I should never have let her on the front of that tandem. It's all my fault.'

'We're all to blame for that, and we're lucky she wasn't hurt more badly. I thought you might use the support, as well as the food.' Dan held up his own burger, and took an enthusiastic bite. 'I wondered if Brando might have arrived to muscle in?'

Jackson pulled a face. 'So far we've been spared that. I imagine he'll be raging, and quite rightly too. I haven't looked after Cherry as I should have, not in any area.'

Dan gave a grimace. 'How's she taking the baby news then?'

Jackson flinched as that major word slipped out so casually. Cherry's initial expression of wild-eyed shock had quickly morphed into ghostly silence and he had no idea whether her increasing pallor was down to the accident or the unexpected discovery. They were in this together, they'd have to talk about it sometime, but tonight they'd somehow run out of words.

'Very loud denial at first, then stony silence after the scan. You know Cherry, she never likes to be proved wrong.' Jackson raked his fingers through his hair.

'How about you?' Dan gave him a searching stare.

Jackson poked at a chip and stared into the middle distance. 'Let's say I'm fighting an indescribably strong instinct to run for the hills.'

'Understandable.'

Was it? How could it be? It was the worst instinct a man could have, and yet Dan sounded unperturbed.

'Actually, it's worse than that.' Jackson frowned, and focused on the small groups of people standing by a side door to the hospital, chatting and smoking. This morning his life had seemed rosy and exciting and wide, and suddenly, at a stroke, one nurse asking an innocuous question, and it had narrowed down to nothing. This was easier to say when he was looking away. 'I'm not sure I can do this at all.'

'Hey, come on…' Dan flopped an arm across Jackson's shoulder. 'It's completely normal to feel that now because of the shock. Every guy in the world who finds he's going to be a dad for the first time is shitting themselves. It's the biggest deal there is, it has to be up there as one of life's scariest moments. But the good guys all come through Jackson, you can do it, and what's more, you will. And like everything else in your life, you'll make a damned good job of it too.'

'But the whole pay-off of me giving up the racing was supposed to be the freedom.'

'You can take kids anywhere you know. They're pretty transportable, at least they are until they're teenagers and that's a long way off.'

'I guess I'm not exactly thrilled at the idea of pushing a baby buggy around the Pacific Rim.'

Dan frowned. 'Just a detail, but you do know a buggy won't run on a beach?'

Jackson looked nonplussed. 'Why the hell not?'

'The wheels get stuck in the sand, you have to carry them.' Dan gave a sniff. 'One person at the front, one at the back, it's no big deal, but you need to know, if you're planning a beach trip that is.'

'Holy crap Dan, I'm hardly at the planning stage; I'm talking hypothetically here.'

'What part of the Pacific Rim are you thinking of, anyway? It's a very wide area.'

'No idea. I saw it on a restaurant menu, it sounded good.' Jackson shrugged off Dan's incredulous stare. 'Don't look at me like that, you're the one who taught me the importance of a good sound-bite.'

Now he was sounding like he hadn't thought this through at all.

'At least you weren't thinking of heading off there on your own.' Dan narrowed his eyes, and took another bite of burger. 'So great you're thinking of traipsing round the Pacific, and tucking into that bottomless of ice-cream. But the biggie is, who's there with you, holding the bucket?'

Jackson gave a grimace. 'Cherry. Every time.'

'There you go.' Dan sent him a triumphant grin. 'I knew you'd fallen for her. There had to be more to you giving up on your career than wanting to be free, and consume ice-cream. It was the thought of spending every day with her that made you give up, wasn't it?'

'Where the hell did you get that from?' Damn to the way Dan knew him, better than he knew himself sometimes.

'I've been trying to make you see sense about giving up on the racing for months, and suddenly you do. It has to be because this amazing woman you've met has made you realise there's more to life, and nothing less than love would do that. And if you're in love, together you'll find a way through anything. So there really isn't a problem.'

Easy for Dan to say.

'But I've always seen the whole two-point-four kids, Range-Rover-on-the-drive package as a living hell.'

'That's only because you've only ever looked at it from the outside, as a footloose guy. When it's happening to you, the reality is that you've got the woman of your dreams to wake up to every morning, and it's all good. As for kids, as soon as they arrive, you're smitten.'

'Maybe.' True, the thought of Cherry being with him every day filled him with a warm, fuzzy feeling. When they'd come back from their trip to Cornwall, and he'd headed off to Spain without her, he'd felt like he'd lost a limb.

Jackson stared back at the bulky hospital building, and the lighted windows glowing in the dusk. Somewhere inside there, Cherry was being operated on. He picked up his burger, then put it down again. No way could he eat until he knew Cherry was out of theatre. He held it out to Dan. 'Can you manage this?'

'Sure.' Dan took the box from Jackson. 'In the meantime, chill. You're in love, and the rest will follow. It'll all be fine. You'll see.'

Jackson raised his eyebrows, and the corners of his mouth plummeted doubtfully. 'Thanks mate, I wish I had your confidence.'

## Chapter 46

'I think you've got everything there that Bryony might want in the morning, Jackson. She'll definitely appreciate having her make-up, and that loose cardigan will be practical and easy to put on to come home in.' Phoebe sent Jackson an affectionate smile as he zipped up the hold-all.

'Thanks for your help. I'd never have thought of taking hair straighteners.'

He'd left Cherry at the hospital around midnight, woozy, but comfortable, her arm newly plastered, with the promise to return first thing complete with supplies.

'Believe me, to some of us straighteners are indispensable.' Phoebe crossed the room, then paused for a moment as she reached the bedroom door. 'I know you're probably struggling to get your head round all this, Jackson, but it isn't just the guys who struggle. Remember, for a newly-pregnant woman there's a lot to get to grips with too, especially when it's come as a surprise. Don't mind if Bryony takes a while to get used to the idea.'

Jackson clung on to Phoebe's womanly insight. Maybe that explained the reticence. 'I thought she was desperate for kids, but she looked pretty gob-smacked when she heard.'

'That's exactly what I mean, Jackson, and her hormones will be all over the place too. Just don't take it personally, and prepare to be patient.'

'She's not joking there.' Dan rolled his eyes, and sent Jackson a meaningful stare as Jackson and Phoebe wandered into the living room. 'But kids are great, I mean you love Daisy, don't you?' Dan hurled out a joke. 'When she isn't screaming, that is.'

'Don't listen to him Jackson.' Phoebe was adamant. 'What you feel for your own kids is different altogether. It's like falling in love all over again.'

'Right.' Jackson sounded doubtful. He wasn't totally sure he'd nailed the love thing for the first time yet.

'Jackson's already over the moon, aren't you?' Dan's punch, decidedly too energetic for two in the morning, made contact with his arm.

'Getting there.' Jackson gave a grimace. 'Except…' This one was another biggie, which had been bugging him all the way home from hospital. 'What if I turn out like my own dad? I wouldn't want to inflict that on any child of mine.'

Dan shook his head. 'That's not going to happen, you really aren't like him.'

'What, I'm not a hard, limelight-seeker, who will drive his kids for his own gain, or worse still hammer them?' Jackson gave a sour guffaw. 'I just have this nightmare thought that I'll have a kid and turn into him.'

'No way. You've always been like your…'

Jackson rounded on him. 'You weren't going to say I'm like my mother, were you?'

'I was.' Dan gave an apologetic grunt. 'But only because it's true.'

Phoebe broke in. 'You two still not in touch?'

'Nope.' Jackson couldn't keep the bitter note of his voice. 'My mother walked, she got her new life, end of.'

'It's a long time ago now.' Phoebe's calm hand arrived on his arm. 'Who knows, you may find a grandchild brings you together, Jackson.'

Now he'd heard it all.

'I think we might be expecting a lot too much from this child.' Jackson shook his head at Phoebe.

'Don't underestimate it, little ones can be very powerful. Whatever, you're going to make a fabulous father.' Phoebe grinned up at Jackson. 'Isn't he, Dan?'

'Damn right he is.'

Jackson reeled at another hearty slap on the back from Dan. 'Thanks guys.'

'We haven't exactly done a lot.'

'You made me see it's possible. Earlier this evening I wanted to get on a bike, and not stop pedalling. Whereas now…' He hesitated. It seemed too much to give a name to the butterflies playing round his stomach. 'I feel much better about it all.'

But as he waved Dan and Phoebe off across the moonlit gravel, making their way back to the main house, he knew he wasn't going to get much sleep that night.

Jackson pushed his way out of the lift, arrived in front of the Nurses' Station and rested the hold-all on the floor. If the clock on the ward wall was right, he'd arrived at 9.30 sharp, just as they'd instructed him last night.

The duty-nurse put down the papers she was shuffling through, and looked up from behind her console. 'Lovely flowers – some-one's lucky.'

The cellophane crackled as he transferred the huge bouquet from one arm to the other. First thing Monday morning, one mention of a pregnant casualty, and the florist had super-sized the already gigantic bunch he'd ordered.

'They went a bit overboard with the bows.' He gave a shrug. 'I'm here for Bryony Marshall. Is it okay to go through?' Silently he cursed his stomach. It had been churning gently all through his sleepless night, and now it was whirling like a washing machine on full spin. Surely morning sickness was what expectant mothers got, not fathers.

'Ms Marshall? Right.' The nurse pursed her lips, doubtfully, and got up. 'One minute, I'll just check for you.'

She headed off down the ward.

Jackson tapped his foot impatiently, shifted his hold on the bouquet again and hoped he wasn't putting too much trust in horticulture to smooth the way with Cherry. No idea what reception he'd get this morning, but he was in this for the long haul and somehow he needed to let her know that. To take his mind off the wait, he began to study the wall posters. He read every poster on the wall at least five times over, in detail. By the time he heard the squeak of the nurse's shoes on the lino, announcing her return, he knew every sign of cancer by heart, and how to have a good time being healthy too.

'I'm very sorry.' She arrived at his elbow, slightly breathless. 'Apparently Ms Marshall signed out earlier.'

'What the hell?' Jackson's gut hit the deck. 'Are you sure you've got the right person? Bryony Marshall? She's broken her wrist.' He tightened his grip on the flowers, and the scent of freesias seeped out into the air.

'I'm afraid so.' The nurse gave him a sympathetic look. 'It caused quite a stir. Someone came and picked her up in a helicopter, it landed on the roof of one of the office buildings opposite apparently. She's definitely gone.'

Brando's flying squad. Jackson opened his mouth, then closed it again, tried to swallow away the instant urge to vomit and dragged his phone out of his pocket to check for messages.

Nothing. He blew out his cheeks.

'Fine. Thanks for that, and if that's that case I may as well leave these with you.' He balanced the flowers on the desk with a bitter laugh. 'Doesn't look like I'll be needing them.' Then he turned on his heel, and strode towards the stairwell.

# Chapter 47

'You know what Brando's like. He waltzed on in, hauled me away and here I am.'

Bryony held the phone away from her ear and screwed up her face in self-disgust at the way she was telling Jackson it was Brando's fault that she'd landed up at here at Edgerton. Hiding out in the Cotswolds was not her usual style. She could have easily stood up to Brando when he came blustering into the hospital ward, given she'd spent a lifetime perfecting the art. Any other time she'd have told Brando exactly where to stick his interference, but this morning the offer of being airlifted right out of trouble had simply been too tempting. Brando had caught her in a moment of weakness and she'd given in. Never before had his huge, rambling country house offered her so much refuge. Somehow she just needed time to come to terms with the idea that there was a baby growing inside her. Who'd have thought that something which was still only the size of a bean could turn her whole world upside down like this?

She didn't feel proud of herself for leaving Manchester, in fact she felt like the worst sort of coward for bailing. And then she'd compounded the crime by dithering, completely undecided on whether to ring Jackson, or message him, and while she was agonising over what to say he'd tracked her down and called her, so now she was in a worse position than ever.

'You can't just run away, Cherry, you're having our…'

Jackson's words would have stung more if they hadn't sounded so desolate.

Maybe he had a point, but for the time being at least, by being here she could blank out what was happening.

She'd managed to cut him off before he said the b-word. 'B', stands for baby, for bombshell. 'I know that Jackson, and I also know it's time I took responsibility for my actions. It's completely my fault I broke my wrist yesterday, and now I'm paying for my bloody-mindedness, insisting I could ride that tandem when I obviously couldn't.' Diverting him in any direction other than the obvious one here, because no way was she ready to talk about *that* situation when she hadn't started to get her own head round it yet. Her immediate rush of feeling about actually being pregnant was of surprise and delight. It was the rest of the complications that made her head for the hills.

'Yes, but I should have stopped you going on the front of that tandem, I should have protected you, that's the point.' Great. He'd taken the bait, and was running with it. 'What I'm trying to say is from now on I want to be here to protect you, and I'm going to make damned sure I look after you. You *and* the…'

Dangerous territory! She swooped in to cut him off again. 'You don't need to worry, I *am* being looked after. I had a medical check when I got here, and I'm fine.' Saying that Brando's doctor was waiting, stethoscope in hand as she'd stepped from the helicopter made it sound like too much fuss. She swallowed hard as her heart fluttered towards her throat. No way was she ready to talk to Jackson about the baby, because it would acknowledge his involvement, and she wasn't sure she could cope with that. Not yet. There were too many other things she needed to get straight in her head first. Her chest tightened at the sense that he was closing in. 'Shea's here to help too and you're flying to Spain this afternoon, so we're all good.' No need to mention that sister-in-law

Shea, having given birth herself twice in two years, had all things pregnancy-related covered.

'Holy crap Cherry, don't be ridiculous, I can't go to Spain now.'

'Sorry?' She reeled as he raised his voice. Not what she wanted to hear. 'You need to prioritise, Jackson. Dan said it's important you go to Spain to wind things up.'

He began again, more calmly. 'I'm categorically not going to Spain until I know...' He broke off, and when he spoke again his voice was grating with frustration. 'You can't just pretend this isn't happening, Cherry.'

Maybe not. But she had to be firm here, buy herself time to think and plan. She hauled in a breath, dug deep for the long-suffering, patient tone that really said don't mess with me.

'I'm fine, and there's nothing that can't wait.' Nine months – or was it seven now – was a long way in the future. Plenty of time. She shuddered and gave a mental grimace. A twang of guilt at the veiled desperation in Jackson's voice made her throw out a last reassurance. 'We'll talk when you get back.'

With any luck he wouldn't try to pin her down on that now.

'Hmmmmph. We'll see about that.'

One disgruntled groan, and he'd put down the phone.

'You know Jackson is very welcome to come and stay, anytime.' Shea put down the tea tray, pushed a stray curl behind her ear, and gave Bryony a worried smile as she sat down. 'For as long as he wants.'

Bryony quaked. Shea was a fabulous hostess, but something in that last comment sounded way too welcoming for someone who was practically a stranger to her.

'Thanks, but he's very busy. He's off to Spain, and after that he's got a whole stack of other commitments.' Bryony was surprised how convincing it sounded when she said it out loud.

'Right. So he's not exactly figuring in your immediate plans then?' Shea hitched towards the edge of the sofa and began to pour the tea.

Fleetingly, Bryony wondered why there were four mugs on the tray. 'He just retired because he wants to be free, and no way am I going to get in the way of that. And he hates the idea of families.' However comfortable she'd been feeling with Jackson, and however happy she was to be having a child, she couldn't bear to think he was only with her out of honour. Pushing him away would free him from that obligation.

'I see.' Shea's eyebrows lifted. 'So, are you two an item?'

Bryony raised her eyes up to the twinkly chandelier, gazing around the elegant spacious room that served as Shea and Brando's snug. She gave a don't-know-where-you-got-that-idea-from shrug, and wished she hadn't when pain zipped up her arm. She had to stamp on this idea, and fast.

'No, we're not even seeing each other. I was in Manchester for a dinner, but that was a total accident, and I kind of accidentally stayed on for the weekend.'

'Hence the gossip page reports Brando was hopping about?' Shea's forehead furrowed, but she still flipped Bryony a reassuring smile. 'A big weekend all round for accidents then.'

'You could say that.' Bryony grimaced. 'Jackson was appalled by the gossip reports though. I knew from his reaction to those he wasn't even ready to be a couple, let alone anything else…' Bryony's voice trailed to nothing. Where the hell had her feistiness gone?

'Here, a slice of Mrs McCaul's lemon drizzle will make things seem better.' Shea leaned across, and passed her some tea and cake. 'And I know I'm asking too many questions, but I wanted to get things straight before…' Shea hesitated.

When exactly did everyone start acting like they were treading on eggshells?

'Before Brando comes?' Bryony looked at Shea over her mug, and took a sip of tea.

'No.' Shea pursed her lips, and took a breath. 'Before Jackson arrives.'

Bryony's splutter sprayed tea across the carpet. 'What?' Her voice was a strangled shriek. This couldn't be happening.

Shea pushed back her hair, bit her lip. 'I'm sorry to be the one to break it to you, but Jackson got in contact, and Brando's flying him in, although I'm not certain it's an entirely friendly gesture. Brando seems to feel it's his place to question Jackson's motives. I'm slightly worried that Brando's only bringing Jackson here to give him a hard time. You know how Brando always wants to fight your corner.'

This had to be the last thing she wanted to hear.

Bryony dabbed the tea-soaked carpet with a tissue, then put a finger on her temple to stem the sudden throbbing. 'Why the hell are they making such a big deal out of this?'

'Well, they're men...' Shea gave a sigh. 'And often men who care jump in with both feet.'

Worse and worse. The word 'care' sent a shudder right through Bryony.

'Jackson and I don't have that kind of thing. Caring doesn't come into it, Jackson's more about...' She broke off. Hot sex wasn't what she wanted to reveal, even to Shea. 'Well, that's just not how Jackson is and I'd never ask him to change.'

'Don't underestimate Jackson. Despite their big blundering feet, men can surprise you, and sometimes they change all on their own, simply because they want to. Remember Brando?'

Bryony had to admit that three years ago, when she'd thrown Shea into Brando's life, Brando had undergone an unbelievable transformation. But this was very different. Brando had been way past ready to settle down and he'd made a free choice, whereas Jackson was just about to taste freedom for the first time in his life, and had every reason to feel compulsion here. No way did she want that on her conscience.

'You worked your own spell on Brando, Shea.' Bryony smiled across at her small, pretty sister-in-law. 'I'm not in your league, and some days Jackson is so arrogant he makes Brando seem like a lamb.'

'He should be here any time now.' Shea glanced at her watch, and flashed a rueful grin in Bryony's direction. 'Strong wills run in the family, I reckon you'll be able to swing whatever outcome you want.'

Easy to say. If only she knew what outcome that was.

'This really isn't necessary Brando.' Bryony leaned back against the sofa cushions and exhaled wearily.

'You're having his child and the guy was running out on you.' Brando stood by the tall sash window, tapping the sill.

Bryony reeled at that. One headstrong, interfering brother on high alert, so anything could happen here. Weak and floppy as she was, from somewhere she had to find the strength to rein him in. 'Technically I ran out on *him*, when you whisked me away from hospital.'

Brando gave a grimace. 'Whatever. I assume you know he's disappearing to Spain?'

So like a man to read it all wrong.

'He *has* to go, he's got work to finalise there, but if you must know he ran it by me.'

'He seemed very anxious to come here on the way.' Brando put his hands on his hips, and gave a derisory sniff. 'I'll be interested to hear what he has to say for himself. It better be good.'

Brando was *so* overstepping the mark here. Bryony picked her jaw off the floor, to plonk him firmly back in his place. 'You need to butt out. You're talking like a Victorian father, about something that's none of your business.'

At least the prickles of fury that stabbed at the back of her neck were fuelling her with energy. Brando jumping to defend her honour was not good news. He and Jackson meeting like angry bulls, both behaving like numbskulls. What an awful thought.

'We'll see.' Brando craned his neck to get a better view of the sky. 'Sounds like he's here now.'

She let out a hollow laugh. 'Unwanted guests, being flown in by chopper? Does it remind you of anything?'

Brando made a leap for the door. 'You stay here, I'll bring him in.' He bolted, and this time he didn't grin at her over his shoulder.

This was Brando getting his own back for the way she'd flown Shea in, much to his horror. Only that had worked out for the best, because she'd been in charge, whereas Brando really had no idea what the heck he was doing here. As the thrum outside got louder, she sighed, got up, and made herself saunter to the window. Definitely no need to rush.

Outside, Jackson, blasted by the down-draught from the rotor-blades, was running across the grass, all dark dishevelled hair and cheekbones, and her pulse went into overdrive. How wrong was that? Then their eyes locked, he raised his hand into a vigorous wave and his face broke into a smile that almost flipped her heart clean out of her chest.

Jackson. Beautiful, amazing, Jackson. Who hated families and longed to be free.

It had taken her all of five minutes to fall in love with the idea of having a baby. But like the world trip, a baby was her dream, whereas for Jackson it was his idea of hell. And no way could she trap him into that.

## Chapter 48

'Great place you've got here.' Jackson knew he was stating the obvious, but any conversation was good if it filled the chasm of silence that had opened up in the room. He might have been overawed by the understated luxury and understated good-taste, but one unfortunate splodge of what looked suspiciously like tea in front of Cherry's feet on the otherwise immaculate white carpet made the room feel instantly less intimidating.

It was hard to get his head round the fact that his baby was actually growing inside Cherry, when she barely looked any different, but the knowledge made him want to go and wrap his arms around her. Fat chance of that now that he'd been shown, very formally and deliberately, to a seat across the room.

Unusual for Cherry to have her feet on the floor, given that she was tucked in the corner of a sofa, and would usually have had her feet firmly folded underneath her. As it was, she was slipping her feet distractedly in and out of her Jimmy Choos. He awarded himself a silent point for brand recognition there. Maybe not quite so sure of herself as her high head and jutting chin suggested, given the way she was fidgeting. If he'd been next to her, instead of in the armchair he'd been directed to by Brando, he might have tried a whispered quip about thinking he'd landed at Downton Abbey by way of an ice-breaker. As it was, the expanse of floor between them stretched like a polar sea and her eyes were cool and guarded behind their invisible ice-wall of defence.

Jackson muttered a silent curse for whatever he'd dropped himself into here. Brando hadn't sounded unreasonable when he'd spoken to him on the phone, but judging by his face now, the helicopter ride that Brando had pressed onto him earlier was a long way from the friendly and helpful offer Jackson had assumed he was accepting.

He drummed his fingers on the soft grey velvet of the chair arm, and his wandering glance alighted on a guitar, propped casually against a sofa. Brando's glowering glances in Jackson's direction suggested he'd happily smash this over Jackson's head. There certainly wasn't going to be any matey small-talk about engines today.

'Sorry to keep you waiting.' Shea pushed through the door, and as she slid onto a sofa next to Brando she pushed back a mass of chestnut curls and slipped Jackson the hint of a sympathetic smile which he held on to very tightly. God knows he could do with some support here.

Brando leaned back, flexed his shoulders against a pile of cushions, and cleared his throat. 'So, Jackson, thanks for coming.' Brando cracked his knuckles, narrowed his eyes. 'Facing up to your responsibilities from the outset will make things easier in the long run.'

Jackson noticed Brando's cheek muscles clenching as he went straight on the attack. Across the room, Jackson saw Cherry's mouth drop open, mirroring the shocked sag of his own. He tried to find a suitable reply, but Cherry had already jumped in.

'Jackson's going traveling, so it really won't concern him.' He noted the word 'it.' So, she was still avoiding saying the word baby then. And she seemed hell-bent on getting him out of the way, unless this was her way of getting him off the hook.

If Cherry had claimed Jackson was about to embark on a spree of mass infanticide, Brando's expression couldn't have been any

292

darker.

Brando turned on Jackson. 'A time like this, and you're disappearing?'

'Yes, no, I mean…' Jackson, aware he was stumbling, fought to get a grip. 'We'd talked about a trip.'

'You're going to the Pacific Rim, Jackson, you know you are.' Cherry's protest came through gritted teeth.

'Where exactly?' Brando screwed round, and his black eyes pierced Jackson. 'It's a big place.'

Under Brando's sudden scrutiny, Jackson wasn't certain he even knew where the Pacific Rim was.

'It's not a reality, it came from a restaurant menu.' Jackson shook his head, and blew through his teeth. 'It sounded a good idea at the time.'

'You were very excited about it for something that wasn't real.' Cherry was nailing him down now. She and Brando, both gunning for him.

'You know world tours are your dream, not mine, Cherry, but I was enthusiastic.' He owed it to Cherry to be honest here, but somehow explaining he'd only been up for it when he thought she'd be coming too was setting himself up for a fall. He dragged in a breath, felt his voice grate as he spoke. 'I'd thought we'd go together.'

It was out there now – not so hard. Obviously a futile hope, though, given the dagger-looks Cherry was slinging in his direction.

'So, you two *are* together then?' Brando swooped on the word, and snatched it triumphantly, then his face softened and his shoulders dropped.

At least it appeared to have had a calming effect on Brando, whereas Cherry's eyebrows peaking towards the impressive plaster-work ceiling suggested she was becoming more irate by the second. Jackson locked eyes with her, took a breath and swallowed. 'I'd like to think we could be together, yes. I'd hoped so before, but it's even more important now she's having our child.'

Cherry's eyes broke away from his and rolled towards the chandelier above her head. 'Now you *are* being ridiculous, Jackson.'

Jackson's stomach dropped, and though he'd known it was a tentative suggestion, he still felt his chest deflating at Cherry's downright dismissal.

Brando dived in again. 'Bry, you have to give the guy a chance to do what's right here.'

Jackson gave a grimace. He might be mistaken, but it felt like Brando's hard line softened by a miniscule amount.

Shea, sitting next to Brando on one of the sofas rubbed Brando's forearm, pursed her lips and sent Jackson a helpless shrug. Meanwhile, given the way Cherry was chomping her lip and pulling at her hair, all Brando's anger appeared to have transferred to her, and then some.

Her brows descended, and she rose in her seat as she pulled her spine rigid. 'You all seem to be forgetting I'm old enough, and responsible enough to handle this myself.' Cherry, mouth welded into a horizontal line, torched them with her glare.

'Fine.' 'Whatever.' 'Of course.' Brando, Jackson and Shea replied as one.

'Well, back off, stop crowding me then.' She growled at them, through gritted teeth.

Shea leaned forwards, and put her hand on Cherry's knee. 'It's only because we care.'

'Whatever.' Cherry's scowl deepened.

'Right, well now that's cleared up, we should give you a moment…' Shea stood, yanked Brando to his feet and propelled him in the direction of the door.

'Jackson's just leaving…' Bryony's words hit the door, as Shea pulled it firmly closed behind her.

Jackson leaned forward in his seat. At least if he kept his butt on the chair, he'd be harder to dismiss. 'We'll talk when I get back from Spain then.'

'There's nothing to discuss.' Bryony appeared to be examining the huge modern oil painting hanging over the fireplace, in great detail.

'What about meeting up?' It was understandable she should blank him on the baby if she was still in shock, or denial, but he wasn't going to let her drive him out of her life that easily. 'Given what we're going to share, shouldn't we work towards something more permanent?' Noting her appalled expression, he threw in a calming qualifier. 'Maybe.'

What had he just said? If he hadn't been sitting down, hearing *those* words, coming out of *his* mouth might have made him fall over in shock. But he was pushing the boat out here, given there was so much ground to cover.

'Jackson, we're practically strangers.' Not happy with that then, given the way her eyebrows and her voice soared. Cherry was doing a good impersonation of Incredulous of Edgerton Manor. 'We've spent two weeks together all told.'

Somehow it seemed longer to him.

'Don't underestimate it, Cherry. Two weeks, together all the time, and it certainly changed me for the better.' And from where he stood, Princess Cherry hadn't come out of it too badly either, so long as you overlooked the pregnancy part, obviously. 'And I like being with you.' One afterthought, thrown in only because it was true.

'Liking someone isn't a basis for *permanence*.' She visibly shuddered as she said the word.

She was missing the point. 'Okay, tell me what is then? All your friends, who've had their Vera Wang moments…' He hesitated, sought to lock eyes with her, to see she got what he was talking about. Her eye roll wasn't quite the confirmation he'd had in mind, but it would have to do. 'Somewhere along the line, all those women had to take a leap of faith, to get to that point.'

'But Jackson, this is different, I hardly know you at all.'

And maybe she had a point, because this pale, stony, intractable woman, clutching her cardigan sleeve, blocking him at every turn, had very little to do with the fun, feisty woman he'd sparred with six weeks ago. Only the sensation of banging his head against the brick wall of her will was agonisingly familiar. She still appeared to have the ability to drive him right around the bend but in a different way this time.

He gritted his teeth. 'Okay, I get that you don't want to see more of me, but where do I fit in with the baby?' Harsh, flinging it into the open like that, but given he suspected she was seconds away from ejecting him, he had no alternative.

He'd expected her to flinch, or falter, but she came right back at him.

'Basically you don't.' She drew herself up high, against the cushions. 'I've thought about it a lot. The world is full of single parents and with the presenting work I'll easily be able to support a child. And Shea and Brando are in London a lot, and with Cressy and all my other friends I'll be absolutely fine. Leaving you free to explore your tropical paradise.'

Why did she bang on about this paradise? He tried to fight the sensation that his chest was disintegrating.

'Cressy?' His voice cracked with derision. Cherry had to be scraping the barrel there. 'Given the way Cressy legged it on Friday with the first guy she got her hands on, somehow I doubt she'll be much help.' And no idea where that random observation came from other than a frantic need to retaliate for the way she'd excluded him so neatly. Wild images flashed through his brain. Cherry, in a hospital gown, a baby in her arms. Him on a sunlounger on some palm-fringed beach being force-fed coconut ice-cream. He didn't even like coconut ice-cream dammit. Or sand. Hating every second. Why the hell would he head off to the other side of the world when the thought of walking out of the room and leaving her here now was making him feel like he had iron bands clamped around his head?

She rounded on him. 'Are you implying I'm not competent to choose my own child's babysitters?' Her shout shrilled up an octave and ended in a shriek. 'This is exactly why I have to do this on my own.'

He opened his mouth to reply but she'd gathered her momentum now, and she was in before he'd found any words to say.

'As for you condemning Cressy, what about you and your track record?' She stabbed the air with one finger of her good hand. 'Jackson Gale, blowing in, blowing out, a different woman every night.'

And she had him there. What's more, he'd walked into that one.

'I know it looks bad, but…' His half-formed excuse was obliterated by her howl of disdain.

'How the hell are you going to commit to being a father, when you can barely bring yourself to commit to a one-night stand?'

For a second her eyes bored into him, brimful of recrimination, then she dropped her gaze, shifted, and re-cradled her plaster-cast in her good hand. She may look helpless, but she had him on the ropes here.

'Good point, well made, Cherry.' In the face of that devastatingly accurate hit, any protest from him would sound hollow. He'd come here hoping they could work something out, and she'd wiped the floor with him. How the hell had this gone so wrong? He swallowed to get rid of the saliva pooling on his tongue.

'I think I'd better go now.' He pushed himself up out of the chair, limbs like lead. 'Sorry for crashing in, I was only trying to help.' He needed to find the refuge of the helicopter before he did any more damage, dammit. And he was kicking himself now because he hadn't done as she'd asked and stayed away. 'I'll maybe call you when I get back?' He hesitated in front of her, took in her bare feet, resting on top of her shoes, pink nail varnish on her toe nails.

'Whatever.' She grasped a cushion, pulled it onto her knee, hugged it to her with her good arm, but didn't meet his eye.

'I'll be off then.' His hand connected with the door knob, and his heart lurched as he saw her lips part. One tiny, crazy part of him was still hoping she was going to ask him to stay.

'Just don't expect you'll ever make me change my mind, Jackson.'

His heart-rate subsided again. One more statement from her, winding him like a punch in the guts. He grabbed one last glimpse of her, as her face slid behind a curtain of hair. Two months ago she'd been the strongest, most vibrant woman he'd ever set eyes on. Now all that was left was her grim determination, and dammit that it was him she was fighting. He clamped his jaw closed, swung out of the room, and strode towards the entrance hall.

One time he'd been a winner, but now he felt like the biggest loser ever. As for making Cherry change her mind? Somehow he doubted anyone on earth would have the power to do that. And the fact she was having his baby only seemed to make her more determined to have nothing to do with him.

## Chapter 49

'You do realise you're behaving like the bitch queen of all time here?' Cressy, perched on the desk edge and stabbed her lunchtime baguette towards Bryony in frustration. 'You're having his baby and in a whole month you haven't returned one of Jackson's calls?'

Bryony frowned, and took a bite of her third sandwich of the morning. 'There haven't been that many.' This last week her wobbling nausea had been replaced with a cast-iron constitution and an insatiable appetite. Somehow she'd expected him to be more persistent. She'd been ready to shun his flowers but they never came, and no way was she going to admit that had left her with a more than a pang of disappointment. Nor was she going to say that despite being tied up with bouts hanging over the toilet, the excitement of going for baby-scans and coping with working with her arm in a cast, she'd had a gnawing in her gut which she suspected had a lot to do with the fact she was missing Jackson like mad. She'd hoped it would go away, but it hadn't, dammit.

'If a guy looked at me the way he looks at you, there's no way I'd be giving him the brush off.' Cressy's baguette was wagging at Bryony again. 'I'd ditch my no-commitment rule and grab him by the boxers with both hands. On those gala evening photos he looks ready to devour you.'

'Jackson does a great line in lust.' Bryony wasn't about to admit how many evenings she'd spent staring at those pictures. All alone in her flat, deep down she wished there was a way to be with him without her feeling that she was forcing him into it. If they'd only got together first that would have been so different. She'd almost felt that was about to happen, almost felt ready to let it, but being pregnant was pretty irreversible, and it changed everything. She knew how resentful men could get long term when they'd been press-ganged into something, especially footloose guys like Jackson, and even if he was hiding those feelings now, they might come out later. Her dad had run out on her mum, and left a marriage he'd gone into willingly. From her own experience at home, men were unpredictable. Now it came down to it, would she put her trust in someone as unreliable as a man? It was agonising to know how much she liked him, and at the same time know it was impossible to make this work. If a tiny part of her longed for him to come back and over-ride all her objections, she was trying to ignore it. She couldn't remember a time when she'd felt this vulnerable, and she had to think of the baby, as well as herself. Hard as it was, it was surely easier all round for her to go it alone now, and avoid all three of them getting hurt later.

'No, that's a lot more than lust in Jackson's face. I know caveman protector slash total devotion when I see it.' Cressy flashed her a significant grin. 'There's no doubt about it, he's in love.'

Bryony flinched. Putting Jackson and love in the same sentence was ridiculous. Everyone knew guys like Jackson didn't do love. The bottom line was she couldn't have chosen a worse guy to get her pregnant. And damn that he still made her heart contract every time she saw his picture.

'I always wanted a family, whereas Jackson always wanted freedom.' Not that Bryony ever envisaged getting pregnant via this route, but now it had happened and she'd worked out a way forward, she was not exactly happy, but she knew it was the way it had to be. 'This way I'm saving him from what he doesn't want, and isn't cut out for. Jackson buckling down to fatherhood is a laughable thought.' And she wasn't putting either of them through that. Compulsion of this kind wasn't on her agenda, especially for Jackson. The two of them complete with pushchair, struggling over rocks to the sea. Why the heck did that picture keep flashing through her brain? She gave a decisive nod to close the subject.

'Do you have any idea how annoyingly overbearing you can be?' Cressy had her terrier-with-a-bone look about her. 'It's not your place to decide what's best for Jackson. He's a big boy – you might have to let him decide for himself.'

'And I might not.' Bryony stuck her chin in the air. If she did the deciding she stayed in control. It had been really hard to come to this point, to give up all thought of being with the only guy she'd ever truly enjoyed being with. They'd had such a great times together, even if time had been short. But she'd come to this decision to protect both of them. And if she let Jackson into the mix again, who knew what might happen?

'Jackson, what the hell are you doing here?'

Bryony's heart leapfrogged into her throat as she opened the flat door and found Jackson, one shoulder propped casually on the door frame as he waited for a reply to his knock.

For one lovely moment his eyes rested on her face. Then they slid down to her stomach, and stayed there. His Adam's apple bobbed as he swallowed hard.

It didn't take a mind reader to know, despite the lack of bump as yet, he was honing in on the baby. She smoothed down her dress self-consciously. 'Jackson…?'

'Okay, right…' Back in the room now. 'I'm here for a delivery.' He bobbed, picked up a large, flat parcel.

Relieved that his scrutiny had passed, she eyed the tall brown paper package suspiciously. 'Why didn't you ring?'

'Would you have answered if I had?'

He was right about that. Of course she wouldn't. 'You're lucky I'm even here, I'm usually out with the gang after work on a Friday.'

'I thought I'd chance it.' He spun her a nonchalant grin.

Somehow she doubted chance came into it, and she'd be having firm words with Cressy about that later. 'So what's this?' She sent a silent prayer to the God of accidental pregnancies, pleading that it was nothing baby orientated.

'Something to remind you what you're missing.' He marched past her into the flat, threw down his bag, put the parcel on the table, tore off the paper and held up a picture.

'The photo of you from the gallery! Brilliant!' Great on the one hand, but she gave a long inward groan for what it was. Jackson, larger than life had to be the last thing she needed when she was trying so hard to get him out of her system.

'That's the one.' Pulling a hammer out of his messenger bag, he marched through to the bedroom, and by the time she arrived, he was already bashing a nail into her wall. 'There you go, this is to help you get used to having me around – and to remind you that I always won because I was good at reading my opponents. I'll put it here, opposite the bed, so you'll see it when you wake up.'

So much for her perfect plaster. He flipped the picture into position, and stood back to see if it was straight. One glorious colour picture of Jackson, larger than life. As a tactic for making sure she didn't forget him it was hardly subtle. Nor was it lost on her that with one bang of a nail, he'd managed to take up virtual residence in her bedroom. Trying not to dwell on the metaphorical significance, her stomach lurched again as he shot her a pointed smile.

'You think I'm an opponent?' She tried to ignore the way his heady scent was already permeating the room.

'Right now we're opposing each other when we really should be on the same side here, Cherry.'

'Right.' Except there was nothing right about this at all. Jackson at the end of a phone she could stall and control. Jackson the whirlwind in three dimensions, rampaging around her flat was an altogether different matter.

302

He looked at his watch. 'There's another delivery arriving any minute. I got you that vintage dentist's chair you always wanted. Remember, you told me about it when you were staying at my place, we were supposed to be going to the retro shops look for in Manchester the afternoon Dan hijacked our plans. I got it to say sorry for that awful day at Brando's, I hope that's good?'

She reeled. Flowers would have been so much easier.

As for getting an eyeful of him, every time she woke up? Halfway through her despairing sigh about that one, the door buzzer went again.

'Here we go! I'll get it.' Jackson brushed her arm as he sprang past her towards the door.

Damn to the way that smallest touch set her skin vibrating. And damn, that whatever she pretended, it felt so easy having him here, even if he was annoying the hell out of her. And crap to the way she kept thinking of him as the father of her baby. But the biggest damn of all was for the shivers of need, which were slithering all the way down past the pit of her stomach, and settling like an aching chasm between her legs. What the hell that was about, she had no idea. Right now she'd have given anything to have thrown up, to have had the excuse to dash, retching, into the bathroom. But for the first time in ages, her guts were stable, which was a lot more than she could say about her lurching heartbeat, or her soaring libido.

'One dentist's chair, in position, if you're sure the bedroom's where you want it, so are you going to give it a try?' Jackson posted her a grin, and patted the leather seat.

Why the hell did he have to be so fanciable? Why the hell did he have to be so nice? Why the hell was he making her want to be with him so badly, when she'd already decided it was a completely bad idea? At least she could blame the mixed up feelings on her pregnancy hormones. She just hadn't expected the 'mixed up' it talked about in the pregnancy book, to translate into anything so

303

humongous and difficult in real life.

'It's meant for atmosphere, and as a clothes rest, it's not for sitting on.' She intended to resist, but given how patient Jackson had been, lugging it from place to place whilst she decided where it looked best, she found herself sliding on anyway, leaning back, rubbing her fingertips along the arm rests. 'It's great, just what I'd have chosen myself, thanks so much.' How the heck had he got this so right?

'And I'm so sorry for barging in on you that day at Brando's…'

Only a month ago, but it seemed much longer. As he shifted, his thigh almost brushed her elbow and her eyes slithered across his artfully faded designer polo shirt, hungry for a glimpse of skin. Tanned torso? No luck. Her gaze snagged instead on his thumb, broad and rugged, hooked into the top pocket of his jeans. Swallowing hard, she slammed the brakes on her roving eyes before they got any further. Mouthwatering maybe, but Jackson's zip was so out of bounds she shouldn't be looking at it, let alone imagining sliding it down inch by teasing inch, so her finger could slip to find the firm heat of him. Yes, she could see that too. *Holy crap, she was out of line here.* Instead she skewed her gaze to latch onto a patch of pink cloud, scudding across the evening sky.

'Brando's helicopter – three outings in a weekend!' She clutched for a thought that might head Jackson off. 'I used to commandeer it all the time when I was younger.'

'Didn't he mind?'

Great, Jackson had bitten. You could always rely on a guy to grab anything aeronautical and run with it.

'He was usually too busy to notice.' She was comfortable enough to let out a rueful grin. 'And I guess I grew out of it, I try my best not to steal it these days.'

'I should have known you needed space…pregnancy is a huge thing to take on board.'

Damn. Back where he'd started. His was voice low, and he was scarily close to talking about the baby, but the sincerity she saw as his dark hazel irises locked onto hers, knocked the bottom out of her stomach and sent a fluttering right through her torso to bang on her throat. She wasn't sure she could handle a contrite Jackson.

'I'd rather not drag it up, it wasn't the best day.' She locked her gaze back onto the sky, hoping her flat reply would stall him. She couldn't start the baby arguments again.

'I was way out of line coming when you'd asked me not to, and you had every right to question that I'd stick around, but it was good. What you said about my inability to commit set me thinking.'

She gave up on the sunset, shifted her neck against the headrest, honed in on the tiny waves of hair on his temple. 'Inability to commit' was a great euphemism for someone who went out and singlehandedly tried to shag most of the women in the world, not that she was going to point that out. She fiddled with the ragged edge, where her plaster-cast sat on her knuckles, wished she wasn't aching for him to snog her.

'Itchy?'

Dammit. One gravelly word from him, and shudders were bumping down her spine.

'Itchy as hell, but it's easier without the sling. Hair tongs are a bit difficult, but it turns out I *can* work the festival look when I'm forced to.' She ruffled her annoyingly messed-up hair.

'It suits you.' He swallowed hard.

'Not really, but thanks anyway.' She let out a sigh. A sigh for how goddam beautiful that mouth of his was, a sigh for how easy it was to talk to him, and yet another for how much she'd missed him – more than she'd even thought, now he was here. His voice, his broad shoulders, the contours of his face, his smell, already making her head giddy.

'You see I never thought about what I did with my dating, or why, before.' He raised an eyebrow. Obviously picking up the unreliable theme again here. 'But a child on the way changes every-thing, and what you said pulled me up short, so I've been working on it. It's taken me a while but I hope that's given you time too.'

305

She reeled momentarily at the way he slid the 'child' in there, then just carried on. And 'child' sounded so much more than just 'baby.'

Stretching out his hand, he wound one errant lock of her hair around his finger and gave it a gentle tug that sent rainbow tingles rippling through her scalp. She parted her lips as his face moved towards hers, pulled in a ragged breath of anticipation, half-closed her eyes, making the world blur.

'I missed you, Cherry.'

One husky whisper, hot against her cheek, that set her heart galloping. She raised her hand towards his chin, aching for the scratch of stubble on her palm, ran her tongue over her lips, waiting impatiently for the pressure of his mouth over hers. Desperately even…

He cleared his throat, and she sprung her eyes open in time to see him veering away from her, jack-knifing across the room.

*What the heck?* She shook her head to clear the chasm of disappointment, rubbed her knuckles over her bottom lip, to fill the gaping space.

Almost out of the door, and he came to a sudden halt, wedged his shoulder against the frame. 'Coming for a walk?'

'Sorry?'

What did walking have to do with anything? Was her head playing tricks with her? She was so sure he was about to kiss her back there, and it just melted into nothing. Was it just a figment of her hormone driven imagination? Given the way her morning sickness had morphed into this out of control, knicker-pumping lust, while she was looking the other way, she probably *had* imagined it. Oh, crap. She needed to find her sensible head, and fast. Because if a kiss was a bad idea, anything more would be a total disaster – and disaster areas were what she was studiously avoiding. She was pregnant. She was going to be a mum. She should be behaving responsibly here.

'There's stuff I need to tell you – it's still warm, we can go by the river.' Despite the laid back words, his face was grave, and his eyes were anxious. 'It'll be easier to explain when we're out.'

Hard to resist a look that worried, that imploring. Impossible, when he came back towards her, grasped her good hand and tugged her fingers. Pulling her, yet somehow keeping her at arm's length? Nice move. And she should be grateful for it, given that snogging him was the last thing she should do. Anything physical could only complicate an already out of hand situation.

'Fine, I don't need to change.' Somehow taking any of her clothes off with him in the same flat seemed like a very dangerous idea even if he was in another room. The way her lust-fairies were working, undressing when he was in the same city would seem like folly.

'I'll just grab the hammer before I forget. I borrowed a baby one to bring, in case you didn't have one.' He scooped it up off the bedroom console as he passed. 'Sorry, bad choice of word, jumping in with my size elevens again.'

Damn, she'd hoped he hadn't noticed her reaction. 'What are you talking about, Jackson?'

'I felt you flinch when I said the word baby.'

Nothing so small – she'd practically jolted his arm off. She needed to explain, and fast. 'Even though I'm happy, I still get a bit of a shock every time I'm reminded. I'm trying to think of it wherever I can though, trying to live up to my new responsibilities.' Saying it out loud might make her act them out more, and think about jumping him less. 'No worries, so long as you aren't about to whip out a Babygro, I'll be fine.'

She watched his eyebrows descend as his eyes flickered in a guilty arc towards his messenger bag.

*Holy crap.* He *had* come with a Babygro. She'd stake her life on it. And not only a Babygro, but enough pheromones to drive her libido round the bend. He was the human equivalent of dynamite, fully charged, poised to blow her carefully crafted solo existence into orbit.

'Ready to go, Cherry?'

Tilting his dark head against the wall as he waited by the door, one raised eyebrow, and a whole armoury of slow blinks, turning her entire day upside down and shaking it. Hard.

'Whenever you are.' She grabbed a jacket, kicked into a pair of open boots, with heels stable enough for a night-time of pavement tramping.

The sooner she got Jackson out of her danger zone the better.

# Chapter 50

'I love the city at dusk. It's magical when the lights come on even though the sky's still blue.'

Jackson stared across the Thames to the twinkling outline of the Millennium Wheel as they sauntered and let Cherry's running commentary flow over him. Ridiculous, but somehow he'd expected her to be looking more pregnant, acting more pregnant, acknowledging it more. She didn't even have a hint of a bump yet, from what he could see, and yes, despite his best efforts, he couldn't keep his eyes away from her stomach. No, definitely no bump, even from this angle.

Her chatter was incessant, yet soothing as he let it wash over him.

'There's a whole city around, but somehow this stretch of pavement alongside the river is really quiet.'

She was keeping an acre of pavement between them, which maybe was no bad thing, given he was finding it impossible to keep his hands off her. Crowding her was the last thing she needed, he had to give her space, and back there he'd almost blown it by diving in and snogging her face off. Hardly his fault, when she did look practically edible, especially with her rumpled hair giving her that extra sexy come-to-bed look. But if he was here for the long game, he had to play it cooler than that. He definitely needed to stick his fist in his mouth every time the word child was about to come out. There was too much at stake to rush this. He was thanking his lucky stars he'd managed to coax her this far without getting kicked into touch.

'The river is brilliant in the evening; I love the way the lights are reflected in the water. I often come down here when I want to have a quiet think.'

Nothing quiet about her fast forward chatter tonight.

'Walking's good for talking if the last ten minutes are anything to go by, not that I've managed to get a word in edgeways.' He bowled that across the wide stone pavement towards her, further away than ever now and wondered if she was even close enough to hear.

'Sorry, I'm just a bit…' She swallowed her words, shuffled her shoulders, and shot him a sideways glance. Nervous, edgy, ill at ease? Whatever it was, she wasn't about to admit it. 'Here I am rattling on, and you're the one we're supposed to be listening to. So, how was Spain?'

If that was a diversionary tactic, it wasn't going to work.

'Spain was great, thanks. Dan was right, it was good to go and it brought a lot of issues into focus. I went, knowing I was giving up, and this time I was like an outsider, looking in on the whole cycling world. That was really useful. It made me aware of a lot of things I hadn't even noticed before.' He screwed himself up for what was to come, and took a deep breath. Speeches about himself were the last thing he was comfortable with but there were times when you had to step out of your comfort zone. 'When you're eighteen, and winning cycling races, there's no shortage of girls taking an interest in you. Winners are sexy, they're attractive, they're alpha-males, there to be picked off and the more successful you get, the more women throw themselves at you. It's like you become a trophy lay. The guys who have relationships find this whole scene puts a lot of pressure on them, because however hard you try to avoid them, there's always some hot babe draping herself over you, and more often than not, it's a lot more than one. There's a whole heap of temptation, and a whole lot of reasons for jealousy, especially for partners who often aren't there. If you stay a free agent, at least you sidestep the difficulties.'

'Hmmm'

That had brought her chatter to a halt, and caused her to veer across the pavement slightly, this time bringing her closer to him, although she was still staring firmly at her feet.

'It's flattering, it's fun, guys are susceptible and I was no different. I hold my hands up to that. But you're right to imply that most guys grow out of it, or at least learn to handle it, and get into relationships.'

'But you didn't.'

'Nope. And I'd never really questioned why before. I admit when we met I was trying to clean up my bad-boy act but only to make my life easier by getting the press off my back. I'd never stopped to think seriously about it, until the day you put me under fire and I didn't have a leg to stand on. So when I went back to wrap up with the team in Spain I dropped in for a chat with the psychologist. They're mostly there to help with confidence and motivation, but they know about other stuff too. Apparently, boys whose parents split up when they're teenagers often find relationships hard.'

'That's you, isn't it?'

'My mother upped and left when I was seventeen.' He shrugged. Out there again, but this time he knew their future depended on him opening up. The thought of having a child of his own, becoming a parent himself, had made him see his own parents in a whole different light.

She was close by his elbow now. 'I know, you told me that day in the park, but I knew you didn't want to talk about it then. How did you feel about it?'

The sweet scent of her hair tickled his nostrils.

'Angry mostly, because my life had been ripped apart. Before the split, home life was always dominated and driven by my dad, but my mum made home comfortable. She always waded in to

311

protect us from his harsher side when we were younger, but after she left, it was rough. Connor, Nic and I stayed with my dad, and with four guys it wasn't exactly homely. He bad-mouthed my mother incessantly, and we never questioned that because she was the one who'd left. I suppose we held her responsible for all the hurt and when she wanted to see us we wouldn't have any of it. And I guess what I took into adult life was that it wasn't worth investing in a relationship, if it was only going to come crashing down. As a winner, there were always new girls queuing up for my attention. By avoiding relationships, it meant I never had to trust anyone, and I never risked getting hurt. It's like I was too scared to trust, so I made sure I never had to, not that I ever thought that was responsible for the way I lived my life.'

'Jackson…' Her hand landed lightly on his forearm, making every hair on his skin quiver.

'When my parents split I went right off the rails and there was no one to stop me. I went wild, partying round the clock. Drinking and faceless sex were an oblivion that helped to blot out the pain. But I had no idea those patterns were going to be set in stone for the best part of the next twenty years, or that it would take the thought of me being a parent to realise I should have changed my ways years ago.'

'And what happened to your mother?' Cherry's wrapped her arm through his, and her hip swung in rhythm with his own as they walked.

'I didn't see her, I locked every thought of her away, kept her in a box in my head along with the hurt and the blame. When I saw the psychologist, he suggested I needed to give her a chance to tell me her side of the story. She's living in France now, in Brittany. So I screwed up my courage and called in, on my way back from Spain.'

'Oh my.' Cherry's exclamation was little more than a breath. 'How was it?'

'It was hard at first, but at least now I understood exactly why she left. My dad bullied her, like he bullied us, and made her life a misery but she didn't have success to hold his attention and soften his harder side. She put up with hell, she stayed until she knew we were old enough to survive without her, and yet all these years I blamed her, for something that wasn't her fault. I was old enough, I should have seen the truth, I should have kept up the contact and I feel so guilty for that now I understand better.'

'That's so awful, but I bet she's so happy to be in touch with you again.'

'We have a lot of lost years to make up for. But do you know, she had every race clipping. Ever since she left she'd carried on following our progress, even though we'd cut her off. For all those years I thought she'd ditched us, when in reality it was pretty much the other way around.'

'It's making me cry…' Cherry sniffed, pushed a tissue to her nose, and rubbed her cheek against his chest.

'I expected to meet a stranger, but instead I found someone who had left, but who never stopped loving me.'

As Jackson paused to swallow the lump that was blocking his throat, Cherry swung around in front of him, and the warmth of her cheek banged soft against his neck. Burying his face in her hair, he dragged in a breath.

'And I have you to thank for that. You were strong enough to point out my shortcoming, and by facing up to it and trying to sort myself out, I found my mother again.' With one finger, he tilted Cherry's head back and met her clear eyes, shiny with tears. 'But in the end, it's not sad; it's good, because talking to her set me free, just like the psych hoped it would. All this time I thought I couldn't trust, because of the way she let me down, but actually she didn't let me down at all. She was there for me all the time, I just didn't choose to see it. Knowing that, I have no reason not to trust, and no reason to fear commitment, and that makes me confident I *could* be there for a child. I wouldn't have any reason to run out, because more than anything, I *want* to be there for our child.'

He wasn't even going to talk about being there for *her* – that was one step too far for now. That part he had to keep to himself. No way could he risk scaring her. Cherry had her face turned up to him, her lips slightly parted, and this time, whatever the risk, he had to bring his mouth down, to taste. Softly, gently, the lights across the river blurring in his peripheral vision, as he closed his eyes. Tentative, tender, delicious. Warm, like coming home. Easy, like a summer day. And then as she responded, hot and strong and hungry, her tongue delving deep, her body thrusting against his, their two lusty libido's kicked in and all hell broke loose.

'Hey, get a room…'

No idea how long they'd been devouring each other when that shout, from some passing skateboarders, forced them to break that kiss. Move their heads apart.

'Maybe we should…' Jackson's voice was gruff.

Cherry standing on tip toe, hissed in his ear. 'There's hot chocolate at home if you fancy?'

Reeling for a moment, he could hardly believe what he was hearing. Not that he'd dared to hope for this, and his pumping chest was aching in case he did something to blow it. 'Now you're talking.'

He slid his hand down and closed his fingers around hers, then he slowly whirled her around and eased her in the direction of her flat.

# Chapter 51

Trying to keep her hands off Jackson as they walked home had been one big problem, but necessary, seeing as any PDA's were likely to get entirely out of hand, given the gaping ache that was throbbing between her legs. Allowing him back to the flat, inviting him even, was a huge about turn for her, and she knew it had big implications. She really didn't want to lead Jackson on, to imply an involvement with him she couldn't follow through on. She might be opening herself up to a lot of hurt here, but he'd put in so much effort on his part, trying to sort out the tangles of his past so he could step up for his new role. That had to show a level of commitment and interest on his part. She hadn't forced him into going to see his mother, which must have been hard for him, and since he'd put himself through that it seemed only fair that she should rein in her fears and give him a chance, just for this evening. Give a little, without getting into too much danger. She'd reined in her wildest excesses and managed not to flatten him against the wall of the stairwell and jump him as they came up to her flat. Note that sensible girl she was, she'd avoided the lift altogether, putting confines like that in the 'way too dangerous' category. To think she'd been alarmed by those teensy tweaks of desire when they'd been at the flat before, whereas now this was lust with a capital 'L'. Lust, with the caps lock stuck completely

315

on, more like, and where the hell had this come roaring in from? And more to the point, how the heck was she going to handle it? She pushed her key into the lock, swung into the flat ahead of him, and took refuge behind the kitchen counter simply to gain a bit of thinking time. Not easy when your brain felt like blurry, cotton-wool, due to your body screaming 'yes' and every bit of your sensible mind yelling 'NO, NO, NO.'

She clattered a couple of cups down onto the counter, flung open the fridge door and made a grab for the milk.

'Tell me you're not…' Jackson arrived, put both hands on the granite counter edge, and smouldered across at her.

Glad that Jackson had moved to the less dangerous side of the counter, she slammed down a saucepan and slopped in some milk. 'Not what?'

'Making hot chocolate?' His gritty voice was low enough to resonate through her.

'Stop undermining me, and go and sit on the sofa.' At least she'd stand more of a chance of resisting him if he was further away, and didn't blast her with his scent at every turn. Maybe she was feeling like this because back there she felt so sorry for Jackson and all she'd wanted to do was wrap her arms around him and make his hurt go away. Perhaps this was her crazy pregnancy protection hormones surging into action hoping to make him feel better. Or maybe too, it was her wholehearted appreciation for what he'd put himself through to make himself good enough for the job ahead. If ever she'd seen a guy man up, this had to be it.

'Fine, I thought you might need some help that's all.' He lowered himself onto the sofa, threw one careless arm across the back, stuck one foot on his knee. All delicious and relaxed then. 'Distant memories of when you set off every smoke alarm in Dartmouth trying to make cocoa?' Rubbing his thumb pensively on his bottom lip, he flipped her one decidedly dark grin and shifted his hips.

Damn those creases in his cheeks. Damn the man for his easy, knee-wobbling sexuality, and the way he was so obviously flaunting that giant bump in his trousers. And damn to how goddam irresistible it was, and that she really wasn't going to be able to stop herself from going to touch it. Except she had to, given she was trying to keep this simple and no more horribly complicated than it already was.

'Smoke alarms? That was ages ago – there's been a lot of water gone under a lot of bridges since then.' And gallons of hot chocolate consumed in the name of keeping her nausea at bay, not to mention a whole month of no sex. No sex, coming straight after enough sex in one weekend to last most people a lifetime, and maybe her body was just needy for a tiny bit more. Needy in a desperate, ravenous way, okay, but needy being all it was, and one bang with Jackson might just sort that out. She squirmed, momentarily stunned by the base nature of that thought and the involuntary contraction volley it set off between her thighs.

'I know you have a weakness for firefighters, but there's no need to call in the fire-brigade when I'm completely happy to take on the job myself.' One more delectably awful shift of his hips. 'Just saying…' Another heart-pummelling grin.

Oh no. She set down the milk, walked deliberately around the counter and crossed the room. Already imagining how it was going to feel rubbing her breasts across that stubble. Just for a moment, she paused in front of him, on the sofa. Then, thanking God that she'd put on a skater dress, she lunged, caught one tanned hand in each of hers, flipped her skirt aside and, as she crashed her crotch onto his, she pinned down his arms. 'That's enough…' Except now she was here, the thrust of him against her pants, through the soft denim of his jeans, was already sending her to heaven, one glorious grind at a time. She made herself steady her hips.

'Hey, careful, mind your arm…' A pained expression passed across his face, and as he withdrew his defences, his body went limp, in all but the one, most crucial, area.

'My arm's almost mended, the plaster's coming off soon.' She shook her hair over her eyes, feeling a little exposed here, but couldn't help settling herself further onto him.

'And how have you been, apart from your arm? Aren't pregnant women supposed to feel like death and throw up all over the place?'

She gave a low laugh. 'I've managed to do all of that, and a lot of sleeping. As for the throwing up, I've no idea why it's called morning sickness, because mine went on day and night.' Noting his horrified expression she hurried to reassure him. 'But it's suddenly eased off, and now I'm eating like a horse. What about you, how's your retirement going, what are you doing?' Small talk, albeit about things she wanted to know, was a good way of avoiding the issue pushing up so nicely between her legs.

'Leaving the team isn't as much of a shock as I'd anticipated.' He rubbed a finger gently up and down her inner thigh as he spoke. 'I'm still going to work with the younger riders on and off until my contract runs out. The British team have been in touch about coaching too, maybe even full time. Dan's gone into over-drive sorting TV appearances and public speaking stuff. I'm hardly going to have time to get out on my bike.'

'Hey, that's great.' How could one finger grazing her thigh make her ache for him so badly? She settled further down onto him. 'I told you it would work out, didn't I?'

'And what about…?' He sounded very unsure. 'Is this even allowed? Should I even be touching you at all? Jeez, what if I…?'

Something about his rush of concern sent a warm glow firing through her body. 'It's fine, Jackson, the doctor said as long as I'd like to, it's actually beneficial.' Noting how they were carefully missing out all the more loaded words, skirting around actually saying it out loud, made her smile.

His voice was gruff as he sent her a loaded smile. 'I hear hormones can work wonders on your libido.'

'Hear from where?' Sheesh, if he'd googled 'pregnant and desperate for sex' and read the same results she had, he'd be expecting her to eat him whole.

'Dan and Phoebe have been through this twice don't forget,

you women aren't the only ones who share information…' He gave a guilty grimace. 'And I couldn't help noticing a certain toy on your bedside earlier.'

'What?' As she squirmed under the scrutiny of his deeply searching gaze, she knew, from the heat, that her cheeks were scarlet. Damn the man for crashing into her private space, and an even bigger damn that she hadn't tidied up after herself.

'Nothing to be ashamed of, Cherry.' His lips twitched, as if he was holding in his laughter.

'I'm not ashamed.' She gave a carefree toss of her head. 'Except maybe for how messy the flat has got with me operating one-handed.' She aimed for nonchalant and no way could she begin to admit to him that the toy in question hadn't come anywhere close to satisfying her need.

'Personally, I see messy as a good thing, if it means you're easing up on the control.' Funny how the resonant burr of his voice soothed her. 'And anyway, I seem to remember you enjoyed a bird's eye view of me in the shower one time…'

Soothing, and then he comes out with that? 'Crap, Jackson, why bring that up now?'

He was laughing openly. 'Well, doesn't it kind of make us equal?'

She pursed her lips, shook her head. 'I really have no idea.' Except she did, because he'd made the perfect observation.

'So would you…like to?' His voice, like rough sandpaper, sent shivers over her body.

'Maybe…' Only the size of what she was sitting on, and the certainty of where it was going, gave her the leeway to feign indifference. Suddenly aware that her nipples were sticking through the thin fabric of her dress far enough to be practically poking his eyes out, she dipped her shoulders, lowered her mouth to his ear. 'Once might be *exactly* what I need.'

# Chapter 52

Bryony woke next morning from the deepest sleep she'd had in ages, satiated and deeply comfortable. Stretching a lazy arm across the bed, her tummy lurched in alarm when, instead of warm man, she found cold space. Prising her eyes open, she jumped at the view of Jackson's line-crossing face grimacing on the opposite wall. *Oh my. This to look forward to on a daily basis?* Then, as she scanned the pillow beside hers, her lips curled into an involuntary smile and she let out a sigh of relief. Even if the clock showed she'd been mistaken in that it was afternoon not morning, at least the indentation in the pillow was proof that she hadn't slept alone, proof that she hadn't dreamed the last twelve hours. No way was her dream imagination capable of conjuring up anything as hot as the non-stop sex they'd enjoyed last night. So that was the old 'one time would be enough' theory out of the window then.

'Hey.' She looked up as Jackson wandered into the bedroom and brought her musings to an abrupt halt.

'I made tea given the kitchen seems to be a coffee exclusion zone. I take it the morning sickness put you off it?'

Nothing quite as promising as a guy in low-slung jeans and nothing else, carrying a full breakfast tray. One time? Seemed like one night hadn't been enough given the twang in the pit of her stomach, announcing that her body was already screaming for an action replay.

'Tea's perfect. You've been out to the bakery? How did you know I'd be ravenous?'

'A calculated guess.' He grinned as he set down the tray, and sat down on the bed. 'I know you better than you think, you know.'

Sideways glances like that she could do without.

'A brave claim, Mr Gale.' She took the mug he offered, bit into an almond turnover, and brushed the stray flakes of pastry off her fingers. 'But then, you're a brave man.'

'Not sure about that.' He cradled his own mug thoughtfully. 'One thing I do know, though – it's good to wake up next to you again.'

*Ditto.* She sipped her drink and wished she didn't agree quite so wholeheartedly.

'Whatever.' If Jackson in her flat was achingly comfortable, Jackson in her bed was beyond delicious, but she couldn't afford to seem needy. 'Being bashed round the head with a plaster-cast in your sleep has to be an acquired taste.'

'You know, maybe it's time to mention, I'm not only here because of the baby, Cherry.'

'No?' Where the hell was he going now? As if there could be any other reason.

'I'm here because I want to be with you, and that's got nothing to do with the baby at all. I'm here because you make my life better, and you have done every minute we've spent together.'

What? The words blurred as her brain struggled to keep up. A guy talking about 'every minute' had to set the alarm bells ringing.

'Jackson…' She fired up her best 'I don't believe I'm hearing this/please shut up' tone, but from the decided set of his jaw, he wasn't about to take notice. She pulled her knees up to her chest, hugged the quilt around them and braced herself for whatever was coming next.

'The day you suggested that world trip, I knew it would be great if I did it with you, because that was the only way I'd enjoy it. But now I know it's more than that, a lot more…'

'Jeez, Jackson…' She heard her voice squeal in protest as her throat constricted. How the hell had he got here? This wasn't how it was meant to be. She took a nervous slug of her drink.

'All this heat that won't go away, the fact I can't get you out of my head, that every day I spend without you is hell – I'm definitely not an expert, it's taken me long enough to work it out, dammit, but in the end I'm here because of one thing, and one thing only – I love you, Cherry.'

'What…?' The tea she'd just gulped hit her windpipe, and returned across the bed in an accelerating spray as she coughed.

'I love you, I'm trying to tell you that I…'

As her body gyrated as she choked, the rest of the mugful of tea slapped all over her plastered arm. 'Oh crap, now look what I've done.'

An immediate flight response kicked in as adrenalin coursed through her body. Before she knew it she'd hared across the bedroom, and was sitting on the floor in the en-suite bathroom, breathing heavily and listening to the echo of the slamming door.

Omigod. Had she really done that? She threw her hair back off her face, banging her head against the bath side, shaking with self-disgust. Jackson had put himself out there, and all she could do was to spit tea in his face and run away.

What kind of a cow did that make her?

A scared one, given the way she was shaking, and a confused one – because although it had been bliss having him back for the night, and she liked him, and life without him seemed like it had a hole the size of the South America in it, the idea of him loving her was frightening beyond measure. She had no clue in the world how to cope with him loving her, or, so much worse, loving him back. She'd sometimes wondered if she already loved him, but love was always safe, so long as it was only one way. If he loved her, that might mean she'd fall in love with him too, and that was too much to handle, too much to risk. Because the moment she liked him too much, or worse still, loved him, all she could think of, was that he was going to walk away, and she couldn't bear the thought of the hurt that would cause her. Strangely, she could have been with him more easily if she hadn't liked him, and didn't care. But she had a feeling that she liked Jackson too much, way too much, to risk the hurt of losing him. And love was one of those explosive things. One-way love was safe. She'd loved Matt for years with no danger of getting hurt, because a) it wasn't mutual, and b) the feeling wasn't real love, and deep down she'd always known it. Matt was safe as houses, and by the time he'd shown any interest, she'd come to her senses and seen him for what he was. But two-way love was a different matter entirely, a total unknown. Loving someone, and finding that love reciprocated? That was a recipe for disaster. Because just one time, there was that one man she'd loved, who also loved her, but then he'd left. And that had smashed her heart into a thousand aching pieces that left her broken for years. No way was she letting that happen again.

She'd needed to do this slowly, and on her terms, and maybe even then she wouldn't have got there. Now, all her control had gone right out the window. Sad to say, as soon as Jackson had said the word love, he'd pretty much blown it for both of them.

# *Chapter 53*

The chaos of the fracture clinic on a Friday morning was some-thing Bryony was willing to endure simply because she knew it was the only way of getting her plaster off, but it definitely wasn't the place she'd have expected Cressy to tag along to, even in the name of being a BFF. Pub crawls, parties, anything involving hot available men would have been right up Cressy's street, whereas X-ray, well, not so much. And morning was fast becoming after-noon, as progress was very slow.

Today, Cressy was pulling out all the stops to try to cheer her up. Despite the fact that Bryony wasn't in the mood for games she'd insisted they play their all-time fave sitting around game of giving out rankings to guys as they walked through the door. In the end it wasn't going so well, and nothing to do with Bryony having a face like a wet weekend, nor all the candidates being old or broken. If Bryony anticipated that would be the main drawback of playing in an x-ray department, she was wrong. Contrary to her expecta-tions *and* the law of averages, most of the guys coming through the door looked to her as if they might have got lost on the way to a Vogue photo shoot. If past experience was anything to go by, and yes, Bryony was an expert given Cressy was more addicted to this game than she was to *Flappy Bird*, most of the guys should have been scoring at least an eight on Cressy's dedicated hottie scale. And strangely the guys Bryony – acting in her completely uninvolved, yet expert due to long-time experience capacity – had down as dead cert tens were only getting sevens from Cressy.

As the nurse with the shouty glasses and the clipboard came out and called someone else rather than her, yet again, Bryony decided it was time to query.

'So what's with all the low scores then, Cressy?'

Another time, another place, with less waiting space to ponder, Cressy's out-of-character behaviour might have escaped Bryony. But here, three hours in, even pre-occupied Bryony began to analyse, and once she considered it carefully, Cressy hadn't seemed herself on the man front for quite a while.

'What do you mean low scores? As usual I'm bang on target, no way that last guy merited anything more than a four even if he hadn't been on crutches.' Cressy's squawk of protest woke up the woman two seats away, who ironically dropped her *Pick Me Up* magazine.

Bryony studied the hunk in question again and concurred. 'Fine, I'll let you off with that one, because basically it's not the fours I'm talking about, it's the nines and the tens. From where I'm sitting there's been a shedload of those, and yet the most you've scored anyone is a seven.'

'What is this, a moderating meeting?' Cressy sent her a defiant scowl. 'Attractiveness is a subjective thing.'

'Possibly, although I'd argue we've been studying it long enough to make it an objective science.' Bryony feeling suddenly guilty for being too wrapped up in her own worries to notice, gave Cressy a softening nudge with her elbow. 'Had any nice ones lately then?'

Cressy pulled down the corners of her mouth. 'Not especially'

Also out of character, given Cressy usually needed a gag her to stop her sharing every last gory detail with the entire office. When Bryony came to think about it, the last time she remembered seeing Cressy with a guy was at the Gala Evening, when she'd been pretty wrapped up to say the least. Bryony gave an inward groan. Talk about being blinded by your own problems – this was majorly significant. How had she missed this?

'So, what about the guy from Manchester?' With the pregnancy and her broken arm, Bryony had neglected to do immediate catch up. Usually where Cressy was concerned, one missed guy was a drop in the ocean as she'd already have moved onto the next.

'What about him?' Cressy's expression was impassive.

What, no information dump? That was a giveaway in itself. Bryony wasn't letting her get away with this – something was definitely going on here.

'You went off with him after the Gala didn't you but you never said what happened? So who was he, where was he from?' Bryony tried to make the enquiry sound casual.

'No one important.' Cressy looked away, uncrossed her legs and stood up. 'Fancy a coffee?'

'Great idea.' Bryony sent her a grin to let her know she was completely busted. 'Nice try, Cressy. Sit down and spill. And *then* we'll talk about coffee.'

If Cressy was being evasive this had to be big.

Cressy sat on the edge of her seat and leaned towards Bryony. 'He's a doc, he lives in London, his name's Charlie and he didn't put out.'

'Right.' Bryony tried to stop her eyes widening. No guy had ever *not* put out for Cressy. Most of them were pressing themselves onto her, often literally, within seconds of meeting her. 'So, is he gay?'

'Nope. Just playing hard to get.' Cressy's smile was perplexed yet determined. 'But I will get him, it's just taking me longer than I expected.'

'So you're seeing him while you wait then?'

'Yep. It's quite a few weeks now.'

Wow, this was a first. Bryony reeled and tried to play down how excited she was on Cressy's behalf. Almost sounded like it constituted dating. Turn up for the books or what?

'So, is he a ten then?' Bryony had to ask.

Cressy sighed wistfully. 'Nope, I'd say he's nearer a fifteen.'

And obviously no one else was coming close, hence the tens being downgraded to sevens.

'Oh my. I guess it had to happen sometime.' Bryony gave Cressy's hand a squeeze. 'I hate to say it, but welcome to my world. Shall we get that coffee now?'

# Chapter 54

'If a guy tells you he loves you, the *last* thing you do, Bryony Marshall, is kick him out, especially if you're pregnant with his baby.'

All the more reason if you're pregnant with his baby, and you're trying to keep two of you safe. Obviously, Bryony hadn't made any progress making Cressy understand that.

As Cressy's incensed shout boomed round the waiting area, Bryony made a grab for a magazine, and cowered behind it. How did such a small person have such a huge voice, anyway? Not that Bryony had planned to tell anyone at all about what happened that dreadful Saturday morning two weeks earlier, and in fairness she should have kept her guard higher, knowing that Cressy would be straight back onto her own case after she dragged Cressy's secret out into the open. It hadn't taken a mind reader to know that Bryony had been low, and given that perfect excuse Cressy had swooped and finally wheedled it out of her. But whereas Bryony had been uncharacteristically restrained with Cressy's news, once Bryony had shared, Cressy didn't return the discretion.

'There wasn't any kicking; I was very polite.' Bryony's insides still shrivelled every time she relived the agonised expression on Jackson's face, when she'd finally emerged from the bathroom and quietly asked him to leave. Stone-walling his attempts to find out what was wrong had wrung her heart out, but in the end, it had been a matter of self-preservation. Had to be done.

'Eventually you were polite.' Cressy gave a disgusted snort. 'Meanwhile, spitting tea over someone, then screaming and locking yourself in the bathroom is neither mature, nor attractive.'

Exactly when did Cressy become the authority on being mature when it came to men? Finding one she fancied enough to see more than once counted a lot less than Cressy thought it did.

'Surprisingly, appearing attractive wasn't top of my priorities at the time.' Feeble sarcasm wasn't going to get her far in stopping Cressy's tirade. It was such a bad mistake to rake this up again when she'd already mentally buried it, and made a monumental effort to move on.

Although waking every morning to see Jackson in glorious four foot high Technicolor close-up on the wall opposite her bed, and knowing that she couldn't bear to be with him was agony, somehow the thought of taking the picture down was even worse. And knowing that she didn't have the guts to be with him was breaking her heart one awful day at a time. Her new-found appetite had disappeared and all she'd been doing was working and sleeping, with no energy for either. She'd thought it would get easier with time, but if anything it was getting harder.

'To be honest, I'm astonished he's even trying to get back with you given the way you've behaved. I'm not sure I would.' Cressy made no attempt to hide her disgust

'There's no getting back, Cressy, because we weren't ever together. And *how's* he trying, I haven't even heard from him?'

'Oh shit.' Cressy dipped, and fumbled in her bag. If Bryony hadn't known that Cressy never blushed, she would have sworn Cressy's cheeks were pink. Without retrieving anything, Cressy sat up again. 'Office full of flowers not mean anything to you? Jackson has to be keeping the London floristry industry afloat single-handed.'

A nurse with a clipboard appeared from behind the reception

desk. 'Bryony Marshall, cubicle three please.'

'Great, Bry, that's you, let's go!' Cressy grabbed her bag, and arrived at the nurse's elbow with surprising speed and enthusiasm, leaving Bryony to sit and ponder.

Something was going on. Bryony wasn't sure what it was, but Cressy's expression was definitely guilty. Cressy had whisked her off on Jackson's behalf once too often, and she wouldn't be falling for that again, whatever Cressy hoped.

'I break my wrist, and I'm fine; they take the plaster off, and I pass out. What sort of a wimp does that make me?' Bryony glanced dejectedly at her cardboard sick tray, and readjusted the pillow on the hospital trolley.

'Pregnant people faint all the time, you might need to get used to it.' Cressy patted Bryony's arm. 'Don't worry, they said it happens to lots of people when they have their plaster taken off too. How are you doing?'

'Better now thanks, and less of the "pregnant people" please. At least having to lie here for ten minutes means I get a chance to ask you stuff.' Bryony sensed Cressy stiffen, which suggested Bryony's instinct was right, so she braced herself and went in for the kill. 'What did you mean about Jackson trying to get back with me?'

Bryony watched as Cressy shuffled on her orange plastic seat, sniffed and then examined the ceiling intently.

Bryony's growl came between clenched teeth. 'Don't think for a minute you'll get away with not telling the truth here.'

Cressy sighed. 'Jackson's desperate to be with you, and it's not just me he's press-ganging, he's been in touch with Shea and Brando too. It's understandable, with the baby and everything.'

'Oh my…' Bryony sagged back into her pillows.

Cressy held up her hands. 'I'll come clean, I'm supposed to be putting you into a taxi this afternoon, as soon as your appointment is over, and sending you down to the south coast.' Cressy rested her chin on her hand.

'But aren't we covering hockey this weekend?'

Cressy's eyebrows touched her hairline. 'Covering isn't the best word choice, given it's men's *naked* hockey, and I didn't put you on the crew, as you're technically spoken for elsewhere.'

'Holy crap.'

Cressy nodded. 'My thoughts exactly, but we'll hopefully be zooming in for face, feet and back shots.'

Bryony's disgruntled growl grew to a wail. 'For chrissakes, Cressy, I'm talking about Jackson, not hockey. What the hell is he playing at?'

'Right.' Cressy shrugged, diffidently. 'Jackson is shooting some programme about sports celebs and designer houses, and Dan's blagged this lighthouse conversion for the whole weekend afterwards, which is where you and your taxi come into the picture. Dan does a damn good job, you have to hand it to him.'

'Well, thanks for sharing that, Cressy.' Bryony bit back the explosion she wanted to unleash and settled for sarcasm. Again.

'You look like you want to nuke me – don't shoot the messenger, I'm only trying to help here.'

'Whatever.'

Help like this she could do without. Right now, Bryony couldn't decide if she was appreciative or cross. But she was damned sure that if she ever got into that taxi, she'd be getting right back out again.

# Chapter 55

'Cressy, hi, I take it Bryony's decided not to come after all?'

Jackson had driven five miles before he'd found a signal, and then he'd waited two hours in the dark in a faceless lay-by beside a hedge for Cressy to pick up her phone. Waiting he could do, if that's what it was going to take, but somehow he hadn't envisaged it would be this hard to get what he wanted with Cherry. He dragged in a breath, and braced himself to hear the worst.

'She didn't arrive?' Cressy, even at this distance, sounded doubtful, and her voice was slightly slurred.

In the background he could hear the hubbub of music and voices, and he could picture Cressy, finger in one ear, hopping from foot to foot in a busy pub, shouting into her phone.

'Nope, she's definitely not here.'

He had an idea he wasn't meant to hear Cressy's colourful curse.

'Any chance she'll be coming tomorrow?' Should he even be pushing it?

'Jackson, I give you my word, I'll try my best to get that woman down to you tomorrow. Just hang on in there. If she doesn't turn up, it won't be for lack of effort on my part, believe me.'

There was being patient and understanding, and then there was downright degrading, that feeling that someone was wiping the floor with you, and somehow he was moving perilously close to the second.

'Well, when I'm at the lighthouse, there's no phone signal, and no landline. I'll be there until two tomorrow, but after that I'll be gone.'

'Right.'

'If you could pass the message on, I'd be very grateful.'

'Gotcha.'

Then the call ended, and he was hurled back into the empty silence of the camper. And for the first time ever, waiting for Cherry seemed hopeless.

'Oi, you! Get here and let me in.'

Behind the vibrating door of her flat, Bryony shrunk back and shuddered at the thumping and the sheer volume of Cressy's complaining. She'd known she'd have to face the music the minute she'd got out of Cressy's taxi, two hundred yards around the corner from where she got in on Friday afternoon, thrusting a handful of notes at the driver to buy his silence. She just hadn't expected that the music would start this soon or be this loud.

Bryony pulled herself up to her full height and hitched up her jogging pants. The banging stopped as she flung open the door.

'Cressy. What a surprise.' Not.

Bryony peered past Cressy. Along the hallway a couple of doors were already ajar, and she posted an insouciant smile to the neighbours who were peering out.

Cressy didn't hold back. 'I *so* do not believe you, Bry. What the hell are you doing *here* when you should be...?'

As if this was any of Cressy's business. 'I could ask you the same?' Bryony pursed her lips sullenly.

'What I'm doing here, is driving back from bloody Basingstoke at stupid o'clock in the morning, getting engine failure on the motorway, waiting two hours for the roadside assistance to arrive and change my points, to try to get you to where you should have been the day before yesterday.' Cressy looked as if smoke might come out of her nostrils at any moment. 'I take it you got out of the taxi I piled you into? Excuse me for asking, but why? What's wrong with a guy who is devoted to you, who, let's face it, is just as stubborn and pig-headed as you are, but it's a damn good job he is or he'd have given up on you months ago? Do you realise most people would give their left nipple to be in your position? So, what's not to like?'

Bryony stood opening and closing her mouth, as Cressy's endless tirade of questions rattled past her.

'On second thoughts, don't answer that. You have about five minutes to come to your senses and get your ass down there, or I've a feeling you may be about to miss one of life's great guys. He'll be leaving at two, and from what he said, that'll be it. There aren't many like him around and believe me, I should know, I've test-driven enough of them.'

Bryony shrank back against the hall wall, but Cressy advanced on her.

'Okay, give me one good reason why you won't go?' Cressy's face would have been inches from hers, if she hadn't been so small.

'I-I-I…' Bryony stammered.

'If I hear one good reason, I promise I'll butt out.'

Bryony took a deep breath. 'I'm not going, because I'm… because I'm scared.' There. She'd admitted it. The whole caring thing scared the bejesus out of her. Out in the open, and she still didn't feel any better.

'Scared of?' Cressy's eyes rolled upwards, but her mouth was one determined line. 'You need to elaborate.'

Bryony sighed. 'How about everything? Scared I like him too much… Scared I'm going to get hurt… And now I'm pregnant I'm making decisions for someone else too.' Somehow it was hard to put into words. 'It's just how much I like Jackson is the most enormous thing that's ever happened to me, no one's ever made me feel like this before. It's huge, it's all engulfing, which means the stakes are massive. I mean, when you feel this much for someone, there's just so much that can go wrong. And having his baby just makes it all so much worse, because for ages I thought he might only want to be with me because he had to be. And it's double the responsibility if things go wrong, because it's not just for me. And that doesn't make me want to go to him, on the contrary, it makes me want to run as fast as I can in the opposite direction.'

'And that's why you're staying away? Jeez, if ever I've heard a silly reason, that has to be it.' Cressy shook her head. 'Man up, Bry. There's only one person who can reassure you on that one, but you have to talk to *him*. And to talk to him you need to see him, and you sure as hell can't do that if you're here and he's in a sodding lighthouse sixty miles away.'

'Mmmm.' Bryony knew Cressy had a point.

'And this huge thing you keep talking about, well I'm no expert, but I'm guessing the engulfing part might just be love. L–O–V–E. From what I've heard that's pretty massive and amazing, a lot like you're describing in fact.'

Bryony felt the blood drain from her face. 'You think that's it? Holy crap, how can I have been so stupid? I think you're right. Maybe I do love him. But if this is love, I pretty much loved him from the first time I saw him. There was this kind of hook that got me, and that changed everything. Since that first day in Scarborough, my whole world has been turned upside down, nothing's been the same since then. It's like the only time that I feel totally whole and happy is when he's there, as if my whole being is tied up with his. It's amazing, but at the same time it scares the shit out of me. At least that explains it, but I'm not sure I'm happy about it. There's just so much potential for disaster. For me *and* the baby.'

'Well, Jackson loves you. That has to count for something.' Cressy, obviously sensing she was making headway, retreated a step. 'He's head over heels, and if he loves you that much, he won't want to hurt you. When you love someone it's all about trust. The idea is you both love each other so much that you can trust that neither of you will do anything to hurt the other. That's why you don't run away, you get together. And together you're strong, together you're damned-well awesome – or so I'm led to believe.' Cressy added the afterthought as she caught Bryony's searching stare. 'But you really need to talk to Jackson about all this.'

'So I love Jackson.' Bryony murmured it at first, and then as a smile spread across her face she repeated the words. Trying them out might help her to get used to the idea. 'Oh my God, I love Jackson Gale. That's it. That explains everything. I love Jackson. And that's why I feel so bad when we're not together, so it makes sense to be with him, if I can find a way around being scared, doesn't it?'

'About bloody time.' Cressy rubbed her nose on her hand.

'I love him, I want to be with him, so I definitely need to go and talk to him.'

'And finally…' Cressy ran her hands through her hair. 'I thought you'd never get there.'

Bryony glanced at her watch, and let out a hopeless sigh. 'But it's eleven-thirty now, so I reckon I've already blown it. No way in the world I can be there by two.' Nothing to describe the pancake flat way her stomach flopped at that thought. She folded her arms, decidedly. 'So that's it then. I've stuffed my whole life up. And it's not just me, anymore, it's all about the baby too. I'm stuffing it up for both of us.' And dammit that her chest was constricting, and a pounding head was making her feel like the world was about to end.

'Or you could take the helicopter?' Cressy flipped her a triumphant smile.

Bryony gave a grimace. 'I gave up whipping Brando's helicopter a couple of years back, I don't even know where it is these days…'

'Usual place and it's ready to go.' Another gloat from Cressy. 'I got in touch with him yesterday just in case…'

'In case of what?' Bryony's voice rose. Incredulous didn't begin to cover it.

'In case there was an emergency like this. Don't forget I know how stubborn you are, I guessed we might be up against the wire.' Cressy gave an unapologetic shrug, going for broke here. 'Brando wants the best for you two, he's behind Jackson the same as the rest of us, and he knows how stroppy you are too…'

'I so am *not* stroppy.' Somewhere along the line Bryony had to come out and stick up for herself again, in the face of so much steam-rollering all around her. Not so long ago she'd been the one with the monopoly on steam-roller tactics, but somewhere down the line, when she wasn't looking, she'd changed.

'Are you going to get dressed or what?' Cressy's eyes slid skywards again. 'And please don't take all day; you've got a helicopter to catch, remember.'

# Chapter 56

'I *really* appreciate you doing this for me, Brando. Driving me down here, letting me take the helicopter and everything…'

Bryony crossed her legs, uncrossed them again, as she'd been doing the whole journey since Brando picked her up. Not that fidgeting helped any, but she was aware she'd left it very late to change her mind about going to see Jackson. Looking at her watch every five seconds wasn't helping either. She dug her fingers into the leather car seat, edged herself forward, then seeing the familiar turn towards the airstrip at long last, she made a dive for her boots.

'It's okay, Bry. If I hadn't stuffed up in the first place I'm not sure you'd be needing me to help anyway.' Brando took his eyes off the road long enough to flash her a contrite grin.

'What do you mean?'

'First I shouldn't have muscled in and snatched you away from the hospital, and second, I shouldn't have dragged Jackson over to Edgerton that day. I've been getting it in the neck from Shea ever since and she's right, I was acting like a class one dickhead.'

'You were only trying to help. At the time I was so grateful for being airlifted out of trouble. I wasn't admitting it, but I was so scared about having the baby that all I wanted to do was hide'

'Maybe so, but if I'd stayed out of it you and Jackson would have had the space to sort yourselves out.' He rubbed his chin pensively. 'I find it very hard to stay back where you're concerned, I always have, ever since we were kids.'

'I had noticed.' Her smile was rueful. 'But mostly it's been great to have my big brother on my side. Whenever you wade in it's only because you care and you're trying to help.'

'Yeah, but this time you'd have been better on your own.' Tapping his fingers on the steering wheel, he gave a sigh. 'You know I've always felt so bad for walking out of home when you were small and leaving you behind. You begging me to stay almost broke me. I can still see you now, wailing and desperate, the guilt for leaving you has always stayed with me.'

Oh my. Poor Brando.

She gave a sigh of her own and wondered what to say to make him feel better. 'You had to go, I understand that now, even if I didn't back then. Going away to school got you out of the awful fights you were having at home. I forgave you.'

'But I think that's why I've always been a bit too strong on the overprotective brother bit – to try to make up for running out on you. And I certainly think it made me completely unable to say "no" to you.'

That confession made her lips curl into a smile. 'And I think I've exploited that to the full over the years too. Big brothers, twisting and little fingers spring to mind…'

He gave a low laugh. 'Maybe so, but you've also done your share of being there for me. Think about the way you stepped in when I inherited Edgerton. You couldn't have been much more than twelve and yet you came in and helped to organise all those annual balls and you carried on right up until Shea took over. Over the years you've achieved phenomenal things there, but I think I might have sometimes overlooked what a strong person you are.'

'That's nice, thank you for that, Brando.'

She wondered where this was leading.

'The thing is, I think it's time I backed off and admitted you're grown up. You can stand on your own two feet and you're

339

completely capable of making your own decisions.' He gave a low laugh and sent her a wry grimace. 'You really have no need for me to come along and mess it all up for you, like I did when I dragged Jackson to Edgerton when you weren't ready to see him. I just want you to be happy, and I think you've got a damned good chance of that with Jackson, but I'm not going to get in your way anymore.'

'Okay.' So this was Brando signing off, because he'd finally realised she was an adult. And for the first time in her life she felt as if she was – all grown up that is.

'So I'll always be here for you, but from now on I'm going to try not to interfere quite so much, okay?' He gave her a smile.

'All good, Brando.'

Then his smile spread to a grin. 'I'll have Shea on my case if I do. So here's your helicopter for today…'

He'd swung the car into the airstrip, and now he was accelerating towards the chopper which was standing on the grass Bryony's heart began to pound in anticipation. *Oh my, this is it then.* Bryony grabbed her bag, preparing to jump out, but as the car came to a standstill a mechanic came across the grass towards them, shaking his head.

Bryony's stomach turned to jelly as Brando's window whirred down.

'Is there a problem?'

The mechanic frowned, wiping his hands on an oily rag.

'Sorry, we've hit a last minute mechanical… We won't be flying any time soon.'

# Chapter 57

'So that's that then.'

Jackson locked the door, shoved the keys to the lighthouse in his pocket. When the hell had he started being a loser not a winner? He'd spent the morning in the spectacular light-bathed living room of the lighthouse, flicking through the Sunday papers, staring out across the expanse of sea. He'd gone out early to get them, in case he missed Cherry's arrival – hollow laugh to that thought – but no way could he concentrate on reading. No way could he even enjoy the changing colours of the water, as the clouds chased across a bright blue sky, which somehow looked like it belonged to a day that was full of promise. Damn that he had ever been stupid enough to believe that one.

All his life he thought he'd been a winner, because he could read people, and he'd hung on to the belief that Cherry would come because deep down he was sure that she did care. But Cherry obviously never had any intention of coming, and it was entirely his own fault for blowing that too. Cherry was right. She deserved a guy who had a track record of dependable relationships, not someone like him for whom the idea of long-term came to hit him like a thunderbolt from the blue the day he finally realised the idea of living his life without her was abhorrent. Talk about late to the party. As the hours of the morning had eased by and the tide had slipped out exposing the rocks around the shore, his hope had ebbed. By the time he got around to making rolls and a pot of coffee for lunch, his appetite had all but disappeared. Now, with the wind snatching at his t-shirt, as he made his way across the grassy cliff top, following the stony path to the camper van, the festive bunting hanging in the van windows seemed to mock him.

Flinging open the van door, he tossed his bag into the back, hauled his body into the driver's seat, and drummed his fingers on the steering wheel. How many times had he glanced at his watch today? Two-fifteen now, and his deadline had come and gone, slipped by when he was gathering the things he'd brought. A gust of wind burst through the open door, caught the Hawaiian garland hanging from the rear view mirror and sent it flapping across the windscreen.

'Damn thing!' One lunge and he snapped it, tossed it onto the floor, and revelled in the instant destruction. He'd deal with the bunting later, because let's face it, he was going to have to wipe everything Cherry out of his life, simply for his own sanity. If she'd wanted him, she'd have come. What part of 'I don't want to be with you' did he not get? Biting away the bad taste, he threw the door closed, then bowed his head onto his hands for one more minute.

Why the hell was he so reluctant to leave?

A shiver rippled down his spine. Because it wasn't just about giving up on Cherry. It was about letting go of his baby too. The ache that had been nagging in his thorax all day kicked into flames. A hundred miles of thrashing on the bike wouldn't touch anger like this. Leaving would put an end to it, but he hadn't thought as far as a new beginning. And he hadn't banked on the pain that was ripping through his torso like an axe.

He turned the ignition key and as the engine roared into life, he slammed the van into gear and began to bump along the track towards the road. Nothing as organised as a plan. He'd drive away, hit the main road, and after that who knew.

The camper banged its way over the potholes along the lane,

quietening as he pulled to a halt at the junction with the road. In the second of silence, he clocked another sound that made his stony stomach lurch – the throbbing of a helicopter engine overhead.

Surely, it couldn't be…? Embarrassingly, he'd jumped in hope at every tiny sound for the past three days. Of course it wouldn't be, couldn't be… What was he thinking? He craned his neck, glimpsed the chopper swooping low over the cliff top fields beside the road, blasting the grass with its down-draught and his chest contracted. Holy crap. Hardly daring to think it was Brando's – there had to be a thousand other blue choppers in the world. His pulse was pumping fast enough to burst, as he slammed the camper into reverse and shot backwards along the lane to the lighthouse. By the time he leaped out he could barely breathe. It was as if the world stopped turning, the seconds stretched interminably as he waited for the chopper to land. Agonising. And then just as he was certain it was about to come down it did one final circle, then slowly turned and veered away.

Jackson's stomach flopped to somewhere around his ankles and for a moment he thought he was going to vomit.

He cursed silently, watching, eyes glued to the blades, half expecting – desperately hoping – that it was an aborted landing, that the chopper would regroup and come back for another go. Then, as the helicopter began to establish a steady course off along the coast every bit of air left his lungs, but still he couldn't stop looking. Mesmerised, he waited as the drumming of the engine faded, stood squinting into the sun until all he could see was a speck against the clouds.

Damn, damn, damn. He stared at the empty sky. Why the hell had he let himself hope? He slammed his fist down onto the stone wall, blotted out the pain that shot up his arm on impact, hurled a random kick at the nearest tuft of grass. More furious with himself than anyone else. Whatever, he was out of here and fast.

This time he hurled himself into the driving seat, flung the van into gear and roared down the lane. Knowing it was wrong to take out his anger like this, but hell, right now there was nowhere else to put it. Bouncing and banging over the bumps, wrenching the steering wheel to avoid the potholes didn't help a bit. As he flew towards the main road he heard one bang bigger than the rest, followed by an ominous clanking.

'Holy crap, what now?' He slammed on the brakes, slewed to a halt, and threw himself out onto the track to investigate the damage.

Just his luck. One tyre completely flat, collapsed in the dust, no doubt ripped where he'd hit a stone at speed, and only one person to blame for that. He closed his eyes, resisted the pressure which was building in his thorax, unsure which was going to explode first: his head or his body. For a moment he rested his head against the cool smooth metal of the camper side panel. There was only one way out of this and it was down to him. Until he changed this wheel, he wasn't going anywhere fast. Wearily he got back into the camper, and gingerly reversed back towards the lighthouse to the flat parking area where he'd have more space to work on the repairs.

So much for a quick getaway. It was at least an hour later when Jackson finally got the spare wheel in place, correctly inflated, and tightened the last nut. A case of more hurry, less speed, coupled with a dodgy jack. Somehow the wrenching and tugging involved in the wheel change had taken the heat out of his anger and turned it to a deep and aching sadness. Regardless of his desire to leave fast, there was no way he could ever face Rik again if he got into his pristine camper with hands covered in grease and dirt, so he grabbed the keys to the lighthouse and went back in to scrub up.

As he emerged into the bright afternoon sun again with hands clean enough to keep Rik off his back, he noticed a sleek car making its way very slowly between the tumbling stone walls along the lane. He cocked an eyebrow as it came to a halt just off the main road. Probably some Sunday afternoon tripper who'd taken a wrong turn, and whoever it was had obviously decided to abandon their attempt. Sensible driver, obviously had more sense than to bring a car like that up a lane like this. He couldn't be sure but it looked like an Aston, a bit like the one Brando turned up in that day at the hotel in Brighton. *It couldn't be…?* There was a slight surge of hope in his chest but he stamped on it hard. More fool him for his pulse rate surging with every passing chopper or random Aston. Once bitten… Anyway a blue Aston meant nothing did it, they were ten a penny weren't they? Not that he'd seen another since, but… *Could it be…?*

Now the passenger door was opening. Not significant. And someone was getting out. He clung onto his heartbeat, fiercely willing it to slow down. The figure didn't close the door, just left it open, made their way to the back of the car, then began running. Running, stumbling, falling, lurching, blonde hair blasted by the wind. Only one person he knew would run in high heels as if her life depended on it…

*Cherry?*

As she raised her hand in a wave that sent his heart hammering hard enough to burst out of his chest, he brushed away the blur of what could only be tears, barely daring to believe what he saw.

'Cherry? Cherry!' And then he was hurling himself down the steps, haring down the lane as she ran towards him, and a minute later he'd swept her amazing, warm body into his arms.

'I can't believe I almost missed you, Jackson.'

Jackson raised an eyebrow. If he hadn't been so pleased to see her, he'd have mentioned that it was ironic that she'd sat tight in London all weekend, then cut it so fine. Downright late in fact. If it hadn't been for the flat on the camper… It didn't bear thinking about. 'So you went for Brando's chopper and it was out of action. That'll teach you. Anyway I thought you'd grown out of stealing it?'

She was here, that was all that mattered. 'Officially, I wasn't actually stealing it, it's just that by the time I came to my senses

345

it was too late to get here any other way. Except when we got to the helicopter it was grounded due to a technical fault so Brando drove me here, but I was going crazy because I thought we weren't going to make it.' Her grave expression said it all, as she leaned back against the balustrade, in front of the floor to ceiling windows that circled around half of the room.

'I feel so stupid for taking so long, but I've been so mixed up. At first, the last thing I wanted was for you to only be with me because of the baby, and I so didn't want to trap you into something that wasn't what you wanted. But once I realised you did care, I've been so paralysed by fear, it's taken me forever to realise how much I care about you. And now I know I want to be with you, but I'm still so scared. Maybe we need to talk.'

Point taken. She might be here, but she was still a million miles from being *sure*.

'So how can I help?' He needed to reach out to her, make it easy. He tried again. 'How have you been the last couple of weeks?'

Brilliant. He watched her mask of composure disintegrate.

'Crap actually.' She pulled her mouth into a line, gave a shrug. 'How about you?'

He raised his eyebrows. 'Pretty much the same.' Playing it down here, given the truth was more like the worst he'd felt in his life, ever, to the power ten.

'Both in the same place then?' Now her strong front had wilted, he could see from the dark circles under her eyes that she looked pale and strained.

'Looks like it.' He gave a nod. 'So why didn't you come?'

'I couldn't.' Biting her lip, as the word rushed out. All that sea behind her, and she was staring at her feet.

'Any particular reason?' Staring across the room, and out at the ocean behind her, he rolled back on his heels, hands deep in his jean pockets. 'We were apart, we were both unhappy; doesn't it make sense to be together?'

She dragged in a breath. 'I was scared, Jackson. I am scared. I

346

so want to be with you, but I'm terrified to be with you, because I like you too much, and I'm worried that you'll leave me, and I can't face the hurt.' The words tumbled out of her mouth.

Wow. He blew out his cheeks. No way had he seen that one coming. 'Okay.'

'And it's doubly bad, because soon it won't just be me who'll get hurt.'

The silence that followed that revelation was wide enough for him to reflect, long and hard.

As she raised her face to look at him, the sharp pain in her eyes brought a lump into his throat, and threw him right back to that day, so long ago, when he'd crashed in like an idiot with both feet, and she'd told him about her father.

Two steps and he'd crossed the floor, reached out and brushed a tangle of hair off her forehead.

'This is about your dad, isn't it?' Suddenly it was obvious. This had very little to do with his past as a player, and everything to do with her childhood. How the hell had he not thought of this before. 'He left, and you think I'm going to do the same?'

She nodded, slowly, and swallowed hard. 'In a way my dad left me twice – once when he walked out, and again when he died. It sounds like a cliché, but it broke my heart both times. All that's left is this deep fear that it'll happen all over again. I know it doesn't sound rational, but it makes me rigid.'

Seeing her eyes, shiny with tears, he pulled her onto his chest, rubbed his hand on her shuddering back.

'And it wasn't just my dad...' She was choking on her sobs as she spoke. 'It was Brando too – he left me, and went away to school. I know it sounds silly, but the only two guys I've ever cared about ran out on me.'

He spoke quietly into her ear. 'You know, it's not so bad to be scared. Scared means there's a big risk, but it can also mean it's something that matters a lot.'

'Mmmm.' She sniffed, but didn't sound convinced. 'I thought

347

if I stayed independent and alone at least I wouldn't get hurt, and I'd protect the baby too.'

He could understand where she was coming from with that.

'It's natural to be afraid of what we don't know, but if we don't have the courage to try it, we might miss the best thing in our life. You might think I'm not worth trusting, but if you knew how much difference you've made in my life you'd have every reason to believe I won't run out on you. You're the only person who has ever stood up to me, the only person who has really challenged me, the only person who pushed me to be myself. Wanting to be with you gave me the courage to face up to life after cycling. My old life was a long way removed from real life, but now I want real, because I want a life with you and there's no way I'll be running out on that.'

Another gulp from Cherry. He was skirting round the L-word here, but he was going to have to bring it out sooner or later, grab for his hard hat and take whatever flak came his way.

'I'm used to being a winner, but the reason I win is because I've always put in the effort to read people. I can tell from the look in your eyes that you care about me. That look is why I've hung on in here when you tried to send me away, but for me it's about much more than just caring, it's about love. I love you Cherry.' There, the words were out there, and Cherry was still here. He took another breath, and crossed his fingers hard. 'I think I fell in love with you the first time I saw you. But the love I feel now is very different – it's about wanting to spend my life with you, it's about wanting to protect you, it's about wanting to build a life together.' Burying his face in her hair, breathing in the soft scent of her scalp, he knew he felt better for saying it.

'You are right, I do care about you, I care so much and that's why I'm so scared.' She smiled up at him, still a little doubtful. 'And it's because I care about you that I really didn't want to hold you back just when you had your chance to be free.'

'Freedom is like a prison if you're not with the person you want to be with. Being free is about being happy, not about being alone. I made so many sacrifices to be a winner and I want to enjoy myself now, but the only way I see that happening is if I'm with you.' Taking her by the shoulders, he spun her around to face the sea, wrapped his arms around her ribs, and squeezed. 'Remember last time we were in that lighthouse in Devon, looking at the horizon, and talking about the future? The line between scary and exciting is a fine one, and exciting is good. A future together could be so exciting, for both of us….' Sliding his hand downwards, he spread his fingers over her tummy. 'For all of us, even – don't you think?'

Not that he wanted a reply. Instead he spun her around again, this time, tilting her chin upwards, capturing her mouth as she came to face him. Warm, hot, delicious. Soaking her up.

Made his insides go molten every time.

## Chapter 58

Bryony rubbed a hand over her lips, and clung onto Jackson's shirt for stability as they slowly broke away from each other. Jackson nudging her behind her knee? Jackson with his hand on her fledgling bump? Jackson giving her that 'floating on a feather bed' feeling? If she could trust Jackson, could go with her gut instinct here and not her fear, there was so much to be gained.

'You know, Jackson, I think you might be right.' She watched his face stretch from a contented smile to a full blown grin. 'If I can get over the fear bit, then we could have the loveliest time.'

'It must have taken a lot of guts for you to come here, feeling as you did.' His smile had faded and his voice quietened to a husky whisper, achingly full of concern. That low growl of his always sent goose bumps down her spine.

'Yes, and no – I had to screw up all my courage but I was having such a horrible time at home. Thinking I couldn't be with you made me feel ill and waking up every morning to your picture made it all the worse.'

Something in the flicker of satisfaction that crossed his face made her think that could have been his plan with the picture all along.

'Whatever the reason, I'm so pleased you came, even if the helicopter let you down.' He pushed back her hair again, and

350

stared gravely into her eyes. 'We can always get a helicopter, if that's what you'd like?'

That random thought made her lips twitch in amusement. 'Thanks, but I got over helicopters a long time ago and today just reinforced that.'

'And I promise that we'll travel – I have this image in my head…'

Jackson was going for broke here, pulling out all the stops.

She interrupted him. 'Let me guess? Us with a push-chair on a Pacific beach?'

'Something like that – except push-chairs won't run on sand, did you know that?'

'As it happens I did, but there'll be two of us remember, we can carry it.' She reached up and cupped his cheek with her hand. 'Really, I don't want a helicopter, Jackson, and I'm not even sure I'd actually like traveling. I think just being with you will be fine.'

He wrapped his arms around her and gave her ribs another squeeze.

'And you're sure you're okay about the baby?'

More gruff concern from him, meant another rash of goose bumps for her.

'I've been hankering after a baby for ages, I thought you knew, you picked up on it often enough.' As she remembered it, he'd been merciless, and a little of that made her dare to push it here. 'So how do you feel about the baby? Really?'

Throwing it out there, then waiting, hardly daring to breathe for what seemed like an age. Only when his face cracked into a smile did she exhale again.

'I'm truly looking forward to the baby, and to us being a family. Dan and Phoebe were great at helping me through the initial shock.' He gave a guilty grimace. 'I already bought a Babygro, I just haven't found the right time to show you yet.'

Rumbled. She stifled the smile that was ready to burst out of her. 'You had it in your bag the day you brought the picture round, didn't you?'

'Yep.' He closed his eyes, blew out his cheeks, then opening his eyes again he rounded on her. 'How the hell did you know that?'

'Feminine intuition.' She gave her smile full rein. 'Or maybe, when I said no Babygro's and you went bright red and stared at your messenger bag, it might have been a giveaway.'

He gave her a gentle chiding nudge with his hip. 'You'll like it, it's got camper vans on it.'

'What if it's a girl?'

'Girls like camper vans too.' Then his laughter faded into an even more apprehensive grimace 'I'm still shit scared I'll turn into my father, and that's something I'd really hate.'

'You mean the way he bullied and grabbed the glory?'

So he did have his own fears. Somehow, knowing that made her feel a whole lot better. 'You're strong, but you're not a bully. Your dad's probably a full blown sociopath, and you certainly aren't that, believe me.'

He gave a heartfelt sigh. 'It's more than that. From what my mum said, I get the impression he used to hit her. I suspect that's why she left, although she's still covering for him, even now.'

'Oh, no, how awful for her.' She frowned, groped to find the right thing to say. 'You're so different from him, there's no reason to think you'd be like him. And you've brought it into the open, that's good.'

'I can only hope....' His gloomy doubt wrung her heart out.

'I'm sure you'll be a wonderful dad, and you're already making *me* feel great. Funny how all along I thought you hated the whole house with two point four children thing.'

'It's true, I did hate the idea as an abstract. I was sure it was the last thing I'd ever want to do, but when I think of doing it with you, there's nothing I'd rather have.' His brow wrinkled as he considered further. 'I guess I'd still prefer to live in a lighthouse than somewhere conventional. It's up for sale you know; you don't need to decide right now, but it's a thought....'

Comments like that reminded her Jackson would always be a

handful, but she was more than up for the challenge.

'When you said exciting, I didn't *immediately* imagine living in a lighthouse. Hardly practical either, given there isn't anywhere to keep your collection of bikes.' She posted him a grin. 'The strange thing is, in my childhood I always had material things, but emotionally I was very insecure. I guess that's why I always tried to control things.'

'So that explains your Ms Bossy thing?'

Straight on her case there, and she loved the way he always pushed her. Rolling her eyes was enough reply to that. 'I shied away from the relationships that might have filled that gap, but somehow, you began to satisfy that need without me even realising. When I'm with you, for the first time in my life, I feel secure enough to relax and let go.'

'But when you talked about your past before, you said that sometimes all a child wants is two parents that belong to them. If you can trust me to stay, we can give our children that.'

She wanted to throw her arms round him and hug him forever for remembering that, and for being patient enough to wait long enough for her to work out that they could be together.

'Now we've got here, it does feel like we belong together. I just felt very vulnerable before.' She leaned into his side, moulding her body against his.

'The times when we're vulnerable can be when we learn most.' He gave her a half-nod.

'Wise words.' She smiled up at him.

'Your words not mine.' He gave her a wink. Her heart squished again. She was so lucky to love a guy like this. Love? Such a big word, but so definitely the right one, and maybe it was time she screwed up her courage to let him know. She slid her arm up around his neck, pulled him down towards her.

'I love *you*, Jackson.' She rubbed her cheek against the rough stubble on his chin, then as she slipped a kiss onto the corner of his mouth, she could already feel his lips stretching into the widest smile. Now she'd dared to say the words out loud to him, they sounded so right she didn't want to stop. 'I love you, I love you, I love you…' Her heart was banging hard enough to explode. Happy didn't begin to cover it.

'I hoped you might, but I can't tell you how happy it makes me to hear you say it.' His voice was husky as he dropped a kiss on top of her head, drew her to him, and squeezed her very tightly. 'You have no idea how much I love you.'

He drew her into a velvety snog that made her feel like the room was turning.

When, finally, their lips parted, she traced her finger down the delicious crease in his cheek. 'It does feel like we belong together, as if it couldn't have been any other way.'

'You've done it for all your friends, now it's your turn, our turn.'

Those dark lashed eyes of his, so soft and full of love.

'All I needed was the right man, and the confidence to make that final leap.' Now she had done it she had no idea how it had been so difficult. 'Somehow, now I'm here, I feel like I've just done that very last bit of growing up.'

'Spending time together has changed us both – I've grown up too. But the big question is, do you think you might be ready for your very own Vera Wang moment? Will you have that Vera Wang moment with me?' He was looking down at her, and she couldn't hold in her ear-wide grin.

She stared at him open mouthed, hardly believing what she was hearing.

'So, will you? Will you marry me, Cherry?'

This time she found her voice.

'Jackson, I'd love to.' She swallowed down a lump in her throat, and then Jackson's mouth found hers and she abandoned herself. It was long dizzying kisses when later they surfaced again and Jackson spoke.

'Shall we ride off into the sunset on a tandem then? To be honest, that's exactly what I wanted to do that first day.'

Her heart was still bursting here.

'Or we could just drive off in your camper – that would work too, so long as you remember to pull into a hotel before dark.' With Jackson she knew it was important to get the ground rules established early.

'What, so you can starch your knickers?'

She braced herself for a confession.

'Wouldn't need to today, I was in such a rush I came out without any.'

She watched his face light up even more.

'I didn't think it was possible to get any happier, but as you do so often, you just proved me wrong. I may need to verify this, before we go anywhere…' His warm hand slid down the back of her jeans, and he gave a growl of approval. 'Exciting. So if the future Mrs Gale would like to kick off those Jimmy Choos, and step this way…'

'You wouldn't be suggesting sex with a view of the sea would you – again? You know I've still got the fossil you gave me that first day on the beach, in my purse.'

'Sea view sounds good to me…' He delved in his pocket for a second, then held up his own fossil between his thumb and finger. 'That was the night the baby happened, wasn't it?'

She nodded and smiled some more. 'I think it was.'

'Couldn't have been be a better first date.' From the decided way Jackson said that there was no doubt he meant it. 'Happy?'

'Couldn't be happier…' She nodded again, and he bowled her a sideways grin that melted her insides. '…or more excited about what's coming next.'

And somehow that was it – the moment that marked the very end of growing up, and the beginning of the rest of their lives, the moment they went off towards their new horizon. So she kicked off her boots, and began to walk slowly across the bleached-wood floor to the sofa, all wrapped up with her very own Mr Right.

Printed by RR Donnelley at Glasgow, UK